The Nickel Man

IN THE SAME SERIES

The Nickel Man
and Other French
Scientific Romances

translated, annotated and introduced by
Brian Stableford

A Black Coat Press Book

Visit our website at www.blackcoatpress.com

ISBN 978-1-61227-445-4. First Printing. January 2016. Published by Black Coat Press, an imprint of Hollywood Comics.com, LLC, P.O. Box 17270, Encino, CA 91416.

TABLE OF CONTENTS

Il se fit enduire de plombagine. (Page 10.)

Original illustration from *The Nickel Man*

Introduction

The first story in this anthology of French scientific romances, "Mademoiselle de La Choupillière," was published in a collection of *Nouvelles* (1832) by the archeologist and paleontologist who signed his works Jacques Boucher de Perthes, although his full name was Jacques Boucher de Crèvecoeur de Perthes (1788-1868). It is one of numerous fanciful stories extrapolating ideas inspired by the activities of Jacques de Vaucanson (1709-1782), the famous builder of automata, whose machines were long gone by the time the story was written but had left behind a legacy of rumor whose marvels were exaggerated by the passage of time.

The anthology contains two other stories in the same vein. The earlier of the two, *L'Automate, récit tiré d'un palimpseste* by Ralph Schropp, initially published in 1878 and reprinted as a booklet by A. Ghio in 1880, here translated as "The Automaton: A Story Translated from a Palimpsest," takes up an older legend relating to the manufacture of an artificial human being, crediting the achievement to the 13th century scholar Albertus Magnus. The legend originally related to the magical creation of a "homunculus," but Schropp updates the supposed method employed to place it in a scientific rather than a supernatural context.

It was reported in 1896 that Léon Daudet (1867-1942) was working on a new novel entitled *L'Automate*, not long after he had published his first novel, *Les Morticoles* [literally, The Death-Cultivators; metaphorically, Doctors] (1894). The short story of that title, here translated as "The Automaton," was presumably originally intended to be the opening section of the novel in question. It was reprinted in the posthumous collection *Quinze contes* (1948) but probably appeared in a periodical long before then, perhaps being rewritten for that purpose a few years after first being drafted (there is a refer-

7

ence in the story to a book published in 1898). As with the previous item, it draws upon the legend of the homunculus, and, although it retains a supernatural context in the creator's conviction of diabolical aid, it addresses the question of the possible psychological make-up of the homunculus in a more philosophically-sophisticated manner than Schropp's tale, with which it forms an interesting contrast.

In between "Mademoiselle de La Choupillière" and the Schropp story, placed there in order to maintain the chronological order of the inclusions, is *L'Uraniade, ou Ésop juge à la cour d'Uranie, scènes dialoguées au sujet des hypothèses Newtoniennes: songe scientifique* [The Uraniad, or Aesop judges in Urania's Court; dialogue scenes on the subject of the Newtonian hypothesis: A Scientific Dream] signed Père Brémond, first published by the author in Avignon in 1844, and here translated as "The Uraniad," which recommends itself for consideration in the context of the history of *roman scientifique* by virtue of its eccentricity and its determined combativeness. So far as can be ascertained with the current state of search engines, the phrase *roman scientifique* [scientific fiction] was first used by Élie Fréron (1719-1776), a diehard opponent of Isaac Newton's theory of gravity, as a pejorative characterization of that theory. In 1844 the term had not yet been adapted for application to new kinds of literary work that appeared in the 1860s, so Brémond's work is a notable example of literary protest against what he considered to be a *roman scientifique* in the original sense of the phrase.

We now know, of course, that the criticisms leveled against Newtonian theory by the unorthodox theorists featured in *L'Uraniade* are utterly mistaken, and one suspects that any modern schoolboy could poke the holes in them that Newton's defenders conspicuously fail to bring up when invited by the fabulist and *ad hoc* judge to argue their case—the real individuals on whom those characters are based could undoubtedly have put up a far more robust and devastating show—but that only adds interest to a debate that is interesting not so much in regard to the problems it addresses but in respect of the issues in the philosophy and sociology of science that it raises in the process.

Little seems to be known about Brémond except that his first name was Pierre and that he was a Jesuit, and his supposed *magnum opus*—or *pièce de resistance*—criticizing Newton's theses, which *L'Uraniade* was written and published to advertise, never did see print. Whether the manuscript that he left on deposit in his local library in Avignon still exists, I have no idea. It is highly unlikely, however, that the earnest work in question could have had the saving graces that allow *L'Uraniade* to retain some interest above and beyond its status as a literary and philosophical curiosity: its enterprise, its liveliness and its sheer bizarrerie.

Also placed between two of the stories of automata is "La Mort de Paris" by the prolific writer Louis Gallet (1835-1898), which first appeared in 1892 in *La Nouvelle Revue*, here translated as "The Death of Paris." It is a slightly offbeat addition to the rich tradition of stories featuring the ruins of Paris, offering an account of how the city and its remaining inhabitants perish from suddenly-accelerated climate change—the advent of a new Ice Age—rather than poking fun at the mistaken conclusions of far-future archeologists. Its conscious affiliation to the tradition, however, adds an extra gloss to what might otherwise have been an ordinary disaster story, equipping it with a delicately ironic elegiac quality. The author was best known for his operatic libretti, and "Le Mort de Paris" has a kind of operatic sweep and flourish about it that suits its theme very well.

In the interests of diversity, the short novel following the Daudet story, *L'Homme en nickel*, here translated as "The Nickel Man," is an item of popular pulp fiction, initially published as a feuilleton serial in *La Science Française* in 1897 and reprinted in book form the same year. It was the work of one of the most prolific contributors to the periodical in question, and it appeared there under the pseudonym "Georges Bethuys," one of several signatures employed by the military historian and journalist Georges-Frédéric Espitallier (1849-

1923) (who also used the pseudonym of "Pierre Ferréol"). Like most of the fiction published in the popular science magazines of the day, it attempts to place scientific notions in the context of a plot that reproduces many of the standard features of the feuilleton fiction of the day, in this case borrowing abundantly from the nascent genre of detective fiction.

One suspects that the puzzle with which *L'Homme en nickel* confronts the detective who functions as its main protagonist would not have confused Sherlock Holmes for more than a few minutes, and the fact that the reader knows the answer from the very beginning only serves to make the policeman's deductive powers seem even weaker, but the story tries as hard as it can to make up for that rickety logic with zest and fast-paced movement, in a manner that was to become familiar in pulpish speculative fiction; in consequence, deserves some credit as a pioneering exercise in a hybrid genre that was to become far more sophisticated as it became much more prolific during the 20th century.

The anthology is concluded by five brief stories by Pierre de Nolhac (1859-1936), which were reprinted in book form in the collection *Contes philosophiques*, published by Bernard Grasset in 1932, although they had presumably appeared in periodicals previously. Nolhac was a prolific writer, best known as a historian, although he also had some reputation as a poet, and he wrote very little prose fiction, but what he did write tended to be inspired by his reflections on the way the world was going, informed by the clinical eye of a narrative historian. The speculations embodied in the stories are small-scale and handled with a deft and delicate wit, representing the end of the literary spectrum opposite to that of the unashamedly populist Espitallier, and illustrating the breadth of the spectrum in question.

The translation of "Mademoiselle de la Choupillière" was made from the version of *Nouvelles* reproduced in Google Books. The translation of *L'Uraniade* was made from the copy of the 1844 edition reproduced on the Bibliothèque

Nationale's *gallica* website. The translation of *L'Automate, récit tiré d'un palimpseste* was made from the copy of the Ghio edition reproduced on *archive.org*, except for the four pages missing from that version, which were filled in from the Kindle version of the ArchéoSF reprint of 2012. The translation of Léon Daudet's "L'Automate" was made from a copy of the undated Guy Boussac edition of *Quinze contes* published in 1948. The translation of "La Mort de Paris" was made from the version in the Kindle edition of Philippe Éthuin's ArchéoSF anthology *Paris futurs* (2014). The translation of *L'Homme en nickel* was made from the feuilleton version reproduced in *gallica* in the relevant volumes of *La Science Française*. The translations of the five stories by Pierre de Nolhac were made from a copy of the Grasset edition of *Contes philosophiques*.

Brian Stableford

Jacques Boucher de Perthes: *Mademoiselle de la Choupillière*

(1832)

In a great and very beautiful city, which counted, as well as six thousand inhabitants, a sub-prefect, a president, a king's prosecutor and a lieutenant of gendarmes—in brief, everything that could contribute to utility and pleasure—there lived a curly-haired, clean-shaven, neatly-brushed fop of the species of those who, in the capital as elsewhere, turn around in a single movement for fear of disturbing the economy of their cravat.

A creature of new invention, wearing a corset and forming the intermedium between man and woman, Baron Léon de Saint-Marcel, twenty-six years rich, with a pretty face and an annual income of thirty thousand livres, playing society games and singing a ballad passably, had everything that constitutes a great man in the beautiful city of B***. Thus, he was the favorite of all the mothers who had demoiselles to marry off, and the target of every spinster or widow in want of a husband. There was not a single dinner party, ball, afternoon tea, lunch, picnic in the woods or excursion in a char-à-banc in which he was not obliged to take part.

The Baron was, in consequence, the busiest man in the arrondissement: putting on his morning suit, his midday suit, his evening suit, visits to receive, visits to make—he did not have a moment to himself. If, by chance, he had a few spare minutes, they were scarcely sufficient to read a fashion magazine, or make tender or polite replies—which were always costly, because he needed to consult the dictionary frequently, as much for thought as for style. Having left school early, he had only got as far as the fourth form, in which one does not learn orthography. He was, therefore, not a scholar; nor was he an intelligent man—which mattered little to him, because he believed himself to be both and, as three-quarters of the city also believed it, he enjoyed all the rewards of science and intellect without experiencing any of the embarrassments.

As we have indicated, Léon had illuminated profound passions among the young women of the locale; but as the demoiselles of our days generally have sage and mathematical views, the primary aliment of the conflagration was the Baron's annual income of thirty thousand livres; he would probably have turned ten times fewer heads had that figure been missing a zero. It is unnecessary to conclude that it was the love of money that made the hearts of those ladies beat—no, people think more nobly than that in the city of B*** , and in any case, to love a rich man is not precisely to love the gold in his cash-box. One loves the proprietor because he is surrounded by all the prestige that makes a person appear lovable: fine clothes, beautiful jewels, lovely furniture; if he does not have all that, one knows that he can have it, or that one could have it for him, which comes to the same thing. That is why, in all civilized countries, the richest futures really are the most beautiful.

Monsieur de Saint-Marcel, whether for moral or political reasons, had not ceded to the seductions of his female compatriots. Although they were generally very nice, he had remained the master of his heart; only one woman had made any impression on him. That was Mademoiselle Louise D***, his cousin, a charming young person who had conceived a sentiment for him that seemed to authorize the projects of the two families. As good as she was beautiful, she possessed exactly what the Baron lacked: intelligence and education; but, her father's fortune having been successively reduced by unforeseen events, Monsieur de Saint-Marcel's passion had diminished in the same proportion, and in the epoch of which we are speaking, had fallen almost to zero. In vain, his mother, on her death-bed, had made him promise to contract that marriage; he was no longer looking for anything but an honest pretext to break off the engagement.

One day, he thought he had found it. After a ball at which Louise had danced with an officer of the garrison, he claimed that she had an intrigue with the soldier.

Thus defamed by the man who was the oracle of society, the unfortunate orphan soon found herself rejected by all the mothers and all the daughters for whom she had previously been an object of envy. Her despair was frightful; the ingrate was still dear to her. She fell ill and, instead of feeling sorry for her, her cousin said that she was play-acting. She played well, because she died.

Petty people who calculate nothing and marry like brutes, for the sentiment of simple nature, criticized the charming Léon severely; they considered him a hard and heartless man. People of status, however—which is to say, people with income—approved of the firmness that he had shown, and the innocent victim, dead of grief, was cited as an example of divine justice, which is always pronounced against young women who dance with soldiers devoid of fortune.

Rid of a redoubtable competitor, the demoiselles redoubled their provocative glances and flirtations. Unfortunately, in the arrondissement of B***, the largest landowners, apart from the Baron, had no more than a hundred thousand écus of capital; that is doubtless a tidy sum in the provinces, but it often happens that a pretty girl whose father and mother are thus provided has little sisters and little brothers, an insupportable rabble for a brother-in-law; or, if she has few or no co-inheritors, the parents are young and do not seem at all inclined to give pleasure to their son-in-law for a long time.

Léon had not, therefore, been able to fix the irresolution of his own wishes; he contented himself with those of all hearts, without granting any of them, which guaranteed him the continuation of politenesses, smiles, diners, compliments, handshakes, and even love letters—for a few sensitive individuals, whose only dowry was their virtue, ventured as far as that.

In that epoch, the arrival was seen in the superb city of B*** of one Monsieur de La Choupillière, a former émigré, former tradesman, former député, former prefect, former chamberlain and former gentleman of the chamber, for the moment simply a malcontent, but still a Comte and worth a million.

Everyone knew what the Comte had been, but no one understood the Comte at all. He was a man like no other, who gave the impression, absolutely, of a human machine. His gestures were regular and compassed, like those of a pendulum, or those of an actor trained in the royal school of declamation. Always on time, to the minute, nothing made him deviate from his route or his habits, and if by chance he made a false step, one might have thought that it was in the place where he intended to make it. He was often very taciturn, and not for anything in the world would anyone have caused him to unseal his lips, because when he began to talk, it was necessary for him to continue throughout a time that he seemed to have determined in advance, and, interruptions and incidents notwithstanding—including, sometimes, the departure of his listener—he carried on talking. His movements were firm and rectangular, as if moved by a spring, and his cycles seemed to be organized on the same principle. His voice, whether by dint of having spoken as a député, announced as a chamberlain, protested as a malcontent or sworn fidelity as a prefect, was exactly as sonorous as the mechanism of a turnspit.

The Comte was a widower; he had an only daughter who was absolutely the same model as her father—which does not happen often, but which ought to be the case invariably, for the facility of family recognition and the convenience of genealogists.

Mademoiselle Colombe seemed at first glance to be the antiphrasis of her name. Nothing in her physique was reminiscent of a dove. With regard to morality we cannot speak, but, leaving all resemblance aside, Mademoiselle de La Choupillière was pretty nonetheless, and very pretty, especially in the light, for her eyes were slightly ringed and her complexion slightly lustrous—certain signs by which one can recognize ladies of high society and the wearing effect of long

16

plays, waltzes, gallops, and, in sum, all the nocturnal recrea-
tions slightly injurious to the general effect. However, the
beautiful hair of the heiress, her pearly teeth, her forehead,
neck, arms and hands whiter than alabaster, her nymph-like
figure and her exceedingly tiny feet soon made one forget
what the freshness of her coloration lacked. If nature was not
present, at least there was art, taken to full perfection.

Mademoiselle de La Choupillière's intelligence, of
which she was said to have a great deal, was of absolutely the
same genre as her face; everything appeared to have emerged
from the hand of the same maker. When she spoke, one believed one was reading a correctly-written book; when she
sang, the ears were filled agreeably, but it was the song of a
Barbary organ; one would have liked less precision and more
soul. Her dancing was analogous; it was the elegant translation
of her father's leaps and bounds. In brief, the entirety of her
person seemed to be the finished work of which the Comte
was merely a sketch.

The arrival of Monsieur de La Choupillière, who had
rented a beautiful residence in the area, was, as one can imagine, a great subject of conversation. All the mothers trembled
on learning that he was rich and had a daughter, and it was
even worse when the demoiselle had been seen, and her
charms were further emphasized by a beautiful carriage, elegant lackeys and a superb hunter.

By a strange circumstance, that retinue had the same nature as the master and the mistress; the horses, as well as the
valets, had something stiff and jerky about them, which was
initially striking. However, as everything was admirably well-
chosen, well kept and perfectly regular, the eye adapted without difficulty to that eccentricity, which was attributed to the
English origin of a part of the staff and the apparatus, and to
the rather long sojourn that the family had made in the British
Isles. In fact, English men and women, horses, dogs and
mules—everything that originates from that country—all have
a mechanical appearance, and an angular character that is not
found elsewhere. Where does it come from? Is it the climate,

the habits, the coal, the porter or the plum pudding? Chemists, anatomists and physiologists will decide.

When Monsieur de La Choupillière was installed in his château, had made his visits to the authorities and the principal families, and had sent cards to the others, he wanted to celebrate his arrival with a party. All the high society of the city was invited, and Baron Léon was not forgotten.

Before he had even met the young woman, her title of heiress had seduced him; as soon as he saw her there was, as one would expect, a veritable surge of sympathy. Never, since Pyramus and Thisbe, Petrarch and Laure, the old and the new Héloïse, had a more violent passion set a heart ablaze, and when the superb silverware was deployed and he had heard its proprietress sing, and seen her dance, and was able to convince himself that the diamonds with which she was covered were not paste, what did he not experience? His bosom pounded as violently as if he had run a race on the Champ-de-Mars against the horse Phoenix or the mare Atalante. So he was all care and attention for the lovely young daughter, and manifested his admiration to the father, who, with a smile that one might have thought hewn with a chisel, replied: "She's the very image of her late mother."

Monsieur de Saint-Marcel, occupied with his new passion, had greatly neglected his old acquaintances during the evening—he had not even spoken to Mademoiselle O***, with whom he had danced regularly at every ball for ten years—with the result that the following day, there was a unanimous outcry against him.

The young men, excited by the others, and perhaps naturally aggressive in the city of B***, thought it appropriate to pick quarrels with him. They were all the more disposed to do so because Léon had just been deprived of his firmest support—his right arm, so to speak. That is a circumstance that it will not be futile to make known.

Our Baron, although very skillful with the épée, as with a pistol, did not like fighting, because he had noticed that one never gained anything whether one killed or was killed. In order to enjoy the pleasure of impertinence, however, and, at the same time, only to have to submit to its consequences as rarely as possible, he had for his second in all encounters a kind of cutthroat, a professional swashbuckler and the terror of honest folk for ten leagues around. One could not seek a quarrel with the Baron without having to answer to Captain Lapierre, a beast as malevolent as he was venomous, who had already murdered many a family's scion.

No one knew what regiment the Captain had served in; it was whispered in low tones that he was a former fencing-master, expelled from the capital for his evil deeds, and that all his campaigns had been fought in penal battalions. He had actively assisted, by means of malicious talk, in the ruination of the unfortunate D***, and prevented anyone from defending his memory by virtue of the fear he inspired. The young lieutenant, an innocent victim of calumny, having wished to give it the lie, had been challenged to a duel and killed by the said individual.

However, that redoubtable man was, for the moment, unable to fight.

The Captain had the habit of going every evening to the only café in the neighborhood, drinking and gambling at the expense of flatterers—for, whether by virtue of fear or something else, everyone has them. When he went in, he always put his hat on a table, where no one dared disturb it, under penalty of an immediate explanation, after which it was necessary to put the hat back where it had been found, or accept a rendez-vous for the following day—an encounter that no one sought, convinced that there was neither honor or profit to be gained therein.

One evening, when the terrible Lapierre and his redoubt-able headgear were in their customary places, a stranger had come in, who, only seeing one vacant table, had removed the hat and sat down there.

The swashbuckler cries: "Respect Captain Lapierre's hat!"

At that interpellation the stranger looks up, not knowing whether it was to him that it was addressed. The other repeats it, adding a coarse oath. The impassive stranger approaches the stove, and puts the hat on it, to the amazement of the entire assembly, trembling for the imprudent, who probably did not know what he was risking.

As for the Captain, he stood up like Achilles, and the most terrible threat, accompanied by the obligatory challenge, emerged from his mouth.

The stranger's only response was to open the window, seize the arm of the unfortunate captain with an iron grip, and, without further ado, hurl him into the street.

It is difficult to fall on to a road from the first floor, however lacking in elevation it might be, without an inconvenient result, so the valiant Lapierre had his head cracked and his arm broken. He had been confined to bed for a month, vomiting fire and flame against the brute who had put him out of a condition to assume a fighting stance, while his pupil and protégé, Monsieur de Saint-Marcel, found himself the target of the animadversion of all the brothers and cousins of the ladies of the locale.

The Baron was sensitive to his situation; he had always been reckoned brave in the minds of fathers and mothers—which is to say, the people who did not know him—and it was important for him not to lose that salutary reputation. Knowing, therefore, that someone would definitely pick a quarrel with him, he thought it prudent to warn his enemies, and having examined the question of which of them might be the most maladroit and cowardly member of the coalition. He took advantage of the first opportunity to provoke him.

The rendezvous having been agreed, they went to the dueling-ground. As the Baron had anticipated, his adversary was afraid, and there was talk of lunch. The victor accepted, and took the opportunity to invite all his rivals, whom he treated to truffles and champagne.

There is no intimity that can resist fine cuisine; the anger of young men is not tenacious, especially when it is only artificial and second-hand. It was, in any case, unimportant to them that Monsieur de Saint-Marcel adored demoiselles and was adored by them. He cleverly made them aware of that, and the peace treaty, whose preliminaries had been presented with the first course, was signed with the second.

With matters thus arranged, the elegant Léon was able to abandon himself entirely to his amour. The charming Colombe appeared to welcome all her admirers with equal kindness, but as she saw the Baron most frequently, it was to him that she listened with pleasure most frequently. The father did not seem at all inclined to oppose his daughter's inclinations; he had no scruples about leaving her alone with her visitors. Someone having made an observation to him in that regard, he replied that he had every confidence in Mademoiselle de La Choupillière, who was the image of her late mother.

One day, Monsieur de Saint-Marcel found his inamorata sitting on a grassy bank under a honeysuckle arbor. Everyone knows that arbors and grass are appropriate to sentiment in all countries, and they were no less so in the fine city of B and its environs. As soon as Léon had touched the bracken he felt suddenly inspired, and to be frank, he should have been; the semi-obscurity of the boscage, the simple and skimpy attire of the young woman, including the dress whose indiscreet folds allowed treasures to be divined, all seemed calculated to seduce him, if he had not been seduced already; I even believe that he would have fallen to his knees in his admiration if the tight trousers he was wearing had permitted him the possibility.

He commenced with a sigh, which was followed by a question that is slightly vulgar, but which had always been positive in the locality of B***: "Have you ever been in love, Mademoiselle?"

"I've heard a great deal of talk about it, Monsieur," Mademoiselle de La Choupillière replied.

"It's a burning passion, Mademoiselle."

"That's what everyone says, Monsieur."

The Baron had started badly, for he remained tongue-tied, as often happens during a matrimonial declaration—further proof of the malice of the demon that always murmurs accurately and effectively to us when it is a matter of an evil motive.

It was necessary to get out of it. What good was it to Monsieur de Saint-Marcel to have been the daring of all the local beauties for such a long time, only to remain mute, like an infatuated fifteen-year-old, on the day when it was most important for him to speak?

The second attempt was no more fortunate. He embarked on a definition of love. He was not very strong in the descriptive genre, and he took almost all of it from the valet in *Le Joueur*.[1]

Mademoiselle de La Choupillière could have said to him: "Love can no more be defined than air or light; it is sensed; it is inspired," but she did not, for she was very modest and reserved."

Finally, Monsieur de Saint-Marcel, after a profound sigh, exclaimed: "Adorable Colombe, it is futile to disguise my wishes any longer. I adore you; I offer you my heart, my life, my name, my fortune. Speak: it is my sentence that you are pronouncing."

"Monsieur," replied Mademoiselle de La Choupillière. "I'm extremely flattered by what you've done me the honor of saying to me, but, as you have had occasion to remark. I have a father; it's to him that you ought to have gone first to ask him for authorization to declare sentiments to me that, honorable as they might be, are entirely irregular at this point in time."

That was a perfect response, and as there is nothing to add when all has been said, the Baron found himself halted again, as if he had had less presence of mind.

"Oh, Mademoiselle," he continued, in a despairing tone "what would be the use of your father's agreement, if I did not

---

[1] Jean-François Regnard's comedy of 1787.

22

have the joy of obtaining yours? In the name of pity, for I do not dare to speak any longer in the name of love, pronounce your verdict; it is life or death."

For a second time he had the idea of throwing himself at her feet, but the wretched trousers still restrained him, and he swore that he would put on more ample ones when the opportunity presented itself.

"Monsieur," replied Mademoiselle de La Choupillière, "my father's wishes are always mine, and the will of a good child cannot be other than to obey."

That manner of expression was somewhat less than romantic, but, as we have said, the daughter and father alike only spoke in ready-made formulas, sentences and phrases, such as are found in all almanacs, gazettes, posters and announcements.

Léon hastened to respond as one responds in such cases, to wit: "Mademoiselle, it's not obedience, but love that…etc." His ardor carried him away to the point that he forgot the inconvenience of his attire, and the genuflection occurred.

Immediately, that which had to happen happened: the inflexible cloth was rent, not in the heart but in a less appropriate place—and that disconcerted him to such an extent that, although not timid by nature, he blushed, went pale, and could only retire, covering the vestment laid bare with his hat.

Having returned home, cursing the fragility of modern fabrics, he could think of nothing better to do than follow Mademoiselle de La Choupillière's instructions o the letter and address himself to her respectable father.

Meanwhile, the mothers, who were not unaware of the Baron's projects, were suffocating with chagrin. It was, in fact, hard to see a stranger winning such a victory over their daughters, merely because she was richer, more beautiful and more amiable, so it was necessary to hear what they were saying about the Comte and his progeniture.

After having exhausted all the resources of ordinary ill-speaking they came to calumny. According to the ladies, no one knew where the Comte had some from, although he had been many things. It was said at first that he was a nonentity, or even less, and was not even a man at all. It was claimed that at certain time, words suddenly failed him completely, and then movement, and that neither were returned to him until a certain agent, who accompanied him everywhere, had subjected him to some mechanical, chemical or surgical operation.

Such a rumor had nothing that could disturb a son-in-law greatly, but it was added that Mademoiselle de La Choupillière was in precisely the same state, and that during these accidents, no one was admitted to the house. It had also been noticed that on the days of balls, at a fixed time, the senior valet or steward, the only one who did not have the strained mannerisms of the rest of the household, came to extinguish the lights, and that at that signal, the Comte and his daughter wished their guess goodnight and withdrew. That had initially been taxed as arrant impoliteness; then people had got used to it, and now everyone was convinced that the master's health required it thus.

It was therefore believed to be an attack of catalepsy, which is nothing but a perfected epilepsy, and it was alleged that Mademoiselle Colombe was afflicted with the same disease. But Monsieur de Saint-Marcel saw nothing in these allegations but malevolence, and did not believe a word of it. In any case, the fortune was there, and with a few precautions, catalepsy could not have any effect on it.

The amorous Baron, having prepared his request carefully, went to see Monsieur de La Choupillière one day, and presented himself in the most respectable and filial manner that he could imagine. The Comte recited, one by one, all the words that do not say yes or no, and sent him back to Mademoiselle de La Choupillière, with his accustomed remark.

Sparing readers, mercifully, from preliminaries that would be as tedious for them as for the lovers, we shall say that after having been from daughter to father and from father to daughter, Monsieur de Saint-Marcel obtained the consent that he desired, with the aid of the steward, who seemed to have great credit with both of them. Convention dictated that the marriage would take place in a month, and a mutual agreement was signed, under the guarantee of a large sum.

Now, it has long been embarked that, in counties where one wants to marry, everyone hears the news of a marriage before anyone has mentioned it; that is what happened in the great city of B   . The next day, it was the talk of every drawing room.

The anger of the mothers and daughters was terrible, and many might perhaps have died of it if, the day after the publication of the banns, the rumor had not spread that the Comte had just lost half his fortune in a major lawsuit.

The future spouse ran to his future father-in-law, who confirmed the verity of that unfortunate circumstance, and added. "But you still have Mademoiselle de La Choupillière; she's the very image of her late mother; you can't fail to be perfectly happy."

That reasoning, and the certainty that half of the Comte's fortune could still pass for a complete fortune, partly dissipated the disappointed Baron's concerns.

A few days later, it was said that the Comte had become involved in an affair on the Bourse, which had removed the other half of his capital. A further visit by Monsieur Marcel brought forth a further confirmation on the part of the Comte, who, after having addressed a superb speech to him, repeated: "But you still have Mademoiselle de La Choupillière."

That was, in fact, a great consolation. The future was still rosy. And then, the furniture, silverware and diamonds were worth a lot of money. The next day, however, it was said that the tableware had been sold and the diamonds seized.

A further race by the son-in-law followed, to whom the father-in-law replied with the same formula. Now, the contract had been signed, so there was a considerable forfeit; there was no more going back. In any case, it is necessary to say, Monsieur de Saint-Marcel was in love, and, even had he been free, he might have hesitated before renouncing his inamorata.

The wedding took place the following day. In spite of the Comte's misfortunes, a feast had been prepared; the entire city was there, some out of curiosity, some out of interest for the family, of which no one was any longer jealous now that it no longer possessed anything. The evening was quite cheerful, and, whatever the amorous Léon did to prevent it from being prolonged, it was nearly midnight when the steward, as usual, came to extinguish the lights and send the company away.

Monsieur de Saint-Marcel retired immediately to his wife's apartment; at that moment he forgot all the blows that fortune had struck him; he was the possessor of the most delightful of creatures, and an air of abandon and languor that he had not remarked before rendered her more seductive than ever. She was on a sofa; she sat down beside her; he removed the light gauze covering her shoulders, and those pure forms appeared to his enchanted eyes. Then his love burst forth in burning expressions.

She responded to it with a sight, and said "I..."

Then midnight chimed.

She stopped.

Léon thought that emotion alone was the cause, and even more smitten, he repeated his protestations.

To that his young wife made no reply. A curl of blonde hair tickled the amorous husband's cheek. He wanted to touch that charming hair; he asked to press it to his lips. She kept silent; that was a consent; He drew nearer, but at the first effort the curl came away from the forehead.

Astonished, he seized another; same effect. What! Was the interesting Colombe wearing a wig? He interrogated her; she remained mute. He took her hand; the hand did not respond to his own. He shook it.

Surprise! The arm came away.

The husband made a gesture of terror, and that movement, agitating the sofa, caused the head to slump. He tried to support it; it fell on to the floor.

Griped by horror, he thought that a baleful vision had troubled his reason.

He runs to the father's room. The latter is still up; he bombards him with questions; he comes to reproaches—the same silence. In his anger, he strikes him, and experiences a sharp pain. He repeats the blow; blood flows from his hand.

He returns to his wife, thinking again that he was deluded. He seizes the inanimate body, which yields to his efforts and separates into a thousand pieces. In a trice, he sees the parquet covered with cogwheels, screws, nails and springs, which collide with one another and roll around, with a silvery sound—and nothing remains in his arms but a dress and the stick of a doll.

He wants to escape that infernal house. In the antechamber he sees the lackeys arranged against the wall, upright, like mannequins after a performance at the opera. He calls them by name, and orders them to prepare a carriage, but not one budges. He launches himself into the courtyard; it is silent. He runs to the stable; he recognizes the coachman, the horses, the dogs, stiff and motionless, all seemingly deprived of life.

Beside himself, no longer knowing what he is doing, he wanders at random. Finally, he finds himself in front of his house; into which he goes, harassed and half-dressed. His servants are astonished and wonder what accident has set the Baron roaming on his wedding night.

Prey to a feverish delirium, he throws himself on his bed, but, ready to belief in magic, shades and revenants, he cannot chose his eyes.

When daylight appears, determined to clear up his doubts at any price, he arms himself, mounts a horse and, followed by his valet, goes to the château.

When he goes into the courtyard he hears a loud sound of hammering. In the vestibule he sees a great many workmen and crates, some sealed and others ready to be. Searching with his eyes for the master of the house he arrives in the nuptial chamber, where he finds the steward picking up the pieces of the Baronne.

On seeing him come in the steward presents him with an invoice signed *Roberson, mechanician*, demanding 10,545 francs 25 centimes, for the cost of repairs to his two best automata.

Pierre Bremond: *The Uraniad or, Aesop's Judges in Urania's Court*

(1844)

Advertisement

The Uraniad should not be regarded as an ordinary play. I have not pretended to write a comedy, for then it would have had to be constructed on another plan and circumscribed by narrower limits. I am not writing for the theater. There is nothing here but simple dialogues on very dry and abstract matters, which I thought I ought to cheer up with a few fairly innocent jokes; and as there are several interlocutors who are not always necessary, they naturally appear and disappear, which has constituted veritable scenes. To place myself within the range of all kinds of readers I have tried to explain myself clearly while talking about very abstract things. I shall be satisfied if I have been able to achieve that aim; in any case, this little bagatelle will form a kind of commentary or preface to the manuscript work entitled *On the Search for the Truth in the Sciences*, which I have deposited at the Bibliothèque du Musée Calvet d'Avignon on 25 March 1843.

As it is alleged that the philosophers of all centuries resemble one another, and that once imbued with an opinion, even if it is erroneous, almost all of them want to defend it until the end of their life, closing their eyes to the most lucid demonstrations, I have therefore thought that by cheering up scientific assertions with jokes, I might more efficaciously engage young astronomers to mistrust theories, even the most lauded, and not allow themselves to be seduced by the striking renown of the scientists who have preceded them, but above all to think for themselves by making use of the doubt that served, before them, Copernicus against Ptolemy, Descartes against Aristotle, Kepler against Tycho Brahé and Newton against Descartes.

CHARACTERS

AESOP
NEWTON, English geometer-astronomer and physicist
HEROMONDAS, astronomer, partisan of Newton
SGRAVESANDE, Dutch physicist, partisan of Newton
PEMBERTON, English geometer, partisan of Newton
MAUPERTUIS, French geometer, partisan of Newton
COPERNICUS, German astronomer
PLUCHE, French physicist
BERNARDIN DE SAINT-PIERRE, French litterateur
VOLTAIRE, French poet and philosopher
POPE, English poet
Monsieur JOUROUFLE, partisan of Newton
The CONCIERGE of Urania's palace
A retinue of astronomer-geometers and physicists.

The scene is under the portico of Urania's palace.

Scene One
Voltaire, Pope

VOLTAIRE: Ah, there you are, my dear Pope! Who would ever have believed they would encounter you under the portico of Urania's palace,[2] you who have constantly been seen inhabiting the verdant arbors of cheerful Helicon. What fortunate hazard brings you here?

POPE : A motive very praiseworthy in an Englishman: to see Newton, to admire and contemplate his glory. But my dear Voltaire, what have I just learned? Ignorant minds have dared to raise their voices to depreciate the immortal theories of that profound genius!

VOLTAIRE: Yes, Pluche,[3] who has come to sustain before Urania that Newton was not a physicist and only merits the name of calculator, and Bernardin de Saint-Pierre,[4] who has arrived unexpectedly, has also claimed that several of his theories are erroneous.

POPE: What audacity in paltry French scriveners. And Urania has not imposed silence on them?

VOLTAIRE: No, for Criticism, crouched at her feet, has obliged her to suspend her judgment by blackening a notebook with his scribbling, which she has promptly sent to the terres-

---

[2] Urania is the muse of astronomy.

[3] Abbé Noël-Antoine Pluche (1688-1761), author of a pioneering work of the popularization of science, *Le Spectacle de la Nature* (1732).

[4] Jacques-Henri Bernardin de Saint-Pierre (1737-1814), best known for the romance *Paul et Virginie* (1788), left for posthumous publication a three-volume study of *Harmonies de la nature* (1815).

trial surface. More than one author has doubtless taken possession of it, since several writings have reached us here attacking the theories of the great Newton unsparingly. The key to the phenomena of nature has been seen to enter those lists, where it is claimed that the greater part of Newton's algebra is nothing but charlatanry.

POPE:
What fatal destiny is pursuing our immortal Genius? Do you not think as I do, my dear Voltaire, that there is nothing but merit and truly sublime science in our Englishman?

VOLTAIRE: Can you doubt it, since I have always been seen to denigrate my compatriots because they were French? But it's necessary not to despair. We, the admirers and copyists of Newton, in order to oppose a dyke to this torrent of criticism, which threatens to engulf the reputation of that only great man, have obtained from Urania that she will hold her court today, and you can see that she has already had her tribunal set up beneath this portico. Now, we want and intend that she shall sanction by her decrees all the theories of Newton—good or bad, let it be said between ourselves—and that in the person of Pluche and Bernardin de Saint-Pierre she shall condemn the detractors of our illustrious genius to silence, and above all the recent anonymous writing still in manuscript entitled *On the Search for the Truth in the Sciences*, which has been deposited in the Musée Calvet d'Avignon.

POPE: To succeed in that project it is only necessary to form a powerful cabal. The honor of both of us is very much at stake, for will it not be remembered that after having praised Newton to the skies you taunted the Angels, saying: *Are you not jealous of the great Newton?* And have I not written, in my enthusiasm: *God said, let Newton be and all was light?* What is more sublime? All those fine phrases, however, will be nothing but bluster if Newton were not the most extraordinary genius. But do I not see Aesop the fabulist coming?

VOLTAIRE: What does that Phrygian want with us?

Scene Two
Aesop, Pope, Voltaire

AESOP: Don't be astonished to see me here. A simple motive of curiosity brings me to this portico. I have learned that there is to be a great debate between geniuses on the subject of the phenomena of nature, and I wanted to know whether reason will be able to applaud their logic and their arguments.

VOLTAIRE: The subject of their disputes is beyond your range, or do you know, poor Phrygian, what a plus b minus c is worth?

AESOP: When one has to talk about the marvels of the universe, it's pointless to bring the grimoire of algebra into it. Simple common sense suffices in questions of that sort. "The practice of that science is doubtless good to ensure by calculation a verity already recognized by reason, but you can take it for certain that any proposition that cannot be demonstrated without algebra is not admitted by nature."

VOLTAIRE: You have become another's interpreter, then? That is one of the reflections made by the author of the key to the phenomena of nature; but our geometers do not let him speak.

AESOP: Whoever the author might be, the reflection is no less true, and I shall see today whether your new philosophers are like those of my century, who reasoned a great deal and observed very little.

VOLTAIRE: Were they very ignorant, then?

AESOP: They were, to such a degree that I could only find one who knew that dogs moved their tails and their ears; and Bernardin de Saint-Pierre, one of your most celebrated observers, told me not long ago that your philosophers bear a strong resemblance to those of times past.

VOLTAIRE: We shall see; but in the meantime, I advise you, great block of ancient flesh, to hide in some corner to escape the gaze of our sages, in order not to make nature blush, in their eyes, at her formless production. Here they come. What! Heromondas is with them? So much the better. He's conversing with Newton and Pemberton.[5]

Scene Three
Newton, Pemberton, Heromondas, Aesop, Pope, Voltaire
Retinue of astronomer-geometers and physicists

NEWTON: What an infinite pleasure your coming gives us, my dear Heromondas! Newton could hardly wait to see you in order to thank you, on behalf of the physicists here, for the zeal that you have shown in the defense of his systems. What does the scientific world say now?

HEROMONDAS: The scientific world is enthusiastic to have named you as its dictator with one voice, and the geometer Bailly,[6] who came to this region before me, must to have told you that himself in presenting you with his *Histoire de l'Astronomie moderne*, which is filled with eulogies to you.

NEWTON: It's necessary to admit that if I have acquired the fine title of dictator, it's principally to the French geometers

---

[5] Henry Pemberton (1694-1771) was a physician, one of Newton's few personal friends. He edited the third edition of the *Principia Mathematica*, which appeared in 1726.
[6] The astronomer, mathematician and Revolutionary Jean-Sylvain Bailly (1736-1793)

that I owe it. They are the ones who have borne me to that pinnacle, without paying any heed to what love of their fatherland might demand. Oh, what thanks do I not owe them? But tell me, illustrious Heromondas, what is it necessary to think of the annoying news that arrives here from time to time, and which causes me to fear for the fate of my theories?

PEMBERTON: Merit is not always shielded from envy. But after all, what does the sound of distant clamors matter, which are promptly stifled by the reiterated acclamations of your worshipers?

NEWTON: Yes, dear Pemberton; but those cries are alarming nevertheless. Besides which, they are growing gradually louder, and might intimidate those who publish our renown.

HEROMONDAS: Have no fear, O sublime Newton! Your detractors cannot form a band like us. And then, do we not have the journalists of all lands under our sway? Who is the man among them who would dare to raise his voice against us? In any case, who can resist our skillful tactics? Sometimes we exalt the genius of those who march in your footsteps; sometimes we affirm that no scientist of merit refuses to adopt your theories. Who does not desire to see the fruit of his genius praised? Who is not ashamed not to be counted among the scientists of merit? Furthermore, if someone prepares a work favorable to your hypotheses, we inform the world via the voice of the press that a book is about to appear that will be epoch-making in the annals of human intelligence. When it appears we announce that the scientific world was waiting for it impatiently and had received it thankfully. In fact, all that is false, but our goal is achieved. We praise one another mutually; we intimidate the depreciators of the theory of universal gravitation; we sustain the zeal of its propagators; and renown is accustomed only to call marvelous and sublime the writings that reflect the radiance of your genius.

NEWTON: But it is said that a certain manuscript work has recently appeared that tends more than any other to darken our glory.

HEROMONDAS: You doubtless mean the work entitled *On the Search for the Truth in the Sciences*?

NEWTON: Yes, have you read it?

HEROMONDAS: Purely by chance, for it is not one of the writings that we seek for preference. Our honor is interested in allowing them to grow old in forgetfulness, and if it happens that we read one we do not admit it, in order not to excite the curiosity of others, which would only turn to our detriment.

NEWTON: But who is the inconsiderate scientist who, in the path of the sciences, has dared to serve as the guide for the author of this disastrous work?

HEROMONDAS: None, and it appears that the author has drawn it almost entirely from his own brain, for he says things that have always been unknown to scientists both ancient and modern, and his manuscript contains discoveries of which, let it be said between ourselves, we have never thought, observations that we have neglected—I don't know how—and experiments that we have made or explained in a contradictory fashion.

NEWTON: Is that possible?

HEROMONDAS: Yes, quite possible, and I assure you that if you and I had been aware of these observations and experiments at the outset of our scientific career, we would have avoided following the route that we have taken, and where we have made a thousand false steps; and I fear that young minds deprived of prejudices, which launch themselves on the path of the sciences, might finally perceive our errors, which might even allow them to acquire a great renown.

PEMBERTON: What! We have taken a thousand false steps? No, certainly not. You'll never make Pemberton believe that.

HEROMONDAS: My dear friend, I would very much like to doubt it myself, but it is only too true. And there are examples, which we must carefully conceal from the public and new adepts. You cannot deny that a convexo-convex or plane-convex transparent substance magnifies the objects that one observes through it. Well, the terrestrial atmosphere is diaphanous and plano-convex relative to us; it ought therefore to have the property of substances that possess those two qualities.

PEMBERTON: Which is to say that it ought to amplify the apparent diameter of stars?

HEROMONDAS: Precisely—and we never thought of that.

NEWTON: O Heaven! What blunders we might have made in ignorance of that property!

HEROMONDAS: Yes gross blunders, for we have never imagined that the sun, the moon and the other heavenly bodies would appear almost half as small without that atmosphere;[7] and yet, it is on their volume amplified by an optical illusion

---

[7] The figure of "half as small" seems entirely arbitrary, given the author's loathing of mathematics. Had he been able to apply measurement and calculation to such vital data as the thickness of the atmosphere, the angle of rays of light striking it and the supposed refractive index of the "lens" constituted by the atmosphere, he would surely have realized that this claim, the lynchpin of his argument, is absurd.

that we have founded most of our calculations. Thus, we have mistaken appearances for realities.

Another example. We have sustained, after you, O excellent Newton, that the celestial spaces were empty, or almost empty. If that is the case, they ought not to oppose any obstacle to the expansion of the terrestrial atmosphere, which is so elastic. Thus, our atmosphere ought naturally to dissipate, by the effect of its own elasticity, and the Earth ought to be devoid of an atmospheric envelope—and by a necessary consequence, if that expansive atmosphere remained coerced around the Earth, it is because there is a fluid substance beyond it that contains it.[8] Thus, if that matter exists, the void is no more than a chimera. What can we oppose to that?

A third example. A stone, dropped from a certain height, falls on to the terrestrial surface. Now, you inform us, incomparable Newton, that it is our globe alone that attracts it.

NEWTON: Of course—but as a hypothesis or supposition.

HEROMONDAS: Well, your assertion, although hypothetical, is entirely contrary to experience. In fact, you know the phenomena of the magnet. You know that that matter attracts iron, but that it sometimes loses its attractive virtue. Furthermore, numerous facts have been assembled regarding electricity that you were never able to know. It has been discovered that a glass tube rubbed in a certain fashion attracts any light substance to which it is approached. But that attractive property cannot be inherent to them, since they are often deprived of it. Thus, if magnetized or electrified substances can lose that virtue, it is not to them that the attraction they exert is due, but only to a substance that has arrived temporarily in their vicinity, which is very sensible when one approaches one face to an electrified globe. Thus the atmosphere that envelops the globe

---

[8] This argument only holds if Newton's theory of gravity is false, so there is a suspicious circularity about the attempt to use it as evidence of that falsehood

might, like the substance that surrounds those bodies, attract the heavy objects that one abandons to their natural weight. But by the effect of a distraction, O admirable Genius, when absorbed by your meditations of the causes of weight, you saw an apple fall to earth, you were only thinking about our globe and not about its atmospheric envelope. Without that unfortunate distraction, would you have neglected to ask yourself in what environment that little mass was gravitating? In the terrestrial atmosphere, you would have replied. Thus, there are two agents, the globe of the earth and its atmosphere, which might have snatched the fruit from its branch. But before concluding that it is the globe alone that has detached it, it is necessary to see whether there is any contradiction in thinking that it might rather be the atmosphere that is the cause of the fall. Now, as that contradiction does not exist here, since the phenomena of the magnet and electricity prove that bodies only attract one another by virtue of the effect of an atmosphere, you would inevitable have recognized that terrestrial gravity only occurs because of the attractive property of our atmospheric fluid.

NEWTON: I admit that the consequence is accurate.

HEROMONDAS: A fourth example. After having affirmed that the Earth exerts an attraction on bodies plunged in its atmosphere, you have advanced, O sublime Newton, that that attraction must extended as far as the moon and the planets. Your theory was so seductive, and its adoption has procured us so much glory, that we have made every effort to corroborate it in seeking proofs endlessly by means of numerous experiments. But those proofs, unfortunately, have been vain, and those experiments have turned against us, without our even perceiving it. In fact, by his experiments on the second pendulum, Bouguer[9] has recognized that in the mountains of

---

[9] The geophysicist Pierre Bouguer (1698-1758) measured small regional variations in the Earth's gravity due to density

39

Peru, the diminution of weight was already very sensible at low distances, and one can see that if he had been able to continue his experiments at a greater height, he would have been obliged hasten his pendulum to zero at a height no greater than half the diameter of the Earth. At that limit, therefore, gravity would no longer have exercised its empire over the pendulum; thus, it is restricted to our atmosphere and cannot extend to the moon, let alone the planets.

NEWTON: Oh, how theories, the savorous fruit of our imagination, deceive us! But can they all be false? No, no, and I hope that my theory of colors and light, at least, is sheltered from the darts of criticism.

HEROMONDAS: Unfortunately, that satisfaction is also refused to you, O supreme dictator!

NEWTON: If that is so, it is necessary to abandon those theories with a good grace.

HEROMONDAS: Not at all. On the contrary, it is necessary to hold firm, scorn the storm that is threatening us and try to intimidate our adversaries with our bold countenance—for otherwise, what would become of our celebrated names?

NEWTON: I consent to that; but then we ought to maintain ourselves purely on the defensive and abandon the project of having the manuscript *On the Search for the Truth in the Sciences* judged, for how can that which is sound be condemned?

HEROMONDAS: Is that the truth? You're going to have that writing condemned?

---

variations in underlying rocks—with the result that the "Bouguer anomaly" is named after him, but the variations were nowhere near as spectacular as this claims asserts.

VOLTAIRE: Yes, we've almost obtained that from Urania, by presenting her with a copy of the work, which a Genius was able to obtain. Look, here's another copy.

HEROMONDAS: You delight me! Courage! Pursue your enterprise; it's the sole means of ensuring our honor.

NEWTON: But what if the public overturns the favorable judgment that Urania will pronounce?

HEROMONDAS: The public? Ha! How can it be a judge in cases of this kind? In matters of science, it criticizes or applauds without knowing, and it reads very few essays that treat subjects of his sort, which are beyond its scope. So criticize, judge and condemn as much as you wish; the public will always share your opinion, because these matters are mysteries so far as it is concerned; it is accustomed to regarding us as oracles, especially when we talk geometry and algebra. In any case, in scrutinizing your decisions, it fears giving proof of great ignorance. But what's this? Do I not see Pluche and Bernardin de Saint-Pierre? How can you suffer those two detractors among you?

PEMBERTON: They have come to defend *On the Search for the Truth in the Sciences*.

Scene Four
The previous, Pluche and Bernardin de Saint-Pierre

PLUCHE: When did you arrive, Heromondas? Newton must certainly have a singular pleasure in seeing you here, for that scientist has no athlete who has fought more valiantly for his cause than you. But if I can believe certain unfavorable rumors, that cause is beginning to decline on the surface of the Earth.

HEROMONDAS: You're mistaken, Pluche. Only those who do not know where scientific beauty resides do not admire the illustrious author of the theory of universal gravitation, but any mind that has even a mediocre education would be ashamed not to yield to Newton the tribute of homage that his divine genius demands.

BERNARDIN DE SAINT-PIERRE: If the news that we receive from France is not apocryphal, it appears that the divine genius is already the object of severe criticism. Have we not heard mention of a certain manuscript in which the author makes known the optical property of our atmosphere?

HEROMONDAS: What silliness are you saying, my dear Bernardin de Saint-Pierre? Is the terrestrial atmosphere a telescope?

PLUCHE: In that regard, however, the author's reasoning seems convincing.

HEROMONDAS: To you, no doubt, but not to us. In any case, if our atmosphere had that optical property, would we be unaware of it?

PLUCHE: Is anything more lucid than what he says about the amplification of the apparent diameter of heavenly bodies, which, without the atmosphere, would appear to us as small on the horizon as at the zenith?

HEROMONDAS: Crazy talk! The author does indeed strive to prove that amplification, but we're incredulous and will not let him say it. He's talking to rocks. But to show you that the manuscript, a copy of which was given to me when I arrived, is only good for trampling beneath the feet of the assembly, I'll throw this copy into your midst. Woe betide anyone who picks it up!

AESOP: Well, Aesop will be that unlucky man; I'll take possession of the manuscript in order to find out for myself whether what it contains is good or bad, true or false, and I'll read it attentively over here.

HEROMONDAS, *to Newton and his adherents:* Aesop is among us! Why didn't you warn me, inconsiderate Geniuses? I would have held on to the work, and would have refrained from chattering as I did in the first moments after my arrival, because that ape once showed in servitude that he has excellent common sense.

VOLTAIRE: What do you have to fear?

HEROMONDAS: Nothing, but it's not good to reveal certain secrets that one ought to keep hidden.

VOLTAIRE: Undoubtedly, but what use can that runt make of it? Let him absorb himself in reading the work that will be condemned by Urania, for her judgment must be favorable to us; I say that before its defenders.

PLUCHE: Hope so, but don't count on it, for Urania won't judge the text without hearing us, and we'll be able to defend it—we're French.

POPE: And we're English.

PEMBERTON: English, French—that's irrelevant in this matter. Newton's detractors will have to submit to their condemnation without recourse, and that's so certain that I'll wager a thousand guineas on it.

BERNARDIN DE SAINT-PIERRE: There's a cabal here, Pluche, but let's not be discouraged. Let's defend the work that contains so many new and undoubtedly true things. The honor of the fatherland might be at stake.

PLUCHE: You can count on me. However, let's not insult Urania by thinking that she might show herself to be unjust. No, she'll weight the reasoning of both parties equitably in her balance, and the truth will prevail.

VOLTAIRE: Perhaps. But in the meantime, you're isolated and not very numerous; we're united and very numerous; and as we shall try to have votes counted, our cause will triumph.

PLUCHE: If it's the more just

VOLTAIRE: It must be and it will be. But what are we doing here? We're wasting time in futile discussions. The hour of judgment has come. Let Urania appear, judge and condemn our adversaries. Let's speak to the Concierge. Hey, someone!

PEMBERTON: Someone's opening it's the Concierge.

Scene Five
The preceding, and the Concierge of Urania's palace

CONCIERGE: What do you want, O Geniuses?

VOLTAIRE: That the powerful Urania should mount her throne to strike down with her decrees the vile contradictors of our incomparable Geometer, and above all to condemn without recourse the recent text entitled *On the Search for the Truth in the Sciences*.

CONCIERGE: I was waiting before notifying you of Urania's will for you to put an end to the vain declamations with which you're making the palace walls resound. I've been ordered to choose a judge from among you.

POPE: What luck!

44

NEWTON: By that signal favor Urania has shown her equitable impartiality, and we ask that it please her to name for a judge the celebrated Heromondas, freshly arrived here, and whom you see before you.

CONCIERGE: That cannot be. That scientist has long shown the greatest partiality for you, and it is to be feared that his prejudices would influence the judgment he pronounced. Would you like Pluche or Bernardin de Saint-Pierre?

POPE: Neither. If Heromondas is a declared partisan of the illustrious Newton, they have not hidden the fact that they are his contradictors. In any case, they're French and would doubtless be glad to see the balance tipped in favor of a text that seems to be the work of a Frenchman. Appoint Pemberton.

BERNARDIN DE SAINT-PIERRE: We challenge him.

CONCIERGE: Why?

PLUCHE: Because he's English and a friend of Newton, the same suspicions might be born in the mind of a Frenchman that an Englishman has conceived against the French.

CONCIERGE: That's true.

PEMBERTON: Install the physicist Sgravesande,[10] then, who is coming toward us accompanied by Monsieur Jouroufle. That physicist belongs neither to France nor Great Britain, so

---

[10] The Dutch lawyer Willem Jacob s'Gravesande (1688-1742), who was appointed professor of mathematics and astronomy at the prestigious University of Leiden in 1717, became one of the leading popularizers of Newton's work in continental Europe. He designed numerous experiments to demonstrate Newtonian principles, and greatly impressed Voltaire.

he will be neutral. How can he give umbrage, since, being Dutch, he has no interest n tipping the balance unjustly. You can take my word for it.

PLUCHE: I challenge him too.

CONCIERGE: For what reason?

PLUCHE: Because he was the first to raise the trumpet to publish the excellence of the English geometer, and he did so with such effrontery that even a Newtonian has not been able to avoid calling him a fanatical partisan of Newton.[11]

CONCIERGE: Before condemning him it's necessary to hear him. Let him approach in order that I might ascertain what is in his soul, but let no one speak to him before I do.

Scene Six
The preceding, Sgravesande, Jouroufle

CONCIERGE: Sgravesande, you doubtless know that in order to repress the contradictors of Newton, we are to pass judgment today on *On the Search for the Truth in the Sciences*?

SGRAVESANDE: Yes, that is the subject that brought me here.

CONCIERGE: What do you think of Newton?

SGRAVESANDE: That he is an excellent, divine mind; that he has never been mistaken, that all his conceptions are imprinted with the seal of immortality and that his slightest ideas

---

[11] Author's reference: "Paulian's *Dictionary of Physics*, 8th edition, article Sgravesande." The text in question is by another important pioneer of the popularization of science, Aimé-Henri Paulian (1722-1802),

are strokes of genius. So I have come here to stand up against his critic, and have the latter's work condemned. But in order that the affair can be expedited sooner, I have drafted the edict of his condemnation and have brought it to Urania in order that she can sign it immediately without reading it.

CONCIERGE: Good, that's sufficient; let's look for another judge.

PEMBERTON: You'll search in vain throughout the universe. If you take one from among the geometer-astronomers, he'll think like Sgravesande, because Newton's merit has convinced and delighted them all.

PLUCHE: And also because, having divided his work between them, they have an interest in defending his glory; in going to war for Newton they're fighting for themselves.

CONCIERGE: Well then, it's necessary to eliminate the enthusiasts and contradictors from the tribunal; I want to establish as a judge a man who, having known nothing about his theories until today, will be exempt from all prejudice or partisan spirit. It will be sufficient that he judges in accordance with veritable common sense.

PEMBERTON: I advise you to go to look for that judge among the geniuses of antiquity.

CONCIERGE: Pemberton, your advice is good and will be followed. Indeed, I see Aesop here, who lived in remote centuries. I appoint him as your judge. Approach, Aesop, mount your tribunal, and show in that new dignity the same intelligence that you manifested in slavery.

HEROMONDAS: Aesop is our judge?

SGRAVESANDE: What! That grotesque individual?

VOLTAIRE: Yes, him! Quickly, fetch a sculptor; tell him to come with his chisel and promptly rough-hew that formless mass, in order not to frighten the amiable companions of Urania.

POPE: He'll never make an Adonis of him.

CONCIERGE: No, he's no more an Adonis than you are, but he has his share of common sense, which is worth more than all the graces of the body.

HEROMONDAS: But remember, illustrious guardian of the palace, that Aesop is not initiated into the elevated mysteries of geometry, and in order to be able to weigh the merit of the great Newton, it is necessary to begin by adopting his ideas and making use of his principles and methods.

CONCIERGE: That is exactly what you have all done, and that is what has led you astray. To judge in a case that ought to revolve around the natural phenomena exposed to all eyes, it only requires intelligence and common sense, and in that regard, Aesop does not cede to any genius. Aesop, here is your tribunal; remember that you have been appointed a judge to disentangle the false from the true and hold the balance accurately.

NEWTON, *to his friends*: Not wanting to witness the debates, I shall retire for a while, Defend my cause yourselves.

Scene Seven
The preceding, with the exception of Newton and the Concierge, the latter having gone back into Urania's palace

AESOP: What is it about, Geniuses that I see present here?

48

PEMBERTON: We have come to defend Newton, the incomparable English geometer, and we request the condemnation of *On the Search for the Truth in the Sciences*, which has dared to attack his divine systems.

AESOP: Who are his accusers?

PEMBERTON, SGRAVESANDE, HEROMONDAS: Me. Me. Me.

AESOP: There are three of you, then?

JOUROUFLE: And me too, Seigneur Aesop; I would like that honor.

AESOP: What is your name?

JOUROUFLE: I have the advantage of being named in all letters Monsieur Jouroufle.

AESOP: That name announces nothing good, but appearances are often deceptive.

JOUROUFLE: Yes, Monsieur Aesop, and one can spin one's yarn like anyone else, for such as you see me, I'm a former porter of an academy in Auvergne, profound in the science of numbers, and hence savant in all genres, endowed with an admirable loquacity, and advantaged by an exquisite discernment.

AESOP: That's as may be. Who are the defenders of *On the Search for the Truth in the Sciences*?

PLUCHE, BERNARDIN DE SAINT-PIERRE: We are.

JOUROUFLE: Good! They're only two, and we're four.

AESOP: You, accusers of *On the Search for the Truth in the Sciences*, what grievances to you allege?

PEMBERTON, SGRAVESANDE: Several. Several.

AESOP: Enunciate them—but each speak in your turn.

SGRAVESANDE: One would never finish if it were necessary to list them all. They are constant, numerous and damnable. What sin is greater, in fact, than that of criticizing the great Newton? The text that we are denouncing has committed it; it is therefore guilty, and you cannot dispense with condemning it. Hasten, then, to pronounce its condemnation, and if you judge it worthy of the fire, I shall execute the sentence myself.

AESOP: You're going very quickly, Sgravesande. You want to burn the book without having heard its defense! The passion you're showing in this affair warns me to be on my guard in order not to be taken by surprise.

JOUROUFLE: O Sgravesande, Monseigneur Aesop is right to be annoyed. What, you begin with insults? Do you not know that at the beginning of a speech it's necessary to handle one's judge with velvet gloves? Then again, an exordium ought to be simple, polished and modest. Oh, if only I had spoken!

SGRAVESANDE: And what would you have done? Clear water!

JOUROUFLE: Clear water? Oh, Monsieur de Sgravesande, you do not know all of my little talent. In your place, I would have softened up my judge with my caresses, in order that I could bring him to my feet. Try.

HEROMONDAS: Well, since your talent can bring about this miracle, we cede the floor to you. Speak, but speak well. Raise yourself up to Newton's height.

JOUROUFLE: Allow me; I shall raise myself up as far as the eye can see rather than trail on the earth in speaking of our great geometer, and I know by heart all of Bailly, who is full of such beautiful things in favor of that supreme dictator. I shall begin.

Monseigneur Aesop, how consoling it is for illustrious Geniuses to have to speak before the most celebrated of all Phrygians, before the admirable intelligence that was the honor of his century and who, by his allegorical conceptions, made fortune blush for having so disadvantaged him in terms of his birth, wealth and physique.

AESOP: Let's leave my good and bad qualities there, and get to the point.

JOUROUFLE, *emphatically*: I am here and I shall speak for Newton.

"Nature wearied of the importunity of men during so many centuries, and errors that disfigured the truth, only demanding an interpreter worthy of her. But such an interpreter could only be a unique benefit to that nature, and it was necessary for her to provide him; finally, no longer able to resist the interested wishes of so many mortals, and wanting to unveil herself entirely, she summoned and produced Newton." Oh, Monsieur Aesop, what a man was Newton! And what a fine spectacle it was to see that scientist smoothing the initially-fluid Earth, prescribing the form that it ought to receive of equilibrium and calculating the power of the stars over the waters of its consolidated mass, enchaining those very stars to an immobile center by a force that Kepler had imagined, explaining all the phenomena of nature and tracing those phenomena back to the simple and unique cause from which they derived. What a distance between him and his great precursors, as much for the universality as the accuracy of his ideas! The latter have had to blush at numerous failures, and their glory has been stained by a few errors, but according to us, Newton has produced only truths, because, "his genius having transported him to the center of nature, he has been a tranquil spectator there, and has recounted what he has seen."[12] Let us breathe for a moment.

PEMBERTON: What eloquence!

PLUCHE: What amphigory!

VOLTAIRE: What sublime speech!

BERNARDIN DE SAINT-PIERRE: What pompous speech!

HEROMONDAS: That's declaiming Bailly really well.

JOUROUFLE: I've got my breath back. I'll continue. Oh, Monseigneur Aesop, if you could only conceive all the sublime ideas of our great geometer, see through his eyes like us, think with his own intelligence, reason in his fashion, you would admit without difficulty that it is in Newton's head that all human intelligence has lived. In fact, I see that scientist towering like an oak in the midst of all the great men who have existed, dominating them all by the strength of his brain, embracing everything with the extent of his genius, "endowed above all with a wholeness in ideas, like the one who resides in the universe, assembling before him all phenomena, tracing them back to the causes that were reserved to him, and devel-

---

[12] Author's reference: "See Bailly, *Histoire de l'Astronomie*, reduced to 2 octavo volumes, vol. II, pp 299, 322 and 333." The quotations in this paragraph and in Jouroufle's next speech come from what was originally a separate work, published in 1779, on modern astronomy, following up the first volume, from 1775, on ancient astronomy.

oping in an admirable manner the general phenomenon of nature."[13] Oh, Monseigneur Aesop, how sweet and pleasing for us it would be to see your mind at the level of his sublime ideas. Then, yes, then, delighted with more and more admiration for your supreme merit, we would take pleasure in praising it without measure in our assemblies and charging it with renown by publishing its excellence everywhere.

PEMBERTON: Can one say anything more true?

BERNARDIN DE SAINT-PIERRE: Can one advance anything more false?

JOUROUFLE: Shut up and I'll conclude. Finally, Monseigneur Aesop, since, after what I've just said, it's established that Seigneur Newton has grasped nature in action, and has enunciated nothing but the truth, in accordance with what Bailly says, I request the condemnation of the work entitled *On the Search for the Truth in the Sciences*, which has dared to sustain that the scientist I question was grossly mistaken.

AESOP: Monsieur Jouroufle, you have just pronounced a pompous panegyric, but you have not articulated any fact that could provoke a condemnation.

SGRAVESANDE: Is it not sufficient that we are sure that Newton was incapable of being mistaken, and that nature has revealed all her secrets to him? If you are in doubt, all the Newtonians here are ready to affirm it. In any case, have we not often put into the crucible of calculation the phenomena invoked by Newton in favor of his hypothesis, and after having operated following the genius of the great man, have we not recognized that his propositions were infallible?

---

[13] Author's reference "See Bailly, especially book XX, entitled *Newton*."

JOUROUFLE: Yes Monseigneur Aesop, that's very true; I can assure you, word of Monsieur Jouroufle; for I have done all these calculations rapidly myself.

SGRAVESANDE: What more is needed?

AESOP: Sgravesande, your reasons are not convincing. Your manner of seeing and certain prejudices might have made you believe in Newton's infallibility, but if you have nothing better to say I'll pronounce, and acquit your adverse party.

HEROMONDAS: Is that possible, in spite of the large number of grievances that we have to articulate against our adverse party?

AESOP: Articulate these grievances then.

HEROMONDAS: Here they are, then. Firstly, it is a fact that until now, it has been recognized that the terrestrial atmosphere has no other properties than transparency and elasticity, but by a signal malevolence, the text of *On the Search for the Truth in the Sciences* gives it in addition an optical property by which the apparent diameter of heavenly bodies is augmented by almost half. If we suffer that usurpation, everything about the planets—mass, volume, distance—is overturned, destroyed, and it would be necessary to reconstruct astronomy on new foundations, which would tend to pulverize our theories and systems, which we desire to be adopted permanently.

AESOP: But in matters of astronomical and physical theory, does not everyone have the right to follow the one that appears most plausible to him?

JOUROUFLE: Yes, in the lands of ignorance, but here we shall never permit it. Newton has spoken; *Magister dixit*. It is therefore necessary to be silent, no longer arguing but believing in his word, as we have done—and all under the penalty of being deemed ignorant and rendering oneself culpable of the most unworthy calumny against that divine geometer.

AESOP: Where are you, Monsieur Jouroufle?

JOURUFLE: I am in beautiful France.

BERNARDIN DE SAINT-PIERRE: Monsieur Jouroufle, since you are in beautiful France, ought you not to do something in her favor, and above all, not seek to depreciate her by defending false hypotheses?

JOUROUFLE: Certainly! When one has undertaken to sustain a thesis, it is necessary for one's honor to sustain it until the end. Look, Monsieur Bernardin, you're doubtless a man. Well, if I took it into my head to claim that you're an animal with two feet and devoid of feathers, I would sustain it against everyone, and I would even go so far as to demonstrate that you are nothing but a plumed…cockerel!"

BERNARDIN DE SAINT-PIERRE : A fine talent.

PLUCHE: It's that of a charlatan. But before going any further, I ask Monsieur le Président to permit me to make a few observations. First of all, I remark that Monsieur Jouroufle is reasoning very poorly in making Nature a moral, powerful and intelligent being, and advancing that she has established laws. Nature does not make them, she receives them, since she is merely a passive agent, and composes everything that there is in the universe: waters, rocks, lands, animals, plants and minerals, stars and planets. Now, all of that is incapable of imposing laws on the universe, for I think that Monsieur Jouroufle, who is part of that nature, has never cooperated, with all his genius, I don't say in the creation of the entire world, but even in the formation of a single moss or grain of sand. Thus, nature, instead of being the legislatress in the vast space of the heavens, on the contrary, receives the laws that her Creator

55

has given her, which she is obliged to follow exactly, without a single point of deviation. The jargon that Nature has done this, that Nature has wished that, and other phrases of the same species, which reek of materialism, is a ridiculous language, which science, for its honor, ought to banish forever from its writing and its assemblies, in order not to induce error in the weak and ignorant.

Finally, since mention has been made of Newton's infallibility, I summon my adverse party to declare whether that scientist has never been mistaken.

SGRAVESANDE: Either way, what does it matter?

PLUCHE: Since our adversaries do not want to reply categorically to my question, I ask the president, in order to clarify the matter, to deign to interrogate some other geometer who is able to speak according to his conscience, because, if Newton made an error once, it ought to be permissible for us to ask whether he might have been mistaken on other occasions.

AESOP: I saw Maupertuis[14] mediating not far away; let him be summoned.

A PHYSICIST *in the retinue*: I'll go and find him.

Scene Eight
The Preceding

AESOP: Maupertuis will doubtless not be suspect to the two parties, since, on the one hand, he has embraced the theories of the English scientist throughout his life, and on the other, having terminated his career in the bosom of an austere virtue, he would not belie his last moments by betraying the truth. But here he is.

---

[14] Pierre-Louis Maupertuis (1698-1759).

Scene Nine
The Preceding, Maupertuis, the Physicist

AESOP: Illustrious Maupertuis, is it true that Newton was never mistaken?

MAUPERTUIS: No, unfortunately, for his most enthusiastic partisans have been forced to admit that he was strangely mistaken in his calculation of the precession of the equinoxes,[15] and that on the subject of the difficult problems offered by the system of the world, he was often given to uncertain observations.[16] Furthermore, in the explanation of the delay of the tides in relation to the passages of the sun and moon, the reasoning of the scientist is unsatisfactory, and contrary to the results of a rigorous analysis.[17] Finally, his theory of light is not sheltered from sane criticism. Newton claims that it only comes to us by emission, and several first-rate scientists have been convinced for a long time that that theory is erroneous.

PLUCHE: Important admissions, which give us the right to doubt the infallibility of the English geometer and to believe instead the phenomena that give the lie to his hypotheses.

SGRAVESANDE: I challenge those phenomena.

---

[15] Author's reference: "See Lalande, *Abrégé d'Astron.* no. 1064, and Bailly, *Histoire de l'Astronomie*, vol. II, p. 311 of the edition reduced to two octavo volumes." The former reference is to the French astronomer Jérôme Lalande (1732-1807), whose 1802 history of astronomy updated and replaced Bailly's, but the citation is an earlier work, *Abrégé d'astronomie*, published in 1774.

[16] Author's reference: "Bailly, *ibid.* vol. II p. 312."

[17] Author's reference: "*Exposition du système du monde*, vol, II p. 127." The text cited, published in 1808, is by Pierre-Simon Laplace (1749-1827)

AESOP: Why?

SGRAVESANDE: Because those phenomena only came to us or were explained to us after we had established our hypotheses, in favor of which we invoke the law of prescription.

AESOP: In the matter of scientific theories one cannot invoke the law of prescription, because it is a property of science to tend toward perfection and always to move forward.

BERNARDIN DE SAINT-PIERRE: That is what is happening here. When Newton forged his theories, he did not give any thought to atmospheres, and never thought that by virtue of its optical property, our atmosphere augmented the apparent diameter of the heavenly bodies outside its bosom; thus, in discovering that optical property of the terrestrial atmosphere, the text of *On the Search for the Truth in the Sciences* seems to have enabled science to take a great step forward.

AESOP: In fact, our atmosphere being diaphanous and convex, ought to enjoy the property of all the substances that have those two qualities.

JOUROUFLE: Look, Seigneur Aesop, I don't like to make you a liar because I know my duty, but how can you expect us to believe in that optical property of the terrestrial atmosphere, since we've never ever thought about it?

AESOP: There's no reason to reject a discovery because one has never imagined it. Tell me, Monsieur Jouroufle, before the discovery of magnifying glasses and telescopes, could one have reasonably sustained that those instruments could never magnify the objects at which one gazes through them?

JOUROUFLE: Oh, no, Seigneur Aesop, I wouldn't have sustained that. I'm not such a bad physicist.

AESOP: But that's what you've done, you and Newton. You haven't thought about that magnifying property of our atmosphere, but does that mean that it ought not to exist? To affirm that, it would be necessary to prove that the optical property in question does not belong to the diaphanous convex substances among which our atmosphere is included.

SGRAVESANDE: We're incredulous.

PLUCHE: President, since we're summoned to defend the optical property of our atmosphere, we summon Sgravesande and his colleagues to tell us what makes the sun and the moon appear larger when they are rising or setting than when they reach their meridian?[18]

PEMBERTON: You're very demanding! What's the point of that question?

PLUCHE: To make you show your science as well as us.

SGRAVESANDE: We don't want to; you're too curious.

PLUCHE: Ah! You've been caught wanting, Messieurs?

JOUROUFLE: My party caught wanting! Oh no, Monsieur Pluche, you're mistaken, and if Monsieur de Sgravesande and Monsieur de Pemberton don't want to reply, don't you know that the learned Monsieur Jouroufle is here, who knows how a philosopher ought to proceed when he's interrogated? Have I not before my eyes the example of the Philosopher Monsieur Galileo? Good people asked him one day why the water in the

---

[18] If the author had not been such a determined enemy of measurement and calculation, he might have bothered to check to see whether this familiar phenomenon might be an optical illusion caused by the proximity of points for comparison when the sun and moon are close to the horizon.

tube of a pump didn't rise up beyond a certain height, since, according to him, nature had a horror of a void. Although he didn't know the true cause of the phenomenon, which depended on the weight of the air, he replied without hesitation that nature only had a horror of a void up to a certain elevation, which filled those good people with admiration, who looked at him as an admirable genius. Now, it's always necessary to follow the example of Monsieur Galileo, even when the explanation one gives is the antipodes of the truth. A bold response and not to be caught wanting, that's the quintessence of philosophy. One cuts the Gordian knot if one can't disentangle it. It is, therefore to follow the example of the Monsieur the philosopher of Florence that I say to my adverse party that the sun and the moon appear to us to be larger when rising or setting than at the zenith or toward midday because, although they're really further away from us than they are in the former instances, we nevertheless think that they're closer, and it's that false belief that amplifies their volume in our eyes.

AESOP: Monsieur Jouroufle, are you speaking on your own behalf or on behalf of your colleagues?

JOUROUFLE: Of course I'm speaking on behalf of everyone.

PEMBERTON: Shut up, Maroufle.[19]

JOUROUFLE: Me, Maroufle! Pemberton, know that my name is Monsieur Jouroufle. Is it thus that you repay, with insults, my generosity and all the ardor that I'm putting into defending your hypotheses, which are perhaps not worth my trouble? If I had known... But...

PEMBERTON: You're annoyed? Calm down. Would you like to see yourself expelled from our learned body, which has

---

[19] *Maroufle* means "bumpkin" or "simpleton," but I have left it untranslated to preserve the pun on Jouroufle's name.

made you shine until now like a luminous sun and will give you a passport in due form to traverse all of posterity with honor?

JOUROUFLE: If that's the case I'll calm down, but I beg you, no more words that wound the self-respect of a man of genius like me, especially when he's right. For after all, don't you all explain that amplification of the heavenly bodies on rising and setting, as I do? If you give me the lie, I'll cite the astronomy of Monsieur Lalande and the physics of Messieurs such and such, who will testify against you.

PEMBERTON *in a low voice*: You're right, but on occasion, it's necessary to be able to keep quiet about explanations that might make sensible people laugh.

PLUCHE: President, can science be glorified by the explanation that Monsieur Jouroufle has just given?

AESOP: Indeed, who could ever believe that a distant object would appear larger because one imagines that it is closer? What is more implausible?

JOUROUFLE: What, then is the cause of that apparent augmentation in the apparent size of heavenly bodies when they're rising or setting, which they gradually lose in proportion to their distance from the horizon?

PLUCHE: Monsieur Jouroufle, *On the Search for the Truth in the Sciences* informs you of the cause, and that cause cannot be an imaginary optical illusion, but is real. Now, we have in that regard veridical witnesses that testify in our favor.

AESOP: What are these witnesses?

PLUCHE: These glass bottles full of water we have brought, and which we summon our adverse party to interrogate—

which will be easily done by placing a little ivory ball half way between the edge and the center, to represent the position of the observer of the Earth with regard to our atmosphere. Then we shall see whether the little ball does not appear larger than before, and finally, placed to the right or left to represent the horizon, and then looking obliquely through the bottle, whether its apparent size is not further augmented.

AESOP: That's sufficient. Monsieur Jouroufle, I instruct you to carry out these experiments.

JOUROUFLE: It's not to make me fall into a trap, at least?

AESOP: No, my friend, it's merely to furnish you with the means of knowing the truth. Try.

JOUROUFLE, *transported by joy*: Indeed! The little ball, put into the water in the bottle and brought nearer to the edge on this side of the center really seems magnified, and its apparent dimensions increase further when it is moved to the right or the left; which does seem to prove that our convex and diaphanous atmosphere ought to have the same effect on bodies that are observed through it.

AESOP: That's evident.

SGRAVESANDE: Perhaps to you, President, but not to us. And in any case, let our adverse party not sing victory yet; for if by chance the optical property of our atmospheric fluid seems to us to have made us run into a little snag, we have other hypotheses that ought certainly to make our cause triumph. I therefore request that *On the Search for the Truth in the Sciences* should make an authentic reparation to Newton for having sustained in the second part of its third book that the Earth has another shape than the one that the scientist has attributed to it.

AESOP: And what form has Newton given the Earth.

PEMBERTON: A shape flattered at the poles.

AESOP: Be careful, Newtonians, not to misinterpret the phenomena, which is very common in those who have embraced false theories. A second error might be less pardonable than the first.

JOUROUFLE: Have no fear of that misfortune, Seigneur Aesop, for we Newtonians, having been able to consider the Earth from all sides, have even been able to determine its form in their fashion. What is that fashion? It is this,

Monseigneur Newton, having created his magnificent theory of universal gravitation, supposed—for who can take away the right, so convenient, to make suppositions?—that the Earth had been fluid before having received a movement of rotation about its axis. According to his theory of universal attraction, all the particles of matter having to attract one another mutually, he concluded, nevertheless, that because of the effect of the circular movement the poles of the Earth would be closer to the center while the equator would be further away. Why? Because centrifugal force must be more sensible at the later point than at the poles—but still in the convenient supposition that the atmosphere did not exist, or that it could not compress either the solids or the liquids reposing in the surface of the globe. Is that not conclusive, and does it not demonstrate that the Earth must be flattened at the poles?

PLUCHE: I ask Monsieur Jouroufle when the Earth, fluid at first according to him, became compact and solid; for if it had remained fluid for some time, the dissipation of all its particles would have ensued, by virtue of the rotational movement of the terrestrial axis.

JOUROUFLE: How curious you are! To be sure, the globe became solid when Monseigneur Newton judged it appropriate.

PLUCHE: That's clear, but did the seas also become solid? Otherwise they would similarly have been dissipated by the reiterated action of centrifugal force.

JOUROUFLE: Oh, Newton found by his calculations the point where they ought to stop, and they stopped.

BERNARDIN DE SAINT-PIERRE: Very good! We thank Newton for having preserved us from a great misfortune, for without his far-sighted calculations, we would have no more seas or water. Honor, therefore, to the makers of systems, they are always helpful!

PLUCHE: So it's almost folly to want to inconvenience then; they're accustomed to having their elbows free.

JOUROUFLE: Pluche and Bernardin, you chatter like magpies, but I can see the reason for it. It's because you want to deflect our attention from the question that is now at stake; you're troubled by what *On the Search for the Truth in the Sciences* says about that subject, and don't know how to defend it.

BERNARDIN DE SAINT-PIERRE: You're strangely mistaken, Monsieur Jouroufle, and far from being unable to prove what *On the Search for the Truth in the Sciences* says about the shape of the Earth, we do not blush to assert it ourselves, and to support it presently.

JOUROUFLE: You affirm against Newton that the Earth is not flattened at the axis?

BERNARDIN DE SAINT-PIERRE: Yes, for we're sure that it's slightly elongated.

JOUROUFLE: Behold the obstinacy of these Frenchmen in wanting to deny the most sublime of hypotheses, first imagined by Monseigneur Newton the Englishman, and then demonstrated in our fashion by the most beautiful observations.

AESOP: What are these observations?

JOUROUFLE: What, Seigneur Aesop, you don't know that people have been to Peru and the polar circle to measure the Earth in order to determine its shape? Oh, what a fine result as obtained from those beautiful observations!

AESOP: I had not heard of it until today, but in any case, what was the result of these fine operations?

JOUROUFLE: You shall see. Let's begin at the beginning. While Monseigneur Newton, by means of his genius and his suppositions, determined the form that our globe ought to have, Monsieur Picard in France and Mr. Norwood in England found that the degrees of the meridian were smaller in the first of those two countries, and, in consequence, that those degrees augmented in amplitude in going northwards.[20]

---

[20] Jean-Félix Picard (1620-1682) published *Mesure de la terre* in 1671. Richard Norwood (c1590-1675) calculated the length of a meridian by walking from London to York and carrying out observations of the sun's altitude. Both of their estimates were reasonably accurate, considering the primitive nature of their instrumentation, and did not justify the conclusion drawn here—which is, of course, false, as many subsequent measurements have shown.

AESOP: And doubtless Newton reformed his ideas and saw that the Earth was slightly elongated toward the north pole; for that evidently results from the measurements made.

JOUROUFLE: Not at all. Do you think he would be so gauche? That would have destroyed the generality of his theory of universal attraction, which he wanted to prevail even so. The Earth had to be flattened at the poles, or his theory would have been overturned.

AESOP: And no scientist or Academician saw things differently than Newton?

JOUROUFLE: Yes indeed! Almost at the same time, Monsieur Dominique Cassini,[21] the famous astronomer, measured another part of the meridian which passes through France, and found that in that part of the globe, the southern degrees were, on the contrary, greater than the northern.

AESOP: From that he doubtless concluded that if all the terrestrial meridians similarly had smaller degrees in proportion to their proximity to the poles, the Earth must be flattened in the direction of its poles, because the meridians being shorter there, the line of the axis there must also be shorter.

JOUROUFLE: Yes, that's what he decided.

AESOP: He was right.

---

[21] Giovanni Domenico Cassini (1625-1712) proposed a project to measure an arc of the meridian from the north of France to the south, which was begun in 1683 but soon cancelled. He made a second attempt in 1700, with several collaborators, which produced an erroneous result, as a result of poor collations of measurements taken by different individuals, which Cassini—an opponent of Newtonian theory—welcomed.

JOUROUFLE: According to us, he was wrong.

AESOP: Common sense says that his thinking was sound.

JOUROUFLE: Our geometrical and mathematical principles interpreted in accordance with the mind of Newton...

AESOP: Badly applied, no doubt.

JOUROUFLE: ...Demonstrated that his judgment was false.

AESOP: Here, therefore, is the same figure resulting from two different measurements? That's a curious phenomenon in the history of the sciences.

JOUROUFLE : A curious phenomenon, Seigneur Aesop! Say rather something scandalous! For what can we think of our sublime mathematical sciences on seeing two first-rate scientists, on the subject of the same operation, judging differently and making opposite calculations?

AESOP: That is, in fact, scarcely honorable for the sciences.

JOUROUFLE: So it was to put an end to such a scandal that our scientists went to Peru and the polar circle to interrogate the Earth.

AESOP: And it was mute?

JOUROUFLE: On the contrary, it explained itself clearly, for it's a docile beast.

AESOP: It explained itself for good and all?

JOUROUFLE: Yes, it declared that it really was flattered toward the poles, and in such a manner that no academician in any country whatsoever, and to scientist of merit dared doubt it now. So I don't doubt it, in order not to appear ignorant, for like them, I only see through the eyes of our dear Newton.

AESOP: And how did the Earth announce itself?

JOUROUFLE: Like this. The French geometers might well have followed Monsieur Cassini's opinion, for what did it matter to them whether the Earth's meridians were shorter or longer toward the equator? But, being enthusiasts for Monseigneur Newton's theory of universal gravitation, and wanting to make use of it in order to be illustrious themselves, their desired internally that our globe should have no other form than the one that the English scientist had attributed to it. Wanting to make sure of that for themselves, like conquerors they divided the Earth up in order to measure it again. Some headed for the equator, the others toward Lapland. Full of the object that had gripped their hearts, they began before their departure—note this well—to adopt the ideas of the illustrious Newton, made use of his principles and his methods, and, having the courage o follow him in the career that he had opened, they wanted to show themselves worthy of him in the explanation of phenomena. If you doubt what I've just said you can inform yourself by consulting the celebrated Bailly, who, a supreme admirer of Newton, has consigned all of these beautiful words to his *Histoire de l'Astronomie.*[22]

AESOP: So much the worse.

JOUROUFLE: Oh, rather so much the better. Those geometers could do no less to honor the great Newton, and the good opinion they had of that scientist proves, according to the same author, their discernment and constitutes their greatest eulogy.

---

[22] Author's reference: "Vol. II p. 332 of he edition reduced to 2 octavio volumes."

AESOP: It might well form a contrary proof; and anyway, what happened when these scientists arrives in Peru and the polar circle?

HEROMONDAS: They found that according to their own measurements, that one degree of the meridian in the former country had only 56,750 toises of amplitude, and that, by contrast, in the polar circle, the same degree was 57,438 toises, while the degree determined by Picard in France was only 57,060 toises—which is to say, greater than that on the equator and smaller than that in Lapland.[23]

AESOP: So, the degrees of the terrestrial meridian are more extensive in proportion to one's proximity to the poles?

HEROMONDAS: That's incontestable.

AESOP: So, these scientist concluded from these measurements that the Earth participated in a slight flattening that went from the equator to the pole? For that is the consequence that one ought to draw from the measurements taken in different places.

JOUROUFLE: Not at all. Do you think that those scientists saw like other people? The beauty of modern science was to conclude differently; the respect they had for Monsieur Newton demanded that, especially when they were only seeing through his eyes, as the learned Bailly ingenuously said.

AESOP: They decided, then, that the Earth was flattered toward the poles in the sense of a line backed up to the diameter of the equator?

---

[23] Author's reference: "Bailly, same edition and same volume, pp, 260, 344 ad 345."

JOUROUFLE: Precisely, and that the axis of the Earth was shorter that that diameter.

AESOP: What inconsequence!

JOUROUFLE: Speak more kindly, Monsieur Aesop. Do you take us for fools? Oh, if I displayed all our science for you! Astronomy, physics, chemistry, geometry, algebra, theories, sublime calculations, and what do I know what else? I'll prove to you that we know everything, that we've discovered every-thing, that nothing can be other than we've demonstrated…but it's necessary not to be too proud, in order not to excite the criticism of the severe posterity that does not like one to praise oneself, even when it is well-deserved. Savant and modest, Monsieur Aesop, that's your servant Monsieur Jouroufle.

AESOP: I'd like to believe all that you tell me about your su-preme merit, but you'll permit me, Monsieur Jouroufle, to tell you that in spite of all your science, you're mistaken with re-gard to the question that occupies us at present. For if the Earth had the degrees of its meridians shorter toward the poles than toward the equator, it would have its poles flattened and its axis shortened, as the illustrious Dominique Cassini recog-nized. But on the contrary, must be elongated toward those same poles if the degrees are less great at the equator than toward the polar circle, which the false hypothesis of Newton argues.

JOUROUFLE: Oh, you would think differently, Seigneur Ae-sop, if, in our fashion and in accordance with Monseigneur Newton's theory, we make you a little geometrical demonstra-tion bristling with a little algebra and seasoned with parallel lines, angles and verticals. I'll stun you so forcefully that you'll be unable to respond. Would you like me to commence that learned demonstration?

AESOP: To judge the question of the shape of the Earth, of which has one has measured one of the meridians, it only requires common sense.

JOUROUFLE: Try a little, Seigneur Aesop. Be brave! Don't be so difficult, and soon, like Monsieur Dominique Cassini, you'll be singing the recantation.

AESOP: What! The illustrious Cassini changed his mind?

JOUROUFLE: Not him, exactly, because he was no longer alive then, but his numerous friends did it for him, because we twisted them so much with our algebraic, geometric, mathematical and Newtonian demonstrations that we forced them to correct his writings and to make him say, although dead, that his measurements of the meridian could not constitute the flattened shape that Newton had given the Earth. It was extremely important for us to obtain that retraction.

AESOP: Is it possible that Cassini has been made to say what he did not think?

JOUROUFLE: Yes, and see what miracles algebra can work when one sees through the eyes and thinks with the mind of Monseigneur Newton.

AESOP: That miracle is only illusory, and I blush for the honor of the sciences, for it will serve to prove, unfortunately, how one ought to mistrust your demonstrations, since neither the algebra nor the geometry that you praise so much have been unable to prevent illustrious scientists from falling into your traps, and have not given the any help to disentangle your false sophisms. But that's enough discussion of the question of the shape of the Earth; simpler experiments will soon judge it in an incontestable manner. Let someone bring me three balls of clay of the same diameter and a certain quantity of the same material.

A PHYSICIST of the retinue: President, we have the three balls of clay you requested.

AESOP: Illustrious Maupertuis, I dare say that you would like to cooperate with these experiments. I know that you took part in the voyage the French geometers made to the polar circle and that you have supported the flattening of the poles,[24] but I also know that in your later years you recognized all the deceptive glamour of science. I can therefore believe that you will have listened benignly to all that has been said against the shortness of the axis, and that you will not make any difficulty about giving me your aid to clarify, in a definitive manner, the question presently under discussion. Take these three balls, then, and trace on them the circle of the equator and the line of the meridian. Also mark the poles precisely. By that means, the meridian will be divided into four parts. Then divide one of those parts into ninety equal divisions, which will be as many degrees to represent the quarter of the terrestrial meridian in the case that our globe were to be perfectly round. As for you, Monsieur Jouroufle, I charge you to interrogate these balls in order to obtain a exact response that can indicate unequivocally whether the Earth is slightly flattened or slightly elongated.

JOUROUFLE: Spare me that, Seigneur Aesop, I beg you.

AESOP: Why?

JOUROUFLE: Because I'm not fortunate in the results of my experiments.

AESOP: Perhaps you'll see accurately this time.

---

[24] Maupertuis published a book on the subject of the shape of the Earth in 1738, after the expedition to Lapland, supporting Newton's thesis.

JOUROUFLE: Precisely, that's what warns me not to get mixed up in it, for it might well be that by virtue of seeing accurately, I'll encounter something that will sink our hypotheses.

MAUPERTUIS: President, here are the three balls divided as you desire.

AESOP: Have you measured each of the ninety degrees that form the quarter of their meridian?

MAUPERTIUS: Yes, President.

AESOP: What measure have you found for each degree?

MAUPERTUIS: Fifty-six lignes, which can represent the 56,000 and some toises that constitute a degree of the terrestrial meridian near the equator.

AESOP: Now, leave one of the three balls in its present state. As for the other two, this is what is to be one. Without touching the first three degrees toward to equator, which will retain the same amplitude in order to provide a standard for comparison, it's necessary to swell the poles of one of the other two balls, in such a manner that its axis is longer, and that he diameters of the circles parallel to the equator going toward the north pole are a little larger than those on the round ball. You'll do the opposite for the third ball, so that one will have its axis and the diameter of its parallels shorter than in the round ball.

MAUPERTUIS: It's sufficient.

AESOP: The operation with which I want to charge Monsieur Jouroufle is not very difficult. It's a matter of knowing whether the quarter of the round ball can contain 90 times 56 lignes in going from the equator to the pole.

JOUROUFLE *to Pemberton*: Shall I take the ball?

PEMBERTON: Take it if you wish, but be careful not to betray Newton.

JOUROUFLE: Well, I find that on the quarter of the meridian of that ball I can place ninety times fifty-six lignes.

AESOP: Marvelous! So, if the Earth were perfectly round, all the degrees of its meridian would be equal?

JOUROUFLE: Incontrovertibly.

AESOP: Now take the ball that has just been diminished toward the poles, whose axis in, in consequence, shorter and see if you can place an equal quantity of lignes a similar number of times between the equator and one of the poles.

JOUROUFLE: Not so stupid, Seigneur Aesop. I'd be furnishing a rod for my back by attempting that new experiment, for is it not obvious that, the poles not having as much matter, the diameter of their parallels being smaller, and the axis consequently shorter than in the round ball, it is necessarily the case that the arc formed by the quarter of the meridian will be shorter. If it's shorter, one could never find room there to carry 90 times 56 lignes. If one wanted to conserve the same number of divisions, it would be necessary to diminish the magnitude of the degrees in proportion to the flattening of the poles.

AESOP: This time, Monsieur Jouroufle, you have given proof of discernment and spoken in accordance with veritable common sense.

JOUROUFLE: Oh, Monseigneur Aesop, when we want to, we think just like anyone else; besides which, the matter is so clear that only those who are willfully blind could see otherwise.

AESOP: Would you now care to see whether, on the quarter of the meridian of the ball swollen toward the poles, whose axis is elongated, you can place 90 times 56 lignes?

JOURSOUFLE: Unless it's to lead me astray?

AESOP: No, my friend, it's merely to enable you to reveal the truth. Take the ball and try.

JOUROUFLE, *joyfully*: Monseigneur, there's room to spare. In fact, on that quarter of meridian, one could contain not merely 90 times 56 lignes, but nearly 91 times 56 lignes, and if one wanted to conserve the same number of divisions or ninety degrees, it would be necessary to make those degrees larger in proportion as one approached the axis, or the pole.

AESOP: You're reasoning very well here, Monsieur Jouroufle; and it's evident that the more the degrees are magnified toward the pole, the more elongated that axis will be.

JOUROUFLE: I think so too.

AESOP: In consequence, the Earth must be slightly elongated toward the north, since its degrees have been found to be more extensive in proportion as one approaches the latter region.

JOUROUFLE: Will you permit me to ask Monsieur de Pemberton or Monsieur de Sgravesande? For you've made me jabber like a parrot, and it wouldn't me astonished if, after so many questions, my head were confused.

AESOP: Speak for yourself without consulting anyone. Don't you have enough intelligence for that? You've just made a demonstration of it.

JOUROUFLE: You definitely believe that?

AESOP: Yes.

JOUROUFLE: And that I also sometimes have intelligence?

AESOP: Who can doubt it?

JOUROUFLE: Well, what do you want me to say?

AESOP: The truth.

JOUROUFLE: And in accordance with my conscience?

AESOP: Certainly.

JOUROUFLE: I'm afraid of compromising myself.

AESOP: What risk can you be running in telling the truth?

JOUROUFLE: What about?

AESOP: You've just seen that when the degrees of the meridian diminish in going toward the ole, the latter must be slightly flattened, and in consequence the axis shorter; and that, on the contrary, the axis must be elongated when the same degrees are of greater amplitude as one advances toward the same region.

JOUROUFLE: Yes, I realize that.

AESOP: So, the Earth, which has the degrees of its meridian more extensive toward the north than toward the equator, must also have an axis longer than the diameter of its equator?

JOUROUFLE: Incontestably.

SGRAVESANDE: What are you saying, rogue? Ah! You think differently than Newton? Well, I shall write to your academy and you'll no longer be the porter there.

JOUROUFLE: Not so fast, Monsieur Sgravesande. Since my discourse doesn't please you, why didn't you cut me off?

SGRAVESANDE: I wanted to know the interior of your soul, and see whether you would be faithful to us.

JOUROUFLE: Oh, faithful, as much as you please—but what can one do when the truth urges us to speak?

SGRAVESANDE: It isn't necessary to listen.

JOUROUFLE: It's sometimes so lucid and clear that one would be ashamed not to be its interpreter.

SGRAVESANDE: It's necessary not to reason so much with it. One says to it dryly: Do you think like Newton? Remain. Differently? Decamp.

JOUROUFLE: Where do you want it to pitch its tent?

SGRAVESANDE: At the antipodes.

JOUROUFLE: If it's obstinate in remaining, what can one do?

SGRAVESANDE: Chase it away with a pitchfork.

JOUROUFLE: Would you treat it like that if it came to your house?

SGRAVESANDE: It doesn't know where I live.

JOUROUFLE: But what if it found out?

SGRAVESANDE: Oh, it wouldn't dream of coming if it didn't arrive with Newton.

AESOP: Sgravesande, will you soon put an end to this debate?

SGRAVESANDE: Yes, if you judge that all the experiments you've just made are false.

AESOP: That isn't possible, and in accordance with them I can't avoid declaring that *On the Search for the Truth in the Sciences* is not guilty for having sustained that the Earth is not flattened at the poles, and that our diaphanous and convex atmosphere really augments in our eyes the apparent size of sidereal bodies, especially when close to the horizon.

SGRAVESANDE: President, is that judgment irrevocable?

AESOP: Yes.

SGRAVESANDE: Well, irrevocable or not, we shall persist in our opinion—which is to say, in believing that our atmosphere has no influence on the apparent volume of heavenly bodies, and that the Earth is not elongated but flattened at the poles, and we shall employ once again the tactics that were so successful about sixty years ago, when Bernardin de Saint-Pierre, here present, tried to demonstrate that the poles are not flattened. We let him say it, and our silence was so marvelous that it made our admirers think that Bernardin was wrong and that we were right.

AESOP: What! Bernardin de Saint-Pierre sustained the same thesis against you?

SGRAVESANDE: Yes, and to convince us, he employed calculations, reasoning and diagrams—and the wind carried it all away.

AESOP: You were incapable of understanding his demonstrations, then?

SGRAVESANDE: Capable or not, we didn't want to hear them.

AESOP: That's not praiseworthy.

MAUPERTUIS: President, I don't believe I have anything further to do here. Permit me to retire, in order that I can meditate in solitude on the false glamour of the human science.

AESOP: Illustrious Maupertuis, do as you please. Geniuses, here comes the Concierge of Urania's palace. He's doubtless bringing us some message.

Scene Ten
Aesop, the Concierge, Pemberton, Heromondas,
Sgravesande, Jouroufle, Voltaire, Pope, Pluche,
Bernardin de Saint-Pierre,
the troop of astronomer-geometers and physicists

CONCIERGE: President, Urania would like to speak to you for a moment; let the Geniuses present remain here.

AESOP: I am at her orders.

(*He goes out with the Concierge.*)

BERNARDIN DE SAINT-PIERRE, *to Pluche* : Let's go too, and find what we need to demonstrate the goodness of our cause, for they'll doubtless want to attack *On the Search for the Truth in the Sciences* on several other grounds; and if they desist in the attack we'll be able to have the pretended void, universal attraction and a hundred other hypotheses declared false, if we have the time.

PLUCHE: Yes, let's go.

Scene Eleven
Pemberton, Heromondas, Sgravesande, Jouroufle,
Voltaire, Pope, retinue of astronomers, etc.

SGRAVESANDE, *to Monsieur Jouroufle*: Do you see, Monsieur Jouroufle, do you see? Urania has summoned our President. Doubtless she's going to reprimand him severely for having absolved *On the Search for the Truth in the Sciences* on two counts. And you, who ought to be defending the incomparable Newton, have turned your coat. What will become of you if Urania expels you from her sight and hr place? For you'll be pitilessly cast out—yes, you will be, you can expect that. It's the punishment your felony warrants.

JOUROUFLE, *aside*: O wretched day! What a frightful abyss is opening beneath your feet, unfortunate Jouroufle! Oh, why didn't you turn away from that fatal scientific truth when it came to whisper in your ear? But what an accursed country the empire of the sciences is! One is always in mortal dread there, and one can't think for oneself; it's necessary, whether one likes it or not, to go along with the false opinions of others. The candelabras of science proclaim, night and day, that it's necessary to doubt before believing, but when one wants to use that doubt against them, they cry anathema. The false systems, false hypotheses, and false results they've adopted on the faith of another are sacred things for them, and one can't touch them. That's how error puts down profound roots that

80

all the strength of a Hercules wouldn't be capable of tearing up. Instead of extirpating it, that error, it's necessary to admire it, to praise it; otherwise, adieu employment, pension, praise, adulation; but laud it to the skies, and everything is lavished on you, nothing is refused. Well, that will teach me. Let the beautiful scientific truth come now; even if it's as brilliant as the sun, no thanks!

Monsieur de Sgravesande, isn't there any means of arranging some repatriation with you?

SGRAVESANDE: No.

JOUROUFLE: Come on, let's make peace! I implore you by the supreme infallibility of Monseigneur Newton.

SGRAVESANDE: So you now believe Newton to be infallible?

JOUROUFLE: Yes, the only infallible! Look, Monsieur de Sgravesande, if Newton were to claim that London goes to bed every evening in the Channel, or even that stones rain down on us from the moon, as some of your colleagues seriously affirm, I'd support it tenaciously against anyone, even though I know full well that they're absurd contentions, pure nonsense.

SGRAVESANDE: So, for you, Newton will always be right, and that book, *On the Search for the Truth in the Sciences*, always wrong?

JOUROUFLE: Oh, as much as you like.

SGRAVESANDE: Be careful, then. If the truth… do you hear me?

JOUROUFLE: Let it come! I'll say to it: Get away, quickly! I won't listen to you any more, unless you arrive with a certificate signed by Monsieur Newton or Monsieur de Sgravesande. (*Aside*) Which I shall doubtless never see.

SGRAVESANDE: On those conditions, I'll grant you mercy. But remember to hold firm.

JOUROUFLE: Oh, as firm as a rock. I'm now intrepid.

SGRAVESANDE: That's sufficient. Move away slightly. Here comes Newton, who doubtless has some secret to tell us.

Scene Twelve
The preceding, plus Newton

NEWTON: From a distance, I saw Maupertuis leave, and I've found out that Urania has summoned the man her Concierge appointed as our president. I hastened to come back in order to learn what happened during my absence. What did they want of Maupertuis?

PEMBERTON: They wanted to know if you were ever mistaken.

NEWTON: What did he reply?

PEMBERTON: That you had made several errors.

NEWTON: Certainly. No man, reduced to his own strength, is infallible. Is that all?

PEMBERTON: No, the opinions emitted by *On the Search for the Truth in the Sciences* that the terrestrial atmosphere augments the apparent diameter of the heavenly bodies beyond it, and that the Earth is not flattened toward the north pole, have been judged true.

NEWTON: Didn't you protest?

PEMBERTON: Yes, we did, but the convex diaphanous sub-stances that all magnify objects see through them and the measurements of the degrees of the terrestrial meridian gave evidence against you.

NEWTON: That ruins all my calculations of the masses of the planets, and the fortune that had looked upon me favorably thus far will now cause me to experience its rigors. Oh, how I fear for my hypothesis of universal gravitation! Will it be pos-sible for me to see the condemnation with dry eyes?

SGRAVESANDE: Incomparable Newton, the sadness into which I see your soul plunged breaks my heart, and suggests a useful advice to me. Why persist in demanding justice from that dull-witted Phrygian, who understands neither algebra not geometry, and who only has his share of common sense? Let us decline his jurisdiction and place the affair before Urania— and if we look out for the moment when she is inspired by your divine genius, I promise you a complete success."

NEWTON: My dear friend, if only you're right!

HEROMONDAS: I perceive another glimmer of hope, pro-vided that the foremost restorers of modern astronomy support us. In fact, shouldn't Copernicus, Galileo and Kepler be here to defend our cause, which is theirs? Their testimony would carry great weight, and demonstrate that we have almost al-ways repeated and copied what others have done before us.

NEWTON: I agree with you. Pemberton, go ask the three as-tronomers on my behalf to come and testify in my favor. For what motive could they have for being obstinate in refusing me their suffrage?

PEMBERTON: Your orders will be carried out punctually.

(*He leaves.*)

NEWTON: Adieu, my friends. If the astronomers refuse the favor for which I've asked them, I'll let you know my final will, but be assured that you won't see me here so long as I know that Copernicus, at least, is here in person. Adieu— stand firm.

Scene Thirteen
*Heromondas, Sgravesande, Jouroufle, Voltaire, Pope,
Retinue of astronomers, etc*

JOUROUFLE *approaching Heromondas*: Monsieur Heromondas, I'm shivering with fear.

HEROMONDAS: What are you afraid of?

JOUROUFLE: Can't you see that our general is abandoning the battlefield in the heat of the action?

HEROMONDAS: It's to make provision for the defense of his theories. Don't worry.

JOUROUFLE: Ah! Didn't Pompey quit his army, in order to make provision, as he saw it, for the defense of his camp? And yet, instead of giving orders, he ran to lurk in his tent, in order to decamp promptly at the approach of the victor, without giving any concern to his poor soldiers, whom he surrendered to Caesar's sword.

HEROMONDAS: Be brave.

JOUROUFLE: Hush! Can't you hear a voice in the distance shouting: *Every man for himself?*

HEROMONDAS: No.

JOUROUFLE: In which direction should one flee?

HEROMONDAS: In any direction—but it's necessary to hold firm; our honor is at stake in defending Newton.

JOUROUFLE: I can't. Don't you see that our party is the weaker?

HEROMONDAS: You can't count, Monsieur Jouroufle. Haven't you noticed that we're four against two?

JOUROUFLE: I could see that, but the adverse party has a third champion with them who's a hundred times stronger than us.

HEROMONDAS: What champion?

JOUROUFLE: Reason.

HEROMONDAS: I can't see him. You obviously have better eyesight than me.

JOUROUFLE: If you could see his firm and assured stance! Oh, I tremble in my every limb when I think that we have to fight such an adversary.

HEROMONDAS: Calm down, and remember that it's in great danger that the strong soul is entirely deployed. Then again, don't you see that crowd of physicists and astronomers who are forming the assembly, and who are all partisans of Newton? Besides which, if you think Newton is Pompey, you must be the great Cato.

JOUROUFLE: I'd like to be.

HEROMONDAS: Try.

JOUROUFLE: What will you give me?

HEROMONDAS: Whatever you wish?

JOUROUFLE: What, though?

HEROMONDAS: A position as secretary in an Academy?

JOUROUFLE: French? English? Italian?

HEROMONDAS: Your choice.

JOUROUFLE: I'd certainly like that position, but I can't accept it; I write too dryly.

HEROMONDAS: Would you like to be appointed chief geometer in Urania's court?

JOUROUFLE: With that I'd be content, for I could extol a scientific error to my heart's content in twenty pages of analytical calculations that no one could read and everyone would admire.

SGRAVESANDE: You won't have any more panic attacks, then?

JOUROUFLE: Oh, now I have courage. Look, Monsieur de Sgravesande, even if you or anyone else ordered me to abandon my post, I wouldn't obey; I'd resist, tenaciously, like Cato in Utica.

SGRAVESANDE: You'd do well. Here's Pemberton; perhaps he'll want to talk to us in private; move away slightly.

Scene Fourteen
Pemberton and the preceding

PEMBERTON: I couldn't find Copernicus. As for Kepler and Galileo, they don't want to appear before the Phrygian, who, they say, has too much common sense.

HEROMONDAS: That ruins our plans.

PEMBERTON: So Newton asks you to quit the hearing and only come back if Copernicus, on whom he's founding his hopes, is present at the debate. As for the assembly, they can stay, and will serve to inform our dictator of ulterior results. Let's leave; it's better to be condemned by default.

Scene Fifteen
Heromondas, Jouroufle, the Retinue of Physicists, etc.

JOUROUFLE, *to Heromondas*: Where are you going so swiftly?

HEROMONDAS: Follow us and we'll tell you.

JOUROUFLE: Don't you know that Seigneur Aesop will soon be back to judge from the height of his tribunal?

HEROMONDAS: There's no need to wait; decamp.

JOUROUFLE: Just now I wanted to run away and you didn't; now I want to stay and you're ordering me to decamp?

HEROMONDAS: Believe me, follow my example.

JOUROUFLE: I can see what you're up to. You want me to quit my post, so that Monsieur de Sgravesande has a sufficient reason to take away the keys to my academy, or my position as the first geometer in Urania's court. Not so stupid! I'm here, and I'm staying.

HEROMONDAS: Would you like me to tell you the truth, frankly? It's because it's a matter of the movement of the Earth in the ecliptic; we can't say anything without Copernicus. So, if you want to sustain the combat against our adversaries alone, you'll be defeated; our party is in peril.

JOUROUFLE: Well, like the illustrious Seigneur Cato, I'll bury myself under its ruins, and I'll have a beautiful epitaph set over my tomb that will let the remotest posterity know that I died defending the Newtonian system, true or false, good or bad.

HEROMONDAS: That's your famous genius condemned to the night of the tomb, then. Adieu.

JOUROUFLE: But you're going very quickly. A word in your ear, at least.

HEROMONDAS: What do you want?

JOURNOUFLE: When Seigneur Aesop sits on his tribunal, how shall I speak? What shall I put forward? What has still to come up in the trial? What accusations is it necessary to bring against *On the Search for the Truth in the Sciences*? What do I say? What do I do? What do I reply?

HEROMONDAS: You don't know?

JOUROUFLE: No.

HEROMONDAS: Well, guess, if you can. Here's Pluche and Bernardin de Saint-Pierre coming back, laden with various instruments of physics, and Aesop's coming out of Urania's palace. I don't want to wait for them. Adieu.

Scene Sixteen
Aesop, Pluche, Bernardin de Saint-Pierre, Jouroufle, etc.

AESOP: Urania wanted to know the judgment I had rendered on the subject of the optical property of our atmosphere, and the shape of the Earth, and she has deigned to confirm them. I would have liked her to discharge me from the difficult employment that she has confided to me temporarily, for there's nothing most annoying that being obliged to condemn as erroneous the opinions of illustrious scientists for whom one has infinite esteem, but instead of granting my request she has ordered me to remount the tribunal in order to regulate the complaints of the two parties. I'm now ready to listen to both. Accusers of the text of *On the Search for Truth in the Sciences*, appear.

JOUROUFLE: Here we are.

AESOP: Where are your colleagues?

JOUROUFLE: I don't know.

AESOP: Shouldn't they have waited for me?

JOUROUFLE: Well, if they're doing as the knights of the great Pompey did on the plans of Pharsalia, how could they have waited for you?

PLUCHE: Why hasn't Monsieur Jouroufle done the same?

JOUROUFLE: And who would defend the great Newton?

BERNARDIN DE SAINT-PIERRE: The great Newton must certainly be glorious, to have such support!

AESOP: Will you continue to be the accuser, Monsieur Jouroufle?

JOUROUFLE: I'd like to, but I can't.

AESOP: What's stopping you?

JOUROUFLE: It's that I'm not a sorcerer; I'm only a disciple of the sublime science, or, in a word, a geometer.

AESOP: I don't understand what you're saying. Explain this enigma to us.

JOUROUFLE: It's that Monsieur Heromondas, while going away, didn't want to tell me what it was necessary to say. "Guess, if you can," he shouted to me. That's easier said than done, for everyone knows that when it's a matter of discovering the hidden truth or secrets regarding science, a geometer isn't a sorcerer.

AESOP: So you have nothing to say against the text of *On the Search for the Truth in the Sciences*?

JOUROUFLE: No, unfortunately.

PLUCHE: Since Monsieur Jouroufle is reduced to silence, I'll change role, and instead of simply being the defender of *On the Search for the Truth in the Sciences*, I'll become the accuser of Newton, whom I've never regarded as a good physicist, but as a skillful calculator. That scientist has advanced that a void exists in the spaces of the universe, and that the Earth and the planets move through that void. As that assertion is false, being contrary to phenomena, I request its condemnation.

AESOP: And what witness will testify to the falseness of that assertion?

PLUCHE: The terrestrial atmosphere, which would cease to surround the Earth if the void were real, because that atmosphere, being elastic, like a spring, would quickly escape if nothing retained it around the Earth.

AESOP: What proof can you give of that elasticity?

PLUCHE: That the air forming the atmosphere, when compressed, exerts and effort to set itself free, and that a bladder full of the fluid and put in the receptacle of a pneumatic machine dilates and bursts promptly when a void is created—which is to say, when the air contained in the receptacle, and serves to coerce that contained in the bladder, is pumped out. Thus, if beyond our atmosphere there were no matter opposed to its dilatation, is would disappear in the same way in very little time.

AESOP: Monsieur Jouroufle, have you anything to allege against these experiments?

JOUROUFLE: No, unfortunately.

AESOP: Then it's evident that the Newtonian void doesn't exist, for otherwise, we'd have no atmosphere.

JOUROUFLE: Oh, just a moment, Seigneur Aesop! We agree that the terrestrial atmosphere would be scattered in the void if its elasticity were the same everywhere, but to get us out of difficulty we sustain with the famous geometers that since the atmosphere doesn't dissipate, it must be the case that the upper layers are less elastic than the lower ones.[25]

---

[25] Author's reference: "See *L'Exposition du Système du monde* vol. II, p. 12, first edition, and page 179 of the sixth, etc."

AESOP: That's very bad reasoning, Monsieur Jouroufle. Do you see that machine in the hands of Bernardin de Saint-Pierre? It's a long steel strip coiled like a watch-spring, which is fastened with a screw. If, wanting to argue that the steel composing the strip were not elastic, I brought forward as proof the fact that it isn't unwinding, you wouldn't fail to protest against the falsity of the proposition. It's the same with the argument that you've just made. It would be better boldly to claim that the upper air belongs to a different species ha the lower air.

JOUROUFLE: I'd like to sustain that assertion, but I can't, because, by a fatal mischance, the physicists who have analyzed air collected at very great heights during aerostatic voyages have recognized that it does not differ in any way from that existing at the terrestrial surface.

BERNARDIN DE SAINT-PIERRE: It is, therefore, indubitable that the air in the upper regions is the same species as that in the lower regions, and must also be elastic. But tell us, Monsieur Jouroufle, are all the sidereal atmospheres in the middle of our void like the one you attribute to the Earth, elastic lower down and inelastic on high, and do they remain coerced around their planets?

JOUROUFLE: Oh no! If that of the moon, for example, had not been elastic everywhere, it would not have evaporated by virtue of the effect of its elasticity.[26]

AESOP: What leads you to believe that the lunar atmosphere has evaporated?

---

[26] Author's reference: "See *L'Exposition du Système du monde*, vol II, the articles on the atmospheres of the celestial bodies, in which the author says at the end of the article that the atmosphere in question is scarcely detectable, etc., etc."

JOUROUFLE: The fact that we cannot perceive it, either with the naked eye or with our telescopes.

PLUCHE: However, it shows itself in a very sensible or evident manner in annular eclipses of the sun.

JOUROUFLE: That costs nothing to say when one has learned it from *On the Search for the Truth in the Sciences*, but we, to whom no one has confided it, could not divine it.

AESOP: Into what part of space would your lunar atmosphere have gone, then?

JOUROUFLE: Toward the Earth, which would have aspired it, and it would have stayed there, so it's claimed.

AESOP: And has it conserved the same elasticity that it had on the moon?

JOUROUFLE: Perhaps, but no one knows.

AESOP: It seems to me that if the fluid lunar atmosphere was highly elastic around the moon, it ought to be the same in the vicinity of the Earth, and in consequence, if it was not retained about the first sphere, it would not have become fixed around the latter, because a change of location cannot change the elasticity of a spring.

JOUROUFLE: That seems evident, I admit. However, you might think otherwise, Seigneur Aesop, if you could reason in a slightly different manner. For example, our atmosphere exists, and it is elastic; therefore, either it ought to dissipate completely or to be retained by some matter capable of opposing its elasticity; nothing seems more consequent; but then, adieu the void, since the atmosphere doesn't dissipate. However, our Newtonian astronomical system obliges us to sustain that the celestial spaces are void, or almost void. What can we do, then? We say that our atmosphere near the surface is highly elastic, since it tends to dilate there, but we also claim that since it hasn't vanished, it must be that it exists toward its confines in a state of rarity in which the fluid atmosphere has no elasticity.[27] On the other hand, we don't perceive the atmosphere of the moon, although it ought to have an abundant one according to our calculations, so we contend that the lunar atmosphere, being elastic everywhere, has dissipated by the effect of that elasticity. Thus we encounter no difficulty that we cannot resolve to our satisfaction. And that, Seigneur Aesop, is what it is to have a geometric mind."

AESOP: But there are real contradictions in that.

JOUROUFLE: Yes, but without contradictions, how could we fill our books and have our science admired? In any case, who is capable of perceiving a contradiction in a book of astronomy or physics, when it's seasoned with a little calculation?

AESOP: Although your logic is astonishing, Monsieur Jouroufle, it won't prevent the condemnation of the hypothesis of the void.

JOUROUFLE: Before condemning the hypothesis of the void, pay attention, Seigneur Aesop, to the fact that we desire absolutely that the universe be a pure mechanism, which, once set in motion by some cause, continues to move without intervention or any outside assistance. If, beyond out atmosphere, we admit matter, which, although fluid, could coerce that atmosphere, that matter would oppose the displacement of the celestial spheres, whose movement would soon be annihilated by the effect of that resistance; nothing is more certain. In consequence, the entire universe, according to us, would fall into a complete torpor, and we would no longer be able to work our

---

[27] Author's reference: "See *L'Exposition du Système de monde*, vol. II, article IX, 'Des atmosphères sidérales.'"

way back by means of the combined mechanisms of impulsion and attraction, which we have imagined, the force of which would no longer be as powerful. Now, to affirm, as we do, that the entire universe is similar to a machine, composed of cogs and levers, which, being dependent on one another, move mechanically without the aid of the divinity, it is necessary not to exclude the void, or, if one wants to admit into space a few vapors or rays of light, they are so nimble and so rare that they not only cannot compress our exceedingly dilatable fluid atmosphere but cannot oppose any sensible resistance to the heavenly bodies circulating in that space. That, Monseigneur Aesop, is what one might call the express doctrine of our incomparable Newton.[28]

AESOP: Your reasoning, Monsieur Jouroufle, is as false as it is absurd. What! You want to sustain an erroneous hypothesis by defending an opinion that is more erroneous still? Which is to say, to contend that total void exists in the celestial spaces, or if there is some matter there, it is incapable of compressing out exceedingly elastic atmosphere? And why? Because it pleases you to call the world a pure mechanism, which goes by itself without the workman who formed it presiding over its movements. It seems to me that this is a case of building considerations on considerations to more important verities, astronomy furnishing you with the means. You could have said: Our atmosphere is elastic and ends to expand; thus, it would escape if nothing were coercing it; thus outside that atmosphere there is a matter that compresses it, although transparent and fluid. But if that matter has enough force and density to produce that effect, it would oppose resistance to the spheres that traverse it, and the friction that would result would soon annihilate the movement of those spheres. Thus, if the latter have continued their course through space for many centuries without being disturbed in the orbit that they describe, there

---

[28] Author's reference: "See Paulian's *Dictionnaire de Physique*, 8th ed. Vol. IV, p. 88."

must indubitably be a sovereign Master who presides over their movements. A mechanism needs to be reset regularly, and the divinity operates here like the hand of the workman; but he does not operate mechanically, like the latter. His permanent will gives life and movement to the universe at every instant of every hour, and it obliges the stars to cleave the ethereal fluid in which they float, without their rapid course being slowed, even though that ether has sufficient force to restrain their expansible atmospheres.

JOUROUFLE: Do you believe Seigneur Aesop, that if we reasoned like that, we could have as many partisans in the recent centuries, who have been enthusiastic about our systems and have heaped eulogies upon us?

AESOP: Ill-merited eulogies at the expense of being honorable only cover us with shame, and I cannot be sufficiently astonished that astronomy, which ought to bring men closer to the divinity, has, on the contrary, distanced them in recent times.

PLUCHE: It is for want of knowing how our atmosphere was formed that Newton and his partisans have imagined that pretended void. *On the Search for the Truth in the Sciences* gives us a true idea of the formation of that same atmosphere, and it is astonishing that such an idea has escaped, all the illustrious scientists there have been until now, although it ought to have occurred to the minds of all of them, however little attention they have paid to the most ancient and most veridical of historians. In fact, at the commencement of Genesis, Moses announces that God first created heaven and earth. The heaven of which he is speaking there is nothing other than the elastic and transparent fluid in which the sidereal bodies were to circulate, and which can be given the name of ether. God did not want to create the world in a single spurt, but piece by piece, in order that it could not be thought that creation as the work of blind chance. That heaven, named the first, sprang from nothing before the earth and occupied all of the space that was destined for it. The earth, appearing thereafter, expelled the ether from the place that it was to occupy, compressing it, and by virtue of that pressure, obliged it to tighten around it. By that means, its atmosphere was formed, which is of the same species as the etheric fluid, and which terminates where the pressure ceases to be felt. One sees, therefore, that he part of that atmosphere closest to the terrestrial surface has to be the most pressurized, since it experienced, initially, the full effort of the expulsion, and that its density originates uniquely from the pressure exerted by the mass of our globe during its deployment, and not the gravity of the superior layers, as is everywhere alleged. If the Newtonian void had existed, the matter thus expelled would have been disseminated, and we would not have had an atmosphere. In order for the contrary to occur, it follows necessarily that the space in which our world was placed was completely filled with that elastic substance.

AESOP: That's enough, and without longer discussion, it is easy to understand that the existence of the terrestrial atmosphere is incompatible with the Newtonian void. What more do you want, defenders of *On the Search for the Truth in the Sciences*?

BERNARDIN DE SAINT-PIERRE: The condemnation of Newtonian attraction. Without thinking for a moment about what our atmospheric fluid might operate, Newton, having seen a fruit detach itself from a tree and fall to the ground, thought that the Earth had drawn the fruit by means of its attraction, and soon imagined that the attraction in question could be exerted over great distances. He concluded, with the German Kepler, that it extended as far as the moon, the sun, and even beyond the most remote planets; and that was the origin of his false theory of sidereal gravitation, or universal gravity, too lightly adopted by our academicians.

AESOP: What proof to you give of the falsity if that theory?

BERNARDIN DE SAINT-PIERRE: Incontestable experiments, which prove that attraction only exists because of atmospheres.

AESOP: What have you to respond, Monsieur Jouroufle?

JOUROUFLE: That if the weight of bodies is almost as sensible at the summit of mountains as in the plain, it might well extend all the way to the moon, as well as to all the heavenly bodies, and reciprocally, as the great geometers inform us.

PLUCHE: You did not reason in the same way just now, Monsieur Jouroufle, on the subject of the elasticity of our atmosphere, with regard to which you could have said, with more reason than here, that since that atmosphere is very elastic in the inferior regions, it ought to be in the same in the most elevated ones.

JOUROUFLE: That's because then, I needed the atmosphere not to be elastic everywhere, whereas now I need attraction to be felt everywhere.

AESOP: Your logic is truly admirable, Monsieur Jouroufle!

JOUROUFLE: Certainly! Is it not that of the most illustrious Newtonians?

BERNARDIN DE SAINT-PIERRE: For the argument that Monsieur Jouroufle takes from mountains to be valid, it's necessary for him to prove either that mountains are not in the terrestrial atmosphere or that the phenomenon of gravity would also be observed there even if they were outside the atmosphere.

JOUROUFLE: One can't think of everything.

PLUCHE: It's easy to see that neither Newton nor Monsieur Jouroufle, who follows his doctrine, has ever thought about all the experiments of which *On the Search for the Truth in the Sciences* makes mention, which can be made with small, very thin objects floating on limped water, which attract one another or repel one another according to the diversity of their atmospheres, but fall into inertia when that same atmosphere is removed.

AESOP: Monsieur Jouroufle, would you like to know about these experiments cited by Pluche, in order to be able to combat them?

JOUROUFLE: No, experiments made in water make me feel ill.

AESOP: They would, however, have helped you to discover the truth with regard to the optical property of our atmosphere.

JOUROUFLE: I'm very sorry about that.

AESOP: Although you refuse to acquaint yourself with these experiments, they nevertheless allow the argument of the falsity of your system of universal gravitation. In fact, by reading them without prejudice in *On the Search for the Truth in the Sciences*, one is convinced that all the phenomena of gravity that are observed on earth are only due to the attractive property of our atmospheric fluid; since, in causing thin disks of silver, copper or tinplate to float in a dish filled with limpid water, one can represent on a small scale the aforesaid phenomena.

JOUROUFLE: It might be, Seigneur Aesop, that you're right but that we aren't wrong, and this is why. The experiments you mention might well prove that attraction only takes place via the intermediary of atmospheres, but they're carried out in water, and we're n air, so, for that reason, I reject that testimony.

PLUCHE: Well, we have others that are based not in water but in our atmosphere.

AESOP: What are they?

PLUCHE: Here they are.

JOUROUFLE: Fine witnesses that you're presenting there. What, bodies that can be electrified or magnetized? What can they say?

AESOP: Monsieur Jouroufle, interrogate them, if you please?

JOUROUFLE: In what manner?

PLUCHE: See, then, whether this steel rod attracts those iron filings or these needles?

JOUROUFLE: No, it doesn't attract them.

PLUCHE: Now I'll magnetize the rod. (*A pause.*) It's magnetized, Monsieur Jouroufle; let's repeat the experiment.

JOUROUFLE: Indeed! The rod now attracts the needles and the iron filings.

PLUCHE: Now see this glass tube that I've just rubbed. It attracts, as you can see, the little particles of matter that one presents to it. But now that I've de-electrified it, see whether it still attracts.

JOUROUFLE: No, it doesn't.

PLUCHE: Is it, then, the iron or the glass that draws small neighboring bodies toward it, or a matter that one accumulates around the former and which forms their true atmosphere?

JOUROUFLE: Those experiments do prove that one body only attracts another by virtue of some fluid matter that is united with it in imitation of an atmosphere, but that atmosphere isn't ours, and as long as that one doesn't speak, I shall be incredulous.

PLUCHE: Is the voice of the experiments you've just made no eloquent enough?

JOUROUFLE: Not so far as I'm concerned. But tell me about the great and beautiful experiments that one can make in our atmosphere. Yes, those are experiments! And you'll see whether they don't certify, as our astronomers tenaciously affirm, that the law of universal gravitation extends over infinite distances, and will be eternal, according to our orders—do you hear?"

AESOP: What are these experiments?

JOUROUFLE: Here they are. Seigneur Bouguer, having gone to Peru to make the earth say whether it is flattened at the poles, which you can believe today if you wish, solemnly interrogated his clock. Having designated as unity, divided into millionths, the length of the pendulum at sea level, he noted that it vibrated sixty times in a minute. Having then taken that clock to a height of 8,786 feet and then to 14,604 feet, as our Newtonians say, his pendulum no longer made the same number of vibrations in the same interval of time, because the air of the atmosphere, being less condensed than the air at sea level, pressed less upon the earth, which announced that the force of weight had diminished in intensity and weakened. It was necessary, therefore, to have the same number of vibrations, to shorten the pendulum by 751 millionths at the first station and 1184 millionths at the second, Now, the distance traveled between these two points is very small, and yet the diminution in weight was quite sensible. Thus, we have all made this profound reasoning, with Seigneur Bouguer: If the differences found in the length of the pendulum are already very sensible at such a small distance, the force of weight probably extends as indefinitely in space; and from that we have drawn the consequence that the force must extend as far as the moon and even beyond the planets.

AESOP: Monsieur Jouroufle, permit me to tell you that that consequence and that reasoning are most absurd, and depose against you; for if they were true, it would be necessary for the shortening of the pendulum to be hardly sensible and for the distances traveled to be very considerable. But according to you, it is entirely to the contrary, and if one compares the reduced quantities of the pendulum and the distances traveled, one will find that the force of weight, instead of extending to infinite distances, must cease less than five hundred leagues above the terrestrial surface, as *On the Search for the Truth in the Sciences* demonstrates.

JOUROUFLE: Oh, Monsieur Aesop, if my reasoning doesn't please you, I'll gladly abandon it, because this time my sentiment accords with yours. In fact, our dear Newtonians, who have doubtless adopted the hypotheses of Newton confidently without scrutinizing them at length and attentively, and even without confronting them obstinately with the phenomena, observations and experiments that they have made themselves, have perhaps wanted to make fun of me in obliging me to believe that the attraction of brute and inert matter can be felt in all directions at a distance of thousands of millions of leagues and in an indivisible instant, without any disorder resulting from that pulling in all directions. That, I confess now, is a great absurdity—that being said, nevertheless, in my opinion, without any consequence being taken from it. But it's impossible that the sun can exercise such a powerful attractive action on the highest planets; however, sidereal attraction must nevertheless exist toward some point, according to my common sense.

AESOP: Where, then?

JOUROUFLE: Toward the earth, where, it appears to me, the proof is striking for all to see, and is renewed twice a day.

AESOP: And what is that proof?

JOUROUFLE: The tidal flux and reflux of the sea. Oh, on that score, Seigneur Aesop, I've caught you in my nets, and I'll force you to admit that luni-solar attraction cannot have any more convincing proof in its favor, as the Newtonian Lalande, a savant astronomer, assures us conscientiously. Now, this is the superb mechanism that the incomparable Newton found in his brain. According to him, the moon, being closer to our globe than the sun, its energy ought to be three or four times more considerable that that of the latter star, and in consequence, act more considerably to raise the earth and its seas twice a day. The moon, therefore, in passing over our hemisphere, attracts the waters of our oceans, but a little less than the earth and even less than the waters in the other hemisphere. The latter remain behindhand, thus appearing to rise at the same time as our Atlantic Ocean, and hence the flux that, by lowering the waters, is soon followed by the reflux, either for our zenith or for our nadir. Now, these effects, which are renewed, but alternately, when, by virtue of the rotation of the earth, the moon appears in the opposite hemisphere, thus procure us very nearly every day two high tides and two low tides, as the excellent Newton assures us.

AESOP: And do the phenomena of the flux and reflux arrive every day in all the seas at the same time?

JOUROUFLE: Not exactly, for, according to exact observations, the phenomena only take place once a day in a large area of the Pacific Ocean, and even the waters of that sea in the Bay of Panama only begin to rise when the Atlantic tide has ceased to rise and is ebbing.

AESOP: But doesn't the moon pass over the zenith and nadir of those seas every day?

JOUROUFLE: Certainly.

AESOP: Then why are there places where only one tide is observed in 24 hours, when, according to your hypothesis, there ought to be two? Isn't your proof in default there, especially if the tide in the Bay of Panama is also taken into consideration?

JOUROUFLE: Oh, if you still doubt the power that the moon exerts on the seas, ask the compilers of yearbooks and almanacs, and you'll see whether or not they'll certify for you that the movements of the moon are coordinated in any year with the production of considerable tides. Those Messieurs are so certain that, in certain cases, they warn maritime authorities to take the precautions necessary for protection against unusual tides.

AESOP: And do they arrive as announced?

JOUROUFLE: What does it matter? Isn't it sufficient that they predict them?

AESOP: No; it's necessary that the event justifies the prediction.

JOUROUFLE: One ought not to be so difficult in regard to theories; it's necessary to grant something to hypothesis, to let a few suppositions pass; otherwise, one would only ever be regaled by old wives' tales.

AESOP: Could we not have some of these newspapers in which our Newtonians announce these extraordinary tides?

BERNARDIN DE SAINT-PIERRE: Purely by chance, I've kept those of the year 1817, when extraordinary tides were announced for the third of April, the eleventh of October and the ninth of November.

AESOP: Did the predicted high tides arrive on the designated days?

BERNARDIN DE SANT-PIERRE: No, President. On the third of April there was supposed to be a very high tide because of the lunar perigee, but everything passed normally, whereas on the sixth of March, of which no mention had been made, the tide was so strong that it broke the dykes in several places and caused a thousand ravages.

AESOP: And was there no indication of the cause that made the sea rise up in such an unusual manner?

BERNARDIN DE SAINT-PIERRE : Pardon me. It was the storms and impetuous winds that reigned on the sixth of March. On the eleventh of October and the ninth of November, it was as on the third of April. The weather being calm on those says, the sea was not rough and the tide did not frighten the inhabitants of our coastal regions, as it had done so terribly on the sixth of March.

AESOP: What do you say, Monsieur Jouroufle, to these high tides that arrive when they are not expected, and which, in spite of the lunar perigee, fail to arrive on the days indicated?

JOUROUFLE: I say that it's a feminine caprice, for Amphitrite doubtless takes offense at the fact that our geometer-astronomers are casting a curious eye on what she ought to do or not do, and in order to avenge herself she does the opposite—but at other times she is less perverse.

AESOP: Well, when Amphitrite, for your honor and that of Newton, wishes to render herself docile to the predictions of our Newtonian astronomers, you will be right—always provided that in the epochs designed for extraordinary tides they are not excited by furious winds.

JOUROUFLE: If the sun and, above all, the moon, don't cause the tides, what is the cause of such an astonishing phenomenon.

BERNARDIN DE SAINT-PIERRE: The sun, not by its pretended attraction but by its chemical and physical action on the elastic vapors raised in the atmosphere—which would take too long to explain here but can be seen in detail in *On the Search for the Truth in the Sciences*, in the chapter on "Tides."

The same work, President, also identifies as erroneous several other hypotheses that Newton has either adopted or introduced into physics and astronomy, such as those regarding light, properly speaking, its refraction, reflection and refrangibility; the colors of bodies and those produced by the prism, eclipses, etc., etc. As we can't list them without appearing tedious, we'll content ourselves for the moment with provoking the condemnation of the one that relates to the pretended movement of the earth, proposed by Copernicus, and which the English scientist Newton has sustained as one of the principal bases of his false theory of universal gravitation, and which its partisans are also obliged to adopt, because they frankly admit that gravitation cannot exist without that displacement of the terrestrial globe.

AESOP: And what phenomena can you cite in support of your accusation?

BERNARDIN DE SAINT-PIERRE: Among several astronomical phenomena that testify against the hypothesis of the displacement of the earth, as one can see in *On the Search for the Truth in the Sciences*, which we cite for the sake of brevity, is that of the fixity of the pole star in all the seasons of the year, while the earth, in rotating on its axis, changes its position every day by approximately two degrees. Now, if the daily displacement of the terrestrial meridian, which only describes a circle nearly three thousand leagues in diameter produces such a change in the position of that star, how is it possible that it does not cause any during the year, if the earth, in traveling around the sun, traveled an immense circle in that same meridian—which is to say, an orbit whose diameter would exceeded sixty million leagues, according to the calculations of the new astronomers? That is too contradictory, and demonstrates in the most evident manner that although our globe rotates on its axis, it does not change location.

AESOP: What do you have to respond, Monsieur Jouroufle?

JOUROUFLE: That I've lost my voice.

AESOP: And how long have you been experiencing this misfortune?

JOUROUFLE: Since people started talking about the movements of the earth.

AESOP: That's an enigma, Monsieur Jouroufle—explain it to us.

JOUROUFLE: Here's the explanation: on leaving me, Monsieur Heromondas instructed me expressly not to say a word in the absence of Monsieur Copernicus on the subject of the movement of our globe in the ecliptic, because otherwise I would succumb. If you want me to chatter as before, send for the citizen of Torun.

AESOP: Let someone go and ask Copernicus to come here.

A PHYSICIST *of the retinue*: I'll go promptly, and I'll soon find him, because I know the place where the philosopher usually meditates. (*Aside.*) I'll tell Newton what's happening.

Scene Seventeen,
Aesop, Pluche, Bernardin de Saint-Pierre, Jouroufle,
Retinue of astronomer-geometers and physicists

AESOP: Monsieur Jouroufle, does Copernicus have to dictate your lesson to you?

JOUROUFLE: Oh, not to me; but you'll see if he doesn't assure you that the earth visits the twelve houses of the zodiac every year in turning around the sun, accompanied by the moon, which flutters around it, describing annually twelve epicycles on the orbit traveled by its primary, and in my opinion that must be the case. For according to my common sense, sharpened by the beautiful arguments of Monseigneur Newton and his adherents, it seems to me that the sun is a hundred thousand times bigger than the earth, according to the parallaxes that these scientists have been able to find, and according to the calculations of the savant Lalande and company, that star, by the fact of its enormous mass, ought to remain fixed in the center, and by its attraction force the earth to circle around it, because, for reasons so powerful, according to us, in relationships and conveniences, it's necessary that the small body be determined and drawn by the larger one, as the sullen Indian is carried by his elephant.

AESOP: Monsieur Jouroufle, you've already given proofs that your memory isn't poor, but you've forgotten, it seems to me that attraction doesn't surpass the region of the atmosphere and that, in consequence, the sun can't have any empire over the earth by the effect of its pretended size, since its atmospheric fluid doesn't extent as far as us. Besides which, when the geometer-astronomers calculated the mass of the sun, they didn't know that the apparent diameter of its disk was almost doubled by the optical property of our atmosphere and its own. The sun is therefore not as large as they have calculated.

JOUROUFLE: I can't help it if the astronomers are mistaken. Anyway, isn't it necessary to conceded something to a beautiful hypothesis? Otherwise, would our sublime sciences be able to sustain themselves against an exact critic?

PLUCHE: The case of the false theory of the displacement of the globe proves that in that regard people have tried to search for science where it was not, and would have blushed to find it where it really existed—which is to say, in the books of the legislator of the Hebrews. In fact, Moses, in his account of the creation of the universe, announces that God created the earth before all the other spheres, and that he employed three days either in forming it or embellishing it, while in a single day he fabricated and brought out of nothing the sun, the moon, the planets and the stars, which are innumerable. Why did God do that? Doubtless to give us a greater idea of the terrestrial globe, which he destined to be the abode of the humans who were to become its masters, and whom he created in his image. That dwelling designed and ornamented in a fashion appropriate to the excellence of the being that was to inhabit it, it was necessary for the divine being to illuminate, and it was then that he made all the sidereal bodies. The latter bodies, therefore, only came after the earth and for the service of the earth. Only having been created for the earth, they ought not to have any influence over its existence, not to subjugate it by being millions of times larger. On the contrary, their courses have been regulated in such a fashion as to serve as signals and mark the years and centuries for its particular utility. That is how powerful reasons and conveniences ought to be applied, not in terms of size or mass. Compared with the simple and sublime story of creation, what are these false hypotheses, these erroneous theories, children of a vagabond imagination? They are like the frail vessels that, after having sailed for some time without a compass in the vast basin of the seas, finally break against the shore on a dark night. But here comes Copernicus.

Scene Eighteen
The Preceding, Copernicus

AESOP: Illustrious Copernicus, I count on your frankness to tell us, without disguise, what you think of your astronomical system. Are you morally certain that the earth travels the zodiac in circling around the sun?

COPERNICUS: No, what I said was not an incontestable truth. It was a hypothesis imagined to explain in a more plausible manner than before, it seemed to me, the movements of the sidereal bodies, but it's still a hypothesis.

AESOP: Which is to say that there is more than one way of explaining the movements of the celestial spheres.

COPERNICUS: Yes, for the appearances, according to all the astronomers, would be the same whether the sun turns around the earth or the earth around the sun.

AESOP: There is, then, no phenomenon that demonstrates invincibly the displacement of the earth?

COPERNICUS: No, it can only be admitted by supposition.

AESOP: And what persuaded you to adopt that hypothesis?

COPERNICUS: The movements of the planets, whose courses are sometimes direct and sometimes retrograde. It seemed simpler to me to think that those retrogradations were only apparent, and that they originated from the displacement of our globe rather than the backward movement of the planet, which would have been obliged to describe several epicycles around the earth in one of its periods.

AESOP: But must one regard those epicycles as unnatural curves—which is to say, as never taking place in the progress of celestial bodies?

COPERNICUS: Not absolutely, since the moon in my own system must reverse its course several times in the course of a year, apparently forming a series of epicycles.

AESOP: If the moon can trace these kinds of epicycles, why should the other planets not be able to describe real ones? Would that be impossible for the divinity? A workman who has enough talent to make a machine move in one fashion has not, because of that, lost the faculty of making it move in others of the same kind, and also dissimilar ones. It therefore appears to me that you ought to have said, since I cannot remove all species of epicycles, no matter in what fashion I explain the universe, it would be better to allow the planets to describe curves of that sort around the earth than to claim that they circle around the sun.

BERNARDIN DE SAINT-PIERRE: If the illustrious Copernicus had lived after good observations, especially after the discovery of telescopes, and he had seen the moons of the planets tracing these kinds of epicycles in turning around the latter, he would have recognized that those curves are more common in nature than simple orbits, since there are many more moons than planets. From that he would have concluded that the latter might well also describe more or less complicated curves around the earth, while the sun and the moon describe true circles, which appear elliptical because of the position that the earth occupies in their orbits.

COPERNICUS: You're right, but as, in my time, the existence of these moons was unsuspected, I thought that it was more appropriate only to make our moon describe epicycles of a sort than five other planets. In any case, believing that the sun was much larger than the earth, I imagined that it was also more natural that the smaller mass circled around the larger one.

AESOP: But then the displacement of our globe would become apparent in the various points of space, because, in being displaced, it could not describe a great circle without the pole star moving from right to left in the course of the year, since every day, it moves by two or three degrees because of the earth's diurnal revolution.

COPERNICUS: Yes, but I didn't think of making that comparison. The apparent beauty of my system dazzled me and carried me away, and to anticipate the objection that might be made to me with regard to the fixity of the pole star throughout the year, I claimed that the stars were such a great distance from the earth that the angle formed by our globe in describing its orbit because insensible when seen from the star. If I had thought about the daily change in the pole star's position that would have embarrassed me.

AESOP: Effectively, in your hypothesis, a small change can produce an effect impossible on a larger one.

COPERNICUS: That's true, but when one creates a system, one doesn't look at it so closely, and one is often constrained deliberately to ignore certain inconvenient phenomena.

AESOP: Illustrious Copernicus, I'm sure that if you had created your astronomical system after the new observations, you would have left the earth fixed almost at the center of the planetary orbits, and would only have given it a movement of rotation about its inclined axis, making its two poles move as indicated in *On the Search for the Truth in the Sciences*; and by that means you would have been able to explain in a more plausible manner the precession of the equinoxes, the diminution of the obliquity of the ecliptic and other astronomical phenomena that certainly depend on the movements of the earth's poles, as the rising and setting of stars are produced by its diurnal rotations and the seasons by the inclination of its axis, as you were the first to determine. I think, therefore, that you will not take it amiss if I declare erroneous the theory of the displacement of the earth around the star that illuminates it.

JOUROUFLE: You're going to insult Monsieur Copernicus in that fashion?

COPERNICUS: I'm not saddened by it, because I haven't represented that hypothesis as an incontestable truth; on the contrary, I was so suspicious of it during my life that I only delivered it for printing when I had one foot in the grave.

JOUROUFLE: Alas, what will Monsieur Newton say?

AESOP: That humans are not exempt from error.

JOUROUFLE: So I can no longer show off, decorated by the Newtonian livery? Alas, poor Jouroufle, you have fallen a long way from your glory!

AESOP: That is a misfortune that the creators of false systems cannot escape. Ptolemy and Descartes experienced it before Newton, but they have conserved a part of their glory nevertheless. Newton can also lay claim to the praises of posterity, like them, although I must here, in accordance with the power that Urania has given me, condemn and declare false not merely the hypothesis of the displacement of the earth, but also those of the pretended void and sidereal or universal attraction. Copernicus, most of all, will always be welcomed with honor in future ages for having revealed the diurnal movement and the inclination of the earth's axis to explain the seasons, and I am charged on Urania's behalf with complimenting him in the name of the scientific world.

JOUROUFLE: Havens! To be condemned on almost all accounts!

AESOP: I'm sorry, but it was necessary to expect it sooner or later.

JOUROUFLE: Oh! Monseigneur Aesop, change your verdict, I implore you.

AESOP: I have judged in accordance with the truth, and I cannot revoke my judgment.

JOUROUFLE: Please, receive our very humble supplication favorably, and you will be delighted to have rendered us that service.

AESOP: It's impossible.

JOUROUFLE: Remember that we can give you a good place in some academy. I'm not deceiving you, Monseigneur Aesop; I can get you in there—I have the keys.

AESOP: I don't aspire to that honor.

JOUROUFLE: Look, I'll even give you my position and title.

AESOP: I have no need of them.

JOUROUFLE: And we'd let you have a good pension. Oh, good Monseigneur Aesop!

AESOP: I didn't ask for one in Greece; I shan't ask for one here.

JOUROUFLE: And we'd carry you on the wings of renown.

AESOP: I'm content with the renown I have.

JOUROUFLE: But remember, too, that we can annul your merit, and you'll have neither a position nor a pension.

AESOP: I don't care.

JOUROUFLE: And that we'll denigrate you in the scientific world.

AESOP: The scientific world won't always be Newtonian, and serene skies usually succeed nebulous weather.

JOUROUFLE: And that posterity will shame you in consideration for us.

AESOP: I have no fear of that misfortune; posterity will be able to render justice sooner or later.

JOUROUFLE: Go on, quickly, hurry—for I can see Seigneur Newton coming, with his numerous friends.

Scene Nineteen
The preceding, Newton, Heromondas, Sgravesande, Pemberton, Voltaire, Pope, the Physicists, etc.

NEWTON: Your presence is greatly desired, my dear Copernicus; would you leave us here alone when we're defending our cause?

COPERNICUS: Rather say yours, for as your partisans have often confessed, the hypothesis of general gravitation can only be sustained by that of the displacement of the earth.

NEWTON: That's true, but as the two hypotheses corroborate one another mutually, to defend my theories is to care for your glory. So I hope that you will render me a similar service, and will strive to do for me what I have done for you. Let us defend the displacement of our globe with all our might.

COPERNICUS: All my efforts are futile henceforth; I can do nothing for you or for me; the affair has been judged definitively, and your sidereal attraction, as well as the displacement of the earth, has been declared false and utterly false.

PEMBERTON: Entirely?

COPERNICUS: Yes.

HEROMONDAS: And you've accepted that judgment?

COPERNICUS: The fixity of the pole star in all the seasons of the year and other astronomical phenomena have closed the path to any protest.

VOLTAIRE: You've given in too easily.

COPERNICUS: What do you expect me to do, on fining myself in contradiction with myself and with phenomena?

SGRAVESANDE: You ought to have appealed to Urania, to the scientific world, to posterity and to all the devils, if necessary.

COPERNICUS: But after all, I never claimed that my astronomical system conformed in all respects with the exact truth; I've always regarded it as a simply hypothesis.

SGRAVESANDE: That's you're sentiment, then? Well, we have a contrary opinion, and we'll sustain against you and against everyone that the sun is fixed at the center of the world and that the earth rotates around that star, describing a true ellipse. My friends, do you not adhere go my proposition?

PEMBERTON: Yes, we adhere to it heart and soul.

SGRAVESANDE: Will you all swear to it?

PEMBERTON, HEROMONDAS, VOLTAIRE, *etc.*: Yes, we swear.

SGRAVESANDE: There, Aesop, retract your judgment quickly or we'll make such a racket that Urania's palace will be shaken.

HEROMONDAS: And toppled.

PEMBERTON, SGRAVESANDE, JOUROUFLE, POPE, VOLTAIRE, *and the troop of Physicists and Astronomers*: Yes, yes, toppled.

Scene Twenty
Aesop, Copernicus, Newton, Heromondas, Pemberton, Sgravesande, Pluche, Bernardin de Saint-Pierre, Voltaire, Pope, Jouroufle, the Concierge, etc.

CONCIERGE: This is a fine racket you're making at the gate of the palace! What's the cause of all this shouting?

JOUROUFLE: It's because Monseigneur Aesop has just said bluntly to Seigneurs Newton and Copernicus that they've lied and that they were wrong. That's not good, and I have an interest in sustaining at those Messieurs are right. For you see, Seigneur Concierge, I was only appointed doorkeeper of my academy because I praised Newton and his partisans to the skies; since then, I've almost lost my position for having muttered between my teeth that Newton wasn't infallible. Misfortune, it's said, advises a man well. I took it back, and as a recompense have been appointed first geometer of Urania's court, with a fine certificate for posterity.

CONCIERGE: Monsieur Jouroufle, you've been taken in by these sumptuous promises. Urania has no need of a geometer of your stripe, and if you want to be received with honor by posterity, I advise you to get rid of your scientific prejudices and embrace the truth when you encounter it.

JOUROUFLE: Entirely?

CONCIERGE: Yes.

JOUROUFLE: Otherwise, posterity will look at me askance?

CONCIERGE: Most certainly.

JOUROUFLE: That's good to know; I'll take advantage of it, for I don't like surly faces.

SGRAVESANDE: Without beating around the bush, Monsieur Concierge, we summon you to overturn the judgments of your creature Aesop immediately. Do you believe that after having grown old in the sciences we want to go back to school and learn what we've never known or understood? Certainly not. What we have conceived ourselves, or learned from Copernicus, Kepler and, above all, from Newton, our supreme dictator, we want to sustain forever.

CONCIERGE: Who's stopping you? Don't you know that the land of science is a state where opinions are free and entirely independent? If you want to say that it's night when the mid-day sun is shining, you can, but you'll render yourselves ridiculous of you try to force others to say that it isn't day. They ought to enjoy the same liberty that you demand for yourselves.

VOLTAIRE and SGRAVESANE, *simultaneously*: No, no, that's not what we intend. Liberty for us, servitude for others. Let them think and speak like us, or remain silent.

CONCIERGE: But what is it about, President?

AESOP: The Newtonians want to sustain, contrary to the evidence, that the terrestrial atmosphere doesn't increase the apparent diameter of the stars that are seen through it, especially at the horizon.

CONCIERGE: One might perhaps allow that false opinion to pass, if they had never had in their power convex diaphanous objects that increase the apparent volume of objects. But as they know those optical facts, their error is inexcusable. Monsieur Jouroufle, do you think like these Messiers?

JOUROUFLE: Oh no, Seigneur Concierge. Your servant Jouroufle does not want posterity to laugh at him while reproaching him for refusing the optical property of our diaphanous and convex atmosphere.

AESOP: The same scientists also want to sustain, in spite of experiments, that the spaces of the universe in which the sidereal bodies are suspended are void, or almost void, and that the expansible atmosphere exists in the middle of that void without being able to dilate there.

119

CONCIERGE: And you, Monsieur Jouroufle, did you defend that erroneous opinion?

JOUROUFLE: Seigneur Concierge. I am veridical, and I confess that I sustained it once, but in passing and without extrapolating its consequences; but now, my intelligence is better founded, and I'm not unaware that everything elastic dilates and expands if nothing retains it.

AESOP: They also want to make us believe that attraction is an occult and intrinsic quality of matter, and that the stars attract one another mutually at immense distances in an indivisible moment.

CONCIERGE: Have you talked such nonsense, Monsieur Jouroufle?

JOUROUFLE: Yes, unfortunately, and before Monseigneur Aesop made us understand that all attraction depends uniquely on the atmosphere. But now I think more accurately, how could I believe and extol such an evident error? For who is unaware that nothing can be attracted without being gripped? An occult quality is certainly not a hook.

AESOP: And they also say that the sun and the moon attract the earth.

CONCIERGE: From so far away, Monsieur Jouroufle, from so far away?

JOUROUFLE: Right! We say that as a joke.

AESOP: Finally, they are absolutely determined to persuade us that the earth travels around the day star, although the fixity of the north polar star is the same throughout the year, which would be impossible if the earth were circulating in space, since the daily displacement of its meridian, in diurnal rotation, changes the position of that star by about two degrees every day.

CONCIERGE: Oh, Monsieur Jouroufle! You have adopted that hypothesis contradicted by more than one astronomical phenomenon?

JOUROUFLE: You're joking, Seigneur Concierge. Monsieur Jouroufle has too much intelligence not to reject such hypotheses.

SGRAVESANDE: Right! I can't believe what I'm hearing. Is this the way, Monsieur Jouroufle, in spite of your promises, that you betray our cause?

JOUROUFLE: And what should I do, when I've seen that my glory will perish in defending your false theories? Look, when one has some intelligence, one wants to be admired by posterity, but posterity will close its doors to me and mock me if, after what I've just heard. I appear before it in Newtonian colors.

SGRAVESANDE: You're dreaming, I think. Don't you know that, on the contrary, your glory would have be augmented if you had supported our opinions, good or bad, to the end, and that the more obstinate you had shown yourself to be, the more posterity would have admired our genius? By dint of saying that you were right and that Newton's adversaries were wrong, you would have appeared to be the phoenix of beautiful minds.

JOUROUFLE, *to Sgravesande, in a low voice*: Of course I didn't know that! Well, when the Seigneur Concierge goes back inside, I promise you that I'll retract everything I've just said. Is that what you want?

SGRAVESANDE: No, you're nothing but a pedant; we don't need your help, we'll do very well without you. Get out of our sight. We expel you from our society, and we call upon posterity to do likewise before it ceases to be Newtonian. Doubtless it will render us justice, and will judge, first and foremost, that you're a fool.

JOURSOUFLE: Call me a fool if you wish. But I was more of a fool, since you force me to say it, when I followed your theories full of contradictions and suppositions, and too often belied by a thousand phenomena. The posterity on which you're counting so much will doubtless not always be under the rod of Monsieur Newton and his adorers, and it will be all the more severe in your regard because you've been so stubborn in supporting the English scientist's false hypotheses

SGRAVESANDE: Well, if posterity comes to condemn Newton, we'll condemn posterity, and expel it from our company.

JOUROUFLE: Expel it as much as you please, but we'll see thereafter who emerges victorious or vanquished. Let our young geniuses launch themselves into a scientific career exempt from prejudices. Oh, how they're going to mock your *Magister dixit*! Adieu, then, Messieurs. Go on dreaming, if you wish, that stones fall upon us from the moon.[29] I no longer envy your sublime science. Adieu, adieu!

(*Everyone withdraws.*)

---

[29] The author appends to the text of his dramatic dialogues a letter written in October 1816 on the subject of the hypothesis that meteorites are extraterrestrial in origin, which he denigrates—like many others—as the assertion that "stones fall from the moon." As it is not directly relevant to the drama I have omitted it; it features the same complaints about the theory of gravity, and also addresses some severe criticism the theories of Mesmer regarding "animal magnetism."

Ralph Schropp: *The Automaton*

A Story Taken from a Palimpsest
(1898)

The heart is everything.

Preface

During a long sojourn at the Château de Beauregard in the south of France. situated in the middle of an ideally pictur-esque mountainous region, we employed long hours in ferret-ing through the shelves of the vast and rich library of that old manor. The books and manuscripts contained there in such large numbers originate, for the most part, from an old con-vent constructed in the vicinity, but nothing remains today of that spacious monastery but walls and ruins. The vaults under which the numerous and venerable monks with silvery hair ambled slowly while reciting the hours have suffered the de-structive action of time; silent and deserted, one no longer sees anything but climbing plants that hide the fissures. Not the slightest trace any longer remains of the narrow cells that once gave birth to so many manuscripts, sometimes so precious!

One day, while extending our curious research as far as the château's archives, we found a parchment covered in mil-dew and spotted with the dust of centuries. After an attentive examination, we recognized a palimpsest. While striving to divine a few precious fragments of Latin or Greek literature that the sheets might have contained, the original characters of which had been washed away in order to make use of the parchment for a second time, we read, involuntarily at first, the new text that had been superimposed there. The Latin was very defective, but the story it contained captured our attention completely from the very first lines.

We give here a translation as faithful as possible, given the deterioration that time has inflicted on the original. Words that have been effaced or have become illegible have had to be reestablished. The monk Theodulus whose name figures at the end of the manuscript seems to have been a man of the world before his entry into holy orders. He probably composed this story in accordance with the memories conserved in the cloister, based on the relation that was doubtless made by the two monks mentioned toward the end of the story.

Nice-Maritime, 28 November 1878.

R.S.

Albert the Great, the pious Dominican and celebrated magician, had just finished his famous automaton. With joy he considered his work, the fruit of long sleepless nights and profound thought. He had been obliged to sacrifice the best years of his life to numerous trials; now, having almost arrived at the end of his career, the sight of his work consoled him for the past troubles and infinite difficulties that he had had to overcome. A most complete success had surpassed his expectations and crowned his desires. He had succeeded in executing to perfection the ideal that he had borne within him since the time of his youth, when he had concluded his studies in Padua.

Homunculus—that was the name with which the new Prometheus had baptized his creation—left nothing to be desired. He resembled a veritable man of flesh and bone closely enough to be mistaken for one. So, in order to trace his portrait, it is a celebrated mortal rather than an automaton that is to be described.

Albert the Great possessed in his soul, in his capacity as a scholar, no trace of the divine breath of the artist, so his creation, purely mechanical, absolutely lacked the imprint of beauty. He had been content to copy a human face and to reproduce nature exactly, without giving the slightest thought to poeticizing it. The features that he had succeeded in imitating were passably regular and agreeable enough; the physiognomy

124

was more pleasing, in several regards, because he had chosen for models certain plastic figures, but empty of expression, such as one encounters in society, the sight of whom soon engenders lassitude. One could allow one's eyes to linger on the visage of the automaton without experiencing either surprise or repulsion, and one always saw that physiognomy again with an equal pleasure.

He had a good complexion, neither pale nor highly colored, and, as a whole, Homunculus was not remarkable, whether by an excessive stature or an exaggerated stoutness. He was the image of one of those men who can be counted in thousands, people who pass unperceived, giving no purchase to criticism, but not exciting any admiration either.

His creator and master had dressed him in the latest fashion of the era; as regards elegance, his exterior was irreproachable. With the aid of an ingenious and well-designed mechanism, the secret of his inventor, Homunculus executed with facility and grace all the movements indispensable to material life. Everything about him was regulated and studied to such a point that he would never be able, in the sphere of action, to offend or irritate even the most susceptible people by abrupt or thoughtless behavior.

Thanks to mechanisms that only their author could set in movement or return to repose, Homunculus' thoughts took on the imprint of the character, intelligence and sentiments of the person speaking to him. In that fashion, he always found himself in perfect harmony with his interlocutor, and he made the most favorable impression from the outset.

Although superficial, the automaton's education had been well directed and was sufficient to his needs. He possessed notions of all things, and, as his mechanical resources could not let him down, he emerged victorious from the most arduous debates.

His voice, established in a monotonous, indifferent and authoritative register, free of intonations and modulations, was perfectly suited to his nature. For those who make use of it, that manner of expression has something divine about it, for they believe that they are floating above various human situations, as in the time of the creative Spirit floating above the waters.

That genre of conversation, which is merely a studied form in many people, was natural to Homunculus. Nothing was capable of gladdening him or saddening him. Like a god, he could traverse the keenest joys and the sharpest pain without feeling the slightest emotion; a stereotyped smile sometimes wandered faintly over his lips.

Those particular features of his character, enviable in some respects, are easily explicable. The great magician had succeeded perfectly in imitating a human similar to all others in gesture and thought, but he had been incapable of giving him a heart, of causing to spring forth within him the divine spark that warms all beings, as the sun exercises its benevolent attraction on the earth.

The monotony of Homunculus' voice, and the general lack of expression in his person, derived from his irremediable imperfections, caused by the impotence of his master to take any further a work above the range of mere mortals. That imperfection deprived the automaton of the sentiments and passions that ennoble humanity, and which flow from the principle of sensibility that we bear with us from birth, but which produces totally different effects in different individuals.

A man who, living by the soul as well as the body, was put in direct communication with the automaton, would not have taken long, in the presence of those impassive features and that unmoving gaze, to feel a chill penetrating his heart. Albert the Great himself often experienced a pain in his ribs, and the sight of that living and yet artificial being, who was his work, sometimes plunged him into a kind of indefinable trouble and terror.

By the efforts of his powerful intelligence, Albert had arrogated rights that only belonged to the Creator. Now, alas, he was about to suffer the consequences and submit to the immutable rules of destiny, which even a god cannot escape.

The individual who creates always forms his work in accordance with plans based on fixed principles. If he submits his work to certain laws, he imposes them on himself by the power of reciprocity. As a creator, he can doubtless liberate himself when he pleases from those voluntary chains, but only by destroying his work. Thus, by the effect of those primordial laws, the master inevitably makes himself the slave of his creature.

Many a time, Albert had been seized by regret for having conceived his insensate dreams and had forged needlessly, in realizing them, annoyances of all kinds. In his moments of discouragement and overexcitement, only self-esteem, combined with the memory of many lost hours, prevented him from destroying his work.

The automaton was beginning to become a burden to him. He did not know how to utilize him. He could doubtless render him motionless, simply by pressing a switch known to him alone, but he would run the risk, in leaving him for more than a day in that fictive sleep, of causing serious damage to his work. The machine was so constructed that it was necessary, under pain of derangement, for it to be continuously active, for movement developed movement within it, giving heat to its limbs and thus becoming the source of Homunculus' apparent life. He had no need of repose, his artificial existence only being the result of fortunate mechanical combinations.

Those reasons obliged Albert only to immobilize him very rarely; in any case, that was not necessary, because the automaton, docile and diligent, carried out his master's orders to the letter. As he never left he Dominican's cell, there was no reason to fear any misfortune occasioned by his intervention, or that might be prejudicial to himself.

But idleness is always dangerous, even for an automaton. That was what Albert the Great also thought. Not being able, even so, to open a career for Homunculus immediately, he made him his secretary and domestic. He retired to the bottom of a drawer the gentleman's costume in which he had initially dressed the automaton and replaced it with a monk's habit entirely similar to the one he wore in the cloister. From then on, Homunculus devoted himself to all kinds of work. He had no equal as a domestic, for what is more agreeable than to be served by machines? The master's correspondence was also handled by him with a rigorous punctuality, and Albert, thus aided in his everyday occupations, was much better able to devote his time to new research and new inventions.

Several months went by in the most perfect harmony between the master and his secretary, and their union would have lasted for long years but for certain circumstances that came to interrupt them.

Homunculus began to be subject to the common laws that claim their rights over all created beings; he experienced a need to exist for himself, for, from the day that he had been finished, he had been capable of providing for himself. Dependency weighed upon him, since he sensed the faculty of living and acting without outside help.

The letters that he was responsible for writing, and his reading in his master's library, had awakened intelligence and had given him an irresistible desire to see the world. An anxious ardor drove him to leave the cell in the convent, but, never daring to communicate his desires to Albert, he conceived his escape plan in silence.

There is no deep-rooted habit that cannot be surprised by negligence. One day, Albert forgot to lock the door of his cell, or perhaps left it open intentionally, intending to take a walk in the garden of the cloister.

Homunculus quickly perceived that negligence and took advantage of it immediately. From the drawer where it had been deposited, he took out his gentleman's costume and, having made a bundle of it, hid it carefully under his robe. As he had learned that money is necessary to live in the world, which he only knew by name, he took possession of the convent's cash-box, which received alms for the poor, and filed his pockets with the contents. Then, after having left the door of the cell ajar, he solely went down the common staircase. A few moments later, he was outside the cloister and in the world that he had such a keen desire to see and know.

Thanks to his habit he had been able to emerge freely from the monastery. The porter had no paid any attention to him, doubtless thinking that he was a brother going out to collect alms.

Scarcely was he outside the walls of the cloister than Homunculus wondered what he ought to do. To begin with he walked rapidly for some time, with the sole aim of getting away from the convent as quickly as possible. All the unfamiliar objects that struck his gaze only caused him a mediocre astonishment. Because of his lack of a heart, he remained a stranger to all impression. The springs that served him as a soul had been so well designed and executed that the automaton admitted the most astonishing things as simple and natural. Thus, he found himself all the more at ease in the world that he was seeing for the first time because his purely mechanical constitution inspired in him nothing but a superb indifference.

Wandering at random, he had arrived on the bank of a river. Instinctively, a good idea occurred to him. He went to hide behind a bush, took off his monk's habit and threw it, not into the nettles but into the water. Then he put on the gentleman's costume and found himself suddenly metamorphosed and embellished. Over the next few hours he continued his route through the countryside, all the way to a highway, which he followed. After a day's marching, it brought him to the gate of a large and prosperous city.

In the interim, Albert the Great, his unfortunate inventor, abandoned himself to a profound despair. After his stroll in the cloister garden, he had returned to his cell. Finding it open and not seeing Homunculus, he had called out to him and looked for him in the vicinity but, being unable to discover him, he ordered a minute search in the enclosure of the convent. Everyone was put to work to rediscover the automaton. Albert did not believe definitively in his escape until the brother in charge of the door told him that he had opened it to a monk a short while before. Messengers   immediately departed in all directions, but they came back without being able to report any precise news.

Two days after Homunculus' flight, a fisherman brought a habit to the convent. Albert immediately recognized it as his automaton's.

"Alas!" he exclaimed, desolate. "Must I lose the fruit of my late nights, the preoccupation of my entire life, in this fashion? Can I expect a similar destruction of my achievement? I have kept my invention secret; my name will not pass to posterity!"

He continued to lament his negligence and his misfortune for a long time, without being able to resign himself to it.

Meanwhile, the automaton was enjoying the supreme happiness of conducting himself in accordance with his own will.

The great city to which hazard had led him soon offered him countless pleasures. He had taken a room in the principal hotel. A secret instinct having driven him to visit the city's fencing and riding schools, he did not take long to cultivate the best of relationships with the young men who routinely frequent those places. Thanks to his particular organization, he possessed a remarkable aptitude for all bodily exercises that only demanded flexibility of movement. The most spirited horse became immediately docile in his hands, and the most skillful fencing-masters feared his blade.

In a matter of weeks he had made numerous friends. In order better to position himself in their society he passed himself off as the son of a good family whose youthful follies had caused him to quarrel with his parents. He only became more interesting for it. Soon, women of the world, whose friends had described some of his brilliant qualities, desired to get to know him. That was not difficult. Two months after his escape from the convent, Homunculus was shining in the foremost salons in the city. Everyone admired his rare distinction, his exquisite tact and, above all, his imperturbable assurance.

Only a few envious individuals permitted themselves to criticize him. They claimed to have sometimes detected in him the manners of a *parvenu*, contracted in another society than the one into which he had now introduced himself. They suggested that he only paid scant or no attention at all to those who did not have a high position or who were merely his equals. They alleged that he deliberately disparaged all those who were praised in his presence, and that in his conversation he incessantly had the sufficient tone that permitted no reply. They regarded him as one of those people who take pleasure in expressing their own opinions but do not permit others to express theirs. Finally, they reproached him—which was much more serious—for behaving basely and crawling with people of influence superior to his rank, especially with those from whom he hoped for some advantage, if only to receive invitations to dinner or obtain via their intermediation one of those facile decorations not earned on the battlefield, but accorded solely as a testimony of favor.

These calumnies had certainly only been invented by the jealousy of a few rivals. What could not be denied was that Homunculus was generally liked. His absence of heart facilitated the means of worldly success. He was especially able to attract the sympathy of women, and thanks to their protection, which he owed to the sentiments that he was clever enough to inspire in them, he shone in all their salons. To conquer their favors, he had begun by making each of them believe individually that he only burned with passion for her, whereas even the most beautiful was incapable of awakening an elevated love in him. His speech only expressed false sentiments; he could repeat the same nonsense to all women, without running the risk of being caught in the nets of his own lies. His natural indifference always made him the master of the situation. By means of that conduct, which derived from his constitution, it did not take long for him to be invited everywhere.

A great lady, very fashionable then for her supreme elegance and also vary sensible although she was no longer very young, having no fear, in spite of her recent widowhood, of showing that Homunculus had conquered her heart, and she put the cap on his success. Soon, the other women were competing with her to excite the attention of the automaton. From that moment on he was so sought after that he became the object of all conversations, and it was regarded as an extreme favor merely to receive a note in his handwriting.

The perseverance of the beautiful widow carried him away. Homunculus, faithful to his nature—which is to say, his mechanism—had remained insensible for a long time; the exhaustion of his money finally advised him to allow himself to be touched by so much love. He consented to marry the great lady, declaring in a negligent tone to his friends that it was not because he loved her, but because he was madly loved himself, that the marriage had been decided.

By virtue of Homunculus' indifference, the union that he had contracted was untroubled by any cloud. His wife adored him and lavished care and attention upon him. She never perceived, fortunately for her, that no heart was beating within her husband's breast. The only thing that she found strange in him was that sleep never came to close his eyes. After a few months, however, she had succeeded in getting used to the phenomenon, and as Homunculus did not begin to waste away, she ended up congratulating herself for having found a second husband who combined with so many other qualities that of never sleeping.

Three years had gone by since Homunculus' escape, and he had become he father of two delightful children, who took after him and their mother. They resembled her externally, but, having no heart, the same insensibility and egotism was found in them as in their father.

Albert the Great had had time to console himself, apparently at least, for the irreparable loss that he believed that he had suffered. He was now attempting other inventions, without thinking overmuch about creating a second automaton.

Around that time, the story of an unusual event came to trouble the ordinary quietude of the cloister. It was said that the inhabitants of the nearest big city had suddenly risen up against a gentleman of noble birth, and that public tranquility had briefly been in danger, but that calm had been restored.

The fact, however, were sufficiently important for them to have spread of their own accord all the way to the silent walls of the cloister.

One feast day, in one of the busiest streets of the city, an aristocrat's carriage had run over a child. Members of the crowd had immediately hurled themselves in front of the horses, and in spite of all the coachman's efforts, exciting them with words and the whip, had succeeded in holding on to them. Furious people had scaled the carriage, uttering cries of vengeance. The great lady who was inside the carriage was terrified; as for the gentleman sitting beside her, his face had not been pierced by any emotion. He had contented himself with throwing a few handfuls of gold into the crowd, in a negligent and impassive fashion. At the sight of that magic rain, the common people had suddenly calmed down. The horses had been released, and the coachman had taken advantage of that to drive away rapidly.

The manifestation seemed to be concluded, and would have been, in fact, but for an unexpected incident. At the moment when the carriage set off again, the lady, who had recovered her composure, had said a few words to her husband; the latter had replied, in a loud voice and in the most indifferent tone with a remark that had, unfortunately, been overheard by a number of people: "There are enough children in the world without that brat."

That cruel comment had run from mouth to mouth. Toward evening, the crowd had pressed, like the turbulent waves of the ocean, beneath the windows of the house inhabited by the man who had pronounced such harsh words in public. People were crying vengeance, and several agitators were already trying to break down the main door. In order to reestablish order and tranquility, it was necessary to have recourse to armed force, and there had been casualties, some of them fatal. Gradually, however, the multitude had dispersed and the night had rendered calm to minds—except that the gentleman was advised not to show himself in the streets of the city for some time.

When that tale reached the ears of Albert the Great, a sudden flash of enlightenment passed through his mind; his face cleared; the expression of his features, melancholy or a long time, became cheerful, and he cried, full of enthusiasm: "My work is not lost! By that absence of heart, I recognize my automaton! Homunculus lives; I shall go to recover him."

He left for the great city that same day, accompanied by two brothers. In less than twenty-four hours they had arrived at their destination.

Rightly presuming that their habits might alarm the automaton, they disguised themselves as men-at-arms and went, the very next day, to Homunculus' house. Albert, transformed into a knight, asked to speak to the master of the house. Far from inspiring suspicion, their disguised served to facilitate their passage, because, since the recent events. Homunculus had been put under protection of the army.

When Albert was in the presence of the pretended gentleman, he recognized his automaton joyfully. As soon as the valet who had introduced him had withdrawn, he ran to his creation and, rapidly pressing the hidden switch that was known to him alone, immobilized Homunculus immediately.

In a matter of minutes the automaton was dismantled, and, the two brothers, who were waiting at the door, having come in, each of them hid several pieces of the machine under his cloak. Albert took the head and shoulders, and thus, as Roman senators had once caused their first king to disappear, the monks carried poor Homunculus away without being seen.

A few days after that event, the automaton was installed in the cell again, submissive as in the past to the orders of his master and inventor. As before, he fulfilled the double function in his regard of secretary and domestic. Albert was radiant with joy, and now kept watch on his work with jealous care. There was no more chance of escape for the unfortunate Homunculus henceforth. Fortunately for him, his lack of a heart spared him from all regrets and all sadness.

A month after that forced return, the celebrated Thomas Aquinas, nicknamed the Great Ox of Wisdom,[30] came to render a visit to the Dominican convent; he had undertaken the voyage with the objective of seeing Albert and appreciating his marvelous inventions for himself. Scarcely had he arrived than he asked for the celebrated magician. A brother indicated to him the cell he inhabited and then withdrew.

Thomas Aquinas having knocked on the door, Homunculus, following his master's orders, immediately came to open it. At the sight of him, the man inspired by the Lord was gripped by fright; he had immediately sensed the absence of the heart, and divined the artificial man in the Dominican's domestic. He must even have mistaken Homunculus for the spirit of evil, for, having raised a knotty oak staff that served him as a support, he struck the automaton on the head with a blow so violent that, this time, the machine was permanently destroyed.

The arguments that followed the automaticide were violent. Albert did not spare the future saint, but all his anger was futile. The master's work was irredeemably annihilated.

Why had Thomas Aquinas not come to the convent before Homunculus' escape? What annoyances poor humanity would have been spared!

In time, the Dominican succeeded in resigning himself and almost consoling himself for the loss he had suffered. It was not the same for the wife of the automaton. The great lady could not explain her husband's sudden disappearance. Incapable of reconciling herself to that inconceivable separation, she set everything in motion to find him.

Her research was devoid of result. Albert maintained an obstinate silence and the brothers who had lent him their aid in the abduction of the automaton were also constrained to si-

---

[30] Thomas Aquinas was known in his student days as "the Dumb Ox"—a judgment against which Albert the Great, under whom he studied, protested, allegedly saying that his bellowing would one day be heard all around the world.

lence, because the Dominican had compelled them under the most severe menaces. It was only after his death that they talked, and it is to them that the relation of this story is owed.

Many years have gone by since that epoch. The events recounted above have been partly forgotten, but the automaton's descendants are still alive, alas. The two sons he had by his marriage have perpetuated his race. Sometimes it seems to be extinct, but suddenly, be the power of the phenomenon of atavism, individuals entirely identical to the first Homunculus reappear on the world stage.

You ask with astonishment: "Where are they encountered?" Without looking very far, you can find marvelously accomplished specimens; they can be seen in all ranks of society; each sex counts its representatives, and it will be particularly easy for you to find examples among courtiers and men of the world.

Louis Gallet: *The Death of Paris*
(1892)

So, this is what the Seer said:

For twelve centuries Paris had been expanding at the foot of the metal tower that remains almost the sole vestige of the former city, which a very ancient tradition names the Eiffel Tower, without anyone knowing exactly where the name came from, the archeologists having failed completely to reach agreement on the matter. The city was immense, sheltering in its ten-story houses crowned with vast terraces a population of six million souls. Its prosperity was great, although it had no longer been the capital of the United States of Europe for a long time. It had, however, remained famous throughout the world for its worship of pleasure. All the peoples driven away from the North by the invasion of the ice had their representatives there, no longer forming any but a single nation.

Powerful Russia had flowed like a river into Asia; Germany only existed as a memory; all of noble Europe was asleep in polar silence.

The United States of Europe then had Marseille as a capital; those of Africa had Algiers.

Mediterranean and aerial communications already being very rapid in those days, the two cities in question exchanged their correspondence and newspapers several times every day, always full of stories about the admirable Paris that, although then situated at the northern extremity of Europe, dispossessed of its political suzerainty, was still the astonishment of the world. Science nevertheless expressed serious anxiety in its regard. The earth was subject to a cooling whose zone was describing increasingly large circles around the pole. But Paris, well-heated, abundantly provided with all industrial riches,

137

laughed at the prophets of doom. The great city had always had enormous depths of skepticism.

And, in truth, the strength of Paris was marvelous then, able to inspire a boundless confidence in its duration, or at least in its means of salvation if, perchance, the existence of its inhabitants should one day be compromised. Gigantic airships with ten rows of propellers striped its sky with rapid flight; smaller ones, as elegant and gilded as royal galleys, crossed paths in daylight or, by night, fitted at the prow with multicolored beacon lights, constellated the sky like a dust of wandering stars.

In streets sixty meters wide, pedestrians circulated without fear between the tall houses. There were only a few electric carriages by then, airships being much more convenient and less dangerous than terrestrial vehicles. As for horses, they had been ameliorated to such an extent over the centuries that none remained, except for a few specimens absolutely pure in form but incapable of any service. Those masterpieces of plasticity were preciously conserved in zoological museums. Perhaps a few still exist today, but nobody knows where they are. The Museum of Algiers has one, but it is stuffed, exhibited alongside the last elephant, another species vanished in the wake of the pitiless hunting once carried out for the collection of ivory, which has been so advantageously replaced today by compressed paper products.

In numerous gymnasia the population incessantly maintained flexibility with the rudest exercises. The race had become very beautiful, no trace of senility appearing on faces, the incessantly-functioning skin admitting no wrinkles, so it was difficult to distinguish an old man from a young one. As for women, it was as if they were uniformly fixed at the age of twenty, and it was not rare, even at close range, for a grandmother to be mistaken for her granddaughter, so much progress had the art of preservative ointments made.

All of that population, communally rich in amiable intelligence, was admirably healthy. For a long time there had been no more physicians; they had been replaced by chemists and simple physiologists. Having penetrated all the secrets of nature and catalogued all the microbes, those scientists had then rested, sagely content to watch humanity live and die.

There were no longer any public libraries or museums, literature and art having no reason to exist in a society that was attached above all to the materiality of things and had long since done away with sentimental speculations and esthetic theories. The language, moreover, had become very simple, although it was composed of all the ancient languages once spoke by the various races of the two worlds. From the exchange of vocables, syntax and formulae of abbreviation, a universal language had been born, in which the verb only played a minor role, giving ground to the precious noun and the adjective, the only ones indispensable, in sum, to the relations of practical life.

Thus, once-enormous newspapers had been reduced to the dimensions of a minuscule sheet. A few sentences gave the political news or recounted the most recent events; there had been no commentary for a long time, and all polemic had been suppressed. An item announced a fact, nothing more; the readers drew their own conclusions. The old argumentative journalists had been replaced by gymnasiarch-reporters whose renown was that of the aeronef moving with the greatest rapidity and flying most speedily to the theater of events.

A little music was still made in great halls: music in which research and the collision of enemy sonorities was pushed to the highest degree of refinement, and which produced, in the nervous system of its listeners, sensations of an extraordinary acuity.

In sum, the people were happy, and grateful to be so, which is rare. As long as no one spoke to them about God, death or amour, which engender pain, nor about the family, whose affections and proofs are subversive of all tranquility, they confessed themselves content; they went through life with a philosophical egotism that made them as beautiful and as joyful as their rich means permitted.

When it was too cold in Paris, when the snow became too frequent, the ordinary people found shelter in the winter gardens, immense palaces of glass in which spring was restored to them; the richest flew away in some pleasure airship to Algiers, or, if the temperature in Algiers seemed too low, all the way to Lake Chad, already bordered with magnificent habitations. That was a matter of a few hours. Many of those holidaying in Algiers returned to Paris once a week to take care of business.

Over the last few years the cold had increased markedly in the middle of each winter, and the snow had fallen with greater force. Snowstorms had been photographed in which the flakes seemed to touch one another and, so to speak, fuse together. But those snowfalls did not last long, and powerful apparatus loaded with special products melted them instantaneously and sent them in seething streams into the drains, all the way to the Seine, which transported them seawards.

One day, after an entire week of weather so spring-like that a few Japanese plum-trees had flowers in the gardens, which caused Parisians, eternally inclined to enthusiasm, to anticipate an exceptionally mild season, the sky was suddenly covered with exceedingly opaque clouds, so low that the summit of the metal tower disappeared, no longer allowing anything to be seen at night but the glow of its beacon, displayed like a bloodstain in the shifting darkness.

The public airships were obliged to modify their service, and, at times, to suspend it entirely, being unable to travel in the almost-constant darkness without danger of collision. Only a few private craft took the risk; for two hours there was a criss-crossing of vague streaks of colored light in the dirty sky, and the loud blaring of sirens sowing alarm in the air, as sinister as the cries of murdered monsters.

Many accidents occurred; two airships, each carrying a hundred passengers, crashed and fell, broken, on the hills of the Point-de-Jour, bristling with cupolas and iron steeples, from which bloody human rags were soon suspended in a sinister fashion.

A police edict then forbade all circulation, until the menacing clouds had dissipated. The temperature was mild. A slight breeze sometimes rose up, and then a whiteness would appear in the sky, and snow would begin to fall, slowly, in large flakes widely separated at first, but then thicker, so thick that within an hour there would be more than sixty centimeters in the streets. The snow-melting machines immediately went into action then and torrents of water flowed toward the river.

That lasted throughout the whole of one night, the snow falling incessantly and pitilessly, and the machines sweeping it away with mathematical regularity. In private meetings, in elegant clubs, the frightened faces of men and women could be seen at the windows, against the bright background of red wallpaper, gazing at the white shroud falling like an endless bolt of cloth, wondering whether it was going to last forever, and whether they would ever be able to go home. The sage were already asleep, ignorant of the event. A few enraged gamblers laughed, forgetting in the fever of baccarat the vague emotion, the fear of the inevitable unknown that had already gripped the souls round them.

In the morning, it became visible that what had been reckoned an event was about to become a disaster. The policemen responsible for manning the machines were exhausted by fatigue and only working tiredly. At about nine o'clock, when he pale daylight had difficulty piercing the gray backcloth of the sky, the dissolving salts required for the alimentation of the apparatus ran out.

While people ran around all the depots in the city, soon realizing that all the reserves had been exhausted by the exceptional requirements of the night, the snow continued to fall with a ferocious regularity, a scourge more terrible in its mild appearance than a devouring but extinguishable fire or invasive but fleeting floodwater, a pale mass rising in imperceptible layers to disquieting heights, eroding and devouring houses at the base, giving the eye the sensation of an entire city buried in a white immensity.

The electric street-lights, left illuminated since the previous evening, shone at ground level over the snow, sparkling with crystals, when dusk came again; the henceforth-invincible scourge had closed all doors. The sounds of the city were stifled beneath that thick, soft carpet.

A great torpor reigned, when, suddenly, toward midnight, a violent wind blowing from due north traversed space, shaking and breaking up the clouds, tearing them like masses of cotton wool, chasing them across the immense sky. And the moon appeared, cold and pure against the black firmament, where a few rare stars were quivering in the depths.

The thermometer descended well below zero and the snowy mass solidified into uneven ice. Then, clamors rose up from the city, the flames of torches flickered in the streets and the squares, and human masses escaped through windows that had become doors, fearful and dismal, traversed by the shrill cries of women, disrupted by sudden falls, forming terrible eddies in the obscure river of beings in flight.

Forgetting those that the snow slowly buried in obstructed houses, the people ran toward the only possible salvation. At the doors of garages, in the shops where airships, ready rigged, extended in the shadows, awaiting the moment to resume their flight in the open sky, groups collided, swearing at one another and fighting.

There was no longer any right, or law, neither servants nor masters. The supreme struggle for existence commenced.

In the radiant light of the second day the engines of the airships began to make their formidable respiration heard. On the white bed of snow, there were black and red stains, of mud and blood, were crowds had trampled and fought.

Finally, two airships rose up, to the cries of their triumphant passengers. The gigantic machines, of a solid but old model, only had canvas propellers, rendered rigid by the ice, when they tried to turn under the impulsion of their robust metallic armatures, cracks were heard in the canvas, here and there, and the progress of the airships became awkward and heavy. A false impulsion by one of the engineers caused their prows to collide. Both oscillated, drew back, and then resumed their convergent course. Then a collision more terrible than the preceding one occurred. One of the disemboweled ships fell like a great dead bird, and, breaking through the crust of ice, plunged profoundly into the snow, while the other, lurching like a doomed kite, came to plunge, skimming the surface, into the middle of the howling crowd.

No one ran to help the wounded. In any case, the sky overhead was darkening again, snow was threatening. The rigged airships, boarded in haste, were launched into the air. A few soon disappeared into the white depths; others fell, their propellers hanging limply, as if some invisible hunter had pierced them with his arrows. Nothing more: to the first layer of frozen snow a new layer was added by falling flakes.

Outside the suburbs, files extended like caravans of black ants. They could not advance beyond a kilometer; soon, they ran into inaccessible banks, and then, the cold afflicting them with immobility, they stayed where they were, frozen in their march. After a brief interval, everything became white again, and nothing revealed the place where the buried caravan had passed.

In the city—that city of six million beings—the human masses had melted, condensed into a single mass, huddled in the immense central square dominated by the metal tower. Already, the snow had reached half way up the vast arches supporting the first stage. Weary and shivering, men, women and children gazed, waiting for help, incapable of action. Around them, in the immense circle of the horizon, only the summits of edifices any longer emerged. The city had already disappeared, leveled by the snow.

In the air there was no sound, not a single wing.

Finally, among those who were still capable of movement after three days of intense cold and invasive snow, a group formed that began to march toward the tower. There salvation might lie, if the snow continued to fall.

There were cried of "The tower! The tower!" And a counter-movement began among the people, many of whom had not thought at first about that refuge.

The elevators were no longer functioning, already seized by the icy snow. They hastened toward the stairs. There was a frightful struggle there. Before that narrow passage people grabbed one another by the throat or by the hair; in the heavy air, the sound of gunshots was scarcely perceptible, along with a brief flash; and black masses fell, their flesh splashed with blood. With teeth clenched, without a cry, they fought.

Finally, the file of the victorious, pale, their hands red, plunged into the narrow stairway. Shivering in the icy wind, not daring to grip the metal guard-rails, which burned the palms if touched, they climbed the steps. And behind them, and around them, the virgin snow rose too, extending its immaculate cloak over Paris.

When they reached the beacon, night had fallen again: a night as pure as the one before, with a blue-tinted moon, sending darts with a thousand icy points at the earth. On high, in the stairway of the tower and on the platform of the beacon, there was a great and formidable silence. And the moonlight, stiff forms, with convulsed faces, leaned over, through the iron latticework, searching the dark horizon for something that was not there.

At daybreak, on the platform of the beacon, clinging to the bars, there were a few men, eyes terribly open—eyes of stone now—frozen forever, gazing in vain at the four points of the horizon from which something might come.

Paris was dead.

The snow soon changed into an immense glacier. The rains of spring came, which washed the mass and made it shine in the sunlight like a lake of glaucous crystal. And when, in that part of the vast polar desert, a few airships still risked themselves in the south, the explorers perceived quite distinctly, beneath the transparent ice, the enormous mass of the edifices, steeples, bell-towers and terraces of what had once been marvelous Paris.

Léon Daudet: *The Automaton*
(1898)

I was in Hamburg, the most mysterious city in Europe, where one can find a factory of monsters, a repository of ferocious animals, and houses of joy of a magical luxury.

It was winter: a gray or yellow sky replete with snow, and that indefatigable snow buried the old Medieval houses, the laborers' cottages in wood sculpted by decay, the churches, the docks and the harbor. It caused a great silence, and the idea of so much mute life under the snow frightened me.

I spent my monotonous days at the hotel. I had brought with me as a companions the *Introduction à la médecine de l'esprit* by my friend Maurice de Fleury.[31] The new and troubling ideas with which that work swarms delighted me. Although I scarcely believe in doctors, and even less in medicine, I marveled to see the mechanistic theories of Spinoza regarding the movements of the soul taken up again and adapted to the context of modern science by a subtle, clever and sincere mind. I thought that the book inaugurated a singular order of research and avenged literature somewhat for the base scoria of a Lombroso.

The door opened. A servant brought me a card: *Dr. Otto Serpius*.

I knew that unusual name. I got up to go and meet him. He was already advancing toward me, tall and stooped, like an ape; the white hair and beard matched the wan snowy day. The dark eyes sparkled beneath bushy eyebrows. The cheeks

---

[31] The psychiatrist Maurice de Fleury (1860-1931) published numerous books, on topics including neurasthenia, depression, insomnia, "senile hysteria" and the criminal mind. The general textbook cited was published in 1898.

and forehead were broad, engraved with a thousand wrinkles; the features, shriveled like the web of a dead spider, expressed malice and pride. I noticed the hands, large and hairy, animated by a slight tremor.

"I heard that you had arrived in Hamburg," the individual said to me. "I came to invite you to a little visit, which, I think, will interest you." With a slight embarrassment, he added: "Bur it's necessary for you to come with me right away, because today is the one only I have before leaving tomorrow on a voyage."

"I'll come with you, Doctor," I replied.

The people who had recommended me to Otto Serpius had warned me about the eccentricities of the scientist's character; some people thought he was mad, others that he was the greatest genius in Europe.

His eyes, which were inspecting everything, fell upon Fleury's book.

"Oho!" he exclaimed, with interest. "You Frenchmen are on the road to wisdom, then. The medicine of the mind—but it's the only one, my dear fellow, the only one. And has Monsieur Fleury kept the promises of that noble title?"

"You'll judge for yourself, when you've read that fine work. Official science is rampant in my country, but from time to time, a clear audacious and powerful mind emerges that breaks down a worm-eaten door, and one sees admirable horizons..."

After a long and tortuous walk, rendered difficult by the snow, through the sordid and fantastic labyrinth of Hamburg, we finally arrived at an old Gothic building, a town house opening directly on to the street, of which that strange city has many. It resembled a mass of flour beneath the somber crepuscular sky.

"Here it is," said my companion. He took an enormous key from his pocket.

The lock grated. The snow was blocking the door, and I admired the vigor of Otto Serpius as his muscular hands agitated the batten, which finally yielded and let us through.

146

The darkness of the dwelling impressed me immediately. I could make out, dimly, suits of armor: warrior carapaces posed as if holding a lance or a sword.

"My guardians and servants," said Otto, laughing—which showed two gleaming rows of yellow teeth.

We climbed a wooden spiral staircase whose steps creaked and whose handrail was unsteady. My guide opened another door.

We found ourselves in a vast room, suggestive of a workshop and a laboratory. Daylight was coming through a vast bay window. Monotonous files of rooftops extended all the way to the river, where the masts of ships were visible. On a long table, which extended for the whole length of the room, all the instruments necessary for physiological research were accumulated: glass cages, flasks, balances. Sitting before that gigantic display, motionless, very attentive to his work, I saw a bizarre individual dressed in black velvet. There was a little skullcap on his round head. He did not look up when we came in.

"That's you assistant?" I said to Otto Serpius.

He smiled cruelly. "I've forgotten something downstairs. I'll leave you for a moment, if you'll permit."

And I remained alone in the laboratory with the famulus, who did not budge.

The silence and that petrifaction irritated me. "Terrible weather for research," I said, loudly.

Abruptly, the individual looked up, and I perceived the most comical face in the world: a large nose, a black beard, two globular eyes wide with amazement. Then, with a rigidity of movement that puzzled me, he stood up, pushed back his chair, turned toward me and started singing a song with words by Heinrich Heine, to a tune by Schumann, in a grotesque and nasal voice.

When that brief performance was finished, he asked, in German: "Are you satisfied?" And without waiting for a reply, he resumed his work.

I did not know what to think. The strangest suppositions went through my mind. Undoubtedly, Otto Serpius was employing a madman. I took a few steps toward the phenomenon and saw that his occupation consisted of arranging packets of equal size, similar to those that pharmacists make up, in a long and narrow box. He proceeded with that task in a fantastically rapid and precise manner. The packets succeeded one another between his agile and stiff fingers, which superimposed them with a brief flick of the thumb and a delicate push of the index finger.

"You have a splendid voice, Monsieur," I said, by way of a compliment, desirous of hearing the sound that had troubled me so violently again.

Without raising his head, he replied, in his nasal but very correct German: "It's necessary to put on a little performance from time to time."

Suddenly, he stood up again, his round eyes expressing anger. He thumped the table, which rendered a dull sound, and addressed me furiously. "Are you going to let me work, finally?"

A few gross insults followed. And he remained standing, trembling with fury from head to toe, to such an extent that his hairy chin was twitching convulsively.

He really is a madman! I'm in a pretty pickle. He's going to attack me and I have no means of defense.

As I made that melancholy reflection, Otto Serpius came back into the laboratory, and laughed.

"What's this? What's this? You're misbehaving again, Vladislas! Give me the pleasure of sitting down and remaining tranquil. Otherwise, I'll make you sorry."

The monster obeyed.

Otto murmured in my ear: "Well, what do you think of him?" His face expressed malice.

"I expected, on coming to your home, some curious spectacle. I wasn't mistaken."

"He's excitable, but not malevolent," said the doctor, inviting me to sit beside him, in a large armchair. He's a very

148

strange fellow. He doesn't understand French, so we can speak freely in that language. Can you spare me a few minutes?"

"I've nothing better to do in Hamburg."

Then, in that redoubtable laboratory, in the presence of the snow, the dusk and the impassive Vladislas, the doctor said: "That fellow would astonish all my colleagues greatly, but I conceal his existence carefully and only make use of him for my own research. He has no father or mother. Such as you see him, he's the child of the flask and the furnace. You seem astonished! Hamburg is the city of prodigies. Ha ha—I'm an old enchanter myself."

"So Vladislas is an automaton?" I asked, very intrigued.

"An automaton, yes, but of a new kind, made of flesh and bone. More precisely, Vladislas is a homunculus. His manufacture gave me a great deal of difficulty. He's the triumph of my vigorous old age. I'll try to explain my efforts and their miraculous result, briefly."

Otto Serpius commenced, in his colorful language: "Scarcely had I entered the grotto of science than I was struck by the poor research in which my colleagues wore away their brains. It seemed to me that they were afraid of delving into the mysterious grotto, where one could nevertheless glimpse singular dormant miracles—for *scientific darkness*"—he emphasized those words forcefully—"is nothing but a purée of seeds, the fecund reservoir of the possible. I resolved not to follow their example, and to devote myself, body and soul, to some singular order of research.

"I made a pact with the Devil—ha ha!—which is to say that I made him a gift of the energy that was within me, on condition that he would help me to fabricate a homunculus. A homunculus! That was my dream. A being whom I would dose with sensations and sentiments, who would think in accordance with my law, who would gradually, by the wearing away of the springs, increasingly take on an independent existence. For the great spring that governs us, my dear friend, is fatality: *Fatum*. That's where the initial thumbprint of the creator is found.—and haven't you noticed that with age, that

149

fatality distends, that external powers are removed from our route as we fall apart? I can assure you that old men are much less subject to the stars than young ones. *We are gods, in proportion to the energy with which we struggle against the sun.*"

After that singular remark, Otto Serpius fell silent for a few moments, as if to allow his prophetic observations time to influence my mind.

Vladislas continued his work. Every time I glanced in his direction, I experienced a slight anguish.

The scientist continued: "I won't go into the minute detail of my failures, or my recipes. Let it suffice you to know that I recommenced the Great Work twenty times over, with the requisite formulae of conjuration. The house shook. A comet appeared over Hamburg, and great scourges burst forth, for we only wrench the partial secret of life from Mystery at the price of veritable hecatombs. Fortunately, my fellow citizens, prey to the ideas of civilization—the most false and absurd of all—never suspected the true cause of the disasters that overwhelmed them. Amid the horrors of cholera, the death-rattles, in the odor of a universal charnel-house, I continued my rude task. Once—don't laugh—the Devil appeared to me in the form of a mouse. I was hesitating between two acids; he upset the bad bottle. Another time, it was by means of a great gust of wind that the Evil One announced his presence to me. The wind caused a grimoire whose calculations were false to fly away, and threw another on to my table whose calculations were accurate.

"The cholera continued its vengeful work. A great pride entered into me at having occasioned such a catastrophe. The gleam of my furnace, by night, appeared to me as the breath of the disease. The tocsin deafened me. I had to close the shutters of the laboratory for a month. I dismissed all my servants. Who could be taken into such confidence? I worked alone, drinking stagnant water, nourishing myself on exotic herbs brought back from my travels. Those large tropical fruits, dried up but still alive, pouted into my veins the ardent poison of research. My ideas seemed to be burning; the furnace roared night and day, such that I ceased to hear the tocsin.

"Finally, on Christmas Eve three years ago, I understood by certain signs that the great mystery was nigh. I locked myself away in the laboratory. I stopped the clocks whose moaning irritates the powers of life and death. I sat down in front of my furnace, and I went into a trance, like the sages of old. The reasons for everything abruptly filed before my mind's eye, but with such a racket, in such hasty pursuit, that I was unable to grasp them. All of a sudden, my retort exploded, and a kind of howling monster rolled from the furnace on to the floor. That was the so-called Vladislas, making his appearance.

"I immediately plunged him into cold water. It wasn't sufficient to have created him. It was also necessary to give him something with which to occupy his life—which is to say, the keyboard of human sentiments…and here I can be a little more explicit.

"The Homunculus is like a piano. He is endowed with certain strings, whose sonorities form all possible sentimental combinations. Those strings end in a single bar, which is the stem of Egotism. From that stem, like the teeth of a comb, depart Pride, Lust and Dread. From those three secondary branches depart a multitude of subdivisions, which, via the vices and the virtues, terminate in simple sensations that are distributed over the skin of the Homunculus as over the skin of a human being, appended to the ears, the eyes, the nose, etc.

"Two large keys, at the level of the hips, put my fellow in joy or in pain, giving his entire organism a particular inclination corresponding to one of those states. Finally, I've established in him the three degrees that are for my Homunculus what speed is for an automobile: heroism, simple life and bestiality. And now you have the outlines of the theory, let's pass on to the practice."

Having finished his demonstration, parts of which seemed obscure to me, Otto Serpius ran to his automaton, who, at the sight of him, uttered a roar.

The scientist burst out laughing. "I left him in pain last time I made use of him. Look, I'm putting him in joy."

He turned a key near the left hip. Immediately, Vladislas' features relaxed, expressing the most vivid delight. He became incredibly polite. He apologized to me for his earlier insolence. He offered to explain the marvels of the laboratory one by one. Except for a little monotony in his expressions and grimaces, and a slight stiffness in his movements, it was impossible to discern anything artificial or unusual in the origin of the Homunculus.

Meanwhile, Otto Serpius seemed plunged in the keenest satisfaction. He observed, while smiling, the behavior of the individual he called "his son," and from time to time, he approved his speech by means of a little affectionate brutality—a rap on the hard skull, a kick on a leg that sounded like wood.

"Does Vladislas know that he's an automaton?" I asked him.

He frowned. "That question is replete with mystery. In giving my Homunculus the exact appearance of life, I've given him the appearance of the laws and progress of life. Thus, I'm amazed to observe in his various performances a veritable change. I know that the springs are wearing away, but that's not all. A particular mode of existence has formed in that semi-artificial being and—don't laugh—he's on the way to liberty. Yes, toward liberty. When I leave him at rest, with neither joy nor pain, do you know what he expresses in that neutral state? Melancholy! Now, according to my studies, melancholy is the condition of someone obtaining a clearer consciousness of himself, more anxious as to his destiny.

"Stranger still"—at this point Serpius lowered his voice—"is that as time goes by, Vladislas has conceived a hatred for me, his Creator. He has begun to deny my existence. He's on the point of murdering me. That's the way it is. That assemblage of life and springs, which I've grouped together myself, suffers in my presence and my power. Two or three times I've surprised him sharpening knives with a strange expression when the work I'd give him to do was making up packets of bismuth.

"When I catch him I those homicidal reveries, I switch him to pain and let him suffer for days on end. I've noticed that after those harsh ordeals, his intelligence is refined in an extraordinary fashion, and the cruelty in his gaze is reduced. He detests me less. He even comes, like a puppy, to rub himself against me, in quest of my caresses...

"All the same, it's quite possible that you'll learn from the newspapers some day of my sudden death. You'll know then that I've be killed by my automaton."

Vladislas had returned to work; I experienced a kind of indefinable dread. Otto Serpius divined my state of mind and said to me with his usual perspicacity: "Every time a mystery disappears, suffering and anguish increase. I've often noticed that, in the course of my work. After the creation of Vladislas, I was prey to an atrocious mental torture for two months. At any rate, the cholera ceased. My automaton scarcely suspects that his life is made from the death of so many peaceful and honest inhabitants of Hamburg, whose souls have passed into my furnaces. You're right, my dear fellow—we live in a strange city."

Georges Espitallier: *The Nickel Man*
(1897)

I. A Singular Scientist

Pilesèche was a man devoid of ambition.

His present situation was sufficient for him, even though it was humble; he was a mere laboratory assistant to a physiologist who enjoyed both renown and a very bad character—in consequence of which the poor laboratory assistant was more accustomed to being shoved around than kind words.

Népomucène Grillard—for, after all, it is appropriate to provide a portrait of the master before setting out that of the servant—belonged to the category of scientists who are surly and disagreeable to their fellow men. Born a peasant, his boorish behavior had conserved the rustic imprint of his origin. He had isolated himself, struggling against a life that was not easy at the outset, and developed an innate combative instinct. His obstinacy had triumphed over obstacles, but he had not tried to rid himself of his native rudeness, and, as his scientific notoriety had increased, that lack of amenity had seemed to grow, because he did not feel any need to repress it.

His first impulse—the best, it is said—was always to receive anyone who approached him with an initial attack. The burlesque odyssey of his academic visits, when he had thought of trying to obtain a chair in the Institut, was legendary in the vicinity of the Sorbonne. By dint of effort he had then succeeded in putting on an almost smiling face when he passed the threshold of the scientist whose vote he was trying to win in the great struggle, but after five minutes of conversation, the animal inside him found itself unleashed, and, trampling the flower-bed of his future colleague, gradually increasing the pitch of his dry falsetto voice, he would take a stand opposed to his interlocutor's theories, pouring out irony by the bucketful and arguments by the mouthful, and the conversation would end in a dispute, with a loud noise of slammed doors that left him, the last man standing, alone on the academician's landing.

He cut his visits short before arriving at the contest, and renounced forever the hope of ever putting on the coat with green palms.

If he was aggressive with his colleagues, it is easy to deduce what his relationship was like with the students who aspired to learn science in his shadow. His laboratory was an inferno; gradually, a void had formed around the scientist, to whom only the timid Pilesèche remained faithful.

The latter would perhaps have preferred an easier master, but he was a creature of habit, and in any case, he had never had sufficient energy to detach himself from bonds to which he gradually became accustomed. He was a kind of eccentric, a great timid child devoid of will-power, whose only passion was for study, with a certain nonchalance in the fashion in which he devoted himself to it.

The physiology on which he worked possessed him entirely, but when he had poured out his contingent of ideas in the common endeavor, it never entered his head that he had anything to do with the result; never, even in the depths of his soul, did he make any kind of claim to their paternity. Népomucène Grillard appeared to him to be a divinity looking down from on high upon feeble humanity, and one does not collaborate with the gods; one serves them.

In any case, having no needs and satisfied with very little, Pilesèche went through life full of an insouciance that was painted all over his person. He had long, unkempt hair; its gray color might have been natural, but was more probably due to an abundant dust generously spread all the way to the dirty collar of the worn and discolored frock-coat that enveloped, without really dressing, his long bony body. The rest of his costume was in keeping.

Along with his athletic appearance, the man had a timid, adolescent expression; his gestures were gauche and maladroit. For anyone who considered him at a glance, he might have passed for a scholar or a Bohemian; he was both at the same time.

There are bilious individuals who live for a long time, to the misfortune of their contemporaries, but it is nevertheless necessary to recognize that exaggerated movements of bile are not favorably to the principles of sound hygiene. For that reason and many others, Népomucène Grillard, when he reached the age of sixty-five, felt himself declining—physically declining, that is; his mentality was not afflicted, nor his energy, nor, most of all, his character. And yet, the aged scientist had embarked on a whole series of experiments that he would not have wanted to leave incomplete.

As time was pressing, he had the imprudent temerity to test some of his physiological discoveries on himself, which was the surest fashion of hastening his end, for the human body is not an experimental field in which the infinitely small can deliver battle without causing damage to the substratum of that microcosm.

The scientist had also launched himself into the new sciences that claim to approach the problems of hypnosis and life after death, and which solicit so many people nowadays. All that overwork had ended up ruining his constitution, to the point that one day, it was necessary to take to his bed.

With his bulldog manners, Monsieur Grillard had never managed to keep a domestic servant for more than a week, and when he fell ill, he could not abide any other care than that of his laboratory assistant, to which he was accustomed. It was necessary then for the latter to comply with all the old man's caprices and not impose his presence on him more than was necessary.

Occasionally, he risked an observation, such as: "It's imprudent to remain alone at night, my dear master; allow me to stay with you..."

"Leave me alone," the other replied.

"You have to eat; make a little effort, or you'll die of starvation."

"What are you doing? Besides, starvation or something else, what does it matter? I feel that I'm at the end of my tether."

"Oh, my dear master, you're not there yet. You're going to get your strength back—but it's necessary to look after yourself."

"Go away. Stop harping on and leave me in peace. You can't tell me anything, damn it! I know better than you are how I am..."

Sometimes, Pilesèche exerted himself on another subject, perhaps even more scabrous.

"You have a nephew, Monsieur; you need to think about asking him to come..."

"A fine fellow, who makes music!"

"Pardon me, but I'm told that he's given up music for sculpture. I imagine he thought that the change might give you pleasure."

"Ha ha! Music or sculpture, it's all one: I don't like the arts. What is there in them that's positive? Can one find theorems that regulate those strings of sensations? And those statues, fixed and frozen—are they worth as much as a morsel of flesh palpitating under my scalpel? Get away—you can talk to me about all that when the arts are sciences."

Thus rejected, his efforts wasted, the poor assistant, undiscouraged, brought up the subject of an orphan niece, with whom the scientist scarcely occupied himself except for paying her boarding-school fees, even doing good in an egotistical fashion.

"She's in a convent, isn't she?" Grillard interrupted. "Let her stay there!"

Pilesèche was, therefore, quite astonished when the old man, one day, softening his voice, summoned him to his bedside and made him party to his intentions.

"I sense that I don't have much longer to go, and, before dying, I want to see my nephew Népomucène. He's an animal, but he's my nephew, and I want to give him my instructions. Go look for him tomorrow evening and bring him here. If you don't find him, search—I don't want to see you without him, you hear me?"

"What if I were to bring him tomorrow morning?"

"How painful it is never to be understood! Not before tomorrow evening, I tell you. I'm not in the habit of repeating myself!"

A few moments later, the scientist called out: "Pilesèche, prepare me an electric bath!"

An electric bath!

The assistant did not believe in the efficacy of that medical treatment, which Monsieur Grillard had improved for his own usage, but how could he oppose his master's will?

"Are you going to contradict me incessantly?" the old man growled.

In order not to excite his bile any further, Pilesèche heated up the water and, uncovering a long vat that was normally used for galvanoplasty, he poured in the liquid, slightly sharpened with a little acid to increase its electrical conductivity.

While taking his bath, Grillard had the custom of lying down on a rattan trellis placed in the bottom of the vat and serving as an insulator. He gripped the cylinders in both hands. The electric current thus ran through his body, while on slight electrolytic reactions occurred on the surface of his skin. He felt a frisson running over his sickly limbs. It felt like ants swarming throughout his being, which at least procured him a temporary relief.

That evening, he made a new demand. He took it into his head to increase the conductivity of his body by having it coated in plumbago. Pilesèche tried in vain to resist, but it was finally necessary for him to grip the heavy brush steeped in a pot where the black lead was thinned down, and to start daubing the maniac, who had stripped off his last garment.

Grillard stood on the floor, trembling, his hands leaning on the bed, and there was no more lugubrious sight than that skeleton, scarcely covered by parchment-like skin, gradually coated with a layer of black, as shiny as wax.

When the grotesque operation was terminated, Grillard signified to his assistant that he was to go away and leave him alone.

"But what about your bath?" said the latter.

"I can take it perfectly well on my own."

And as Pilesèche was accustomed by habit to passive obedience, he left, while the old man, his back bent, supporting himself on the walls, headed toward the half-full vat.

As he went past the slate-topped table mounted in sliding grooves, however, he stopped, listened to make sure that the door of the apartment had closed behind Pilesèche, and, seizing a piece of chalk with one hand and some pieces of paper lying on the table with the other, he began rapidly transcribing a previously-prepared inscription, the letters of which followed one another in complete incoherence.

Having done that, the ambulant black phantom finally reached the galvanoplastic vat. He poured into it the contents of a bottle full of a glittering crystalline salt, lit a reflector lamp placed nearby, and lay down in the bath, after having opened the tap of a small reservoir, whose water began to flow into the vast in a thin trickle, with a monotonous murmur.

The old man had placed himself in the vat in his usual position. Thus extended, with his knees brought back toward is meager breast, only his face, tilted backward, emerged from the water. He searched with his gaze for a brilliant point that the lamp picked out on a silver ball suspended in front of him. Motionless, his eyes jaundiced by icterus and immeasurably wide open in fakiristic contemplation, he waited...

Silence had fallen, lugubriously. Nothing could be heard but the purr of the stove and the susurrus of the trickle of water that was solely causing the level in the vat to rise. Gradually, the water covered the scientist's closed mouth. Only the nostrils, eyes and forehead appeared above the liquid surface.

Already, however, all consciousness had disappeared from the inert and rigid body. Népomucène Grillard had put himself into complete catalepsy by staring fixedly at the luminous dot trembling on the polished surface of the silvery ball.

The water was still rising, its meniscus climbing to assault the projections of the emaciated face.

And the electricity did its work on the molecules of that exsanguinated flesh, gently and slyly depositing solid particles appropriated from the decomposing salts: an impalpable dust of nickel, which clung on to the layer of plumbago and gradually covered it...

II. A Sinister Discovery

On the 31 December 1890, St. Sylvester's Day, at eight o'clock in the morning, the Rue de la Montagne-Sainte-Geneviève was crowded, in spite of the glacial fog, with businessmen and housewives who were running in quest of breakfast, their heads swathed in wool, clutching the traditional milk-jug in their numb fingers.

Two eccentrics, rather incongruous in their appearance and costume, were striding over the damp and sticky paving stones; they did not seem excessively out of place, however, in the midst of the other passers-by, the stiff slope in question not normally being the rendezvous of the flower of the aristocracy.

One of the two, his figure clasped in a black velvet jacket, had a simple scarf wound around his neck; it was the only concession he made to the rigor of the temperature, for he was holding his hat in his hand in spite of the season, proudly throwing back his long back hair, lustrous a well-groomed, with a leonine gesture.

The other, by contrast, was very negligently clad, with no attention to detail; that was Népomucène Grillard's laboratory assistant, and the succinct portrait previously painted dispenses us with describing the costume he was wearing.

"So, my dear Pilesèche," said the man in the velvet jacket, continuing the conversation, "my uncle has suddenly felt his familial fibers vibrating?"

"He has, at least testified the desire to see you," the other replied, not without a certain reticence.

"I'm still amazed, not being accustomed to such tenderness on his part."

"The sentiments are modified, Monsieur Bémolisant, and soften at the approach of death."

"And you think that the old man is there?"

"I believe that it would be very difficult for him to get better. I think he's worn out. He's developed an extreme nervous sensitivity, and I've been able to observe profound disturbances in his organism of late. However, he might live for a few weeks yet; yesterday evening, when I left him, Monsieur Grillard was not exactly worse; he merely manifested the desire to be alone, and dismissed me rather abruptly, I have to say..."

"In order not to misrepresent his amiable character. You're an angel of forbearance, Monsieur Pilesèche, and in your place, I would have broken his retorts over his head a long time ago."

"Are you astonished, then, that he has quarreled with you?"

"What do the doctors say?" asked the other, after a brief pause.

"The doctors? You can hardly doubt that he's refuse their intervention, and you know how determined he is..."

"How stubborn, you mean. Yes, yes, I know my dear uncle, although he banished me from his presence a long time ago. I know that one can't easily get him to give in. He's doubtless a great scientist, but what an insupportable fellow!"

Pilesèche pursed his lips with an indulgent gesture. "Everyone has his little faults; I'm used to his and I'm no less affected for that by the sad state to which I see him reduced. Oh, since a month ago the laboratory no longer exists. Even before being bed-ridden, the poor man had no heart for anything.

Experiments begun were left incomplete. There was only his most recent research...you know, his research on the occlusion of living beings?"

"The occlusion of...," said the other, nonplussed. "He was working on the occlusion of living beings. What on earth can that be?"

"You don't keep up with the reports of the scientific societies?"

"Eminently unhealthy nourishment, Monsieur Pilesèche—no, I don't read them. The occlusion...ha ha! My dear uncle definitely had a very accentuated crack in the brain. At his age, it's pardonable."

"You can laugh, but I assure you...the results are precise and I myself..."

"What you too? Well, you're a bit touched yourself, my friend. Anyway, it's not astonishing. The great man's laboratory assistant...and it's contagious. But come on, explain it to me: what is this occlusion, of which I've never heard?"

"Artist as you are, you must have heard mention of some recent very singular discoveries. In the course of digging in perfectly virgin ground, incontestably undisturbed for several centuries, it sometimes happens—rarely, I admit—that is breaking blocks of stone, one sees emerging from one of them a toad, which yawns and stretches: a living toad, awakening after a centuries-long sleep..."

"And you've seen that yourself?" said Bémolisant, incredulously.

"No, I haven't seen it myself," the laboratory assistant replied, mildly, "but our experiments prove the possibility of the phenomenon. We've reproduced it artificially; we've hermetically sealed up toads, frogs, even cats..."

"For centuries?" the artist interrupted, holding his ribs.

"For a few days—but that's sufficient to demonstrate the conditions in which a living being can remain like that, without dying."

"You're amazing!"

"No, no, it's quite simple. It's quite evident that it you content yourself with enclosing your subject brutally, whatever it might be, it will die quickly, asphyxiated. But in the multitudinous phases of hypnotic sleep, there's one, still little known, that resembles death but isn't. It isn't catalepsy, properly speaking, in which the subject doesn't cease to breathe and the blood still circulates; it's like a paralysis of the entire organism, a complete suspension of life..."

"And the animal can live without air, without light?"

"It lives…if one can call the complete arrest of all the vital functions living."

"And what do you do to enclose it in its pebble?"

"The prison doesn't matter, so long as it's hermetic; the one that Monsieur Grillard normally employs is a metallic envelope deposited by galvanoplasty."

"It's only scientists that have such ludicrous ideas!"

"Pooh! Have you forgotten your theories about music, then? Do you think that the six-thousand-note scale with which you once wanted to endow us wasn't at least as singular?"

"So I wasn't understood by the men of my time, and in order not to lower my art by vile concessions to the level of my contemporaries devoid of ears, I renounced music..."

"You see..."

"Now I do sculpture…decadent sculpture…you'll see! A revolution, my dear, a revolution! The primitives were nothing, the Byzantines nothing more; the art has never been understood like this..."

"You were talking about cracked brains a little while ago, Monsieur Bémolisant. I have reason to believe that, by virtue of atavism, you..."

"Oh! I'm misunderstood before I've even spoken!"

They arrived at the coaching entrance of an old house of rather sordid appearance, and, after darting a distracted glance at the lodge, deserted for the moment, they climbed the somber staircase whose sticky handrail adhered to the fingers.

The fourth floor landing, to which insipid and nauseating odors rose up from the rest of the house, was illuminated by wan daylight falling vertically through a glazed skylight open in the roof.

Pilesèche took a large key from his pocket and introduced it into the lock of a door painted in yellow ocher.

"My uncle lodges a long way up," said the artist, out of breath after his climb.

"That's because of the laboratory; one can't find appropriate premises to let everywhere."

"And then, admit it, landlords don't like having such a constantly grumpy tenant..."

They went into a gloomy vestibule, which gave access on one side to a small kitchen, and on the other to a room decorated with the name of the drawing room and furnished with four rickety armchairs. At the back was the door to the laboratory, the biggest room in the apartment: the only one in which Népomucène Grillard lived, and which was really useful to him.

The two newcomers were walking on tiptoe, as is appropriate in the apartment of an invalid. Pilesèche gently lifted the latch of the laboratory and pushed the door. The vestibule was suddenly invaded by a violent flood of light and empyreumatic odors.

The laboratory was illuminated from above, like a painter's studio. The raw daylight fell upon tables overloaded with an inextricable tangle of glassware: flasks of various shapes, test-tubes and reagents of all colors in recipients of every form. There was a microscope, and countless items of bizarre apparatus, in chaotic disorder. An enormous chimney-hood, on which iron-clad furnaces, earthenware crucibles and pot-bellied retorts were strewn, completed the encumbrance of the fin-de-siècle alchemist's lair, while various guinea-pigs, cats, frogs and toads were scratching in their cages or beneath bell-jars scattered here, there and everywhere.

The scientist's laboratory also served as his bedroom, but the iron-framed bed, on which a meager mattress was thrown, attested that Népomucène Grillard was no sybarite.

The newcomers approached it with muffled footsteps, in order not to trouble his slumber. Wasted effort! They were astonished—on might almost say frightened—to find the bed empty.

Pilesèche opened his eyes wide in bewilderment, but no exclamation could escape his gaping mouth, so tightly was his throat constricted by that unexpected spectacle.

"Come on, let's pull ourselves together," said Bémolisant, the first to recover the power of speech, passing his hand over his forehead. "If he's not here, he must have gone out, improbable as the supposition might seem. The concierge will have seen him go past. I'll go and question her."

The artist ran downstairs and presented himself at the lodge, where the concierge was in the process of warming up her milk, with his back turned.

"Has Monsieur Grillard gone out?" asked Bémolisant, out of breath.

"Out! Oh, the poor old man. He's not in any state to go for a walk. He's in bed. It's a month, now that he hasn't been down and I haven't seen him. Monsieur Pilesèche gives me news of him every say, for you can imagine that, with his everlasting bad mood, I don't risk going upstairs to offer him my services."

The good woman had turned round, hands on hips. "You can go up confidently. He's at home, in bed…unless Monsieur Pilesèche is putting one over on me," she added, laughing thickly.

Bémolisant had no desire to persist. While going back up as hastily as he had come down, it occurred to him that the sudden disappearance was going to seem singular to many people, to say the least.

Pilesèche was waiting for him at the door, his expression utterly distressed, pale and worn out, his arms dangling. "I've found him, alas," he moaned, in a cavernous voice.

"He's hanged himself, perhaps?" the other queried, anxiously.

"No, worse than that."

"Well, what? You're killing me with your reticence..."

"Come..."

Taking hold of his jacket, the laboratory assistant led him to a corner of the laboratory, where Bunsen piles and galvanoplasty vats were scattered. One of them had unusual dimensions; it was full of a green-tinted liquid in the middle of which one could make out the black form of a human body.

"There he is," murmured Pilesèche, strangled by emotion.

"He's drowned himself!"

"No...he's *metalized* himself."

"What do you mean?"

"Like the toad, Monsieur Bémolisant, like the toad!" He shook his arm.

"But he's dead, at any rate?" said the nephew.

"Oh, it's probable. The human species doesn't have a long life, alas."

They both stood there, immobile and mute before the strange spectacle.

Suddenly, Bémolisant, moved by a sudden inspiration, uttered a stifled exclamation. "But my friend, there's something you haven't thought of..."

"What's that?"

"We're going to be accused of having killed him."

"Oh my God! But that's absurd!"

"It's less absurd than supposing a sick man capable of steeping himself in a galvanic bath all on his own. Think about it! No one has seen him for a month; he's been sequestrated. He's found in that state; there's been a violent death. We're the only ones who've been in here; it's us that will be accused. You and me—both of us."

The other was stunned. "You're right," he moaned, wiping his forehead. "What are we going to do, then?"

"I don't know. Perhaps he's left a note, a piece of paper announcing his fatal resolution. That will suffice to get us off the hook..."

"Alas, he's capable of not having done anything, in order to play one last trick on us."

"Let's look anyway."

Their eyes troubled by anguish, they looked everywhere, on the tables and in the drawers.

Nothing.

Suddenly, however, their eyes fell upon the blackboard, which bore the following singular inscription:

READ CAREFULLY:
bfoomgtqkl ovyesqnuesrsngbnljuefrplfyesqn ugnxglpretkynqitcpsgstknptfzpftifpcfyesk fj gpbutigoskeneruteexrbpdbvetvangnugtjpsutu dvipps.

"It's a cryptogram! To mock us one last time for our ignorance. Can you decipher it, at least?" demanded the laboratory assistant.

"Oh, as to that, no."

"Then we're back with the sword of Damocles hanging over our heads."

After a moment of silent meditation, in which their minds were heavy with pitiful thoughts, Bémolisant said, with a somber expression: "Pilesèche, the moment has come for grave decisions."

At that remonstration, the other straightened up, ready for anything.

"It's necessary for the corpse to disappear," the artist concluded, his voice whistling.

"Ah!"

It will disappear; we'll take it away. And later..." His voice attained the extreme limit of tragic falsetto; one might have thought that it was escaping his brain through his cranium. "...Later," he continued, in the stifled tone of a traitor in a

167

melodrama, "well, we'll be able to explain the disappearance. The most urgent thing is to get rid of the evidence."

The two men leaned over the vat. The laboratory assistant opened the tap.

The liquid ran out slowly, and its soft, musical susurrus contrasted strangely with the sinister situation. Gradually, the contours of the body emerged in their black envelope; one might have thought it a statue emerging from the mold, still covered with a layer of powdered oxide.

Unconsciously, as if he were still in the middle of one of his habitual experiments, the laboratory assistant rubbed the cheeks with the palm of his hand, where the metal whitened, polished without difficulty.

"It's nickel," he said, finally.

The body, clad in its metallic pellicle, was holding two nickel cylinders in its hands, attached to the negative pole of the pile.

"He's heavy," murmured Bémolisant, trying to lift him up.

"How are we going to get him out?" asked Pilesèche.

"How, above all, are we going to get him past the concierge without arousing suspicion?"

"Oh, my head's splitting. I'm not made for conspiracies!" He let himself fall on to a chair, his head bowed—but Bémolisant shook him rudely

"Come on, a little nerve, damn it! Are we little girls?"

"You talk about it so casually…I've never been accused of any crime until now."

III. In which the Peregrinations of the Nickel Man begin

An hour later, a cab stopped outside the door of the house and Pilesèche got out, while Bémolisant went through the arch with three day-laborers he had recruited in the Place Maubert.

The concierge was on the threshold of her lodge.

The laboratory assistant made violent efforts to give his face a smiling expression, the muscles taut, and he saluted her. In spite of his determination not to allow his emotion to show, he was frightfully pale, more gauche than ever, his movements feverish and disordered.

"Bonjour, Madame Paponot," he succeeded in saying, in a strangled voice.

"Bonjour, Monsieur Pilesèche," the stout lady replied. "And your M'sieu, how is he?"

"Uh, he's still nearly…you know…it comes and goes."

Bémolisant started up the stairs; the concierge pointed at him, laughing. "That *artiss* in velvet, all hot under the collar, asked me a little while ago whether your invalid had gone out! Poor fellow! It's not the time!"

"Oh no, Madame Paponot, it's really not the time." He added, by way of correction: "The gentleman is a scrap metal merchant."

"Oh—not an *artiss?*"

"No, no, he's a scrap dealer. One can't turn around up there, it's so cluttered—so I said to Monsieur Grillard, what if we were to get rid of all our superfluities?"

"Good God, what are those? You scientists, you have these words..."

"It means our scrap metal, our old stuff—you know."

"Oh, yes…and the poor man agreed? That must be the first time in his life he's ever agreed with someone."

"When one's ill, you know, one becomes more human. But I'm chatting, and my men are already upstairs. *Au revoir*, Madame Paponot, *au revoir*."

Quickly, he ran up the rickety steps in order to catch up with Bémolisant and the porters, whom he let into the laboratory.

Then, showing them the vat, over which he had nailed a lid of planks, he said: "This is it."

One of the men took hold of the long box by one of its corners and tested its weight.

"Damn," he said, letting it fall back. "It's no feather-weight."

"Of course not," Bémolisant replied, as tranquilly as he could. "Scrap metal is heavy."

Everyone lent a hand to the task, and the box was finally taken down, with a great deal of difficulty, to the coaching entrance.

Pilesèche had no desire to chat; he went past the lodge rapidly, in a hurried manner—but that did not suit Madame Paponot, who stopped him.

"Hey, M'sieu Pilesèche!" she shouted after him. "A bit of advice—today's Saint Sylvester, as you know. It seems to me that I can't decently avoid going up tomorrow to wish the poor m'sieu a happy new year, like my other tenants..."

No, no!" exclaimed the laboratory assistant, precipitately. "He can't see anyone. That might put him in a bad temper...and strokes can arrive so quickly, you know. Don't worry, I'll give you your present, and you won't have to put yourself out."

The box was loaded; the porters were dismissed.

The coachman leaned over toward his clients, already installed in the vehicle.

"Where are we going, bourgeois?" he asked.

That was a question that Pilesèche had not anticipated. Was it necessary to shout out loud he place that they had chosen as a refuge? They might as well put the police on the track immediately.

Fortunately, the artist had anticipated the eventuality, and, putting his head through the window, he shouted an address at the coachman chosen at random. When they reached the Rue des Écoles, however, while the horse continued its rapid trot, he lowered the glass again and, sticking out half his body in order to get closer to the driver, he said to him, without being heard by the passers-by: "I've changed my mind, Coachman—we'll go directly to Avenue Clichy, number..." He pronounced the number so quietly that the coachman could hardly hear it.

When Bémolisant sat down again, he turned to his companion, who was mopping cold sweat from his brow. "The flight is consummated," he said, in a dramatic tone.

The other started. "Are we being pursued?" he said, bewildered.

"Pursued! I certainly hope that nothing will be discovered. It will be as well, moreover, in order that no suspicion arises, if you go back there as usual."

"Oh, I'd never dare! Just think! I'd have to answer the concierge's incessant questions, give her news of the pretended patient, recommence what I did just now, lying impudently. It's beyond my strength."

"Do you want to ruin us, wretch? If you're not seen again, people will become anxious; they'll break down the door; they'll discover everything. It's absolutely necessary to go back…at least until we've found a solution to this inextricable situation. Furthermore, now I think about it, you've forgotten to erase the inscription that will attract all eyes to the blackboard. We've even omitted to copy it."

"What's the point, since we can't decipher it?"

"We're going to dry, damn it! I'm not going to admit defeat. A little energy, Pilesèche."

"I will, I will…I'll go to the laboratory…not today, but tomorrow, when I've recovered somewhat from all this emotion," said Pilesèche, in a tone that contained more resignation than resolution.

After meditating for a while, the artist resumed speaking. "It's no good," he said. "I've thought hard, but everything I've just seen seems strange, and I can't understand how the fellow came to bury himself in that vat. Tell me a little about the premises of the affair, as an examining magistrate might put it."

"Don't talk about examining magistrates! You'll give me the shakes. Anyway, what can I tell you that you don't know? Your uncle had a few manias, but nothing that allowed such a design to be foreseen. He was bad-tempered, not insane. I can only explain his final action by supposing that he wanted to

171

carry out one last experiment on himself. He didn't say anything about it to me. Ill, crippled by pain, he certainly felt that he was on the way out, and it was then that he manifested the desire to see you. You were his nephew and his godson—that's only natural. How could I know that he's planned everything to make you a witness to that sad spectacle?"

"I ought to have mistrusted that abrupt return to good sentiments."

"What else can I tell you? Yesterday, I found him in a bad mood, as usual. I brought him eggs, hoping to make him eat, but he sent me packing, along with my eggs."

"He was obviously not an easy patient."

"He asked me for an electric bath..."

"My God, what's that?"

"It's the bath in which we found him, but instead of a metallic salt susceptible of yielding a galvanoplastic deposit, we normally put in pure water, simply sharpened with a little acid to increase its electrical conductivity."

"Oh, very good! The traitor was preparing the execution of his sinister project."

"Evidently. I'd hardly closed the door, no doubt, than he wrote the cryptogram that intrigued us so much and plunged himself into the bath, after having added nickel sulfate and ammonia."

There's one thing that I can't explain. So long as he was conscious, he wouldn't have been able to plunge completely under the water, where he would have choked—and yet we found him submerged, which would have been indispensable in any case for the deposit to form evenly over his entire body."

"Oh, the explanation is quite simple. Didn't you notice a small reservoir placed above the vat, the liquid from which was discharged through a rubber tube. Your uncle lay down first in such a way that his nostrils were above the surface of the water, and the flow coming from that small reservoir finished covering his face gradually. He would have had to be in the state of special catalepsy that I've mentioned to you by

172

then, but he could put himself into it and he would have prepared himself for a long time by means of his experiments in hypnotism. It was sufficient for him to say to himself: at such a time, *I'll fall into catalepsy*, for phenomenon to be realized by autosuggestion."

"I see now how things must have happened, but that doesn't change our situation. Try telling that to the police commissioner, and he'd laugh in your face. Listen, it's necessary to work out what we're going to do. We'll take the cada...." He stopped and resumed: "...the parcel directly to my studio, but if you run into my wife, don't say anything to her about this adventure. Above all, don't say anything to my mother-in-law. You know how talkative women are; they're easily led by the nose, so that if the police were to interrogate them, I don't know how we'd get out of it."

It was necessary to recruit a few more porters to take the box upstairs.

"It's a bronze statue," Bémolisant told them.

"It doesn't astonish me anymore that it's so heavy," one of them replied.

The studio was situated on the floor above the apartment in which the artist's family lived, so neither Madame Bémolisant nor her mother, Madame Legris, was able to see what was happening in the house.

When the two accomplices were alone in the large room in the middle of which the funereal package lay, they let their arms fall alongside their bodies with an enormous sigh of relief.

"Finally," said Bémolisant, "We can breathe."

"It's only a respite, alas. It won't be possible for us to hide Monsieur Grillard's disappearance forever."

"But thanks to our stratagem, at least we have time to think about it."

"Shouldn't we remove his metal envelope?" hazarded the laboratory assistant, "For after all, if he isn't dead..."

"Get away! Now you're believing in this nonsense. It's one thing for toads to wall themselves up without coming to

173

any harm...no, no, don't worry; my uncle is well and truly defunct, and his cadaver is much less troublesome inside its nickel box than otherwise. If we don't succeed in concealing him from all eyes, well, so far as everyone else in concerned, he's a statue, nothing more."

With these reflections, the nickel-plated man was removed from his vat and placed in a corner, lying down in his natural attitude. While Bémolisant searched for a serge curtain in order to hide him to the extent that it was possible, Pilesèche started rubbing the surface of the metal in order to polish it and complete the appearance of a piece of sculpture.

He had only just finished that task when someone knocked on the studio door.

"Perhaps it's the police," one of them whispered, fearfully.

"What if we don't answer?" added the other, equally anxious.

"They'll break down the door. It's better to be bold."

That boldness did not go as far as to calm their nerves, and they were both wearing singular expressions when Bémolisant went to open the door.

IV. In which an Influential Critic Intervenes in the Affair

Two men were waiting on the threshold, but the newcomers did not seem to justify so many apprehensions. They were perfect gentlemen, art lovers who had come to visit the studio.

"Baron d'Estrèchini!" exclaimed the artist, recognizing one of them.

"In person. You promised me, my dear, to show me some decadent sculpture. I've come to ask you to keep your promise, and I've brought Antoine Leroux, the influential critic, whom you'll have to suborn...if he'll allow himself to be."

"Ah! Delighted," said Bémolisant, still holding the door ajar. "Positively enchanted, but I don't know if I can let you in. I..."

"What! Perhaps you have a model here at present?"

"Yes, precisely."

"That doesn't matter. All the models know us; we no longer intimidate them." And without paying any further attention to the artist's hesitation, he added: "Go in, Leroux."

"After you, Baron."

"Come, come—no ceremony on the threshold of the sanctuary."

Pilesèche, who had taken off his coat in order to take the nails out of the box, had just picked up a feather duster. He was dusting everything within reach feverishly and indistinctly, without daring to turn round, for fear that his distraught features might betray his emotion.

"It's for this amiable fellow that you were going to turn us away?" queried the Baron, perceiving him.

"Not badly built for a model," added the influential critic, looking him up and down with the eye of a connoisseur. "I haven't seen him around. Good muscles...a little gauche, perhaps, but it's up to the sculptor to rectify the pose.

"Let's see these sculptures—show us!" said the Baron, pivoting on his heel and looking around.

The studio was cluttered with mounts and mock-ups. The two strangers started casually lifting up the damp cloths that were preventing the clay from drying out, but the sight of the masterpieces underneath failed to inspire any enthusiasm in the critic, who pursed his lips in a disapproving grimace that did not augur anything good.

Bémolisant had taken possession of the Baron, and was seeking to impregnate him with the extravagant principles of decadent sculpture.

"The goal of art, Monsieur," he said, "is not merely to give a more or less faithful representation of our fragile terrestrial envelope. If it were, the animal painters, who are obsessed with realism of representation, would be the foremost among us. But art ought to aim higher, and, disengaging the human from that which is animal, ought to seek the soul in its hidden folds, to render it visible, tangible..."

"And sensible," finished the influential critic, in a bantering tone, continuing to ferret around while the sculptor continued his discourse.

Terrified, Pilesèche saw Monsieur Leroux coming closer and closer to the nickel-plated man, over which he had hastily thrown a serge curtain. He would dearly have liked to draw his attention in another direction, but how?

Not without a similar anguish, Bémolisant had seen the critic progressing toward the terrible statue, and although he carried on talking, he had absolutely no idea what he was saying, being uniquely preoccupied with those movements. The Baron lent a sustained attention in vain to the nonsense in question; he could not extract any meaning from the string of words.

Suddenly, the critic, perceiving indistinct forms on the floor, enveloped by a serge curtain, lifted up a corner of the cloth.

Bémolisant could not suppress an exclamation. Pilesèche dropped an old plate, which smashed on the floor.

Antoine Leroux uttered an expressive: "Ah!" and took a step back, raising his lorgnon to his eyes. After a brief contemplation, he came, at a measured pace, to take the artist by the arm, and, smiling enthusiastically, said: "Oh, my dear, that's not good of you...no, it's not good to amuse us with bagatelles and these frightful mock-ups when you're hiding a masterpiece in a corner. But it's quite simply admirable! It's marvelous! Better than that: it's a revolution! Oh, if that's decadent sculpture, I accept it; I acclaim it, and you can count one adept more."

Emotionally, he took hold of both the artist's hands and shook them vigorously. "Come," he said to the Baron, finally. "Come and see this marvel." And, dragging him toward the statue, which was gleaming under its white patina, he said: "Look at that! What vigor! And what simultaneous morbidity! How downcast that man is in his suffering! Nature could never have translated it with that precision of genius. It's hollowed

176

out by an energetic thumb, without weakness." He turned to the poor artist. "It's for a tomb, no doubt?"

"Yes, yes," the latter hastened to reply. "It's for a tomb."

"And you've titled it…?"

"I haven't titled it yet."

"Oh! Don't forget that a good title is half way to success."

"But I don't have any intention of exhibiting it."

"Yes, I understand: a tomb is an intimate work. But an artist has a duty to himself and his century. A masterpiece is part of the patrimony of humankind. Oh, but you will exhibit it; moreover, I shall begin a campaign in my newspapers, and I promise you a prodigious, colossal, unprecedented success…"

"But I beg you…I'm frightened by the thought of the public paying attention to my humble person."

"Damn! That's the first time I've encountered such modesty combined with such talent. No, no, I shall force your hand. I'll run to book the hall in the Rue de Sèze, and tomorrow morning you'll hear my first beat of the tom-tom…"

A few minutes later, the visitors took their leave, and the influential critic was heard exclaiming, as they went downstairs: "A revolution, my dear, a veritable revolution in art!"

That scene had completely overwhelmed the two accomplices. They no longer knew where they were, if they were dreaming or awake. Events were dragging them away in a desperate whirlwind, and before they had been able to formulate a plan, or even measure the depth of the abyss open before their feet, they had slid into it invincibly, driven by blind fatality.

Who can tell? But for the arrival of those importunate visitors, they might perhaps have collected their scattered wits and found some means of announcing the entirely natural death of the poor uncle. Yes, that was what it had been necessary to do—but there was no more time.

And, on thinking that, everything that they had just done finally appeared to them as the height of absurdity.

It was while they were still in the laboratory that the solution was simple and easy. What they should have done was strip the cadaver of its metallic envelope by carefully dissolving the nickel; then they should have laid the body suitably washed, in the bed. Who, then, would have been astonished to learn of the death of an old man who had been at the end of his resources for a month?

Could the doctor called to issue the death certificate have found any disquieting particularities, even if he had done a complete autopsy? It hardly seemed probable.

So, the two men had been perfect imbeciles. They finally perceived that, too late to repair the damage.

And they looked at one another, desolate.

"My dear Pilesèche!"

"Monsieur Bémolisant!"

"We have to flee."

"Do you think so?"

"I can't, however, allow that man, that cadaver, to be exhibited in public..."

"Eh! How can you do otherwise? If we run away, people will wonder why. Let's not attract investigation in our direction. You see, it's me who's being reasonable now. I can feel my courage coming back; I feel that I'm capable of the boldest designs, and if it's necessary to be bold..."

He was abruptly interrupted; several raps sounded on the door, and in spite of his brilliant attestation of energy, Pilesèche went pale, anxiously seizing his feather duster, while Bémolisant went to open the door, fearfully.

The artist found himself face to face with his wife, who was anxious because he had not come down at the usual time for lunch.

"That's true!" he replied. "I haven't eaten!" He turned to the laboratory assistant. "Are you hungry, Pilesèche?" he added, in a desolate tone.

"I hadn't noticed it."

"Me neither—but it doesn't matter. Would you like to have lunch with us, Pilesèche."

"Ah! If you like." He seemed to be saying: *Are we not indissolubly linked to one another by this complicity in a crime...that we didn't commit? Can one of us act without the other?*

I am not even certain that, in the confusion of his ideas, he had not managed to convince himself that perhaps they were, in fact, guilty, albeit with attenuating circumstances, so great was the obsession pursuing them.

They went down to the floor below, where the Bémolisant studio was situated: a very modest apartment, redolent with the restricted means of its tenants.

Still preceded by Hélène, they went into the dining room, where Madame Legris, the mother-in-law, was already sitting at the laden table, feeding a baby sitting in a high chair.

"Finally, there you are!" she said, through pinched lips, peering at her son-in-law through her spectacles.

That simple sentence was pregnant with storms. Bémolisant bowed his head. It was necessary to reply, though. "Mother-in-law, I can explain..."

"I know that you always have excellent reasons, my son-in-law."

"What do you expect? It's necessary not to treat artists like other men. Art has its demands, to which its high priests must yield..."

"Oh, I've certainly perceived that, since I've had the honor of being the mother-in-law of a high priest of art."

Hélène wanted to cut short a discussion that was threatening to turn bitter, and while Pilesèche hid himself as best he could behind his host, she said: "Maman, Népomucène has an excellent excuse today. You know that he's been to see his poor Uncle Grillard, who is also his godfather."

"Aha! The reconciliation scene! You can tell us all about it..."

Tell them all about it! The two men were in torment.

"How is your uncle?" the pitiless woman continued.

That was certainly a very indiscreet question, to which Bémolisant was not tempted to reply immediately. He went

179

blank. He remembered, just in time, that he had not introduced his companion, and stood aside in order to allow him to appear.

"This is his assistant, Monsieur Pilesèche, whom I introduce to you, and who will be having lunch with us."

"A guest! Oh, Monsieur, excuse us; my son-in-law never has others. He brings us guests without warning—that isn't done! We have the greatest pleasure in receiving you, and we would have been glad to do so in a dignified fashion. You must take account of the unexpectedness..."

She stood up swiftly and ran to the kitchen, where Hélène was already cooking a supplementary omelet.

Pilesèche was confused. He stammered a few excuses, and would have liked to hide in a hole—but Bémolisant forced him to sit down, and a few minutes sufficed to restore good order.

When everyone was at table and had soothed the pangs of a hunger that could wait no longer, Madame Legris returned to the charge.

"Now, give us news of your uncle."

Madame Legris was a plump individual, quite replete, whose moist lips sketched an eternal smile, the expression of which adapted nevertheless to circumstances. When it was a matter of an illness or some other sad subject, that smile became appropriately tearful, and for the moment, it was with an expression of lugubrious compassion that she asked after the health of the uncle—the dear uncle—who, after having treated his nephew rigorously, had suddenly appeared on the horizon with the physiognomy of a good uncle with a legacy to leave.

It seemed, however, that her question was not addressed to anyone. Bémolisant eluded it; Pilesèche was busy cutting up bits of food for the baby.

It was, however impossible to escape that redoubtable interrogation for long. The good woman took the latter directly to task in his turn.

"You who live in his intimacy, Monsieur Pilesèche, tell us what you're thinking."

"Oh, he's very ill, very ill," replied the laboratory assistant, shaking his head.

"Ah! You fear a fatal outcome, then?"

"I fear so…I certainly fear so," repeated the poor man, at a loss

"To be sure, you see us all deeply affected. Come on, Népomucène, tell Monsieur how affected we are, for after all, he's your uncle. One doesn't lose an uncle without emotion. This one wasn't always good to us, but we practice the forgetfulness of insults."

The good lady paused momentarily on order to let that profession of faith produce its full effect. Then she resumed, in a low voice: "He's rich, isn't he?"

"I believe that he enjoys…that he enjoys a modest ease."

"It's only just that it should remain in the family, and my son-in-law is his only nephew."

"Forgive me, Madame, but there's a niece, at a convent in Fontenay-sous-Bois."

"Oh, that's right! Poor, dear child, now she's alone in the world!" groaned Madame Legris.

"Oh, her uncle wasn't a great resource for her, for he paid very little attention to her."

"We'll go to collect her, pamper her…Népomucène, do you know your cousin?"

"I've only seen her when she was very small, Mother-in-Law."

"Hélène, we're going to go to Fontenay-sous-Bois, aren't we? It's necessary that the child witnesses her uncle's last moments."

"No, no, Mother-in-Law. Let's not get carried away, if you please. My godfather doesn't like anyone forcing his hand, and doesn't want to see anyone he hasn't summoned personally."

"So, Hélène, your wife..."

"My wife, like everyone else, will be obliged to leave him tranquil. I don't suppose, in any case, that that will cause Hélène any mortal chagrin, since she doesn't know him."

"Very well, very well," riposted Madame Legris, slightly piqued. "But if it's not permitted to us to testify our sympathy to the dying man, it's not forbidden for us to take an interest in our cousin, our co-inheritor. She must be bored to death in her convent; we'll go in search of her. She'll live with us, and the regulation of the succession can only be facilitated by good relationships between the heirs."

"But Mother-in-Law, I really don't know why you want to regulate prematurely a succession that isn't open and might well escape us. How do you know what my uncle's testamentary dispositions are?"

"That's right! Come straight out and say that he's disinherited you! So you argued with him? For after all, if he summoned you, is doubtless wasn't with the intention of telling you that he was disinheriting you!"

"I haven't said anything of the sort."

"…On the contrary, it was to be reconciled with you. Come on, have you or have you not been reconciled with your uncle?"

Bémolisant was undergoing torture. That woman, unconsciously, was twisting the knife in the wound. He did not know what to say, and answered obliquely.

"Yes, of course…but does one ever know? Can one ever say? I'm not at odds with my uncle, but…"

"Well, then," Madame Legris concluded, "let's be tranquil. We'll act as we please. You have no understanding of sentimental matters."

In response to that apothegm, to which there was no answer, Bémolisant thought it best to lower the flag, and he finished lunch with his nose in his plate.

IV. A Revolution in Art

All Paris invaded the gallery in the Rue de Sèze, where the Hungarian painter Shaparazzy was exhibiting his works. But it was not exclusively the paintings of the celebrated artist that attracted the elegant and select crowd of première patrons.

Everyone was rushing, in fact, to see—finally—the statue whose praises the entire press was singing, with a great reinforcement of hyperbole, and a great clash of cymbals.

Only one discordant note had been struck within the concert, by the journal *Art classique*—but the tendencies of that specialist periodical being well-known, that very criticism was a certificate of modernity that had to add further advantage to the magisterial work, exhibited thanks to the care of the valiant critic Antoine Leroux.

The latter had set his heart on assuring its success, and, while one scarcely caught a glimpse of the sculptor—this Bémolisant whose name had been unknown yesterday—the journalist multiplied his efforts as if it were a matter of personal importance. It is true that he drew a profit from it that was no less effective for being indirect, for his name was, on this occasion, pronounced at least as often as that of the artist.

The newspapers waxed lyrical in his regard. One read comments such as: "The savant critic whose marvelous flair has been able to discover a modern Praxiteles…" or "We owe to the illustrious critic the opportunity finally to admire, etc…" or "With an abnegation and a disinterest that does him honor, the eminent Antoine Leroux had sworn to reveal this neglected talent to the artistic world; he has kept his word…"

In brief, there was around his name an honest acclaim to which he was not at all averse.

On the day when the Exhibition opened, he never quit the room where the nickel statue had been placed, lying on a pedestal covered in red velvet, in the middle of the principal gallery.

And it was, in fact, a strange and magisterial work, that metal statue representing a man who was tensed as if in the final coma of his agony: the features emaciated by suffering, the skeleton jutting forth beneath the skin, the breast hollowed out by a spasm, the hands clutching two short metal cylinders of which, to be sure, no one could quite explain the significance, and the eyes, finally, wide open to the horrors of surging death.

183

The lovers of prettiness in art had no need to go to that exhibition, but those in search of eternal verity, those whose souls were open to all pity, shivered as they approached that moribund, and felt their hearts squeezed by a dolorous grip.

Antoine Leroux went from group to group, explaining, provoking enthusiasm that never seemed sufficiently spontaneous.

It was a triumph, a stunning triumph. For a week, the newspapers resounded with the name of Népomucène Bémolisant. People were astonished that they had not heard mention of him before, and a few critics occasionally hinted that the artist in question resembled many others who had found a work in a stroke of luck and had emptied themselves in that single effort—one work, and one alone—with no yesterday and no tomorrow. For Bémolisant, who suddenly appeared like a meteor, had produced nothing until then; it was quite possible that his fortune would be exhausted in that flash of genius.

Those prophets of ill-omen, however, were clamoring in the desert—or, to put it more accurately, their voices were drowned out by the concert of enthusiasm and admiration.

Even the government seemed excited, as if by the advent of a Messiah. What! A master had been born, and did not bear the official stamp! What use, then, was the École? What was the point of the Grand Prix? They did not go so far, however, as to hold it against him that he had no attachment, and the director of the Beaux-Arts was already skillfully feeling out the critic and the sculptor, in order to acquire the work for the State.

Monsieur Bémolisant, at the first mention of that, seemed to jump out of his skin. It was as if someone had made a monstrous suggestion. The statue was not for sake; it was destined to ornament a tomb—the tomb of Monsieur X, as the label said.

Who could that Monsieur X be, whose family had commissioned a statue stark naked and in such a state of morbid emaciation?

We are usually pleased to ornament our deceased, to idealize them, to drape them in ample folds in a noble attitude; and the public found the nudity of the dying man a trifle bizarre for the coronation of his tomb. It was admirable as a work of art, but it was absurd when one thought of its destination.

From there to making up stories about that mysterious and eccentric family it was only a short step, and that served to defray the curiosity of the public, as well as filling the columns of newspapers.

The artist's studio was besieged by reporters, to whom he replied as best he could—which is to say, with the first thing that came into his head. By dint of explaining to them his conception of art and the secret thoughts that had led him to conceive that superb work, he ended up taking himself seriously in his role as a reformer, and perhaps ended up believing that he really was the author of the statue—but a cold shower brought him abruptly back to a sense of reality

That irresistible and chilly disillusionment was inflicted upon him by a journalist at bay, Jean Saure, well known for the elegant fashion he had of being indiscreet.

The reporter had forced his door, notebook in one hand, pencil in the other, and without wasting any time, interrogated him. Between the questions and in the course of the interview he let the latest gossip escape.

"Oh, by the way, dear Master," he put in, "in spite of the mystery you've tried to suspend over your statue, we've now finally identified the original that it represents/"

"What! How?"

"Yesterday, in a group of people who had come to see the work and were discussing its anatomical perfection, Dr. Delcourtil suddenly cried out, on seeing it: 'But if I'm not mistaken, it's the image of Népomucène Grillard!'"

"Ah!" groaned Bémolisant, who felt faint.

"Monsieur Grillard might have lived as a misanthrope and hardly ever shown himself, but he's sufficiently well known in the scientific world; a few academicians were sum-

185

moned, who recognized him immediately. This evening's newspapers will be very well documented on the subject. But everyone is crying; 'But the man isn't dead yet; how has Monsieur Bémolisant dared to exhibit his statue...a statue that represents him struggling in his death throes?'"

"That's precisely where the mystery, the enigma begins," Bémolisant stammered, for the sake of saying something.

"That enigma you're going to help me clarify. I promise you a leading article in my paper. You'll never have had such acclaim, such a magnificent success."

"No, no...I beg you...no publicity; I'm the enemy of fame. It offends my most intimate family sentiments. Look, I'll buy your silence with a confidence..."

"Ah! Now you're talking!"

"But swear to me that you'll keep what I'm going to tell you to yourself."

"Word of a reporter!" said Jean Saure, with an enigmatic smile.

"Well, know then that Monsieur Grillard is my uncle. He's very ill...perhaps he's dead at this moment. I wanted to retain his features such as they appeared to me in that supreme illness, to erect a monument worthy of him, to make him, in his final hour, the supreme homage of my talent."

"That's a whole novel in outline. I understand everything: your reluctance to exhibit, your hesitations, which Antoine Leroux only vanquished by trickery, your persistent silence regarding the original of the statue. Perfect, perfect... I'll run along...I don't want to know any more. I'm expected at the paper. It's necessary that the public know your great soul, and finally appreciate you..."

"No, no, I implore you. You swore to me to keep silent..."

"And you reminded me of my oath: thank you!" said the reporter, making his escape before the artist was able to stop him.

Bémolisant was furious. He sensed a vague danger suspended over his head. Without knowing in what form the danger would fall upon him, he was invaded by an extreme anxiety.

No matter; it was the day that his exhibition closed; he was about to regain possession of his work and finally remove it from indiscreet curiosity. It was about to change domicile and be lost to sight. He hoped that, as one fad follows another, Paris would soon forget him in favor of some new attraction at the zoological gardens or the winter circus.

When evening came, therefore, he went to the Rue de Sèze in order to reclaim his statue and regulate his account. The entrance fees had produced a considerable sum, and his share of that celestial manna was rather tidy.

He stuffed the bills and gold coins into his pockets, pinching himself in order to convince himself of the reality of the windfall.

The statue had been carefully packed. In front of the gallery it was hoisted on to a fiacre that was waiting at the door. Bémolisant was about to climb into the cab himself and leave when a man hurtled toward him, shoved him into the fiacre, leapt in after him, closed the door and, leaning out of the lowered window, shouted at the coachman urgently: "To the Gare de Lyon!"

That man was Pilesèche.

Pilesèche, pale and wan, his features distressed, trembling with fear.

Seizing the artist by the arm, sticking his lips to his ear, he whispered, in a voice so distraught that the other started, gripped by the contagion of that fear: "The police are on our heels."

"Wretch! What's happened, then?" he demanded.

"Oh, let me pull myself together first."

He made use of his moustache to fan himself, although it was a cold January day, as breathless as if he had run all the way across Paris.

Finally, reassembling his courage and his idea, he said: "I've just been to the house."

"On the Montagne Sainte-Geneviève?"

"Yes. It's on fire. It's a furnace. There were firemen blocking the street. The steam-pumps were launching torrents of water, but to no avail. The flames were spurting out of the windows, crackling, with black and acrid smoke. It was horrible. And in the middle of it I saw a police commissioner wearing his sash and giving out orders. Madame Paponot came out to talk to him, and raised her arms toward the skies. I wondered if I ought to go up, but quickly reckoned that it was better to keep quiet. That suits my character better—and besides, the fire might have helped us, in sum, by permitting it to be supposed that my poor employer had perished in the flames."

"You're right," opined the artist, "and it's all for the best."

"What, all for the best! But listen—that's not all…unfortunately. I found myself in the midst of people of the neighborhood, who were too occupied watching the fire to recognize me. They were talking about the cause of the disaster. One said that it had begun in the distiller's cellar, the other that it had started under the eaves. 'In any case,' he added, as soon as Madame Paponot perceived it, she immediately thought about the gentleman who's ill that nobody ever sees him. Perhaps it's him, she said, who started the fire. A sick person, you see—that can happen…especially if there's no one looking after him'

"At that moment Madame Paponot was with the commissioner, gesticulating as if she were demanding something of him. Then the commissioner turns to the firemen. 'Hey,' he said, in a loud voice, there's a man in the mansards who's ill and disabled. Is anyone willing to go up and find him?'

"Two or three firemen run forward shouting: 'Me! Me!' They set up the telescopic ladder, which goes up all the way to the fourth. A fireman jumps on to it and goes up it like a cat; he staves in the window-frame of the laboratory, whose panes have already exploded, and disappears into the furnace. The crowd utter a cry of admiration and terror…he finally reappears, alone…"

"Naturally!"

"Then there's an immense cry of disappointment. 'He hasn't got him!' But he, to reassure them, shouts in his turn from the top of the ladder: 'There's no one there!' He comes back down, rapidly. The commissioner is waiting, and questions him. The fireman reports that he's explored the apartment and couldn't find the old man.

"The commissioner shakes his head and is thinking about it, without saying anything, when I hear murmurs in the crowd: 'It's odd, all the same, a man on his death-bed taking off like that on the very day of the fire. There's a mystery in this, for sure...a mystery such as Richebourg[32] never invented, and the police will stick their noses in, have no fear...'

"Those words, you see, Monsieur Bémolisant, are engraved in my brain. I saw everything spinning; I nearly fainted, and I ran away as fast as my legs could carry me. How did I get here? I don't know, for I was running without a goal. Instinctively, I looked for you, and I'm more tranquil now that I've found you."

"But what do you expect us to do?" groaned the artist.

"We have to flee..."

"Flee where? They'd catch us at the frontier. Why take me to the Gare de Lyon?

"To go to Switzerland."

"Fool—we'd be arrested there and extradited without further ado."

"Damn! Let's go to the station anyway; we'll leave the cab there, to put the police off the track. Oh, I'm becoming artful! On the way, we'll think of a means of getting away."

The vehicle was still moving. Finally, it piled up outside the station. The coachman hailed porters, who unloaded the heavy package and put it on a station trolley, not without commenting on the considerable weight of the oddly-shaped box.

---

[32] The enormously popular but now forgotten feuilletonist Émile Richebourg (1833-1898)

The travelers seemed very hesitant about the destination to which they wanted it to go. In the end, they decided to deposit it in the left luggage office; it was a temporary solution, which had no other advantage than giving them time to sort things out—but it was all very well to step back from the edge of the ditch; eventually, they would have to jump it.

Presumably, inspiration came to them, for, half an hour later, Bémolisant came back on his own, drawing a little handcart that he had hired, leaving a ten-franc deposit as guarantee. He took the statue out of the left luggage office and after having it loaded on to his vehicle, he set off in the direction of the Seine.

On the Boulevard Diderot, Pilesèche rejoined him, darting anxious glances to the left and right, and the two of them were swallowed up by the crowd...

VI. *A* Fin-de-Siècle *Detective*

Monsieur Rosamour was smoking a cigar by the fireside. Sunk in a softly-padded armchair, his feet crossed in the American fashion on the marble mantelpiece, Rosamour abandoned himself to the pleasure of daydreaming. He liked that quiet idleness in a cozy apartment, where his artistic temperament had assembled a few paintings and costly trinkets. His gaze wandered from one to another, and life appeared to him in its brightest colors.

Rosamour did not, however, spend all his time doing nothing. He had a métier, or, let us rather say, a profession. He was a detective: a *fin-de-siècle* detective who had broken the mold of the police of old. He was an accomplished gentleman, correctly dressed, clean shaven, perfectly polished and susceptible of cutting a brilliant figure in any society.

His colleagues at the Rue de Jérusalem [33] regarded him with a disdain pierced with a certain jealousy, because, without having the air of being up to much, he had had a few suc-

---

[33] The then-headquarters of the French Sûreté.

cessful cases at the outset of his career, and had treated them with means so unexpected that they wondered whether the young puppy was not about to turn the old methods upside-down—which caused the hairs of the old conservatives of the Sûreté stand on end.

He claimed to be inaugurating the new type of the scientific detective.

"Modern science," he said, when he let himself go in telling the story of his vocation, "has put within our range resources still unutilized, in which it is sufficient to draw with full hands. Unfortunately, the ordinary run of policemen, ingenious and adroit as they are presumed to be, are notoriously insufficient in their education. Personally, I'm a doctor of science and a laureate of the Institut. When I reached the age to choose a profession I said to myself: *What scientific career is as yet unexploited?* And I perceived a lacuna in the police: that was my opportunity.

"Certainly, my honorable colleagues have been able to take advantage of the most obvious conquests of science—railways, the telegraph and the telephone—but science intervenes in many other aspects of our lives every day, and for someone who knows it thoroughly, it is a torch, a sure guide, which it is necessary not to abandon for a single instant. In a general manner, and above all, what I want to introduce into my police research, is the scientific method, and to that end I've worked hard; the study of the masters has permitted me to glimpse the rules of what I might call the great strategy of the art.

"Those rules, which were instinctive to them and which they applied, so to speak, without being aware of it, I claim to have classified in my mind, and I march almost with a sure step along the way, leaning on the experience of the ancients, served by modern scientific methods. No more empiricism: experimental logic! According to the case, I can apply the methods of any of my illustrious predecessors…at least to the extent that our physical means permit me to. Before acting, I always ask myself: what would Vidocq, Lecoq, Macé or Goron have done? And then: what should I, Rosamour, do?"

Was not the young *fin-de-siècle* detective still a trifle lacking in the manner explaining his sound principles?

He even claimed not to limit the scope of his method to classical science, and was not reluctant to seek help from the occult sciences, or those reputed as such—I mean hypnotism and induced sleep, whether he utilized the clairvoyance of extra-lucid mediums or sought to hypnotize suspects himself.

In vino veritas, says the adage, and some people are not far from admitting that it is just as easy to get the truth out of a somnambulist as a drunkard.

One could argue about that endlessly, and sustain that the aforesaid subject is not as unconscious as one would like to believe; that he takes a malign pleasure in parading his medium and his audience through a heap of extravagant stories, and that in the end, especially when his interests are at stake, he will resist suggestions and indiscreet questions with all his might. To that Rosamour replied that nothing is absolute, but, even supposing that hypnotized subject does not always tell the whole truth, it is incontestable that he is not in entire possession of himself, and betrays himself all the more easily by his reticences or his contradictions.

What does a policeman require? A presumption, a clue, a guiding thread, a word let slip that puts him on the track, ready to check the indications given severely and subsequently find their material verification.

A judgment based on revelations acquired in that state, either from the guilty person or a third party, would doubtless be iniquitous, but is it still bad when one only seeks within the revelations a means of investigation?

For our part, we cannot say and almost dare say that the method will only ever prove its worth by the manner of its application.

As for Monsieur Rosamour, he was convinced that he applied it with the greatest prudence, and we have no reason to contest the high opinion that he had of himself.

These delicate problems, where the very essence of our psychic nature—to use the language of initiates—is at stake, without science having succeeded in grasping the link that attaches it to the corporeal world, are attractive by virtue of the marvelous that surrounds them and the element of the unknown that is inseparable from them.

So, Rosamour was in the meditative attitude appropriate to an individual haunted by such grave thoughts. He was smoking his cigar and could, by reaching out his hand, pick up a little book from a table, in which his paper-knife marked the page that he had begun.

It was not a work by just anyone; the book treated the subject of the divining rod and was signed Chevreuil.[34] Such a name guaranteed the value of the contents.

And Rosamour was thinking about what he had just read.

As everyone knows, a divining rod is a forked stick, a simple hazel rod, which water-diviners—which is to say, those who make a particular specialty of detecting subterranean watercourses—hold out in front of them. At the moment when they are directly over the spring, the rod becomes active and bends, twisting the hand, thus indicating the precise spot in which it is necessary to dig.

If the explanation is difficult, the fact is undeniable, and attested by people worthy of trust. The majority of scientists no longer refuse to admit it nowadays, while surrounding it with reticences and circumlocutions tending to protect the infallibility of science.

But if the divining rod is capable of indicating springs, might it not be applicable to other searches? That is what one

_____

[34] The well-known painter and occultist Léon Chevreuil (1852-1939) had not yet built a reputation as a popularizer of occult science in 1890, when this scene is set, and the subsequent reference to "his day" suggests that the intended reference might be to the perfumer Étienne Chevreuil, who had a strong interest in spiritism and associated subjects, but does not appear to have published any books on the subject.

is tempted to ask. Examples abound of people who have sought to discover, by that means, hidden metals, buried treasures, even criminals...

Ah! That was what interested our policeman most keenly, and a medium enjoying a certain reputation had been pestering him for some time with offers of service, assuring him that he enjoyed that precious faculty. Rosamour was seeking to enlighten his religion by rereading Chevreuil's treatise.

In truth, there were fors and againsts in the book, which dated from a era when it had appeared revolutionary to discuss such "nonsense," as people said, and although the illustrious scientist seemed to admit the results obtained with the rod in the search for springs, he was evidently a great deal more skeptical with regard to treasures and criminals found by that means. The repeated failure of a large number of experiments was bound to give him reason for doubt.

In brief, the conclusion of the work was, firstly, that in no case was there any direct action of the object sought on the rod; if the latter moved, it was because of an unconscious action on the part of the men; and secondly, that the rod turned, most frequently, when the operator believed that it ought to turn—which is to say, at the moment when, for one reason or another, the operator was convinced that he was above the object sought.

Right, Rosamour said to himself. *I can admit that the rod is only the tangible sign of the phenomenon, but that it's the man himself, without being aware of it, on whom the presence of the water, when it's a matter of a spring, exerts its action. Which Chevreuil had difficulty understanding, because, in his day, the study of the psychic phenomena that are approached so boldly today, and seem less extraordinary, had not been carried out in depth. When one sees the hyperexcitability of the senses that can be obtained in certain subjects in the various phases of the second life, can one not admit that, by autosuggestion, one can succeed in acquiring a kind of flair, a particular and exceptional lucidity?*

194

The skeptics cry: "What are you telling us, with your rod? That the instrument that discovers water today by undergoing disorderly movements above a spring will, if you ask it for old tomorrow, cease turning when it passes over a subterranean aqueduct in order to agitate over a treasure? That's too obliging."

But that's the confirmation of the theory, Rosamour continued, *for that flair, suddenly awakened, goes toward the object of the autosuggestion, not toward others. Why, then, should one not succeed in also following, using the same means, the tracks of criminals/ Not everyone will be up to it, but it's sufficient for it to be possible, and that there are special constitutions capable of acquiring the necessary flair.*

And Rosamour picked up the book again in order to re-read the instructive and quasi-marvelous story of the water-diviner Jacques Aymard, who had pursued murderers by that means in Lyon, and had put his hand on the real guilty parties.[35]

As if to provide a counterweight to that story, so clear, it had to be admitted that subsequent attempts made by the same operator had been completely fruitless, but it was necessary to take account of the fact that the circumstances were not the same. It had been suddenly announced to him that a crime had been committed in the street, and, full of confidence in his power, the diviner, who had not reasoned as we have just done, proclaimed loudly that he would find the guilty parties, but it seemed that he lacked a point of departure; he wandered at random, and ended up in places where the murderer could not be.

Rosamour smiled; those results did not appear to him as contradictory as people said, and he thought he could explain them simply.

---

[35] The anecdote about Jacques Aymard's attempt to transfer his supposed water-diving skills to the detection of a murder in Lyon, at the end of the 17th century, is reported in numerous 19th century texts.

"To follow a trail," he said, "one needs to be holding one of the ends. Can a dog find an object that is unfamiliar, without having got the scent in advance? In the case of the murder in Lyon, which gave him his success, Jacques Aymard had gone down into the cellar where the crime had been committed. In that circumscribed space he had been put, so to speak, virtually in the presence of the murderers, who had left something of themselves there—their spoor, if you like. He had the trail.

"On the contrary, a crime is committed in a street, at an indeterminate spot; he murder has merely passed by; what permits his trail to be distinguished from those of other passers-by. In those circumstances, Aymard could not find the murderer, because he had absolutely no idea who he was pursuing, and was not impregnated, so to speak, by the personality of that particular individual."

And the policeman drew from all that the conviction the water-diviners—to leave them that name—are capable of discovering any object or person, but that it is necessary to put them in preliminary contact with the object or person in question.

He was, therefore, in no doubt that the practice in question, so singular at first glance, might render great service in certain criminal cases, and he promised himself that he would use that precious means of investigation advantageously when the opportunity presented itself, with a set of favorable circumstances.

He was at that point in his reflections when a whistle-blast summoned him to the telephone that he had taken care to install above his work-table.

The head of the Sûreté ordered him to put himself without delay at the disposal of the police commissioner at the Panthéon.

As soon as he had changed clothes, our man was on his way.

As you will have guessed, the mystery whose discovery the fire in the Rue de la Montagne had permitted was not unconnected with the abrupt summons that had torn Monsieur Rosamour away from his studies in cerebral physiology, to plunge him into the midst of the positive operations of his profession.

VII. On Induction in Criminal Matters

Madame Paponot, the concierge of the burned building, had been singularly disturbed on hearing the cry of "Fire!" resounding in the stairwell.

She was dozing lightly, plunged in her big armchair, wrapped up next to the purring stove.

Suddenly, at that cry, she had found herself on her feet, eyes open, prey to a tremor that she had, however, succeeded in quelling very rapidly, in order to go and see where the fire was.

Already, all the way up the staircase, there was a frightful racket of doors opening and people running down, uttering screams of fear, interjections, appeals for help and lamentations.

A neighbor, possessed of a clearer head, ran to the nearest fire alarm, while someone else closed the gas taps and the tenants began throwing their furniture and bedding out of the windows.

The firemen arrived quickly, moreover; the steam-pumps were set up and launched their sprays at the blaze. The flames had already invaded the stairwell, however; it was necessary to let the fire go and preserve the neighboring houses.

The tenants had been able to get out in time, but the disaster had been so rapid that most of them had been able to save very little by way of possessions.

It was necessary to consider it fortunate that there was no personal injury to deplore—for, all things considered, the disappearance of Monsieur Grillard definitely seemed to be anterior to the conflagration.

That disappearance was nonetheless singularly intriguing to the police commissioner who was conducting the investigation into the cause of the fire. What could have become of the bizarre tenant whom all the witnesses declared to be incapable of quitting his bed? That was what the magistrate asked himself, and which he tried to clarify by means of a confused interrogation, to which Madame Paponot brought her customary volubility.

The excellent woman explained to him with expressive gestures and an infinity of details that she had not seen her tenant with her own eyes for six weeks. She had been told that he was ill, but she could not affirm herself that he was not in any fit state to leave his room. She had been told, however, that he never left his bed, and that same morning..."

"Who told you that?" the commissioner put in, impatiently.

"Monsieur Pilesèche, of course. His helper...what do you call it? His laboratory assistant."

"And where is this laboratory assistant?"

"At home, no doubt. He only comes twice a day to see his boss, give him what he needs and do a little housework. Hold on, though," the doorkeeper remarked, as if struck by a flash of enlightenment, "in fact, I haven't seen him since the day before yesterday."

"Aha!" said the commissioner, and with pressing the point any further, added: "Which physician visited your tenant?"

"He detested them all equally and didn't want to see any of them."

"So there was no one but this Pilesèche who went into his room?"

"I believe so. Monsieur Grillard is something of a boor, and it wasn't a good idea to knock on his door. I, who am speaking to you, Monsieur le Commissaire, even though I'm the concierge of the house, I said: *That's no reason to let someone die like that without help*, but every time I said to Monsieur Pilesèche: *I'll go see to your boss now and again, and take him some soup*—and I'm famous for that, you know, I'm praised for it—Monsieur Pilesèche replied to me: 'Oh,

Madame Paponot, you know Monsieur Grillard; how can you think of going to disturb him? It'll put him in a terrible temper, and you'll be the cause of him having a fit.' You understand, me, I'm a good woman at heart, although a trifle abrupt at first sight, and I wouldn't have wanted any harm to come to that poor man, so I stayed on my stairs, without daring to knock at the door."

"And that never seemed singular to you?"

"In truth, now that you mention it, it does seem slightly shady, but what do you expect. I'm a concierge, I'm not here to spy on the tenants."

The commissioner allowed her to launch into a long speech on the duties of her estate; he reflected, and searched among those elements of information for the conductive thread, which escaped him.

The first hypothesis that he examined was that the invalid, seeing himself suddenly threatened by the fire, had made a supreme effort and had succeeded in reaching the staircase, where he had been suddenly enveloped by the flames. Although it was important not to neglect that supposition, however, it nevertheless ran into implausibility at several points.

On the other hand, was it not necessary to see a singular coincidence between the disappearance of the old man and the fire breaking out suddenly with extreme violence?

Could he have started the fire himself in a fit of delirium, and escaped via the rooftops? That was impossible, in his condition, and by dint of reflection, the commissioner found a combination of facts that suggested something quite different.

No one had seen the scientist for six weeks; his laboratory assistant took care to ward off any unwelcome visit. And what was that laboratory assistant? A menial employee, come down in the world, who, after completing his studies, had never found the energy necessary to get out of his rut and quit the bohemian life into which he had lapsed.

Was it impossible, given those data, to reconstruct the drama? First there had been a sequestration. The shameless bohemian had doubtless wanted to obtain from his ailing master that he should become his heir, or something analogous—there was no shortage of motives; that was for the examining magistrate to determine in a more precise fashion. The other had resisted. In a final scene of quarrel and struggle, the exasperated assistant had seen red and killed him. Suddenly, faced with his crime, he had been seized by a sudden terror; what should he do now? How could he avoid indiscreet questions?

He had hidden the body, and had started the fire in order to destroy the all the traces of the crime.

Was that not a logical deduction of the entire sequence of events? Was it not a succinct summary of a criminal history such as one encounters every day—a banal history, in truth, for the criminal had not any particularly ingenious imagination in deflecting suspicion.

But was the story, in fact, so banal?

Were there not, in those various facts, disconcerting circumstances, mysterious points well worthy of intelligent research by a policeman devoted to his métier?

That was the road followed by the commissioner's thoughts; he smiled at the hope that such an investigation, well-handled and expertly deduced, would do him honor.

To be sure, he did not want to bring the Sûreté into the affair, wanting all the merit for himself, but he did not have any agent on his staff clever enough and capable of carrying out the delicate research that it would be necessary to undertake. It was therefore necessary to resign himself to telephoning the Prefecture of Police in order that a sleuth could be put at his disposal. That was what he did.

Then, after taking time out to regulate another affair and give his orders, the magistrate picked up his hat and got ready to go out for lunch.

On the threshold of his office, he found himself face to face with a very correctly-dressed young man who greeted him ingenuously.

The newcomer might have been thirty; he was a fairly handsome fellow, with a pink and youthful face ornamented by a blond moustache over the full red lips of an amiable philosopher. Beneath semicircular eyebrows, with gave him a slightly naïve expression, gray eyes devoid of any gleam hid behind the shiny lenses of a myopic's lorgnon. Nothing about him attracted attention—not even his costume, which was no less banal for being correct. He was a dull or neutral individual.

He bowed, with an unpretentious smile; then, in a bland and colorless voice, he said: "I've come to place myself under your orders, Commissioner."

The magistrate considered him briefly, trying to put a name to the inoffensive face.

"Why, of course," he said, finally. "It's Monsieur Rosamour. I confess that I didn't recognize you."

"Which proves," said the young man, with an imperceptible hint of satisfaction, "that it's not necessary, in order to put on a disguise, to employ make-up outrageously, as some of my colleagues do. You know my principles: disguises are never very difficult to penetrate; a cunning malefactor who knows that he's being watched never lets himself be taken in. False beard, false wig: there's always a point at which the artifice can be pierced."

"I know that; it's not for nothing that they call you the scientific detective."

"And I'm proud of meriting that appellation.

"Well then, we're going to understand one another perfectly. Come with me, and I'll explain what it's about on the way."

Like a man who can manage his effects, the commissioner recounted the story of the previous day's fire, the mysterious disappearance of the aged tenant, and the sequestration of which he had evidently been the object. He set out, piece by piece, the scaffolding of his hypotheses, and deduced with great logical force the charges that weighed upon the scientist's laboratory assistant."

"And you've mounted a search for this laboratory assistant?" Rosamour put in, toying negligently with his cane.

"Immediately," the magistrate relied, "And if my agents can put their hands on him, they'll bring him to me and put him under lock and key without further ado."

"I advise you not to do that."

"Why not?" replied the other, nonplussed.

"It's obvious. He can be questioned, and will be, but it would be premature to arrest him or make him aware of the suspicions that are weighing upon him. Thus far, for what can he be reproached? Have you see the *corpus delicti*—the cadaver? Where is the man who has disappeared? Perhaps his disappearance can be explained quite naturally. The laboratory assistant will reply to you, like Cain: 'Am I his keeper? I left him yesterday, as usual; he was in bed. If he's disappeared, it's without my knowledge. You want to hold me responsible, but have you any proof that I had anything to do with it? First, find the fellow, dead or alive.'"

"You believe he's innocent, then?"

"Me? Not at all. I don't believe anything. I examine the situation; I feel out the terrain, and I say to you: remember the Gouffé affair.[36] A man and a woman kill a bailiff and get rid of the body. Heavy charges are laid against them; people are sure—morally certain—of their guilt, but the investigation is absolutely paralyzed because there isn't a cadaver. The trunk in which the victim was enclosed turns up, and things change their aspect completely. Are we not in the presence of a similar case? What we need to discover is the man who has disappeared."

"I agree with you, but my conviction is that we'll only find him by following the trail of his laboratory assistant. Monsieur Grillard, you see, wasn't…"

"Monsieur Grillard?" the policeman interjected. "Did you say Monsieur Grillard?" He pulled a newspaper out of his

---

[36] The trial of Michel Eyraud and Gabrielle Bompard for the murder of Toussaint Gouffé in February 1891 was one of the great *causes célèbres* of the period, and the memory would have been very fresh when this scene is supposedly set.

pocket. "Perfect: here's an item of information concerning him."

Unfolding a copy of *Le Petit Journal*, he pointed out an article to the commissioner.

Finally, we have been able to penetrate a part of the mystery enveloping Monsieur Népomucène's masterpiece. The magnificent statue that All Paris has been admiring in Georges Petit's gallery is destined for the tomb of Monsieur Grillard, the uncle and godfather of the eminent artist, who wanted to render him the filial homage of his talent. His idea was perhaps a trifle bizarre, and not everyone will understand how it was possible to represent the image of a man still alive—although very ill, it seems—in the last spasms of mortal agony. Although it is always legitimate for genius to seize nature in the raw, there is in this circumstance a lack of good taste on which it is not appropriate for us to dwell.

"There, it seems to me," observed the commissioner, rubbing his hands, "is an incident that might help us in our research. It's necessary to find this sculptor, and I have no doubt that we shall obtain precious information through that channel."

"I'm convinced of it, as if you care to give me *carte blanche*, I believe I shall be able to bring you an abundant harvest of information in a matter of hours."

They had just reached the commissioner's domicile when a secretary, running after him, announced that Pilesèche had not been found at his habitual lodging and that it had been impossible to discover what had become of him.

Monsieur Rosamour took some notes, wrote down a few names and addresses, and, hot on the trail, set forth at a rapid pace.

It did not take him long to collect the information that seemed to him to be the most urgent, and a few hours later, getting down from a carriage at the commissioner's door, he hastened to the policeman's study.

"Am I on time?" he asked.

"You're punctuality itself," the other replied. "We'll see if you're equally precise in person. Sit down and tell me the result of your investigations."

"First of all, no *person*, if you please."

"Aha! The scientific method!"

"Exactly. Pilesèche, thirty-three years old, a pauper, unsuccessful, whose timidity and gaucherie have always prevented him from mounting to anything. Not in need."

"Eh? Appetite coming and going, one isn't astonished to discover one day, in hidden recesses, needs that one didn't suspect."

"I understand; we'll see about that later. Second individual: Bémolisant, something of crackpot, started out making music; quarreled with his uncle, who didn't like the arts and didn't encourage them. Our artist wanted to renew the methods of music, cursed his contemporaries for not understanding him, and, shaking the dust of old Europe off his boots, went to Tonkin to look for more naïve enthusiasts among primitive peoples. In the midst of hair-raising adventures—if they're true—made the acquaintance a widow named Legris, whose daughter he married. Music continuing not to pay, the handsome Népomucène—for he's a good-looking chap—set up as a vermouth merchant in Haiphong. Returned to France as soon as he'd amassed some small savings, and, returning to the arts, took up sculpture. Suddenly revealed himself by the statue representing his dying uncle.

"In that regard, I don't know for sure as yet whether he was reconciled with Monsieur Grillard, but doesn't that seem to you to be quite probable? That statue isn't a work that one makes up; it's evidently made from nature. He's seen his model; it's even necessary to admit that he's seen him often, which contradicts the concierge's declaration that no one went up to see the old scientist. That's one of the points I have to investigate, and perhaps I'll succeed in elucidating it. As for the artist, unfortunately, I did see him, because..."

The commissioner pursed his lips and said to himself, privately, that it was hardly worth the trouble of posing as a champion of new methods in order to bring in such a poor harvest. This was lyricism, not information; anybody could have done it better. He thought, however, that he ought to encourage the young policeman.

"Well," he said, "you haven't been wasting our time, but we still have a lot to do."

"Wait a moment—I haven't finished."

"Ah! Let's have it..."

"Such was the fashion in which my characters were described to me, and by way of conclusion, they don't seem cut from the cloth of great criminals. They aren't equipped to hurt a fly."

"Beware of angry sheep."

"I understand that, and I'll be wary of taking any premature consequence from such vague premises. We're in the presence of individuals in whom there is no predisposition to crime, and it we were able to examine their heads we doubtless wouldn't find the superb atrophies that are the evident marks of criminal instincts. Nevertheless, one circumstance is sufficient to lead even the mildest of men to crime: poverty, anger, momentary madness. If the investigation of an affair weren't made up of a thousand contradictory elements, police work would be banal. To arrive at the motives that have enraged our sheep, however, it's nevertheless necessary to know their primitive character precisely: that's done."

"Yes, my friend, but we're no further forward now than before.

"Wait! Let me tell you one item of news—a very important item…"

"Ah! Finally."

"Do you know why I can't put my hand on Monsieur Bémolisant

"I beg you not to spare your efforts; don't leave me in suspense..."

"Because he's disappeared."

"Ah! Everybody in this affair has disappeared, then! But that corroborates my suspicions—admit it! There's a link between all these events, no doubt about it, and our artist is mixed up in the affair somehow."

"I'm not denying it. Yesterday evening, when he went to the Rue de Sèze to collect his statue, a man—it must have been Pilesèche; he fits the description—arrived like a hurricane, shoved him into the cab that was waiting for him and got into it after him, shouting "Gare de Lyon!" to the coachman. The cab was number 10,406. I questioned the driver; I have his statement and his description of the bizarre box containing the statue."

"We have to telegraph the frontier."

"What the point? For one thing, it would be too late, as they've had all night to flee. Secondly, it's unnecessary, since our fugitives didn't leave by train. They simply deposited the heavy crate in the left luggage office, which they took out again not long afterwards. Then they went along the Boulevard Diderot, where I lost track of them."

"Good. They wanted to put us off the track and went to the Gare d'Orléans. That's elementary."

"Not at all. No one saw them either at the Gare d'Orléans or the Gare Montparnasse."

"Damn! In Paris, nothing is lost; we need to find them."

"Oh, don't worry; I'm not overly bothered about that, sure that well find them when we need to do so. The scientific method, you see. I don't play the Indian and sniff the traces of moccasins on the asphalt when I have better things to do. For the moment, and before anything else, I have to find my scientist, dead or alive. So I'll leave, after having calmed your legitimate impatience—at least, I hope so. I'll set out on the hunt again."

The commissioner seemed more resigned than convinced. "Go on, then," he said. "And don't waste any time, for if our men are still running, we'll have difficulty catching up with them."

"What do you expect? In any case, they had twenty-four hours start. If they wanted to reach the frontier, they'll have done so. Wherever they are, though, we'll collect them just as easily, when the time comes. Let's allow them to run and not give them any warning before having assembled a formidable body of evidence against them."

When he had gone, the commissioner stood up in a bad mood, and strode back and forth in his office, muttering. He was disturbed by Rosamour's methods. The old game seemed to him to be preferable to all those subtle theories. He could not understand why, having picked up the trail of the two fugitives, the agent had not tracked them until he caught them.

He could easily have imposed his way of seeing on Rosamour, but he would be shouldering a heavy responsibility in case of failure by preventing him from acting as he wished, and he decided to wait for the result of the preliminary investigations.

In any case, it was quite certain, as the policeman had said that the two fugitives would, indeed, be easy to find while they were dragging a hundred-and-fifty kilo parcel around with them.

VIII. How Rosamour Became Increasingly Perplexed

Madame Paponot had sensed that her importance was singularly inflated by being mixed up in this mysterious affair. She gladly told all her neighbors about the police interrogation to which she had been subjected. She even embellished it, adding to her own role, attributing replies to herself by which the magistrate's intelligence had evidently been enlightened.

In brief, without her, the mystery would have passed unperceived. She had just saved society, and, satisfied with her busy day, perhaps slightly fatigued by the incessant talk, she was returning majestically to her lodge, which was almost the only part of the building still intact, when she found herself confronted by well-dressed man with a pince-nez shielding his eyes, who bowed gracefully and said to her, without the slightest hesitation: "Bonjour, Madame Paponot."

"What, you know me?" said the concierge, straightening up in surprise.

"Do I know you! But certainly I know you. I've come to ask you for some information about the fire."

"Aha! You're a *journaliss*..."

"You've guessed it! Well, I wouldn't have hidden it from you any longer."

"You've arrived very late, you know. I've already seen five or six."

"Oh, that's nothing; there's plenty more to recount. I'm the one who put it in the paper that throughout the blaze, the concierge, Madame Paponot, displayed superb courage and energy."

"You put that, my lad? Well, that's kind; you're a nice young man. It's true, all the same, that I wouldn't have believed myself to be so courageous. I came and went-it was all the same to me!"

Rosamour—for it was him—had a bundle of newspapers under his arm. He searched it. "Look," he said. "You can see the article…oh, damn, I can't find it; I must have dropped it. I'll send it to you; I'd like you to read it." At the same time he unfolded some illustrated papers, and stopped, as if by chance, at the portrait of the hero of the day, the sculptor Bémolisant.

"A fine head," said Madame Paponot, looking at it. She leaned over the engraving, and added: "But if I'm not mistaken, I know that face. A funny idea, putting a scrap-dealer in the paper."

"A scrap-dealer!"

"As sure as my name's Madame Paponot."

"There's 'sculptor' written under the picture."

"Perhaps he is a sculptor, but he's a scrap-dealer for sure. I even said to Monsieur Pilesèche: 'Who's that *artiss*,' and he said: 'He's not an *artiss*, he's a dealer come to collect our old scrap metal.'"

"Perhaps it's not the same man. Have you seen him several times?"

"In truth, no. He only came that once on the thirty-first of December. You can see that I remember the date, and then, a face like that, one can't be mistaken."

"Monsieur Pilesèche was making fun of you."

"Monsieur Pilesèche never makes fun of me," said Madame Paponot, stiffening herself, scandalized by such a suggestion. "He'd have a job."

"That's true. And what did the two of them do, that day?"

"They had porters with them, who brought down a big crate full of scrap metal."

"So you saw what was inside?"

"In truth, no, but they said it was—not to mention that it was heavy. The men were sweating."

"And it was big, this crate?"

"Long, mostly—six feet at least. One might have thought it was a coffin.

"Ah! And they loaded the crate on to a carriage."

"Of course. They were going to the Quai des Augustines, from what they said to the coachman."

"I'd be very curious to see how your eccentric tenant was installed, if it's not too badly burned up there.

"One corner's still there, but you'll understand that I can't risk myself on the stairway. I'm a little heavy, and it might collapse. But if you want to, don't hesitate. Go gladly. You'll be all alone."

Rosamour did not need the invitation issued in that picturesque form to be repeated, and set about scaling the shaky charred steps, cluttered with rubbish of every sort.

On the upper floors, the firemen had set up a ladder to replace the demolished staircase, and he reached the landing on which the smoking remains of the floorboards remained, thanks to a few joists that were still intact.

The panels of the apartment door were three-quarters burned, but the lock was still attached to its slot and the policeman observed that it had been locked with a key. It was, therefore, inadmissible that Monsieur Grillard had tried to get out during the blaze, for he certainly would not have taken the trouble to lock the door again.

Administering a thrust of his shoulder to the remaining woodwork, Rosamour passed over the threshold of the apartment and walked with precaution over the beams. The first two rooms had been completely obliterated by the flames. Beyond them, thanks no doubt to the presence of a partition wall, the laboratory still existed in part, encumbered by the mass of rubble that the roof had accumulated there in collapsing.

At the back wall, a cracked section of what had been the chimney-hood still remained. The slate-topped table, which a counterweight permitted to be raised and lowers at will, was intact. In one of the corners was the scientist's iron-framed bed, and nearby, heaped up pell-mell, cages containing the asphyxiated cadavers of animals and broken or twisted apparatus.

The disorder was indescribable. Rosamour took it all in at a glance, and advanced further into the middle of the slates and debris, clouds of black soot escaping therefrom under his feet.

He went to the bed and, methodically clearing away the clutter heaped upon it, examined it carefully. It had not been remade since the scientist had slept in it for the last time. There was no visible trace of blood beneath the stains inflicted by the fire, but the agent was surprised, on lifting the covers, to find a crumpled nightshirt and a cotton bonnet thrown carelessly on to the bed.

Two hypotheses presented themselves to the detective's brain. Either the scientist was dressed when he left the apartment, or, if there had been a crime, the murders had stripped their victim naked in order to make him disappear more easily. In any case, it could not be admitted that Monsieur Grillard had been surprised by the fire in his bed.

Rosamour left it until later to have those pieces of evidence taken away in order that he could examine them more closely. Without concerning himself with hem any further, he continued his inspection.

On the top of the stove, in the midst of broken retorts, he noticed objects of bizarre form, and, on approaching, found that there was a collection of motionless small animals, especially frogs. When he reached out to touch one, he observed that the brown color covering it was due to a thick layer of dust and soot. Underneath, the polish of metal appeared. The strange fauna was nickel-plated.

At first, the policeman only looked at all that out of simple curiosity. What connection could the objects have with his own research? But a sudden reflection stopped him.

Had not these metal animals, nickel-plated like the sculptor's statue, been sculpted by the same hand? In that case, they attested that Bémolisant, the sculptor, and his uncle were not such strangers to one another as they appeared to be.

In any case, it was curious to observe works in the home of one of them that had evidently come from that of the other.

Let's put one of these paperweights in my pocket, Rosamour said to himself, continuing his investigations.

In spite of his attention, though, he did not find a single object that put him on a new track, and he was about to leave when his gaze fell upon the slate blackboard. He noticed the outline of letters there, or, rather, the vague traces left by chalk after a rapid and summary erasure.

A man who knew the importance of the smallest details, the policeman approached again, trying to read the inscription. The string of letters was inconsequential, and made no sense.

It was scarcely probable that a scientist like Monsieur Grillard had wasted time on a handwriting exercise, and as the letters were not reminiscent of chemical formulae or mathematical calculations, our man, very intrigued, resolved to clarify the matter.

He searched for a bit of sponge, which he moistened lightly in the bottom of a dish, and dabbed the inscription, without rubbing it, in such a manner as not to erase is any further.

Immediately, thanks to the greater contrast between black and white, the characters stood out with sufficient distinction. There were gaps, unfortunately, but after a rapid examination, Rosamour remained convinced that he was in the presence of a cryptogam.

The most urgent thing was to collect it, at all costs.

Calmly, the policeman took out his cigar-case, to which, in the place where it is often customary to embed a small watch, there was an orifice closed with a lens several centimeters wide. He aimed that eye at the slate board, pressed a small button next to the catch, and, having completed that simple operation, replaced the case in his pocket. He had just photographed the inscription.

That done, and quite tranquilly, he retraced his steps and went back down to the ground floor.

Madame Paponot was waiting for him on the threshold of her lodge.

"Come in and I'll give you a lick with the brush," she said. "You're a little untidy. Well, did you see anything good in the attic?"

"In truth, nothing worth the trouble of going up there," Rosamour replied, in a disenchanted fashion. "Anyway, I'm wasting my time. All this isn't my business; I'm just a journalist. Well, *bonsoir*, Madame Paponot."

"You'll send me the paper in which there's mention of me, won't you?"

"You can count on it..."

Rosamour took away several precious items of information from the theater of the blaze. None, however, was of a nature to extract him from his perplexity. The cryptogram was so truncated that it would certainly not be easily deciphered.

By way of recapitulation, he went over the facts that appeared to him to be established.

First of all, Bémolisant had come to see his uncle. How many times? The concierge affirmed that he could not have made more than one visit; at any rate, he could not have gone past the lodge often without being seen. During his visit on December the thirty-first—the only one clearly established— with the connivance of Pilesèche, he had concealed his identity and the two of them had taken away a heavy box of unusual form.

What could the box have contained? That was perhaps the nub of the problem.

If the laboratory assistant and the nephew had murdered the old man, was it probable that they had enclosed the cadaver in such a box? No; they would have chosen a recipient attracting less attention by virtue of its length. The concierge had said that one might have taken it for a coffin. One does not choose a coffin to transport a body that one wishes to make disappear. One puts it in a trunk of usual appearance, by folding it up. If the box was long, it was because it contained something long and rigid. Furthermore, the weight of a body was insufficient on its own to make it as heavy as it was said to be.

Was it the statue?

But how had it got into the scientist's abode? A statue of that size does not arrive at someone's home without being noticed. It would have been seen on arrival, as on departure...unless the method used to produce it only permitted it to be contrived in the laboratory...

And Rosamour remembered that nickel lent itself to galvanoplastic deposit.

"Bah!" he said. "Bémolisant would have had to come back often for that operation, as well as to establish a mock-up, and until there's proof to the contrary, it's necessary to admit that his visits were rare."

He slapped his forehead.

"Of course!" he added, continuing his monologue. "One session would suffice for a molding from life; perhaps it was a plaster mold that was transported thus. The fellow does; he's molded; and then his cadaver is made to disappear, one way or another. Perhaps it was burned in the laboratory furnace...

213

"Yes, but a mold cut up into pieces doesn't occupy such a great length. I'd rather believe that it was the statue itself, obtained by galvanoplasty, that the two men took away. When I've visited the artist's studio and observed that he hasn't installed any equipment for galvanoplasty, I'll believe that my deduction is the only logical one. And the proof is the toad that I have in my pocket, and which was obtained by the same procedure...

"Come on, let's not get carried away prematurely in hypotheses, and let's not abandon the scientific method for an instant."

The agent took out his watch.

"Good," he murmured. "I still have time to go see Madame Bémolisant and get her to talk."

IX. What Happened at the Artist's House

The artist's domicile had been in a singular disarray since the disappearance of its master.

Bémolisant had announced as he went out that he was going to fetch his statue and collect the fee for its exhibition.

That operation should not have taken long and could not have retained him beyond dinner time. He had been patiently awaited, however, for he had not accustomed his family to overly meticulous punctuality. At eight o'clock, however, the child had been crying; they had fed him and put him to bed. At nine o'clock the women had decided to sit down at table in their turn, but without any great appetite.

"I wouldn't be anxious," Madame Legris said, "if he hadn't collected a considerable sum of money, but these days, you hear about people murdered in the boulevard, which isn't reassuring."

Weary of waiting, at about one o'clock in the morning, the ladies had resigned themselves to going to bed, but at the slightest noise, Madame Bémolisant, who was not asleep, shuddered, thinking that she could hear someone at the door.

Early the next morning, she went to the Rue de Sèze, where no one could tell her anything; all that anyone knew was that the artist had collected five thousand francs, had taken the statue and left in a fiacre with another man, who had joined him.

She went home and imparted that discovery to her mother, all of whose attention was immediately focused on the high figure of the receipts.

"Five thousand francs!" she said. "That would come in handy, for our capital is considerably eroded. I don't suppose your husband has thought of spending it all on his own..."

"Oh, Maman, you know Népomucène; he's incapable of such an action. He has his faults, I grant you, but he's honest and disinterested."

"Then it's necessary to go to the police and ask that they make the necessary investigation."

Hélène set forth and asked for directions to the local commissariat. When she went in, she approached an employee timidly, who was leaning back in his chair stretching his arms.

"What do you want?" he asked.

"Monsieur le Commissaire?"

"He's gone out. What do you have to say to him?"

"It's just that...I'd like to speak to him..."

"Since I've told you that he's gone out, if you don't want to say what brings you here, you can go away."

He picked up his newspaper "It's just that...it might be urgent."

"Well then, explain yourself."

"My husband didn't come home last night."

"Ha ha ha!" chuckled the clerk. "It happens."

"He'd just collected a large sum of money."

"What a rogue. Go on, make your declaration." He had reached out a hand to pick up a printed form, which he filled in as he interrogated the young woman and as she replied.

When he had finished, he said, by way of conclusion: "That's that. You can go home, little lady, and sleep tranquilly. Husbands don't get lost. They always turn up."

Hélène was no more reassured by that imbecile's comments than by the verbiage of her mother, who found every consolation.

"Listen," she said to her daughter when she came back come. "Népomucène isn't the husband you need. He's a crackpot, and I groan every day over the circumstances that forced me, in Tonkin, to give him to you as a husband. It wouldn't be any great loss, you see..."

"But with all his faults, he's my husband!"

"A colonial husband! The most unfortunate thing is that he's disappeared with the money, just at the moment when—I don't know how—he'd created a certain celebrity. Oh, perhaps it's a stroke of luck after all, for he wouldn't have been able to sustain his renown."

"But since he'd succeeded in making that statue..."

"There's something incomprehensible in that, you know. A statue doesn't sprout overnight like a mushroom. He can say that he wanted to give us a surprise, but we'd have seen him making the mock-up, coming and going, and the model...and the founder...what do I know? I repeat, I scent trickery."

"It doesn't matter. I'm very anxious."

"You're playing your role..."

The discussion was interrupted by the arrival of a visitor, who insinuated himself into the apartment as soon as the door was ajar, and said, as he handed over his card: "Is it to Madame Bémolisant that I have the honor of speaking?"

"Yes, Monsieur," Hélène replied, while she scanned the piece of cardboard with her eyes, and read: *Isidore Boissonnald, Enquiry Agent, Director of Family Security.*

"Madame," said the short man, taking a seat that no one had offered him, "my card indicates to you the kind of business in which I'm occupied: it's principally research in the interests of families. I can say without boasting that I've never taken charge of an affair without seeing it through to the end. My agents are all possessed of a skill that one doesn't encounter in the official police, for the simple reason that it's necessary to pay talent what it's worth. I'm not miserly with them, but, on the contrary, I'm extremely easy-going with families. We get paid by results, and except for a small fee to cover our expenses we don't receive any money until we have succeeded. Finally, you can be sure of our most complete discretion. My motto is *Hush!* and my blazon, a finger over lips..."

During this little speech, Hélène examined the singular visitor, whose broad face framed by slack cheeks was illuminated by a perpetual vague smile beneath a fleeting and uncertain gaze.

"Monsieur," she said finally, "I don't quite understand what you want with me..."

The other took on an expression of afflicted and discreet condolence.

"Oh, my God, Madame, it's quite simple! My agency has learned, at an early hour, of the disappearance…the cruel disappearance"—he emphasized the addition—"of the eminent artist whose wife you are, and I have come to offer you my services to find him."

"I don't believe I should hide it from you that I've already approached the commissariat. Perhaps it's necessary to wait for the result."

"Oh, Madame, don't be under any illusion. The Prefecture won't do anything. Act yourself, don't waste any time, for searches are much more difficult when they're belated."

At the same time the officious individual inspected the furniture which was not of a kind to give a high idea of the resources of the family and the remuneration that might be expected therefrom.

"But in sum, Monsieur," said the young woman, "what do you think of this disappearance?"

"I must confess that we avoid all hazardous and premature hypotheses; we only occupy ourselves with affairs with which we are charged. If you would like to pay us a modest sum of a hundred and fifty francs for our initial research, I will be able to tell you shortly what it is necessary to think of this occurrence. Then, depending on the difficulty of the ulterior research, according to whether there has been a murder, a sequestration or a flight, and, finally, whether it is necessary to operate in France or abroad, I shall quote you a simple, categorical and definitive fee."

"Permit me to consult my mother, for, in truth, I'm very embarrassed," Hélène relied, after a moment's hesitation.

But Madame Legris, as soon as she was brought up to date, hastened to declare the she saw no opportunity for that expense.

"Think about it," said the enquiry agent. "Perhaps you'll reproach yourself later for having neglected such a justified step. The sum for which I'm asking scarcely covers my initial expenses. Anyway, you have my address, and I shall come again tomorrow to obtain our definitive reply.

He stood up and headed for the door, slowly, like a man who still hopes that there might be a change of mind, but he was allowed to depart, and as he went out backwards he collided with a man who was just reaching out for the electric bell-push.

Isidore Boissonnald turned around and darted an oblique glance at the newcomer, a man correctly dressed, who stood side to let him pass.

Madame Bémolisant could not hide. She allowed the new visitor to come in, slightly annoyed by all these disturbances.

"I shall not employ any subterfuge or artifice with you, Madame," said the newcomer, without any preamble. "My name is Rosamour, but that will tell you nothing. I have come to collect some information from you regarding your husband's disappearance."

"I'm desolate, Monsieur, but the agent who his just left has already proposed to make a similar search..."

She held out the card that she was still holding to Rosamour. Without taking it, the policeman darted a negligent glance at it.

"...And I refused his proposal," Hélène continued, before having had a response from the Prefecture of Police, to which I made my declaration."

"Good! Precisely—I've been charged by the Prefecture to ask you various questions that will aid us in the research that you have requested."

"That's different. Please sit down, Monsieur."

"First of all, what indications do you have regarding the present whereabouts of your husband?"

"None, Monsieur, and as he had just collected some money, I can only suppose one thing, alas, which is that he has been drawn into some trap."

Rosamour was perhaps not absolutely of the same opinion, but he did not let anything show and contented himself with asking a few questions about the employment of the sculptor's day.

"I'm obliged," he added, "also to obtain information about your family situation. You must excuse me, Madame, but our task is delicate and seemingly insignificant indications are sometimes flashes of enlightenment for us. You live with Madame your mother and a child. I have no need to ask you whether Monsieur Bémolisant was a model husband?"

"He never went out."

"Good. Does he have relatives?"

"An old uncle that he never sees, because they'd quarreled."

"Monsieur Grillard."

"That's right. Do you know him?"

Rosamour made an equivocal gesture that might have passed for a negation. "But I'm told that the uncle and nephew had been reconciled, to such an extent that Monsieur Bémolisant had made a statue of his uncle. It must, therefore, have been necessary for him to visit him quite often?"

"I don't know; so far as I know, he only saw Monsieur Grillard once."

"On December the thirty-first, no?"

"Precisely. It's an easy date to remember. I even recall that Népomucène came back late and went up to his studio with Monsieur Pilesèche, his uncle's laboratory assistant, so that, when they didn't come down for lunch, I went up to knock on his door. It was one o'clock and he hadn't thought of going to table."

"Did the Messieurs seem a trifle emotional, overexcited?"

"Your question reminds me that they did, in fact, have a slightly singular air. Monsieur Pilesèche had even taken off his coat and dusted it, which seemed bizarre to me. But it's not astonishing that they were a little overexcited, for that was the day when Monsieur Leroux had convinced my husband to exhibit his work."

"Ah! His statue was finished?"

"Yes, it had just been brought."

"Monsieur Bémolisant had been occupied with the statue for a long time?"

"I can tell you that I'd never heard mention of it before."

"That's odd."

"All the odder because my husband likes to talk about the artistic ideas that are on his mind."

Good, thought Rosamour. *There's a statue that no one has mentioned the day before, and whose arrival coincides with the visit to the uncle. That's what was in the box; that much is evident. But it doesn't help us to discover what has become of the original.*

After that aside he resumed: "And you've doubtless informed Monsieur Grillard of his nephew's disappearance?"

"No, Monsieur. I confess that the idea never occurred to me. I don't know him at all, personally, and he doesn't seem to be desirous of making my acquaintance."

"And since then you've had no news of him?"

"No, Monsieur. When the laboratory assistant came here in recent days I asked about him, because the worthy Monsieur Pilesèche never talks about him otherwise. The poor man is very ill, he told me."

"Well, Madame," the policeman said then, in his most solemn tone, emphasizing his words, "I can be more explicit. The house in which your uncle lived burned down yesterday, and Monsieur Grillard has disappeared."

"In the flames?" asked Madame Bémolisant, whom Rosamour was observing from the corner of his eye, but whose face expressed nothing but the sharpest surprise and the most sincere horror.

"I don't believe so."

"But what is it necessary to suppose, then? Monsieur Grillard was ill and couldn't leave his room. Someone must have removed him!"

"All suppositions are admissible; it's all a matter of finding the right one. Who are Monsieur Grillard's heirs?"

"My husband and his cousin Sophie, who is at the convent of Fontenay-sous-Bois," Madame Bémolisant replied, without hesitation. "You believe that a thief...?"

"I don't believe anything, Madame. Until now, I haven't settled on any hypothesis. But I can't hide from you any longer that this disappearance, coinciding with that of your husband and Monsieur Pilesèche, who was with him, permits the gravest suspicions.

"Oh! Monsieur, you're frightening me. You've taken a solemn tone. Good God, what is it? What are these suppositions?"

It was evident that the young woman was sincere and knew nothing; it would not have been possible to play a learned role so perfectly.

"Can one not suppose," the policeman added, measuring the effect of his words, "that the laboratory assistant and your husband have something to do with the old man's disappearance?"

"I don't understand," Hélène replied, with a naivety that was not feigned.

"Monsieur Bémolisant saw Monsieur Grillard on the thirty-first of December. Admit for a moment that the latter received his nephew with some sarcasm; a dispute might have followed. Your husband is quick-tempered, impatient—you recognize that yourself. He might have been carried away, and in a moment of anger..."

"Enough, Monsieur, enough! Your supposition wounds me, and I can't tolerate the formation of such an accusation in my presence."

She had risen to her feet, cold and dignified, her hand extended in an energetic gesture. But Rosamour, without quitting his chair and without departing from his calmness, continued in the same tone of voice.

"You're wrong to get so excited so soon," he said. "One doesn't respond to an explicit accusation with a disdainful silence. I'm pointing out a danger to you; it's necessary to confront it and tackle the enemy hand-to hand."

"My husband, a murderer!"

"Unintentionally."

"No, Monsieur, it's not possible. You're lying..."

"It's not me that it's necessary to accuse, for the hypothesis isn't mine. Furthermore, I will say that I'm seeking the truth without any prejudice. But it's up to you, Madame, since you're sure of your husband's innocence, to help me bring it to light. I've told you the hypothesis that will seem the most plausible to many people; do you have another to put in its place?"

"What do you want me to say? I'm overwhelmed by that frightful accusation. It's a hammer-blow that has stunned me, and I can only cry loudly in the ardor of my conviction that he's innocent!"

"That is unfortunately insufficient to counter the charges against him. But you can see the frankness with which I'm acting toward you; return the favor. Trust me. Be sure that nothing would give me greater joy than demonstrating Monsieur Bémolisant's innocence, if he is innocent. Think, then! Everything accuses him, and I have to destroy that scaffolding. It's a task worthy of me. I'm speaking to you as an artist, after having spoken to you as a man, for I have a heart, you see; I'm accessible to pity, to generous sentiments, and when I see a weak individual in tears, a woman devoid of support, I'm always tempted to spring to her defense...

"It's agreed, then; henceforth, we're allies. You'll help me as much as you can to discover the truth. But it's understood that you'll speak without any afterthought, that you won't hide anything from me under the pretext that it might be unfavorable to your thesis. I'm a confessor; it's necessary to tell me everything."

Finally, resignedly, she said: "Question me, Monsieur. I'll answer."

The conversation was a long one. In spite of the excellent memory on which he pried himself, Rosamour took notes.

When he parted from Madame Bémolisant, he addressed a few words of encouragement to her. "Have confidence," he said, "and whatever happens, don't worry. I don't know whether I'll be able to come back to see you soon; I might be forced to depart on a journey sooner than I would wish—but even if you don't hear mention of me, have no fear; I'll be watching and working."

He headed for the door. "Oh," he said, turning round. "If the gentleman who was leaving as I arrived comes back, send him away—and above all, don't tell him anything. He's one of those swindlers who only seeks to fish in troubled waters."

When Rosamour was back in the street, he lit a cigar philosophically and hummed a tune from an operetta. *It wouldn't take much*, he thought, *for that poor woman's conviction to persuade me. Instinctively, moreover, it seems to me that they're two imbeciles who are running away naively, without having killed anyone. At any rate, Madame Bémolisant is a precious auxiliary in finding them. But where's the body?*

He went into a small restaurant, where he ate a hasty meal, and prepared to make a tour of the editorial offices of the principal newspapers. His principle was that the press ought, for anyone who knew how to play the game, to be the best auxiliary of the examining magistrate and the policemen—but it was necessary, for that, not to let it spread indiscreet information as it liked. The best way to make sure of that was to inform it himself.

He recounted the story in his own fashion, enlivening the details that it suited him to publish and not neglecting to say, in accordance with the well-known fallacious formula, that the police were on the track of the mysteriously vanished individuals.

After which, Rosamour hastened to go to bed. He had nothing better to do. Were the reporters not taking charge of the task now?

The following day, in fact, the principal newspapers published long sensational articles under the headline *The Mystery of the Panthéon*, which imparted to the public the marvelous discoveries of their reporters. It was demonstrated, by peremptory reasoning, that the celebrated artist Bémolisant had not been murdered, but had fled with the laboratory assistant of the eminent physiologist Grillard. What means of locomotion had the fugitives employed? In what direction was it necessary to look for them? As many questions calculated to deflect less skilful individuals.

We have, said one of the articles, *discovered the merchant who rented his handcart, and, furnished with an exact description and the number of the vehicle, it was not difficult to assure ourselves that no cart fitting that description has been abandoned in Paris, or even in the suburbs. On the other hand, the package that the artist was carrying is too singular and recognizable for it to have gone unnoticed at a railway station; in reality, the two men have not taken a train. They must have passed through the fortifications on foot, which seems to be confirmed by the declaration of a customs officer at the Porte de Bercy. We shall know before long where the fugitives are. Our reporters and cyclists are departing in all directions.*

Rosamour rubbed his hands.

The next day, a benevolent reader notified a newspaper that he had encountered two travelers answering the description, in a state of complete dilapidation, at Voves, on the Vendôme line, a hundred kilometers from Paris.

"Where the devil are they going?" Rosamour asked himself—and answered himself almost immediately: "To Saint-Nazaire, no doubt. They're counting on embarking there for America. At the rate they're going, I have a week in hand."

He went to give an account of his initial results to the examining magistrate, Monsieur Fischer, who had been taken the mysterious affair in hand, substituting himself for the commissioner. Then he prepared to continue his search.

In order to obtain more precise information he sent a description of the fugitives everywhere, but without issuing any arrest warrant. He wanted to keep track of them and have them watched, but not arrested prematurely.

That description, which he communicated to the press, was a marvel of sagacity.

The Bureau of Anthropometric Measurements had succeeded in reconstituting Bémolisant's characteristic dimensions with the sole aid of a photograph and clothing found at his home. As for Pilesèche, it had been necessary to do without his photograph, none of which existed. From the size of the footwear left at his lodgings it had been concluded that he was about one meter seventy tall—above average. His garments had indicated his corpulence; the traces left by the friction of jutting bones at his elbows, knees and shoulders had furnished other measurements. That was the scientific method, applied in its fullest extent.

When Monsieur Boissonnald came to knock on Madame Bémolisant's door to find out whether the night had given her advice, the artist's wife contented herself with telling him that, on due reflection, she had renounced any further research.

The enquiry agent withdrew, slightly discomfited by the vanishing of a nice windfall; cases being scarce and time being short, it was important not to miss any opportunities that cropped up, but he was particularly vexed to see the ground being cut from under his feet by the Prefecture of Police—for he was not duped by that defeat, having recognized Rosamour, and not doubting for an instant the part the latter had played in his disappointment. If the Prefecture was going to snatch the bread out of his mouth, his métier was going to become impossible.

Enveloping Rosamour in his resentment, he thought, angrily: *I'll pay you back for this. If I can do you a bad turn, in my fashion, you'll be disenchanted before long.*

X. The Result of a Session of Hypnotism

There was a veritable snowstorm that evening, and the wind was shaking the windows of the Cheval Boiteux inn—said to be the best in the village of Briseval, at the end of the bridge over the Loir—rudely.

The frightful weather was not at all to the liking of a fairground performer whose bright leotard could be seen beneath a threadbare overcoat, and who was counting on putting on a little display of his various skills in the main room, where the local bigwigs ordinarily gathered, with the precious assistance of Miss Adda, his acolyte, who was to submit with a good grace to the most curious, amusing and simultaneously instructive experiments in hypnotic suggestion.

The showman put of the commencement of the session as long as possible, for the audience only consisted of two big fellows playing billiards and a few peasants drinking their mazagrans and chatting around a table in the midst of a cloud of smoke.

Miss Adda was sitting next to the stove, from which a damp mist was rising. She was short and thin, with pale, fatigued features, a sad and pensive expression, hiding her pink stockings and short spangled skirt under a grimy tartan deprived for the fringes that had once ornamented it.

The showman, who called himself Professor Joël, was, by contrast, a solid fellow, all muscles; his black hair was plastered over his narrow forehead by pomade. His sharp face was provided with a superb aquiline nose beneath which extended the long waxed tips of a shiny moustache. He was striding back and forth impatiently in front of the stove, slowly sipping a glass of eau-de-vie.

An old woman was knitting at the counter, indifferent to everything that was not a purchase.

Suddenly, the door opened under a gust of wind, which entered violently, chasing snow and cold into the overheated room, and with it came the two strangest individuals imaginable.

Imagine two tall bodies in long frock coats, their shoulders disappearing under the snow, collars turned up over the icy rivers of their beards, clutching unspeakable top hats. Their shoes were enveloped in muddy snowballs, while long yellow streaks climbed the legs of frayed, worn trousers that were crying mercy.

"The door! The door!" clamored the chorus of young peasants, who knew about city ways.

One of the newcomers, blinded by the light and the warm vapor of the inn turned round awkwardly, grabbed the batten of the door, which was banging on the wall, and sealed the hole though which the wind was blowing.

Then both of them let themselves fall on to the nearest bench, a few paces away from Miss Adda, whom that abrupt interruption had snatched from her reverie and was staring at them with an extinct gaze. They seemed half-dead of cold and fatigue. The shorter one nevertheless stood up and went toward the innkeeper.

"Madame," he said, his jaw numbed by cold and scarcely capable of articulating the words, "be good enough to give us some good hot soup, quickly, and a bottle of wine. After that, we'll see."

The worthy woman inspected their sorry state—but, given the frightful weather, who would have looked any better? She hastened to bring them what they wanted, and when she uncovered the fuming soup-tureen, the man said to the hostess, but not very loudly, as if in a confidential tone: "We have a crate on a handcart with us; we've put it in the shed. Please keep an eye on it."

"People hereabouts aren't in the habit of stealing," the old woman snapped.

"It wouldn't be easy to take away, I know—but still, it's necessary that you know that it's ours."

"All right. Are you staying here overnight?"

"Yes, let us have a small room."

Then they began eating like starvelings, without saying anything more. Miss Adda was staring at them obstinately, and involuntarily. As soon as they had come in, a magnetic force had imposed itself on her will, making her turn her head in their direction. Her gaze was drawn to one of them in particular, whose tall gangling body was bent over his plate.

The two travelers asked what else could be served to them, and in the blink of an eye had swallowed a bowl of mutton stew and a large chunk of cheese.

That substantial repast seemed to cheer them up. They sat back on the bench with a certain air of satisfaction, as hot coffee was brought to them.

"Oof! That's better," gasped the older one. "I was absolutely done in."

"We're not out of difficulty yet, my dear Pil...my dear friend," the other replied. "We're not half way yet."

They were talking in low voices, leaning toward one another.

"In spite of everything, we ought to count ourselves lucky, the way things are going, and if it weren't for those damned newspapers talking about us and making me anxious. I could believe that we'd been forgotten."

"Yes, but you read that note in the *Figaro*."

"Bah! The papers want to seem well-informed. If they were on our track, we'd have been arrested already, damn it."

"I wish I could share your confidence."

At the same moment, two gendarmes came in, immediately followed by a traveler enveloped in an ample fur coat.

The arrival of those worthy representatives of the authority appeared to disturb the two travelers. They huddled over a newspaper, the reading of which suddenly seemed to absorb them completely. The gendarmes paid no heed to them, and went to sit down in a corner, with their usual solemn tread.

The young man who had come in after them began by darting a circular glance around the room, and, perceiving the readers, who did not succeed in hiding their faces completely, he came to sit down not far away from them, looking at them with a satisfied expression.

Well, thought the newcomer, *chance has favored me, and I'll telegraph my fortunate discovery to the paper*.

When he questioned the innkeeper, however, as she poured him a glass of hot punch, he learned with some disappointment that the Briseval telegraph office closed at seven o'clock in the evening, and would not open again until seven in the morning. It was necessary to resign himself, and, as reportage never loses its rights, he resolved at least to interview the people he seemed to be seeking or pursuing. He only needed some incident to give him the opportunity.

He had not overlooked the gendarmes, and laughed covertly as he lit a cigarette. *Those brave soldiers of the law, who are sipping quietly in their corner, have no suspicion that the two criminals who about whom all Paris is talking are four strides way from their kepis. It's not me who'll tell them—I'm a reporter, not a detective.*

As for the two individuals he was considering so lightly as criminals, they had seen the reporter come in, but he had been too well wrapped up in his furs for much of his face to be visible. Now that he was sitting down, by contrast, his overcoat was ajar. Bémolisant, who was watching him from the corner of his eye, could not suppress a gesture of bewilderment, and he leaned toward Pilesèche.

"We're no longer safe," he said. "There's someone who knows us."

"Are you sure?"

"I've seen that face before somewhere. Hang on…the memory's coming back. He's a journalist who came to interview me once."

"And you think he's recognized you?"

"I'd bet on it. Who can tell whether he might be here tracking us, in order to be the first to report our arrest?"

"You're frightening me. That journalist, those gendarmes…we're doomed, then!"

"Keep quiet—but let's try to slip away."

From that moment on, they maneuvered as adroitly as possible in order to leave the room without attracting attention, but to complete their misfortune, the showman, judging that no one else was likely to turn up at that late hour, had taken off his overcoat and was blocking the internal door by means of which the fugitives had planned to escape.

The performer commenced his patter.

"Mesdames et Messieurs," he said, "I have the honor of submitting to your competent attention a few curious experiments that have earned me the suffrage of highly placed people, and even crowned heads. I shall begin by doing a few card tricks and feats of strength, in order to get my hand in and develop my magnetic fluid. After that, I shall have the honor of introducing you to a remarkable subject whom Doctors Bernheim and Charcot[37] have tried to lure away from me with gold. I shall submit you thereafter to experiments in somnambulism, hypnotism, Mesmerism, suggestion and catalepsy; these experiments are absolutely unprecedented and new, astonishing and mysterious creations that have no relationship with those of certain charlatans who call themselves, alas, my colleagues, have been able to put before you. Everyone knows that Professor Joël is no charlatan. I could, like some people I could name, earn a great deal of money with trickery, but I have always preferred the art and the science."

After that brief introduction, the session commenced.

---

[37] The neurologists Hippolyte Bernheim (1840-1919) and Jean-Martin Charcot (1825-1893). The former developed the theory of suggestibility in attempting to account for the phenomena of hypnotism, while the latter made extensive use of hypnotism in his famous investigations of "hysteria" at the Salpêtrière.

The first part, in which only Professor Joël was in play, offered nothing of particular interest, except for the extraordinary dexterity of the experimenter, who juggled with his cards and made them do whatever he wanted.

When he had finished, he announced that Miss Adda was going to prepare for her appearance, while he made a tour of the amiable society, which would want to recompense the skill of his performance and encourage him for the sequel.

The two travelers who had been first to arrive, in whom the reader will have had no difficulty recognizing Bémolisant and Pilesèche, did not have to be begged to put their obol in the bowl; that generous gesture reassured the landlady, who was watching them from the corner of her eyes, that they were definitely not penniless vagabonds, as she had briefly feared.

In the meantime, the young woman had risen to her feet and thrown her tartan over a chair. Her eyes, atonal a little while before, were now shining with a feverish light. She braced herself in her satin corsage, which creaked, and beneath the body of a sickly child, a kind of innate distinction was definable, which the abjection of her métier had not succeeded in obliterating entirely.

She advanced at a languid pace, swaying on her hips with the customary gait of a ballerina. The showman tightened the hem of her skirt with a leather strap.

"We're going to begin," he said, finally, "with a few experiments in catalepsy. Catalepsy, Mesdames et Messieurs, is one of the phases of hypnotic sleep. Similar to death, it gives the body a cadaverous rigidity. The muscles tense with a superhuman force. You're going to see each of this frail creature's limbs become as stiff as a steel bar.

He had grasped her by the wrists, and, looking into her eyes twenty centimeters from her face, he concentrated all the force of his being in the fixed gaze.

The most complete silence reigned in the inn, where all the audience members were waiting, leaning forward, hypnotized themselves, reluctantly intrigued, and holding their breath.

Half a minute was sufficient. Suddenly, Miss Adda fell into the arms of the strong man. The latter made a sign to Pilesèche, who happened to be closest to him.

"Come and help me, Monsieur, I beg you."

At that appeal, the laboratory assistant felt very ill-at-ease, not wanting to put himself so much in evidence, but his companion shoved him—would not a refusal have attracted more attention?

"Come, come," insisted Joël. "You're not going to leave me alone with this charming burden in my arms?"

Pilesèche stood up and advanced toward them.

"Bring up a chair, please. Lift Miss Adda up by the feet and place them on the edge of the chair, while I place her head on a second support.

And the young woman, completely rigid, was suspended like a bridge, only supported by her heels and the back of her neck.

An "Ah!" of astonishment ran round the room.

"Oh, don't exclaim yet. This is nothing—and to give you a better idea of the strength of the tensed muscles, the Monsieur who is helping me will prove to you that a frail woman can carry him without buckling." He had placed a napkin over the subject's body. "Climb up, Monsieur," he added. "Climb up without fear."

The other did not want to.

"Climb up, since he says so," clamored the impatient peasants.

He made his decision, and stood up on the rigid body.

"Weigh upon her as heavily as you like," said the showman. "Are you scared of falling?"

Miss Adda did not budge under the burden, and more than a wooden beam.

"Well, Messieurs, you can see that the subject supports eighty kilos without flinching. What do say to that? But look, solely by the force of my gaze, I shall now return flexibility to her muscles. Don't move, Monsieur..."

He gazed fixedly at certain tensor muscles, which gradually gave way. The body sank down gradually, as of the bridge were breaking in the middle—but when the operator ceased gazing, the immobility became complete again.

"Now we'll return her to her original position—and all, Messieurs, by the power of my gaze alone."

And the body straightened, obedient to the imperious will that commanded it, lifting the laboratory assistant up again.

"Take note that the insensibility is complete," the operator continued. "Approach, Messieurs; you can prick or pinch the subject; she won't feel a thing... Now, if you're completely convinced, we're going to wake Miss Adda up and pass on to recreative experiments in somnambulism and suggestion."

Pilesèche had got down.

Joël blew on the closed eyes of the young woman, and spread out his hands, as if to draw away the fluid. Miss Adda uttered a sigh, and Joël supported her at the moment when, waking up, she was about to collapse on the floor.

The audience cried "Bravo!" and started clapping, but the professor stopped them with a gesture.

"Some of my colleagues, to deceive their audience, make passes and grimaces, roll up their sleeves and assume diabolical attitudes, but Messieurs, nothing is simpler than hypnosis; I'll show you how true savants operate. Pay attention!"

At the same time, he clicked his fingers in front of Miss Adda's eyes. She, suddenly gripped by the gaze, started following the fingers everywhere they went, in abrupt zigzags, twisting her body in order not to lose sight of the digits that had hypnotized her, leaning over backwards in atrocious equilibria, her eyes wide open.

That went on for a few minutes.

After that fatiguing activity, Miss Adda was woken up again, and set forth on a little quest of her own. Professor Joël announced that he was about to go from strength to strength— "as chez Nicolet"—and, in accordance with suggestions with which the audience would collaborate, he would show his

233

gratitude for the flattering attention that was being lent to him by making some experiments in second sight,

That alluring program proceeded with increasing interest, and Pilesèche, gradually forgetting his present situation, recovered his old enthusiasm for science. He had an increasing desire to substitute himself for the charlatan, crying to him: "Friend, what you're doing is merely the infancy of the art. I've known many other things for a long time, Let me take your place, and you'll see!"

Without having to be begged now, as soon as the magnetizer asked for assistance, he presented himself, and as he guessed in advance what the other desired, his actions came to a nominated point neatly and precisely, so that Joël could no longer reckon him a simple curiosity-seeker.

Thus, during a brief pause, the impressed operator whispered in his ear; "You're in the game, eh, my dear chap?"

"Not exactly, but I have a few tricks up my sleeve."

"Messieurs!" cried the professor, no longer worrying about his assent, and turning to his audience, "I'd like to introduce a little diversity into the session, and this Monsieur will show you a few experiments of his own. You'll be able to see that there's no trickery involved, and that Miss Adda is a truly remarkable subject."

"He's an accomplice!" someone shouted.

"Get away!" shouted the others.

And Pilesèche, enfevered, no longer thinking about anything but science, set about realizing the most difficult and marvelous experiments. In his hands, the young woman was an instrument of extreme sensitivity. She shivered as soon as he looked at her, and it only required a simple imposition of his hands to make her pass through all the phases of the strange state, still so little known, in which the human organism seems, step by step, to live distinct lives successively, progressing further and further toward an acuity of perception so keen that it extends across time and space. Miss Adda seemed to be under his complete dependency, drawn to him by

234

an irresistible force, never taking her eyes off him, even during hr periods of lucidity.

"The two of us could do great things," said Professor Joël, his eyes widening in their turn.

"More, more!" cried the members of the audience, stamping their feet in enthusiasm.

The gendarmes had risen to their feet, open-mouthed in surprise at all that sorcery. The reporter brought his hands together in his pockets, with the curious instinct of his métier. Only Bémolisant did not abandon himself to the general fever, thinking that it would have been more prudent to slip away.

The young woman, sitting on a chair with her eyes closed, with Pilesèche behind her, drawn up to his full height, his hair thrown back, his eyes bright and his left hand on the subject's had

"Can you see?" he asked.

"Yes, said the other, softly, with some effort. "I can see a little, but take me further."

Pilesèche pressed down harder on her hair.

"Ah!" Miss Adda continued, as if a veil had been torn away. "I can see! I can see!"

The laboratory assistant extended his right hand. The audience was mute, held in suspense. But suddenly, in a lower voice, in the midst of the silence, and with a gesture of fear, she said: "Oh! Poor man, poor man, save yourself! You're being pursued. Be careful—they know who you are and where you are."

The laboratory assistant shivered. His face went pale, and his entire body was shaken by a nervous tremor.

Everyone's eyes were fixed on him now.

Some were laughing, not knowing what was happening. But the gendarmes were also looking at the singular operator. They looked at one another and started talking in whispers—and one of them, taking a piece of paper from his pocket, seemed to be comparing the individual with a description.

"It's him," he said, in a low voice, to his companion. "There's no arrest warrant, but we can't let the opportunity pass."

And, heading toward the traveler slowly, like a man going about his business who is not about to let his target escape, he said in a loud voice: "Monsieur Pilesèche, I arrest you."

Bémolisant stood up abruptly, He looked for a way out, but the second gendarme, turning toward him, spread out his arms.

"Don't try to leave, I beg you," he said, in his turn.

"What is all this?" cried the audience members, absolutely astounded.

The gendarmes were glad to display their sagacity. "They're the murderers of the Panthéon quarter," they said, simply.

"Oh!"

At that reproving cry, everyone stood back, leaving the two accomplices in the hands of the authority.

"My word!" murmured the reporter. "I had nothing to do with it—but what a fine telegram in the morning!"

"Damn it, gendarmes" cried the professor, gripped by a fit of philanthropy and gratitude toward the man who had lent him his assistance. "Let me at least post bail for the criminals!"

"Thank you very much," replied Bémolisant, in a dignified tone, "but we're not criminals, and we don't accept charity." The artist, who had been so afraid of being caught a little while before, had recovered his courage now that he was a prisoner.

"Brigadier," said the reporter, presenting his card to the gendarme. "I'm Jean Saure, a journalist well known even in this remote region. Will you allow me to ask these Messieurs a few questions?"

"Are you mocking the public force? A journalist? What does that matter to me? Address yourself to the public prosecutor."

"Very well, grim soldier; I shall fall back in good order."

The gendarmes had carefully bound the prisoners' wrists.

"And now, right turn, and march!" said the brigadier. "To prison!"

XI. In which the birds are flushed out

Briseval's prison was the vulgar lock-up that ornaments the Mairie of any self-respecting village: a small, dark, narrow cell wedged under the staircase, designed to hold incorrigible drunkards rather than hardened criminals. It was not used often, not because people were any more virtuous in Briseval than elsewhere, but because there was an indulgent sympathy there for the joyful lovers of the local drinking den.

The principal usage of the cell was to serve as a storeroom for the instruments of the town's brass band.

The corners of the cell were furnished with spiders' webs, with their tenants, and water was dripping down the walls of the low and poorly-ventilated room. It was scarcely possible open the door, let alone close it again.

When the two prisoners found themselves anyone in that obscurity, they let themselves fall on to the dusty planks that served as a camp bed and remained silent for a moment, overwhelmed by the horror of their situation.

The wind was blowing through the ill-fitted planks of the door, and the poor fellows were numb with cold.

"A bad night is soon passed," said Pilesèche, finally, "and we'll be taken before an examining magistrate tomorrow. I'd as soon get it over with as drag out my sad existence along the highways. What do you expect? I'm not made for adventures."

"And as you can't demonstrate your innocence, you'll rot in a cell until they drag you to the assizes, where an idiot jury will convict you, and you'll take your head to the scaffold, for a crime you haven't committed!"

"Brrr! You're sending cold chills down my spine. But what the hell! Since we're caught, let's be fatalistic, and let our destiny work itself out..."

237

"You can say that if you like—me, I'd prefer to save myself if there's a means."

"It's only in novels that one digs tunnels under the walls to escape from prison."

"But this badly-closed room isn't a prison; there must be a way of getting out of it."

Pilesèche shook the door. "It's solid, at any rate," he said, "And the lock's enormous."

"Come on, my friend, my good Pilesèche, we don't have time to waste, and those damned gendarmes are bound to be back first thing in the morning. Think hard. Do you need tools? Here's my knife, for they forgot to search us."

"Listen—I'll give it a try. I noticed that this cell is under the staircase. If the steps aren't made of stone, it might be possible to attack them."

Groping with his fingertips, he approached the declivity formed by the ceiling of the cell. The point of the knife succeeded in chipping away a few flakes of plaster and laid bare a simple lattice, easy to destroy. Behind it there was nothing but a wooden step—but the oak boards were solid and well-fitted; the knife was chipped and there was a risk that it might break.

Picking up a bench, Pilesèche made use of it as a lever, leaning it on a second bench placed at right angles. The step, retained by notch-boards, bent in the middle, and Bémolisant took advantage of that opportunity give a vigorous blow to the vertical plank that served as a counter-step, and which, being less thick, gave way easily enough.

All that made a lot of noise, but people are accustomed to paying no attention to the racket made by a caged prisoner; people in a lock-up do not behave like angels.

The prisoner listened briefly to see of anything abnormal succeed the noise, and then, squeezing through the opening they had contrived, they found themselves in the vestibule of the Mairie. Their captors had thought they had done enough by locking the doors, and, by virtue of habit, had left the keys to the interior doors in the locks. Everything was going smoothly.

The fugitives hesitated as to the direction to take, and finally decided to go out via the gardens, after having locked the door and thrown the key into a field.

The squall had calmed down, chasing away the clouds, and the moon's silvery rays were reflecting from the snow.

As soon as they had escaped the enclosures and were in open country, Pilesèche signaled to his companion that he could not leave the body of his former employer at the mercy of the local people.

"Just think," he said. "What if, by chance, he were still alive!"

"Oh, again…!"

"It doesn't matter—it's a scruple you ought to share. Follow the road, walking slowly, while I go back to the inn. Don't worry—no one will see me. I'll get the cart and catch up with you in a few minutes. If I'm caught, too bad—save yourself, without worrying about me, and...good luck."

Bémolisant hesitated over letting his companion take the risk alone, but the other would find it easier to get himself out of trouble that way, so, all things having been considered, they split up.

Pilesèche started running, sticking close to the walls. The snow stifled the sound of his footfalls.

He had no difficulty reaching the courtyard of the inn and slipped into the shed—but the place where he had left the cart a few hours before was now empty.

Assuming that the gendarmes had taken possession of that piece of evidence, he retraced his steps rapidly, and as soon as he had caught up with his companion they both moved behind the hedge bordering the road, so that they could walk while sheltered from view.

They made haste, to the extent that the fresh snow, in which they sank ankle-deep, permitted.

Suddenly, they perceived by means of the moonlight a vehicle stopped on the road a hundred paces ahead of them. They moved closer with caution.

There, its wheels caught in the snow, was one of those large fairground caravans, whose vast flanks can accommodate an entire family, with the accessories of their trade.

Between its shafts, a single meager horse was striving to drag the heavy machine, and its panting breath, condensed by the cold, was forming a cloud of vapor around its head. A man was encouraging it with a forceful reinforcement of oaths and whiplashes, while a woman was trying to push one of the wheels.

The two fugitives moved closer, and we not a little surprised to see, attached behind the vehicle, a little handcart which bore a strong resemblance to their own, and recognized, in the charioteer and his acolyte, the performers of the previous evening.

They told themselves that there might be some advantage to be gained from the situation, and that in any case, they were not running any great risk in revealing themselves to a man who, by virtue of his profession, must be more often at odds with the police than with malefactors.

Quitting the shelter provided by the hedge, therefore, they leapt out on to the road and marched resolutely toward the performers.

Professor Joël saw them, and recognized them immediately. He was evidently wondering what disposition the two dangerous criminals might have toward him, but he was vigorous and scarcely accessible to fear. At any rate, he remained prudently in position, ready to receive them in case of aggression.

The two men did not seem to be paying any attention to the handcart that had been stolen from them, however, and Joël was the first to speak, in a good-humored tone.

"Well, well, Messeigneurs—so we've given the gentlemen of the constabulary the slip!"

"Monsieur," said Bémolisant, "you don't know us, but we swear to you that we're honest men. There's been a mistake. Help us to get out of it, and give us shelter in our vehicle."

"We're no longer as proud as we were yesterday evening. Personally, I don't see anything in your difficulties with the police, but to offer you the hospitality of my house would be a little risky. The gendarmes are after you, and I don't want them on my back."

Miss Adda gazed at her Master with an imploring expression, without daring to say a word but gripped by a supreme pity.

"It would be so easy for you to hide us in the back of your vehicle," hazarded Pilesèche.

Bémolisant joined in with more solid arguments.

"We're not without money," he said, "and we'd be grateful for your hospitality. Combining actions with words, he took a five-hundred-franc bill out of his wallet.

Five hundred francs!

Joël's eyes gleamed with covetousness. Five hundred francs! These people, so poorly dressed, must be very great criminals to have five hundred francs in their possession. Where the devil had they stolen that money? After all, that wasn't his business. His fingers stretched out toward the blue piece of paper, which disappeared immediately into some pocket or other.

"Come on," he said, "let's not waste time here. Give me a hand to get my wheels out of this accursed snow, and perhaps we can come to some arrangement."

The two men applied themselves to the wheels, while Joël whipped the horse, which, having recovered its breath, put sudden pressure on its collar and succeeded in getting under way again.

"Now let's chat," said the mountebank. "I'd like to get you out of difficulty, but one good turn deserves another. You doubtless still have a few notes in your pocket. Hire my outfit and you can remain my associates, and least as far as Nantes. I'm dreaming of spectacular shows and phenomenal receipts." He addressed Pilesèche. "You play the hypnotist like no one." He turned back to Bémolisant and added: "And you must have some hidden talent?"

"I play all kinds of musical instruments pleasantly," the artist replied, modestly.

"That's perfect." In a detached tone, he added: "I won't hide it from you that I thought to render you a real service by getting rid of the cart and the crate that you neglected to take to prison; all that might have fallen into the hands of the gendarmerie. It's no trouble. I've even committed the indiscretion of looking to see what's in the box. As an anatomical specimen it's not bad. We'll exhibit it and I'll take change of the patter. Now it's time to hide; dawn's about to break. Climb inside with Miss Adda.

They did not need to have the suggestion repeated.

In the depths of the vehicle there was an immense wicker basket. Joël explained to them that it was the nacelle of a balloon that he used for ascensions in large towns where there as a chance of suitable receipts. The two fugitives climbed into the nacelle, over a clutter of objects of every sort. Adda carefully arranged the rigging of the balloon, which succeeded in hiding them from view without inconveniencing them.

"You'll be in clover there," said the showman, laughing broadly. "At the slightest alert, burrow down under that mass of fabric—they won't find you under all that."

The side road that the caravan had been following had joined the highway again, where the snow was not as deep and required less effort from the emaciated horse that was pulling the mobile house. The showman climbed on to the driving seat, with Miss Adda by his side, still silent, but emotional without showing it, turning round from time to time to check that the others were well hidden.

It had been daylight for some time already and they had occasionally crossed paths with carts whose drivers, well wrapped up, cracked their whips to warm themselves up, when they suddenly heard two horses trotting behind them. Joël craned his neck to see who the early morning riders were.

"Look out! This is the critical moment," he said, ducking back into the vehicle hurried. Don't move and leave it to me."

It was the two gendarmes.

The noise of the cavalcade drew nearer, and the representatives of the public force, drawing level with the vehicle, fell into step with it.

"Bonjour," said the brigadier. "Have you seen anything unusual this morning?"

"My word, no. Not many people about because of the cold, and if I didn't have to get to Courtalain in good time, I'd have slept in late at the inn—but what can you do? One has to make a living."

The brigadier darted a suspicious glance into the depths of the carriage.

Without paying any heed to that, Joël continued: "By the way, Brigadier, if you have a yen to take the numbness out of your limbs and have a drop, I've got a nice bottle of rum in the bottom of the basket. Let me offer you two fingers. My beast can get his breath back in the meantime."

He did, in fact, bring his horse to a halt. "Adda, get that bottle and glasses," he went on. And so saying, he leapt to the ground, stamped his feet and stretched his legs.

In her turn, Adda briskly leapt down from the footstep and presented glasses to the two gendarmes. They hesitated, still suspicious, but the fairground performers seemed so innocently confident.

The brigadier placed his horse sideways, in order to get a better view of the inside of the vehicle. It was crammed with boxes and baskets; there was no space wasted and even less disposable.

"Well, what about your amiable crooks yesterday evening?" said Joël, in the most natural fashion in the world.

"In truth," said the brigadier, laughing sardonically, "I was wondering whether you were taking then away in your wagon?"

"No jokes, Brigadier; I don't carry vermin with me. But what do you mean? Has someone stolen them?"

"They've decamped. They're clever fellows, but they can't get very far on foot, and we'll show them that one can't make fools of us twice. I hoped that you might have run into them."

"Haven't seen anything of them. They've more likely cut across the fields."

"Too bad, too bad..."

The gendarmes clicked their tongues, raised their fingers to their kepis as a sign of gratitude, and resumed their trot.

XII. On the Track

Rosamour, a stubborn man, persisted in occupying himself uniquely with finding Grillard, dead or alive.

That was the *corpus delicti*; in its disappearance lay the whole of the mystery that the police had to decipher. Thus, the policeman, without wasting his time running after the fugitives, was collecting the slightest indication, in order to reconstitute, piece by piece, the kind of life that the scientist ordinarily led.

In truth, Monsieur Grillard's relations were restricted and very intermittent. Among the people who might be able to shed some light on the habits of Népomucène Grillard, Rosamour suddenly thought about his notary, Maître Durand, a shrewd fellow who had known him for a long time, having been at the École de Droit when the future scientist was frequenting the laboratories of the Sorbonne, and who, not being afraid to stand up to him, had always remained on good enough terms with him—which is to say in a permanent dispute that never went as far as falling out.

When Rosamour sought to obtain some enlightenment, however, Maître Durand contented himself with smiling and shaking his head, and his mocking eyes sparkled behind his spectacles. He knew nothing more than the public, but "that old devil Grillard was so extraordinary in every way that he was bound to finish in an extraordinary fashion." As for him, all he could say was that he was the depository of his testament.

"Aha!" exclaimed Rosamour. "I hoped so; that document might perhaps tell us something..."

"Not so fast," the notary interrupted. You'll only have access to that information in six months time, at the earliest."

"How's that?"

"I'm only to open it six months after his actual or presumed death."

"Very well—but to inform the police..."

"The police and the notariat are two different things. Professional secrecy, Monsieur—what about that?"

Rosamour had a strong desire to by-pass the lawyer's professional secrecy and obtain a formal warrant from an examining magistrate to search the office that had the pretention of being a tomb of secrets—but that was a major step that would certainly have put him at odds with the entire chamber of notaries, and he went home pensive, cursing the fatality that blocked all his best schemes.

It was in that state of mind that a message from Monsieur Fischer, the examining magistrate reached him, summoning him to the Palais urgently.

Only taking the time to grab an overcoat, our policeman hurtled into the street.

The magistrate as waiting for him, striding back and forth in his office impatiently.

"They've been arrested!" he cried, as soon as he saw him, showing him the yellow slip of a telegram open on the desk.

"Who?" said Rosamour, still thinking about nothing but his cadaver in his distress.

"Eh? Bémolisant and his acolyte, of course. What do you expect me to be thinking about, if not this accursed Panthéon affair—my nightmare?"

"Damn it!" the agent could not help saying. "That upsets my plans. What impetuosity people have, arresting people before it's time! Have you any means of confounding them and getting them to confess?"

245

"Bah! The worthy gendarmes might have been a little hasty, but it's done now. It's a matter of making the best of it. Perhaps it's a fortunate diversion, anyway, since your research hasn't turned up anything."

"Patience! One can't expect to fall on the right track at the first step—but I persist in believing that old Grillard's corpse is the key to the mystery, and that it's necessary, above all, to find it. Anyway, since the two fugitives have been arrested, I'll go..."

"Yes, by talking to them cleverly, you'll certainly be able to tie them in knots, and end up finding the truth—although, to tell the truth, those two fellows appear to me to be much less naïve than they seemed at first. Mistrust, Monsieur Rosamour, mistrust—they're sly ones; they're very clever."

"Oh, very clever," replied Rosamour, with absolute skepticism. "Anyway, I'll go, and we'll see..."

At that moment, someone knocked on the door. An office boy handed another telegram to the examining magistrate, who opened it. On reading it, however, his expression suddenly changed, in spite of the mask of impassivity that was habitual to him. It was with pinched lips, without saying a word, that he handed the piece of paper to the policeman.

The latter read it attentively in his turn, shook his head and sketched a vague smile.

"I see," he said, "that if the gendarmes of Briseval arrest people inappropriately, they let them escape in the same fashion. That doesn't change my plans, if you don't mind. I'll set out anyway, and I won't take long to find our fugitives, be sure of that."

"I suppose, in fact, that they're continuing to make for Nantes and Saint-Nazaire, by a more-or-less roundabout route, still having the intention of taking to the sea."

"I'll follow them step by step."

"Don't let them slip through your fingers at the last moment and embark."

"They won't embark without me."

"Try to succeed—public opinion is beginning to get impatient. The press, which never loses an opportunity to criticize the police, is already shouting from the rooftops that it's another file to be closed and that we can only arrest criminals if they turn themselves in."

"I'd like to see the reporters doing our job!"

Rosamour was particularly piqued by the examining magistrate's slightly sarcastic remarks, but he was forced to recognize their justice. In spite of all his skill and all his steps, the case was no further forward than on the day it had been assigned to him. He had collected an ample dossier of information. He knew every detail now of the lives of Bémolisant and Pilesèche. He had been able to reconstruct their comings and goings throughout the week that had preceded Grillard's mysterious disappearance and the one that had followed it. Only one thing escaped him—and that was the only important one.

What had become of the estimable scientist?

Of him, there was no trace.

He had come to believe that it was definitely his body that had been taken away in the box. But what had become of it thereafter, and where had the statue come from? The sole hypothesis that did not come to his mind was to identify the body with the effigy.

The nature of the metal and the opinion of competent people suggested that galvanoplastic methods must have been used to fabricate that statue, which no founder has cast; that was a conclusion acquired—but no galvanoplastic workshop in Paris or the surrounding area had ever been commissioned to carry out such work.

Learning that Monsieur Grillard's last endeavors had necessitated the employment of those processes of metallization, and that the scientist must, in consequence, have had the necessary equipment in his laboratory, Rosamour, moving from one deduction to another, was inclined to believe that the statue must have been finished there; it must, therefore have been the statue that was in the box, which was more in accordance

247

with the excessive weight than the policeman's first hypothesis.

But in that case, once again, what had become of the scientist?

There was no way out of the dilemma: the box contained either the body or the statue, and in either case, the mystery, for being different, was no less indecipherable—as well as the famous cryptogram on which he had counted momentarily to supply the key to the enigma.

Decidedly, the examining magistrate was right. It was to the presumed guilty parties that it was necessary to go to seek the solution to the problem.

The agent ate a hasty meal and took the train at twenty minutes past midday with a ticket to Gault Saint-Denis, the nearest station to Briseval. There he took a cab, which deposited him at the door of the gendarmerie of the latter village.

The brigadier had just returned, rather discomfited by his fruitless pursuit.

Rosamour showed him his warrants and, without wasting time criticizing him for his inopportune intervention, he submitted him to a routine interrogation. Then he had himself taken to the prison, silently examined the location, gave orders for a locksmith to come and open the door giving access to the gardens, and had no difficulty finding the tracks of the fugitives. The snow had preserved them, and it was easy enough to follow hem step by step.

The two men must have separated outside the enclosing wall of the Mairie. The footprints of one of them were lost on a path leading back to the village, confused with those of other pedestrians, but the other had gone across the fields, going round the houses in order to reach the westbound road to Courtalain.

He had waited there for a few minutes, as testified by the trampling of the snow in that location, but he had eventually been rejoined by his companion, and both of them had continued on their way, following the hedge instead of the road.

All of that was written in a clear and precise fashion on the great white page. There was no mistaking it. Suddenly, however, the tracks stopped again. A further trampling indicated a new halt, and then the two fugitive had leapt on to the road. The imprints of their heels could be seen deeply embedded in the snow by the roadside. From then on, it was difficult to follow them because of the other tracks with which they were confused.

Escorted by two gendarmes, Rosamour continued his investigations as far as a place where there was a muddy dip in the road. The snow was no longer intact there, except between two profound ruts, on either side if which it had been crushed, mixed with earth and water to form a horrible sludge.

A vehicle had stopped there. The white area indicated the place protected by the body of the vehicle. In front of it, the horse had stamped its feet for some time, trying to gain purchase for its hooves, and then had pulled away. The carters, by exciting it or pushing the wheels, had got it moving.

Rosamour examined everything, leaning over the ground, without making the two gendarmes party to his reflections. They were wondering what could possibly there to interest the clever fellow from the Sûreté.

When he had finished his examination, the agent turned to the brigadier and asked him, in an indifferent one: "Since you traveled along this road shortly after the escape, you can tell me what vehicles you encountered."

"Oh, indeed. They weren't very numerous, in any case, given the weather. The first one was saw was that of a conjuror who gave a performance yesterday evening at the Cheval Boiteux. As I told you, it was during that performance that the arrest was made…"

"Ah! Give me a few details. Where was this vehicle when you encountered it?"

"About three kilometers from here."

"Did you look inside?"

"Ah!" said the other, swelling up with pride. "One knows one's métier. I stopped the vehicle, without making any fuss, and I could see all the way to the back. There was no one hiding there."

"You didn't go inside?"

"I didn't think it was worth the trouble."

"Well, my good man, you were mistaken; your two birds were there."

"You're joking," said the brigadier, who was strongly tempted to hold his sides.

"Where was your conjuror going?"

"To Courtalain, where he's giving a performance this evening."

Rosamour looked at his watch. It was too late to think of catching up with the fugitives that day. In any case, there was no urgency since he now knew where to find them. He therefore went tranquilly back to Briseval, telegraphed the examining magistrate to reassure him, installed himself at a small table in the Cheval Boiteux, near the stove—the same one at which the artist and the laboratory assistant had dined—and ordered a comfortable repast, which consoled him for his fatigues.

XIII. An Unexpected Ascension

The entire quarter of Nantes surrounding the gas factory was on holiday. It was the day of the fair, and in the little square the fairground booths were set up, ranging from the humble tents where waffles were spreading the odor of frying to the ample theater whose façade disappeared behind painted canvases.

When dusk came, everything was illuminated, as brightly as by day. Big drums of every caliber began to thunder, with the strident accompaniment of cymbals. The French horns, bugles, trombones and ophicleides all sang their favorite songs. The mechanical orchestras, their hundred flags blowing in the wind, bellowed furiously in the midst of wooden houses gleaming with gilt and facets of mirrors.

And the crowds went by, in a perpetual jostle of elbows, with an indescribable riot of cries, catcalls, exclamations of joy, growls and yelps. Everyone was at the fête, all having a good time!

Among the establishments that the inexhaustible parade passed there was one, in particular, that arrested the members of the public as if it had seized them by the collar. That was a pavilion of restricted dimensions, decorated with paintings in which a superb woman clad in a low-cut dress could be seen, in all the attitudes that somnambulistic sleep can produce. A gentleman in a black suit, wand in hand, evidently represented the skillful operator who realized the marvels in question.

And on the trestles, that same gentleman in a black suit—but in the flesh and bone—with a beautiful smile and beautiful words on his lips, was inviting the crowd to come into the tent with noble gestures.

A rather thin young woman was leaning on one of the tent-poles and occasionally adding something to the proprietor's patter.

"Come in, Mesdames et Messieurs; it only costs ten centimes—two sous! You'll see the most astonishing things. Hypnotism demonstrated! Extra-lucid somnambulistic sight! Come in, Mesdames et Messieurs.

To one side of the platform, a clown with a white face and a village bridegroom with a red nose were making deadening music. The former was banging a bass drum and cymbals with formidable wrist-power, the later blowing into an enormous trombone, with clicks and clacks every time the long slide went in or out to its full extent. The sounds that sprang from the brass instrument, along with the vibrations of the shrill rattle, tore the most hardened eardrums. It was a *danse macabre* of triple crotchets, a hectic jig of delirious triolets, cascading over the broken rungs of a fantastic scale of incoherence.

And the grotesque artiste who was inflating his cheeks to blow into that tube has such an expression of unalloyed satisfaction that the public guffawed, stamped their feet, howled with joy and shouted for more at the top of their voices, with an exhilarating enthusiasm.

But the man in the black suit rang the big bell, and the music fell silent.

It was just in time; the artiste was on the point of collapse. His entire face was swollen and as red as his vermilion nose. He sponged his temples, and while the patter ran its course he leaned toward the clown

"Finally," he said, "I've found an audience that understands my music! I've been all over France, America and Asia. I've given concerts to high society and savages, but no one ever applauded like this crowd."

"This crowd had an instinct for decadent music, my dear Bém..."

"Call me Arthur, I beg you."

The clown also had his share in the success. It was not that he was particularly amusing, or that his sallies were marked with the English humor, reminiscent of an epileptic undertaker, that one loves to encounter nowadays in artistes of that genre. He was absolutely deadpan, sulky and sad, and it was his sadness that was funny. In the bouffant trousers that dressed his legs, with the sun on his belly and a half-moon on his back., he was so gauchely maladroit, so blissfully taciturn and stiff, that one could not look at that white face with its two eyebrows like grave accents without laughing until one cried.

"Come on, Monsieur Clown, say something amiable to the honorable society!"

It was the black suit that pronounced those engaging words, and, taking Monsieur Clown by the arm, he made him do a pirouette, while that unexpected shock caused the marionette to stagger and beat the air with his long arms.

People writhe with laughter, and when the invitation to "Enterrrrr!" resounded again, there as a veritable stampede that threatened to overturn the trestles, stave in the planks and bring down the whole tent.

Inside, the spectators arranged themselves on the benches, poorly covered with red fabric, which was coming away in tatters.

At the back, a platform represented the stage. At the foot of the stage was a red velvet pedestal, over which a muslin veil was thrown, vaguely outlining the forms of a recumbent body.

The young woman who has just appeared at the door was sitting on the stage, with a weary and disenchanted expression. The clown was astride a bench. Finally, when the village bridegroom and his trombone had taken their places in a corner, the man in the black suit advanced toward the audience and bowed, one hand on his heart, like a vulgar comic-opera tenor.

"Mesdames et Messieurs, you must have heard mention of Professor Joël. I can say without boasting that renown precedes me wherever I go. The Académie itself has taken an interest in my work, and I defy anyone, in that honorable society, to carry out experiments more curious than those you are about to witness. But enough preamble! You're impatient—strike up the band!"

The trombone launched a series of furious notes. When the chromatic scale was extinguished, Professor Joël bowed again.

"Before putting on display before you all that hypnotic science has of the mysteriously sublime, let me give you a few necessary explanations regarding the anatomical constitution of the human body.

While pronouncing that emphatic exordium, he lifted the veil that was covering the red pedestal, on which a recumbent body appeared, painted in a cadaveric hue, with greenish tints of advanced decay.

"You have before you, Mesdames et Messieurs," the professor continued, "the reproduction of a masterpiece of statuary, in which the anatomy of the human body is, so to speak, sculpted in the quick."

And to think, thought the melancholy village bridegroom, *that it's me who painted my uncle in those lugubrious colors!*

With the tip of his wand, Joël gave his physiological demonstration, accompanying it with big words and grand gestures, but his audience was primarily griped by the eyes. Everyone stood up on the benches and jostled one another in order to see "the masterpiece of statuary" and that strange thin and pale man whose bones were jutting out through his green-tinted flesh.

That was, however, only a curtain-raiser, and the real performance was yet to commence—but before then, the professor had a recommendation to make to the public.

"Don't forget, Mesdames et Messieurs, that tomorrow, at two o'clock in the afternoon, in the square in front of this establishment, the inflation and ascension will take place of a monstrous balloon. I shall have the honor of performing, on a trapeze suspended below the nacelle a thousand feet up in the air, the most perilous acrobatic feats that you have ever seen. And now, I shall begin..."

We shall not describe that session of hypnosis, in which the clown played the major role, Professor Joël contenting himself with commenting and making speeches, explaining the experiments that his auxiliary was carrying out on the entranced young woman.

Among the spectators there was one young man who had placed himself beside the village bridegroom, and who, while the latter was not blowing into his trombone, did not disdain to chat to the instrumentalist.

At first there were exclamations and expressions of admiration. The experiments impassioned and enthused him. He was a traveling salesman, he said, and had seen all sorts of things, but he had never seen anything as impressive. Then he came back to the anatomical statue.

"Is it made of wax?" he asked, naively.

The artiste shuddered. "I don't know," he replied.

"It's astonishing how much it resembled a drawing I've seen in the illustrated papers. It was a sculpture by Bémolisant—you know, the artist who disappeared.

The other shifted in his chair, with an evident malaise.

"It's said that he murdered his uncle," the spectator continued, in a tranquil and detached manner.

"That's absurd, idiotic...what do you want?" exclaimed the other, immediately biting his lip.

"Me? I don't want anything at all. I'm just saying what there is in the newspapers.—but perhaps you know better than I do, if you know him..."

"If I know him, if I know him...why do you think I know him?"

"Well, no, I don't say that. How do I know? It doesn't alter the fact that the old man can't be found. And yet, if he hasn't been murdered, he could reappear, and then the slander would shut up, wouldn't it?"

"Well, it's easy for you to talk. It's always easy to settle questions. I'd do this, I'd do that—but when one finds oneself in a tight corner, one finds that it isn't so easy to get out of it. In fact, I don't know him, this sculptor; I'm just talking..."

"To make conversation, that's all—understood."

"But I have a sympathy for him. One ought to have, between artistes. And I say to myself: who knows? Perhaps he's in a situation that's too implausible, and, if he tried to make people believe it, everyone would laugh in his face. They'd cry: 'Tell it to the marines, old man! You can't take us in with tales like that!' And all the evidence is against him, everything demonstrates that he's guilty...it's just a supposition, you understand, a simple supposition..."

"Oh, that's how I take it."

"He says to himself then: I've been very stupid to fall into the wolf-trap. I could swear my innocence till the cows come home, but they'd convict me anyway, and I want to keep my skin.' What do you think of that reasoning, eh?"

"That it's sane enough. Unless he's guilty, in which case I'd understand even better why he's running away."

"You wrong to believe that. Anyway, I'm not trying to convince you."

"All the more so as it's not me that it's necessary to convince, but the police."

That observation had the power to make the artiste shudder. In a low voice, he repeated: "The police, the police...yes, it's the police."

When the performance finished, the audience got up to leave, with a frightful hubbub.

The pretended commercial traveler politely took his leave of the trombonist. Scarcely had he turned his back when a head leaned toward the artiste's ear and murmured: "Don't trust the man who was just talking to you—he's a policeman."

The unfortunate village bridegroom started trembling in every limb.

At that moment, the man in question turned round and, perceiving the man who had just spoken to the musician, said to himself: *Why, what can that serpent Boissonnald be doing here? That's not obvious. He'd better not put a spoke in my wheel or, word of a Rosamour, he'll regret it.*

The following day, which was Sunday, the fair was in full swing.

The preparations for the launch of the balloon were being made solemnly, as is befitting when it is a matter of interesting a crowd and extracting good money from its pockets.

Ropes had been extended to form a large circle; within that area several rows of chairs had been set out, in which the most curious or the most fortunate spectators had taken their places.

In the middle of the circle, one of the openings of the gas main had been uncovered.

The envelope of varnished calico forming the balloon was lying on the ground like a huge fishing net, the valve in the center. A broad tube, similarly made of varnished calico, was fitted to the gas conduit, the other end extending underneath the aerostat to the orifice that have it access.

Professor Joël had abandoned his black suit; he appeared in the spangled leotard of a simple acrobat, ready to perform gymnastics underneath the nacelle that could be seen a few paces away, rigged out and ready to be attached to the balloon's net as soon as the inflation was complete.

Pilesèche, in his clown costume, and Bémolisant, the trombone-playing village bridegroom, were there again, along with Miss Adda, who was circulating among the spectators, selling them oranges and barley-sugar.

It was a bright, sunny day with a dry cold that that had not kept anyone away. The audience was numerous and its members well disposed to take pleasure in the spectacle they had been promised, the preparations for which Joël was explaining to them in a stentorian voice.

Two or three employees of the gas factory, in braided caps, were lending their collaboration to the inflation. The gas was gradually introduced into the envelope, which swelled up awkwardly, like the spontaneous generation of an enormous mushroom.

The cords of the net were attached to sacks of ballast, which held the fragile machine in place, preventing it from rising too quickly. The men had to bring the bags closer together, attaching them lower down, as the gigantic ball rose up, forming a gilded dome inside the mesh of the net.

The equator of the thousand-cubic-meter sphere is already visible; it is filling up rapidly now. The pear-shaped neck appears. The time has come to fit the nacelle; it is attached.

With scrupulous care, Joël verifies all the junctions, makes sure that no cleat is faulty, that no mooring-rope will break in mid-air, imperiling the human lives that are about to confide themselves to the frail craft. The material is a little old, but with precautions the ascension will be accomplished without a hitch. The passengers announced in the program are Joël, Miss Adda and a volunteer. While Joël does his perilous exercises on the trapeze, Miss Adda will guide the aerostat. As for the benevolent passenger, he has paid a rather large sum to procure the emotions of a voyager in space.

The aides attach a French flag to the suspension cords; the anchor is hanging over one of the sides of the nacelle, and to maintain equilibrium, the other side is fitted with the guide-tope rolled up into a ball.

Everything is ready.

Joël was in the nacelle, methodically arranging the instruments and sacks of ballast.

Miss Adda was selling the last oranges, and the novice passenger was saying interminable adieux to his family; one might have thought that he was about to embark on a long voyage.

In the meantime, Pilesèche and Bémolisant, in their eccentric costumes, were making furious music—but the artiste did not have the same verve as the previous evening. The immutable principles of absolute music were no longer speaking to his heart. He had many other preoccupations, and it seemed to him that he could still hear the mocking cry: "Look out! It's the police!"

And all of a sudden, his eyes, scanning the circle of spectators surrounding the aerostat, his eyes encountered the enigmatic visage of the so-called traveling salesman who had been denounced to him.

The man's words and gestures came back to his mind. He interpreted and explained them in the worst possible light, while, with inflated cheeks, he blew unconscious notes nevertheless into the mouthpiece of his trombone.

That man had talked about Uncle Grillard!

Was that not enough? Had he not given, himself, and without being solicited, all the reasons that condemned the laboratory assistant and the artist?

Then, leaning toward his companion—his accomplice—between two brazen squawks that split the ears of an indulgent public, Bémolisant spoke in a low voice, confiding his anxieties to him. He showed him the danger that was surging forth like the head of Medusa.

And the spectacle unfolds. The preparations are complete. Joël gives the order to remove the final sacks of ballast hanging from the net, which are keeping the balloon nailed to the ground. Several men put their weight on the nacelle to prevent the aerostat from flying away into the atmosphere, but their number is insufficient. Joël calls for a few volunteers. Oh, there's no lack of them! They emerge from the ranks of the audience and launch themselves into the circle reserved for the maneuver.

Several brush past the two musicians.

At the same time, a voice whispers in their ears: "He's the police!"

And when their haggard eyes go once again to the commercial traveler, the subject of so much anguish, the voice continues, bringing their fear to a peak: "He's going to arrest you at the end of the performance. Save yourselves."

Arrest them! They go pale and tremble in their tight and grotesque costumes. As if moved by a spring however, they have both stood up, dropping the trombone and the big drum. They are face to face, consulting one another with their gaze, in the midst of the crowd, whose members are also on their feet to watch the departure, all gazes fixed on the balloon—for the solemn moment has arrived. Impatiently, Joël calls out to his passenger, who is stretching out his adieux with kisses and compliments.

Miss Adda, with one hand on the edge of the wicker cage, her head turned toward the unhurried traveler, is ready to climb into the nacelle.

But suddenly, abruptly, in the midst of a confusion of aides jostling one another, two large bodies fray a passage through the men still retaining the balloon. Those two bizarre phantoms leap into the nacelle. As if they have agreed to act and speak in unison, they utter a cry in unison: a single, vibrant, resounding cry:

"Let go!"

At that powerful, unexpected cry, the surprised aides instinctively lift the hands that are retaining the aerostat, and the latter, suddenly free, bounds like a thoroughbred whose bridle has been released.

An enthusiastic hurrah rises with it.

The spectators have only seen in that unexpected turn of events a comic effect prepared in advance. They applaud.

The passenger, abandoned on the ground, stares open-mouthed at his vehicle in flight, and Miss Adda, brushed by the nacelle as it escaped, remains motionless in stupor.

In the audience, however, one man had straightened up, surprised and also anxious, while beside him, another man who has approached murmurs ironically in is ear: "You're stumped, Monsieur Rosamour."

"Stumped!" the agent replied. "Not yet. There's the tele-graph for worthy men—but you'll pay for this, Monsieur Boissonnald."

Balloons launched from fairgrounds do not, as a rule, come down far away. Rosamour had no doubt that by tele-graphing the authorities in the region toward which the bal-loon was heading, he would have news of it that same evening.

Now, the balloon had been carried away by a north-easterly wind. It was heading toward the sea, which might force the aeronauts to come down sooner than they would have wished.

In spite of the favorable circumstances, the night did not bring any news.

The following day also passed without anything being heard of the aerial voyagers. They had flown away into the sky, and they had not come down again.

Boissonnald was right. Rosamour was stumped.

He did not want to admit defeat, however, and he went back to the tent, where Miss Adda was awaiting, silently and fatalistically, the denouement of the singular affair.

She did not understand as yet exactly what had hap-pened, and had no doubt that the aerial voyagers might return at any moment. Time was passing, however, and her confi-dence was ebbing away. A dull anxiety had been born within her, and a kind of obsession. It was not the image of Joël that passed through her mind—Joël was always harsh, with never a kind word—but that of the unfortunate Pilesèche, so sympathetic to the young woman's miseries, even though he scarcely talked to her. It seemed that his magnetic power had not only exerted a temporary influence over her, but had installed itself as sovereign throughout her being. When he spoke, she listened, lost in a dream, as if his voice were singing. When he approached, she felt his proximity instinctively, and turned her head. And now that he was no longer there, it was like a great void in the middle of which she was completely disorientated. A part of her had departed with her magnetizer, without her being able to render account of what had disequilibrated her, and that exteriorization, as it were, of her faculties.

When Rosamour came to question her, he found her anxious and agitated. She looked at him suspiciously, without replying. Instead of threatening her, the agent was gentle and insinuating; he was only looking for the truth, the proof of innocence.

At Pilesèche's name she had shuddered, and Rosamour pulled that string, saying that it was in the interests of the young man that he gather all the information that might facilitate his recover.

Then Adda, quite simply and without any evasion, told him the story of the association from the day that Joël had met the two supposed criminals.

Criminals! Who could possibly believe that they were? She had seen them at close range, had lived with them, and she swore that they were not.

She became excited as she said that, and then her speech fell back into calm monotony, as if wearied by the effort.

Certainly, she had told him all that she knew—he had no doubt about that—but what she knew scarcely cast any light on the problem. Rosamour left, discouraged by the conversation; he made a minute inventory, without finding anything in the midst of the gaudy trash cluttering the tent and the vehicle that might aid him in his task. He kept a few papers for examination at leisure, although even they appeared at first glance to be insignificant.

As he did not want to return to Paris empty-handed, however, he invited Miss Adda to accompany him—she was still a witness—and registered as baggage the famous nickel statue, stripped of the layer of paint with which it had been daubed, shining beneath its white patina.

XIV. The Wreck of a Balloon

The idea of attempting the aerial route to escape the pursuit of the gendarmes does not involve any more danger than that implicit in tranquilly buying a railway ticket for a distant location, but it is less practical.

Murderers and other large-scale malefactors do not always have a ready-inflated aerostat to hand, fiacres generally being more common in our streets. The balloon, moreover, is a costly means of locomotion that does not lend itself easily to mystery.

Joël had been utterly astounded on seeing those two fantastic beings leap into the nacelle: a clown and a village bridegroom, two estimable murderers—for it must be said that he if had once listened, with a benevolent smile, to their fantastic explanations regarding their imaginary crime, he had not been duped for a single instant. It was not him, Joël, who could be taken in by such tales; he had seen far too much of the world to be credulous.

"What's got into you?" he shouted, with a formidable oath, when, after that abrupt irruption, the balloon, escaping from the grip of its guardians, flew away into the air.

The wicker nacelle, poorly attached to the encircling net and violently jolted, oscillated like a salad-shaker, and the aeronauts were forced, in order not to be slammed into one another, to cling on to the rigging.

They had made a sudden bound five hundred meters into the air before the acrobat had recovered from his surprise. It was truly a little late to give the crowd, amazed by that unexpected departure, the spectacle of pirouettes executed on the bar of the trapeze that the balloon had lifted up with it and which was swinging furiously. In any case, the incident had been so unexpected and comical that the members of the public, believing it to be a farce cleverly planned to tease their appetite for novel fare, were clapping their hands fervently and crying "Bravo!" with all the force of their combined lungs.

The clamors rose up in discordant gusts all the way to the narrow receptacle in which were crouched the three most singular passengers imaginable: an acrobat, an improbable clown and the most horribly grease-painted of village bridegrooms, with his flowery waistcoat, his gigantic collar shapelessly turned down, his Bluebeard suit with large brass buttons and his beribboned bouquet.

Joël was furious, and he had no lack of reasons to be. Was he not about to lose his reputation, by virtue of not having completed his program?

"But since they're applauding...!" the former laboratory assistant objected, timidly.

"You're nothing but an idiot!" the other interrupted, violently. "What about the passenger I was supposed to bring—is he applauding too? He's been left on the ground...and carrying away his money. Is that the way to do things, eh? I wouldn't care about that, if it weren't necessary to go back to Nantes for the rest of the kit, but we're going to have to do that...and we'll be lucky if the police don't get mixed up in it..."

Bémolisant and Pilesèche lowered their heads and received the downpour without saying anything. From time to time, the artiste tried to get a word in. "Listen...," he said, timidly—but immediately, the insults rained down even harder, and the orator had considerable reinforcements of oaths in his throat.

Everything comes to an end, however, even the great fits of anger of acrobats and professors of magnetism. Joël finally fell silent, breathless, and Bémolisant was able to make his speech.

He explained the cause of their panic. He related the mysterious advice uttered twice over, and the head of Medusa suddenly appearing in the form of an agent of the Sûreté with a mocking expression.

It makes no difference whether one is innocent, there are things one cannot help and, in truth, without reflection, they had both had the same idea, of taking off for the clouds. Perhaps it was stupid, but after all, one could hardly blame them.

"Well, it's very clever, what you've just done," Joël muttered. "As if the telegraph has been created for nothing! You'll be picked up when you disembark from the balloon, and thanks to you, I'll be caught in the net. But if that happens, damn it, you'd better get ready to pay me back!"

During this altercation, rapid as it was, as the insults had followed one another like javelins in some Homeric combat, no one was keeping watch on the progress of the balloon, which had continued rising until it reached an altitude of a thousand meters and then had started flying rapidly southwestwards.

An immense plain of hilly cloud extended beneath the nacelle, pierced here and there by somber holes, shafts of a sort, at the bottom of which patches of brown earth could be perceived.

Above them gilding the yellow cambric dome of the balloon, the sun was shining in the transparent and rarefied atmosphere. In spite of the clouds floating higher in the sky, which obscured it at intervals, its rays warmed the aerial globe somewhat, and it resumed its ascendant trajectory as it dilated in that heat.

Gradually, however, as it continued its course, the aerostat penetrated into a glacial mist in which the iridescent light was scattered by the turbulence of microscopic crystals of nascent snow.

For the aeronauts, all indication of movement had disappeared. The aerostat seemed to be motionless in space, in the middle of a block of unpolished glass, drowned in a diffuse light.

No more earth, no more sky! No noise was rising up from the ground to the nacelle. It was a grim solitude; oblivion in the midst of the golden darts of radiant light.

Bémolisant was shivering with fever and cold, while Pilesèche, his head in his hands, forgot his observer's temperament, unconscious of the marvelous spectacle that was offered to him without his having to seek it out.

The acrobat Joël was certainly not sacrificing himself to the ideal, and his poetic tastes did not solicit him to prolong the voyage for the vain pleasure of contemplating the aerial scenery. A fairground ascension is not exactly an amusement for the man who carries it out; he considers that he has done enough for is audience when he has made a prestigious departure, and as soon as he has disappeared into the clouds he has nothing more pressing to do that return to earth as rapidly as possible, in order to avoid excessively considerable expense in returning by railway. It had required the surprise and the heat of the dispute to cause him to forget those principles of sage economy, in order for him not to have yet determined the descent by a vigorous tug on the valve.

On the other hand, the perspective of the tricorn hats and sashes that he was expecting to appear on landing rendered him rather perplexed and irresolute. Was it necessary to stop, or to gain ground, in order to return to earth in some remote spot where it would be easier to get away?

The atmospheric circumstances took responsibility themselves for answering the question.

The balloon was weighed down by a multitude of spangles and needles of ice. Under that burden, and as the gas contracted by virtue of cooling, the aerostat began to descend. There were no reference points, but in order to be certain of the fall it was sufficient to look at the flaccid fabric, which was hollowing out beneath the huge sphere maintained in the broad mesh of the net.

Joël threw a few pieces of cigarette paper out of the nacelle, which seemed to rise up rapidly toward the sky, simply because the aerostat was descending much more rapidly than they were.

The aeronauts felt a vertical wind strike their faces. Finally—the last indication—the flag suspended from the rigging was lifted up, fluttering under the resistant action of the air.

It seemed that they were heading for the ground at a speed that was already vertiginous. The acrobat judged it prudent to slow that hectic progress by emptying a sack of ballast.

The fog did not permit the ground beneath the nacelle to be distinguished, but a dull murmur could be heard, like the distant rumble of trains in the vicinity of a large train. The noise was rather bizarre in its continuity, and grew in volume as the altitude diminished.

In order better to perceive and analyze it, Joël leaned over the fragile wicker of the nacelle.

The fog seemed to become less dense. The iridescent crystals, charged with electricity, were attracting one another, hastening together and aggregating into snowflakes. That snow was falling on to the balloon, already bristling with needles of frost—a white coat whose layer was thickening and making the aerial vehicle heavier. The danger was imminent, for its speed was accelerating rapidly.

"Damn!" cried Joël. "Ballast, quickly! We're falling!"

It was, indeed, a rapid fall that was now precipitating the balloon toward the earth, and already, through the snow, daylight was visible.

Obstinately leaning half way out of the nacelle, the acrobat tried to catch a glimpse of the murmurous ground, and suddenly shouted: "Damnation! It's the sea!"

The sea! It was the sea that was producing that strange murmur. It was the sea, rolling wave after wave, breaking on rocks.

The shore was close by, but the balloon had already passed over it, and, while falling, it was continuing its course out to sea!

"We're doomed!" howled Joël, his hands clenched in his hair.

"We need to find a contrary current," hazard Pileseche.

"Imbecile! A contrary current! Empty ballast, animal! That's all that you can do..."

And, setting an example, the two men nervously threw sacks of ballast into the sea, without even untying them, abruptly and hastily, each time delivering a shock to the aerostat.

And when the ballast ran out, it was all the instruments there were in the nacelle, and anything that was loose, heavy or light, including the anchor, whose rope was rapidly cut by a stroke of a knife.

As if it had understood the danger, the aerostat, thus unburdened, slowed its velocity, and finally paused two or three hundred meters above the swell that was oaring beneath it. But it did not rise up again, and there was nothing left to lighten it any further.

It was still heading westwards, and toward the west there was nothing but water, as far as the eye could see, and on the water, only a few distant sails that were disappearing over the horizon, without having seen the airship in distress.

His anger passed, Joël, in the face of danger, had recovered all his composure. It was not the first time that he had confronted peril in his adventurous life, and he thought about the best means of prolonging their suspension at a moderate height until a ship, passing close by, perceived the balloon and came to its aid.

But time was passing and the balloon, after a brief respite, resumed its downward movement. he guide-rope hanging from the nacelle suddenly touched the surface, and, gradually plunging into it, lightened the aerostat slightly…but not enough, alas, to interrupt the descent, which continued irremediably.

The aeronauts had nothing more to throw out. Then discouragement gripped them: what was the point of delaying the fatal outcome? No ship appeared that could pick up the unfortunates, and now they were waiting, instinctively clinging to the rigging...

Abruptly, an impact!

The wicker nacelle dipped into the sea, which submerged it momentarily, soaking the unfortunates to the skin.

Joël, with his knowledge of the métier, had climbed into the circle of the net, but, pushed by the wind, the balloon lay down on the sea, leaving its rigging trailing in the waves, and the acrobat with it.

Under the deballasting effect of the nacelle dipping into the water, however, the gas recovered a little force and lifted the entire rig, which, with a new surge rose up fifty meters—only to fall again immediately.

And those lugubrious somersaults, the last bounds of an exhausted horse, were repeated until the balloon, having used up all its energy, flaccid and convulsed, stood up by the wind like a huge body without a soul, resumed skimming the waves, only slowed down by the heavy burden that it was still dragging, half-submerged, hollowing out a long wave behind it.

That envelope of cotton fabric, bloated and undulating, in which gusts of wind hollowed out pockets with sinister flopping sounds, resembled, in the light of the setting sun, a monstrous octopus sustaining in its tentacles three condemned men, just sufficiently to prolong their agony.

Every shock that plunged them under water gave them a vision of the anguish of death.

Pilesèche and his companion had tried to escape the waves by climbing up to the net as well. With their feet on the edge of the nacelle, they hoisted themselves up as far as they could—but their position was even more atrocious there; they were rolled in all directions, only hanging on to the ropes by their stiffened hands, battered by the waves, blinded by the icy mist...

And, letting go, they fell, devoid of strength and courage, into the bottom of the nacelle, losing consciousness and perception of their surroundings.

Were they not already in the strange slumber that resembles the vestibule of death? How many minutes separated them now from eternity?

XV. An Agents' Square-Dance

As he boarded the train that was to take him back to Paris Monsieur Boissonnald found himself torn between two contrary sentiments, and, according to whether he turned his ideas heads up or tails up, he found a face that was cheerful or sad, like the double image of Heraclitus and Democritus.

In him, Democritus was weeping for the lamentable outcome of the particular affair that had brought him to Nantes—for, in truth, it was only a fortunate combination of circumstances that had allowed him to stumble by chance on to the tracks of the fugitives.

Heraclitus was laughing in thinking about the nice trick he had just played on his colleague Rosamour, whose somewhat arrogant manner had the gift of making his hair curl.

He counted, moreover, on not leaving it there, and working to discredit the "scientific detective" by all the means at his disposal.

Who could tell? Perhaps there was a place to take there, and the private enterprise that he had undertaken had not been sufficiently successful that he would disdain an opportunity to return to the administrative bosom, if some striking coup could open the door to him.

That is why Master Boissonnald, as soon as he arrived in Paris, thought that he ought to present himself in the office of Monsieur Fischer, the examining magistrate in charge of the Panthéon affair.

Boissonnald had assumed his most hypocritical expression and his most enigmatic smile. He found the magistrate in a state of nervous overexcitement, easy o understand, for he

269

had just received a telegram from Rosamour announcing the aerial flight of the two criminals. Did that fact not corroborate all his suspicions? A further telegram informed him, moreover, of the negative result of all the agent's attempts to discover where the balloon had landed. Finally, Rosamour announced his imminent return, and more ample verbal explanations.

Boissonnald therefore arrived in time to be the first to furnish details of the incident. In doing so, he took a malign pleasure in charging his colleague with all possible stupidities, so effectively that the magistrate, who drank in his words and was already quite prepared to depreciate the conduct of an unsuccessful agent, was convinced that he was dealing with a complete idiot.

In the meantime, Rosamour was on his way to render an account of his lack of success. That is never a situation full of attractions, and we would be lying if he said that he was not crestfallen.

As for the welcome that waited him, he was under no illusions in that regard. The method that he had thought it best to employ in the affair had never pleased the examining magistrate. One success could legitimate his initiative. He had failed; it only remained for him to pay for the breakages.

Such were the reflections that were agitating him on the cushions of the express between Nantes and Paris, but as, all things considered, he was not lacking in a certain dose of philosophy, our policeman ended up going to sleep and dreaming that he had stolen Icarus' wings and was improbably giving chase to the fugitives through the skies.

On arrival in Paris, the time had not get come to go to the Prefecture of Police. He therefore occupied himself with lodging Miss Adda in a nearby hotel, in order to have his witness near to hand when needed. As for the nickel statue, as well as the other items that he had thought he ought to retain from the acrobat's frippery, he had them transported to his own apartment. The rest had been left under seal in Nantes.

When Rosamour decided to go to the Prefecture he was not surprised to be received coldly by the head of the Sûreté, who nevertheless held him in particular esteem.

"My good friend," the latter said, "the scientific method has not held up. What do you expect? You've made too much noise with your operations. Of someone else one would be content to say that he'd been unfortunate; of you, they'll say that you've been maladroit. That's what comes of wanting to reform humanity. Now, I advise you not to go to see Fischer for the moment. He's furious with you. It's necessary to say that you've demolished yourself throughout this affair—a child of fifteen wouldn't have had your naivety."

"But nothing is lost," Rosamour protested. "Our fugitives have escaped into death, for it's obvious that they've fallen into the sea; otherwise I'd have picked up traces of them. The affair is therefore liquidated in that respect. There now remains the other aspect of the problem to resolve, the victim to recover. Let me disentangle that—I'll take responsibility for penetrating the mystery. We'll see then whether or not I'm maladroit..."

"Ta ta ta...if I were alone, free in my movements, I wouldn't say no, and you'd be able to get your revenge, but anything I can do would be futile. Someone else has been found for that task."

That declaration fell upon the agent like a cold shower. "Ah!" he said, finally. "And may one know to whom the affair has been entrusted?"

"Yes, indeed...all the more so as Monsieur Fischer felt obliged to go over my head in order to go in search of that idiot Boissonnald."

"Well, well...so it's Boissonnald!"

Rosamour was perhaps about to say more, but he stopped, prudently, thinking that the moment for confidences had not yet come.

"As for you, my dear," the head of the Sûreté added, "my advice is that it's time to disappear and wait in solitude for things to pick up again." With the skepticism of a man accustomed to the perversity of things down here, he added; "Your time will come."

"To put it another way, I've got the boot."

"Sorry…you understand. Such a resounding failure—the court requires a scapegoat."

"Fair enough. I know how to occupy my leisure."

"Then all's for the best. No hard feelings and, when the time comes, when all the noise has died down, count on me open the door."

"Much obliged."

As Rosamour as leaving, he turned round. "There's no point, then, in going myself to report…"

"Absolutely. Boissonnald has rendered you the service of sparing you that trouble by reporting your actions in detail—he happened to be there at the moment of the escape."

"Oh, I know, and I'm far from sure that he didn't have anything to do with it."

"Aha! He's a sly one…"

Rosamour stuck his hat on and left the Prefecture of Police in a state of complete exasperation. With his hands in his pockets and his teeth clenched, he strode along the quais at a rapid pace, with no objective in mind, trying to reassemble his ideas and settle on a line of conduct.

What could he do?

Rancor is a poor adviser, and for the moment he was all rancor, only seeking the best means of putting one over on the examining magistrate and the successor who had got him so briskly sacked.

Someone was about to poach on his preserves! And if that individual found the key to the mystery, he, Rosamour, would pass for a naïve fool!

All was not said and done yet, of course, and he was not about to let go. There were two players in the game, if you please; it remained to be seen who would reach the goal more rapidly, and in the meantime, he would use all cunning of a Mohican to put Boissonnald off the rack, mystify Fischer, and roll over the police and the court alike, to snatch their prey from them if the aeronauts ever reappeared on the horizon and especially—above all!—to prevent them from finding the old scientist, the pivot of the entire affair.

To start with, he did not feel any urgency to hand over to the clerk the few pieces of evidence that he possessed and to make known the only interesting witness that had been involved in recent events. Miss Adda was in a safe place; he had taken great care not to mention her to a living soul; no one would know who had caused her to disappear, and Boissonnald might search for her for a long time. It was more probable, however, that the latter would be much more interested in the two fugitives, unless he had accepted once and for all that the unfortunates had perished in the waves.

As if to corroborate ht hypothesis, the newspapers announced that the wreckage of a balloon, deprived of its nacelle, had been found in the sea, and that the balloon could not be any other than the one from the Nantes fair. And indeed, as soon as that news reached the court, the file on the affair was hastily closed, there being no point in further pursuit since the guilty parties—who could doubt now that they were guilty?—were indubitably dead. It was, in any case, an honorable fashion to finish with an annoying investigation on which no one had succeeded in casting any light. There would always be time to take it up again of new circumstances required it.

Even Boissonnald was not overly keen to follow such an obscure trail, which did not augur anything good. He had got the job and was quite comfortable there, what point was there in risking committing some stupidity in a complicated affair that had sunk his predecessor?

Everyone was, therefore, satisfied—even public opinion, which, not doubting the culpability of the two fugitives, finally had the denouement of the drama—a picturesque denouement in which the crime had been punished by ineluctable fatality, as was appropriate.

Rosamour was the only one not to be content, doubtless because he was too difficult to satisfy: the only one not to bury the affair, because he judged that his self-respect demanded that he provide a different denouement, his goal having always been before all, to find the old scientist and explain his disappearance.

While those in official regions were occupying themselves with other matters, Rosamour, in the shadows, was setting up new batteries.

Only one thing worried him one cannot make war without funds, and funds were lacking now that he was no longer drawing a salary from the Prefecture. But it is not with a mind as inventive as the former detectives that one allows oneself to be stopped by such details. He had already glimpsed the means of procuring the necessary resources. Had he not brought back the nickel statue that everyone thought admirable? Would it not be possible to sell that uncontested masterpiece?

He thought, in addition, that there was a certain Madame Bémolisant in a corner of Paris to whom he had promised news of her husband. The moment had come. He had a definite sympathy for the poor woman, and judged that it was time to put her in the picture regarding the artist's fate.

Privately, Rosamour thought that, if the latter had found death as a way out of his adventure, it was no great loss, estimating that, as a husband, Bémolisant had always been more of an encumbrance than an asset—which was perhaps a reckless judgment. The agent wanted to convince himself, at least, that the widow would only be according him the just tribute of regret that convention demands in our society, steeped in conventions of evident absurdity.

He promised himself, at any rate, to console her as best he could, not wanting a pretty woman to weep for too long.

At the house in the Avenue de Clichy he found the two poor women desolate, firstly because they had had no news of the vanished artist, and secondly because they were running short of money. For one of them, at least—I mean Madame Legris—the second reason even surpassed the first, the grief of losing a son-in-law being unable to compare with a financial wound.

"Oh, I was right!" cried Madame Bémolisant's mother, the respectable Madame Legris, the very model of mothers-in-law. "Could one found the least confidence on that artist's brain? There he is, running around the world, leaving his wife and child behind without a care."

"But mother," he young woman pleaded, mildly, "why accuse him when he's doubtless the victim of an inexorable fatality?"

"Ta ta ta. I know what I think: he's a simple imbecile."

He two women hardly ever read the papers. They were therefore unaware of the latest events, and Rosamour, with a hypocritically saddened expression, was obliged to pick up his story at an early point.

What Madame Bémolisant wanted to know first of all was whether, if her husband had not fallen into a trap, he was still alive,

"Alas, Madame," said Rosamour, avoiding the question, "there is still some uncertainty as to his fate, but I saw him not long ago..."

"You've seen him! He's alive, Monsieur?" she interrupted, leaning toward him anxiously.

"He was, at least, alive a few days ago—but let me tell you about my journey."

Briefly, he passed in review the various incidents in the flight of the two men whom no one, to begin with, was pursuing; their unfortunate arrest in Briseval; how they had escaped from prison, and how they had associated themselves for a few days with Professor Joël.

Perhaps he insisted more than was necessary on the moral decadence of the two unfortunates who had not hesitated to deliver themselves, as grotesque marionettes, to the mockery of the public. Was he hoping to kill affection and regret in the heart of the wife by means of the ridicule of the situation?

Finally, he recounted the final episode of the odyssey: the flight in the balloon.

"But after all, why were they running away?" Madame Legris objected, yet again, not daring to add: *if they aren't guilty?*

"I don't know," Hélène replied, mildly, in her stubborn fashion, "but what I do know is that my husband is incapable of a bad action, much less a crime."

The policeman took pity on that superb confidence. "You're right," he said, "but one can kill without being a born criminal. One can also run away without being guilty, for fear of being accused. If one sees an entire body of evidence loom up against one, and cannot perceive, on the other hand, any way of proving one's innocence, that's enough to make a man lose his head, unless he has an exceptionally strong mind. One runs away then, like a hare, without thinking that the flight itself furnishes a further argument to the case for the prosecution."

Madame Bémolisant followed his argument avidly, which responded so well to her own thoughts. As Rosamour spoke, it seemed to her that the evidence was shining bright. She acquiesced with a gesture; her eyes lit up with hope; tears were scintillating in the lashes.

"Yes, Monsieur, yes," she said, finally. "That's definitely it; he was afraid, and he fled. It's not necessary to seek elsewhere for the explanation of his conduct. And Monsieur Pilesèche went with him. Weren't they both timid and fearful individuals, as naïve as children, and knowing so little of life!"

"They might have made one another afraid," Rosamour continued. "One coward is nothing, but two cowards are capable of going to the ends of the earth by pushing one another. They were faced with a *fait accompli*—an inexplicable death. They suddenly saw the accusation looming up before them, inevitable and irrefutable. In the impossibility of responding to it, they thought to escape by flight..."

"That's evident. I'll go tell that magistrate. I'll tell him..."

"Don't take the trouble. It's too simple to appear plausible. In magistrates' offices, they look for more subtle motives, and you'd be wasting your time. Then again, there's no urgency now; the unfortunates might have found supreme deliverance in the waves to which their balloon transported them..."

"Do you think so, Monsieur"

"Who can say? In any case, if some ship has picked them up they're doubtless safe now, out of reach of the law, which has abandoned the chase. Let's allow all the noise to die down, then."

"But Monsieur, the rehabilitation—it's for me that it's necessary, and for my fighter, who bears his name..."

"You shall have it...you shall have it in full. I want to prove the innocence of our two scatterbrains—but give me a free hand; it's by finding the old uncle that I'll succeed in that. Don't worry; the honor of your name isn't indifferent to me. The more I get to know you, the more I feel borne toward you by the respectful sympathy that first made me your ally."

And gradually, he consoled her, like a child that one soothes with kind words; that music rose from his heart to his lips, and even intoxicated him.

He showed her the future open before her, full of radiant sunlight, succeeding the morose past. Could one despair, at her age? Her heart would awake on day, of its own accord, to the joy of living, in the midst of those who loved her, when time had done its work. She had had the strength to suffer, would she not have the patience to wait for the new spring in which everything within her would be reborn?

Was she listening to him, her eyes fixed and her cheeks pale and sad? Or were her thoughts wandering in the distance, over the waves where the treacherous nacelle had sunk?

XVI. In Search of the Cadaver

"A *labadens*![38] Rosamour, my friend!"
"Jean Saure! Is that you, old comrade?"

---

[38] A *labadens*, in Parisian argot, is an old friend from school or university.

277

"The king of reportage in person. Ah! The recognition scene always make a sensitive heart beat faster."

"It's been such a long time since we ran into one another. And then, like this, unexpectedly, on a street corner..."

"To be frank, my dear friend, the encounter isn't absolutely fortuitous; if I'm in these parts it's partly to look for you. I need you."

"Aha!" said the other, without blinking, but bracing himself to withstand the rude assault of a man wanting to borrow money.

He was mistaken, though; the comrade did not have designs on his wallet, and all anxiety vanished as soon as he spoke again.

"Aren't you in charge of the investigation of the Grillard-Bémolisant affair?" the journalist continued.

"Um," said Rosamour, with compromising himself.

"I'm on the hunt for news; I need you to give me some. Go on, talk: my paper is waiting."

"Well, whatever it costs me, I'll make you a confession..."

"A confession free of all artifice..."

"Absolutely free of all artifice..."

"Make your confession, then—but you know, I don't trust myself; it's not in my métier to let myself by taken in."

"All men, in all métiers, have the same pretention...and they get taken in all the same. No matter...it's quite clear that I have an idea at the back of my mind, and I'll tell you what it is..."

"Without beating around the bush?"

"Without beating around the bush. I'm a policeman; you need me. You're a journalist; I need you. Let's join forces, and all will be for the best."

Jean Saure linked arms with the detective. "Golden words," he said. "Come and have a beer. There's nothing better to aid confidences."

The two men stopped under the awning of a café, and Rosamour was finally able to formulate the confession promised with a mysterious expression.

"You know, my dear Jean, since the papers have said so, that my two fugitives slipped through my fingers and took off like sparrows. That small misfortune would be nothing, but for the wrath of the court, which has got me the boot. Now, you know that I'm rancorous, vindictive and not patient; you can therefore conclude that I'm not taking my disgrace as benevolently as people would like to believe. For want of being able to do official police work, I shall launch myself into opposition. I have my plan; I'll let you in on it. The two of us will undertake the counter-investigation. The magistracy is searching for the murderer; we're searching for the victim. I need Père Grillard, dead or alive. We'll demonstrate the perfect innocence of Bémolisant and his acolyte..."

"What! You think they're innocent!"

"Until there's proof to the contrary. I'll tell you my reasons. We demonstrate that the examining magistrate is a blockhead, that Boissonnald is a murky individual, that Rosamour is a great man, the rival of the great policemen of the past..."

"Who were decorated!"

"I'll be content with a simple statue."

"You shall have one."

"It's a veritable campaign that I'm undertaking against the Sûreté and the Court; I shan't be content until I've ground my enemy into the dust."

"Go, Redskin!"

"But for that I need a newspaper—a newspaper that will take the lead and won't be afraid—and that's where our role begins."

"Oh, my friend, I'll introduce you to my editor, who likes nothing better than slinging mud at the administration. You can make your pitch; your natural eloquence will seduce and persuade him. All the reporters on the paper are ready to launch themselves on the various tracks you indicate. As for me, I'll take charge of putting the boot into your examining magistrate. I'll be mocking, I'll be mordant, I'll prick him and harass him. It's a task, at least, and not banal."

"Is your editor capable of putting funds into the enterprise?"

"Don't worry about that—to get one up on the police, he won't back off."

And as ideas come in the course of conversation, the two friends quickly fell into agreement regarding the first operations of the campaign.

First of all, it was necessary to interest public opinion, to prepare for a turnabout in favor of the suspects. Now, great humanitarian sentiments do well in newspapers headlines and columns; a subscription in favor of Madame Bémolisant could not fail to have a prodigious effect. Given a little push, the public, in its turn, would feel sorry for the undeserved fate of the unfortunate woman and the innocent baby struck so cruelly by the unjust accusation leveled against her husband.

"Yes, unjust. Hasn't the investigation been marked by the most evident prejudice. Where's the evidence of culpability?"

And all the usual speeches about judiciary errors...

There was an entire war machine on which the two friends counted of making use like a catapult to batter the defenses of the Sûreté that had so ludicrously sacked the most scientific of its detectives.

And what a racket there would be around the subscription, to come to the aid of the pitiable victims of an unmerited insult!

And finally, the statue! Did they not have the statue? That statue was a flag, as Joseph Prudhomme would have said. They were going to exhibit once again the marvelous work of the sculptor whose disappearance in such mysterious circumstances attracted so much attention.

The dispatch-room of the paper seemed entirely indicated for that manifestation, which would take on the color of a charitable intervention in favor of a tearful family. Was it not in that dispatch room that once could see, every day, the flower of current affairs, to which the paper, raising the trumpet to its lips, never failed to give a noisy publicity?

Tombolas, charity sales, pictures to hang on the wainscoting, autographs by the man of the hour, with his photograph in his latest cravat: to that kaleidoscope, the public willingly applied its eye.

In truth, that was the drumbeat that the two conspirators needed.

And in the meantime, Rosamour went to establish his batteries solidly, before unmasking them and battering a breach in the theory so briskly erected by the examining magistrate

What he had not said was that he counted on inaugurating, in order finally to discover what had been the fate of the unfortunate Monsieur Grillard, a method as bold as it was unusual.

The story of Jacques Aymard, the "sorcerer" of Lyon and his divinatory wand was running through his mind. Was this not the case on which to try out the singular means that had succeeded so well in that circumstance?

Rosamour also thought that Miss Adda might be useful to him in realizing that project.

She was, to begin with, the "sensitive individual" described by the Baron von Reichenbach,[39] for whom the nature has manifestations unknown to common mortals. The policeman had witnessed experiments that left no doubt as to the sensibility of her nerves.

---

[39] Carl von Reichenbach (1788-1869) was a scientific researcher who made several notable discoveries in chemistry and was a significant pioneer in research into the relationship between electricity and magnetism, which he attempted to associate with a universal field of energy he called "odic force." He also supposed the latter to be responsible for the phenomena of hypnotism.

Without even being plunged into a provoked trance, she perceived the odic effluvia that escape from the asperities of various bodies, but which are only detectable by a few individuals. If someone raised a hand in a dimly-lit room she saw a kind of slight flame springing from the fingertips, and that flame differed in color according to whether it was emanated by the left or the right hand.

It was sufficient for her to hold a glass in her left hand for a few minutes for the water it contained to take on, for her, an insipid and disagreeable taste and make her feel nauseated, whereas water appeared pure and agreeable to her when she held it in her right hand.

One would never finish if it were necessary to identify all the bizarre and unhealthy sensations that the young woman experienced, which made her a remarkable subject for study.

Rosamour judged that all these precious faculties might finally find their application. It was only necessary for him to be able to put Miss Adda on the track of the old scientist. With that end in mind, the policeman assembled a few clothes that had belonged to Monsieur Grillard and, making a package of them, went to the cheap hotel where he had lodged the young woman, having given her instructions to show herself as little as possible.

The instruction has been almost superfluous; after the overworked existence that she had dragged out on the road, the former ballerina was avid for repose and tranquility. She lived in her little fifth-floor room, only descending occasionally to buy a cornet of fries or the few sous' worth of cooked meat that constituted the bulk of her nourishment.

She stayed there, often in bed or sprawled in an old armchair with worn-out springs, doing nothing, motionless, her gaze lost in a dream...and her dream went into the distance, all the way to the sea, where she thought she saw a balloon floating, disaster-stricken. And among the passengers in the frail nacelle, she only saw one: the one who had so much empire over her; the unfortunate clown, Pilesèche.

Her imagination concentrated then on that singular spectacle; her vision darkened; her entire being became numb, as if, even at a distance, she could feel the effluvia of her former magnetizer passing through her.

Was that not because he was still alive?

That conviction invaded her entirely, and when, with a violent start, she woke up again, agitated, excited by fever and nervous overexcitement, she conserved that belief that the aeronauts had not perished. She tried to make Rosamour share it, but he shook his head. No, no, the sea did not return its victims; anyway, they would have heard mention of it.

And what was the point in paying any more attention to the unfortunate shipwreck-victims? The key to the problem was the vanished cadaver; and it was the cadaver that it was necessary to find, at any price.

Putting her into contact, therefore, with all the objects that had belonged to the scientist, he questioned her, pushing her lucidity toward that sole question: where as the old man's body?

She did not reply.

Large beads of sweat testified nevertheless to the efforts she was making to see with the eyes of her soul and the grasp a trail that was incessantly hidden.

He decided to make one last attempt, and took her to the former dwelling of the mysterious victim.

The rubble had been partly cleared; the walls had been shored up, but the repair work had not progressed beyond the first floor. He was nevertheless able to hoist the young woman up to the former laboratory, which remained in almost exactly the same state as on the day after the fire, except that the charred beams had been supported by stays, and planks had been thrown laterally to make an almost continuous and accessible floor.

Silently, Adda went along the walls, feeling, sniffing, her eyes staring beneath half-closed lids, folded into herself, and sometimes shivering.

Suddenly, she stopped, her neck taut, her nostrils dilated, as if she had perceived the distant odor of the object for which she was searching. Her hand extended forwards, pointing at an invisible phantom that was fleeing before her, zigzagging like a pursued hair; then she started walking.

Adda went down the ladders that she had had so much difficulty climbing without any assistance, marched through the streets, without hesitation, without stopping…marching continuously, until, at the top of the Avenue Clichy, she stopped for a few seconds outside Madame Bémolisant's door; then, as if picking up a fresh trail, she resumed her curse, going back down toward the great boulevards; hesitated again at the intersection of the Rue de Sèze; set off again more urgently in order to steer toward the house where Rosamour lived, after detours and backtrackings that had taken her all the way to the Gare Montparnasse...

Rosamour, who was following her, was exhausted.

Miss Adda did not seem to feel the fatigue of that hectic course, and her feet skimmed the ground, hardly touching it. Her pace accelerated, while unfortunate detective ran out of breath following her and it was with a flagellating stride that he climbed the stairs leading to his apartment.

In front of the closed door she stopped, breathless, and banged on it violently with her fist until the policeman had opened it.

Adda went in like a hurricane, with an "Ah!" of relief and triumph—but, immediately vanquished, her entire being relaxed, as it were, abruptly, and she fell, inert, outside the cupboard in which the nickel statue lay...

Oh, poor Rosamour scarcely spared a thought for that statue, as he let himself fall in his turn into an armchair, his face convulsed and streaming after that hectic steeplechase.

For a moment, he had been hopeful: the somnambulist had such an inspired expression. She was walking with such a sure and rapid pace toward her invisible goal! But on seeing her climb the stairway of his own house...

Good! thought the disappointed policeman, laughing humorlessly. *You're going to see that the cadaver is hidden in my apartment! I'm hiding Père Grillard, or giving shelter to his murderer! Too bad—my subject isn't as brilliant as I hoped, and I'm back to square one....*

Regathering his wits, he went on: *I only have one hope left: the indecipherable cryptogram contains the key to the enigma; it's up to me to bring it out.*

He was tired out by such a gallop, however, and incapable for the moment of stringing two ideas together. He was still mopping his brow and panting when Adda woke up and rubbed her eyes, also exhausted, her limbs aching, incapable of moving them without crying out, and utterly unconscious of what had happened.

Rosamour was still under the impact of his failure when his friend Jean Saure came to find him. The news that he was bringing was not made to comfort the poor detective.

To be sure, the press campaign was going well; public opinion was already showing a benevolence toward their cause, while the court was under vigorous attack. But time was passing and the need for money was making itself felt. Madame Bémolisant had confessed, blushing, that her resources were almost totally exhausted, and the war could only be continued with the aid of new subsidies.

It was necessary to sell the statue.

An Englishman, a kind of Barnum, had made an enticing offer. They might be able to do even better by organizing a public auction.

The agent acquiesced to all his friends proposals, leaving him complete liberty to act, without the strength to think and devoid of courage.

He only had one idea left: to harness himself like a Benedictine to the deciphering of the cryptogram. That was where salvation lay. The rest scarcely mattered...

XVII. Saved from the Waters

On the deck of the little steamer *Francine* two streaming bodies lay, clad in grotesque costumes, which the waves had lacerated in a bizarre fashion.

The drowned men were lividly pale, insensible to any stimulation. They scarcely had a pulse-beat, and no breath was emerging from their breasts.

Sailors and passengers surrounded them with muffled exclamations, while two or three crouching men strove to re-animate them, massaging them in order to restore some warmth to their icy extremities, imposing rhythmic tractions on their tongues in order to reestablish the automatic move-ment of human respiration, which maintains the hearth of life.

A physician, without saying much apart from issuing brief commands, was presiding over that work, and listening at intervals to see whether the hearts had begun to beat under the violent stimulation of napkins soaked in boiling water and abruptly applied to the epigastrum.

Standing up, his legs apart, with his hands in his pockets, a short broad-shouldered man, solid and thickset, was smoking his pipe. He was the commandant of the vessel, Captain Carbagnac, a southerner of good vintage, who had no need to proclaim the fact; his accent did that for him.

"Stand aside, the lot of you!" he cried, in a stentorian voice, to the sailors whose circle was getting tighter, intercept-ing the daylight and the respirable air. "Nevertheless," he said, addressing the doctor, "We interrupted their bath at a good time."

The doctor, very busy, only replied with a grunt—but the other had no need of an interlocutor; his loquacity could do without replies.

"Look—one of them moved... It's not so bad... With good fur gloves and vigorous rubbing, you can wake the dead... Poor fellow, they don't look so good, all the same... Well, it would be a great pity, old man, if Captain Carbagnac was deflected from his route for corpses... I have confidence, me... I said to myself: Doctor Caudelot is no fool, he'll get these fellows out of it... What desolates me, damn it, is not to have saved the balloon. I'd gladly made a captive ascent...a don't worry old man, a *captive* ascent...Captain Carbagnac owes it to his crew, his passengers, and his family...but nevertheless, imagine how delighted these worthy fellows will be with our rival. Go sound a fanfare! Trying to disengage the nacelle, the damned balloon found a means of flying away with the remains of the net, and that buckle of gas flew away as if it were neither more or less than a soap-bubble..."

One of the drowned me opened haggard eyes and his lips moved, murmuring softly: "Where am I?"

And that question, escaping like a breath, they divined without hearing it.

The other came back with a spasm. "The police! The police!" he repeated, pursued all the way to the coma of asphyxia by an obsessive anguish.

And they both fell back into their unconscious immobility—but their hearts were finally beating; their breasts were rising, aspiring the oxygen of life, and falling back in irregular somersaults.

The doctor stood up and readjusted the sleeves that he had rolled up. "Now I'll answer for them," he said, finally.

"So much the better, thank God," exclaimed the captain, in a voice that he had doubtless borrowed from the thunder of his homeland. "Hey!" he continued, "You four lads, here! Lift these fellows up for me and stick them in hammocks with good blankets. We'll chat later."

Although a trifle abrupt, Captain Carbagnac was a good man. If he did not present a tender appearance and sacrificed nothing to sensitivity, he was nonetheless humane in his fashion. While continuing his pacing, therefore, hands behind his back and the wind in his face, he smiled, content with the fortunate result of the rescue, the smile broadening within the superb collar of beard that framed his broad full-moon face.

And, resuming his customary preoccupations, he went back to his daily inspection, like a man who knows the importance of detail, barking orders to port and starboard, darting a glance through the open hatchways all the way down to the engine room, not disdaining to check the propriety of the *houteilles*—which is the name by which the place designated with the initials W.C. is known on the deck of a steamship.

Finally, having given a cabin boy who got under his feet a clip round the ear, he went down to the lower deck.

There, side by side in two hammocks, the two drowned men were trying to recover their thoughts, and the same words came back to their unconscious lips incessantly.

"Where am I?" said one.

And the other, agitated, as if he were trying to escape an obsession, repeated: "The police! The police…!"

The first was parading bewildered eyes around him while his hammock swayed in the swell "Bémolisant!" he murmured, on perceiving his companion. And, after searching his memory for something that gradually came back to him, he added: "Where's the other one?"

"The other one, the other one?" the captain repeated, between his teeth. "It appears that there was another one…well, my friend, he's gone to the bottom. I haven't seen him."

He turned toward the doctor. "The brave fellows seem to me to have come through it; we'll be able to submit them to a little interrogation. I'm curious, at least, to know their stories, these actors…"

Did one of the shipwreck-victims understand those words. Perhaps—he turned over in his hammock as if to escape the announced interrogation, while the other muttered more loudly: "The statue…! The statue…!"

That excitation was followed by the most complete prostration; the unfortunates remained unconscious for twenty-four hours.

They emerged from it at the same time. When Pilesèche opened his eye and learned toward his neighbor he encountered the other's atonal gaze.

"Are we alone?" he murmured.

"Yes," replied the other, nodding his head.

288

And in fact, that part of the deck was deserted, everyone being busy with his duties.

"Where's the ship going?"

"I don't know."

"Are we discovered?"

"Alas!" said Bémolisant, without answering the question. "Pilesèche, what have they done with my uncle?"

"What must he be thinking, if he's still alive inside his nickel envelope, in being himself submitted to such ordeals?"

"We need to find him and free him," Bémolisant added, with a start. "But how do we get out of here?"

"How do we get back to France...in spite of the gendarmes and the police?"

"As long as they haven't signaled our capture by semaphore…"

"What if we were to throw ourselves in the water?"

"What would have been the point of making so much effort to save ourselves?"

"I can't live like this..."

There was a momentary silence then, and Pilesèche, propping himself up on his elbow, without saying anything, swung his long thin legs out of the hammock.

His poor empty head could scarcely hold itself upright, and slumped from one shoulder to the other. Everything around him was spinning, while the pitching and rolling of the vessel swung the hammock back and forth above the floor, which seemed to be fleeing. But his eyes fixed persistently on a pile of neatly-folded clothes, doubtless destined to replace the rags that had survived their shipwreck. He gazed at the small objects that had been removed from their pockets: their knives, their purses, and finally the wallet in which the poor laboratory assistant and opportunist clown had stuck a few papers, among which he had so carefully folded up the copy of the famous cryptogram taken from the scientist's laboratory.

He had never had time to try to decipher that cryptogram, and had ended up forgetting that it was in his wallet—but an obsession, brought on by illness, drew him back to it now.

Who could tell whether the key to salvation might be contained therein?

All kinds of methods came to mind by which it might be easily deciphered. Finally, it seemed to him that he only had it before his eyes, reading it would be straightforward.

Moved by that obsession, stiffening himself against the numbness that was invading him, he leaned out of the hammock and stretched out his arm in order to reach the wallet with his fleshless hand. Just as he grasped it avidly, however, a pitch of the vessel caused him to lose his equilibrium.

Pilesèche tumbled on to the floor, where he remained unconscious until a sailor, passing by, came to lift him up like a feather and replace him in is hammock, without perceiving that the invalid was clutching the precious wallet in his clenched fist, and pressing it against his heart.

As soon as he thought he was alone Pilesèche took out the piece of paper, soaked by sea-water, and absorbed himself in the contemplation of the half-effaced hieroglyphs...

The two castaways were well cared for. They were administered cordials and soups that formed a delicious diet after the wretched fare of their life as fairground performers. Only one anxiety clawed at them, and that was wondering whether their identities had been unmasked and the news of their capture had reached France.

When Captain Carbagnac came by, they usually pretended to be asleep, as much to listen and try to overhear some indication as to avoid questions. They only risked opening their eyes when they judged that their incognito had definitely not been penetrated.

"Well, my sleepers who've woken up," said the captain rubbing his hands. "That was a nice snooze! And now, my little sinners, it's time to tell me whether you want to going all the way to the Congo or whether you want me to drop you off in cow country.

"Are we on the coast of France?" hazarded Pilesèche.

"Oh, as to that, no, and if Captain Carbagnac hadn't had bad weather and the wind in his face, the *Francine* would have passed Madeira by now, at least. All that I can do for you, if you want to leave us, is deposit you preciously on the coast of Portugal. A little far from Paris, it's true, if that's your destination. All the same, it's still Europe, and by addressing yourself to the French consul, you could be repatriated gratis, with all the honors due to you."

Address themselves to the French consul? That did not seem to them to be advice to follow. But bah! Once ashore they would be able to get out of trouble. They still had enough money in pocket, which simplified things.

The two unfortunates therefore accepted the captain's offer, and while the Francine set a course for the little port of Vila Nova de Milfontes, Pilesèche and Bémolisant got ready to leave the ship, dressing in costumes that were half-naval and half-civilian, which they owed to the munificence of their rescuers, the passengers and he captain.

One morning, the ship dropped anchor in the harbor, and the two castaways immediately took their places—not without having thanked Captain Carbagnac and the doctor warmly—in a launch that was going to take advantage of the unscheduled port of call to renew the provisions of fresh food.

It was a good opportunity to take a stroll on *terra firma*. The worthy captain of the *Francine* spruced himself up a little and, in company with Dr. Caudelot, had himself taken ashore; they were both glad to stretch their limbs and to have news of what had been happening in the world since their departure.

After an hour spent chatting with the French consul, the two friends went to install themselves on the veranda of the best local hotel, for a little siesta and to catch up with their correspondence.

Facing large glasses full of iced cocktails, while the captain wrote a letter, Caudelot started reading newspapers in various languages. Before the rest, however, he scanned the French papers that the consul had lent them, following them in chronological order, devouring the detail of news items, important and petty, that had captivated public attention for an hour while they were at sea.

Suddenly, the excellent doctor uttered an exclamation that made Carbagnac jump in his rattan armchair.

"Damn it, my dear," exclaimed the commandant of the *Francine*, "you must have encountered something phenomenal!"

"Phenomenal—you said it!"

"Make me party to this sensational news, then."

"Do you know who we saved from the waters?"

"Two fairground performers, I suspect..."

"I'll give you a hundred guesses."

"No idea, my dear doctor—don't leave me in suspense."

"We've saved Père Grillard's murderers!"

"Good God! I don't believe it."

"Just read the story of their escape in a balloon..."

"In truth, it's a strange case. But it's not my job to tip off the police about the villains they've let slip through their fingers. Anyway, they can't be far away, and if the consul's got his wits about him, he won't have any difficulty recognizing the famous Panthéon murderers in the heroes of the story we've told him. It's his business, not mine. All the same, though, I'll tell the story to my brother while I'm writing to him—they'll have a good laugh on the Canebière when they hear what specimens Captain Carbagnac took the trouble to save."

XVIII. In which we encounter arrieros *and smugglers*

Meanwhile, the fugitives had judged it prudent not to stay too long in the town.

They had regularized their presence, thanks to declarations and statements signed by Captain Carbagnac, who had explained their situation. One cannot requite shipwreck-victims to be carrying on their person all the necessary documents establishing their identity, and by avoiding certain indiscreet questions by people who were devoid of suspicion, they were soon able to continue on their way.

In order to conserve their resources, while thinking that they might occasionally be able to use diligences and railways, they departed on foot, all their luggage tied up in a handker- chief on the end of a stick.

They walked without saying anything, doubtless mulling over the same thoughts in their heads.

In front of them stretched a dusty road bordered by stunted trees, curved toward the east by the sea breeze.

The sunlight was sparkling on the reddish dust that was kicked up by the hooves of mules, and the road extended like a long ribbon, plunging into the depths of ravines and scaling hills. It seemed to them that they could already perceive, in the distance, on the blue mountains, the vague silhouettes of French customs officers...

Without looking back they marched, drawn toward their native soil by an unconscious force, in spite of the menacing storm that they sensed before them.

Could they hope to pass unperceived through the mesh of the net extended along the frontiers, where the hundred eyes of Argus inspected new arrivals, no matter how insignificant they seemed?

And if they succeeded in crossing the dangerous line, would they still be sheltered from all danger as they ap- proached Paris, to which they would be fatally drawn back?

But their present security, after the moments of terrible anguish that they had passed through, produced a physical relaxation in them that they had not previously known. When they had passed a restful night in a rather smelly inn, in the midst of innumerable insects that constituted a disagreeable permanent garrison in the straw extended for sleeping, they found themselves back on the road to France, refreshed and replenished, no longer thinking about anything, under the ar- dent sun, which was making the cicadas sing in the long grass.

Pilesèche was still depressed, in consequence of which he did not say much; he has less resilience and a less supple imagination than his companion, and a brief encounter with a picturesque gypsy camp was insufficient to distract him from his preoccupations.

By contrast, the new impressions chased away the impressions of sad past ordeals in the artist. He was dreaming about fandangos glimpsed in the evening by the tremulous light of the moon and the stars, and the old popular songs, mocking or sentimental, were singing within him to the accompaniment of guitar and castanets.

Where were the nebulous principles of decadent music, then, and the famous scale of six thousand notes whose apostle he had been? Was Bémolisant about to convert to the musical religion of the old race that sang to coming into the world? Or was that old race about to bring Bémolisant back to a taste for its naïve melodies? An arduous problem, no doubt, about which one could argue for a long time, for the time was lacking for a conclusive experiment—but it is worth noting that the artiste bought castanets and a guitar, and started to sing, during the pauses in the voyage, the old *romanceros* that have never been written down and are transmitted from mouth to mouth, with the warm accents of old heroic dialects.

Unfortunately, music and the fandango had no purchase on the scientific mind of the former laboratory assistant. Physiology had no truck with such nonsense, and he had been nourished on the xs and ys of vivisection. While his companion scraped the taut strings and pinched arpeggios or sad diminished sevenths, resolving ironically into broken cadences in order not to conclude in banal perfect chords, Pilesèche labored on the translation of his cryptogram or stirred in his head the alternatives contained in the question: "Is Monsieur Grillard still alive in his nickel envelope?"

Let us confess that he dared not make a definitive response, and remained in a dolorous perplexity.

They went by, however, and the voyagers crossed, one by one, the sierras that constitute the skeleton of ancient Iberia, reaching the foothills of the Pyrenees.

As they got closer to the frontier, they felt increasingly invaded by heavy apprehensions. The stages of their journey shortened, under the most various pretexts, and the voyagers scarcely dared advance, invincibly retained by the dread of the vague peril that they were about to confront.

On coming out of a village, they encountered a small band of men following the same route, driving mules laden with rather voluminous bales. Those *arrieros*, cigarettes in their lips beneath their vast sombreros, darted suspicious glances at them, hardly inclined to encourage conversation.

The two fugitives, however, experienced such a keen need to ask questions and find out which was the best road and the surest means of deceiving the surveillance at the frontier that they approached the muleteers and tried to strike up a conversation with some banality regarding the heart and the oppressive sun—an eminently insinuating exordium familiar in all countries.

The man who appeared to be the leader of the band and who was marching proudly, with his hand stuck in the leather buckle of his hazel-wood *maquilla*, only replied in monosyllables, with a sullen expression which would have put off his interlocutors if they had not long since double their dose of philosophy.

Bémolisant was well aware that he did not inspire confidence in the Spaniards, but necessity has no law; he needed the aid of local people; these looked somewhat like smugglers, which was not injurious to his program, and it was necessary to take advantage of the fact, at all costs.

Taking the bull by the horns, therefore, he told them that he did not know the country, and asked if he might join them to follow the road—to which the leader replied, summarily: "*A su disposicion de Usted!*"

To the *Usted*, it was a matter of bowing graciously as a sign of mute gratitude, his repertoire of the Castilian language not being very rich in appropriate formulae. Above all, he was careful not to appear to perceive the decidedly mediocre pleasure that the offer of his company seemed to cause the descendant of El Cid Campeador;[40] and, as the other did not unclench his teeth, he began a monologue aloud, asking questions and supplying replied.

They stopped to eat in the hollow of a valley where the fresh water of a stream was cascading, and each of them took his provisions from his sack. Bémolisant ever amiable, emitted a few coarse pleasantries in a whimsical Spanish that had the privilege of bringing a smile—was it a smile?—to the Olympian face of his mute companion.

The latter deigned to open his mouth and interrogate the Frenchmen as to their civil estate—after which, without allowing the impression left by that suspicious interrogation to be divined, he stretched out on the grass, turned his back on the honorable company, and dozed off for the siesta.

There was nothing to do but follow his example, but Pilesèche did not have Bémolisant's superb confidence. He dared not close an eye, thinking that the brave men of Navarre, with their ferocious eyes as sharp as the daggers stuck in their red belts, looked more like bandits than honest transporters of merchandise.

Gently, he nudged his companion's elbow to recommend prudence, but the insouciant artist was asleep.

When the sun was in decline again, the entire caravan, upright in response to a guttural summons, set forth again. The leader seemed to have lost his mistrust; Bémolisant, judging the moment favorable, told himself that he was not risking anything, after all, and started tell him his story—or, at least, a romance sufficiently adapted to the circumstances.

What the other understood from it, quite clearly, was that the two young men had come a long way—their papers said so, at least—and that they wanted to get back into France, with some reason for not wanting to attract attention there; and that, in sum, they wanted his help to cross the frontier incognito.

---

[40] The 11th century hero Rodrigo Diaz de Vivar was known both as El Cid (the Lord) and El Campeador (the Champion).

The Spaniard gradually relaxed. He explained to them exactly what métier he was following, with his band. He took confidence so far as to tell them his name, which was Juan Calcadores, a native of a little posada near Sos. All that was of no fundamental importance, but what interested the fugitives most keenly was that they were about to reach a small hamlet populated by people who made a habit of traversing the frontier for the requirements of their commerce. In spite of the euphemisms it was easy to understand that it was more a matter of smugglers than globe-trotters—but Calcadores reckoned them to be resourceful men, and that was sufficient.

Furthermore, they were approaching their goal. The path climbed up with abrupt bends, suspended on the flank of a mountain overhanging a deep and sheer ravine. Dusk had arrived and the moon was at the zenith, over the narrow fissure that some Roland's sword had carved into the mountain. The men were marching behind their mules, slowly but at a steady pace, without breathing more rapidly.

Unlike them, Bémolisant did not have legs hardened to that kind of exercise; he rubbed his thighs and sponged his forehead, looking forward to the blessed threshold where he would finally be able to get a little well-earned rest.

It was the furious barking of half a dozen dogs that first signaled the strange little hamlet, composed of a few small huts wedged in the hollow of an overhanging rock. Through narrow and smoky windows a few rays of light filtered, which were abruptly extinguished in response to the noise, and in the darkness a voice shouted: "Who goes there?" in a tone more menacing than amicable.

Calcadores responded in his turn with a few sonorous interjections that resembled a password, and the little troop continued to advance. While the *arrieros* disappeared with their mules beneath the somber arch of a portal, however, Juan told the Frenchmen to stay where they were for a minute and allow him to warn the person who was to be their host about their presence.

Fortunately, the negotiations did not take long, and following a little old man, bent with age, who appeared to be the master of the place, Bémolisant and Pilesèche penetrated into a room of moderate size, into which people of all sorts were already crowded, some eating and drinking around a massive table, others lying down along the walls, wrapped in rags that had been cloaks, with the hoods pulled down over their eyes.

Pilesèche advanced hesitantly, his eyes blinded by the light that suddenly struck them. The sordid room gave him the impression of a brigands' cave, from which he had little chance of emerging alive. Meanwhile, as all eyes—and what eyes!—peered at the newcomers, the master, sitting them down at the table, pushed toward them a large loaf of black bread, already considerably eroded, and a bowl of milk full of *migus*—pieces of bread fried in unpurified oil—which emitted a nauseating odor of rotten olives.

It would probably not have been a good idea to venture into that place with the air of cosseted nabobs, but our two companions did not have the look of fortunate aristocrats in quest of the unexpected, who might be robbed profitably.

When they had attempted to appease their hunger with a few unspeakable concessions to Spanish cuisine, the two Frenchmen were taken to a corner by their aged host, who made them a speech with all the nobility of which he was capable

"Señor Juan tells me that you desire a guide to traverse the frontier by night, and that you are counting on our help—but that is a perilous enterprise for us; how much will you pay?"

"We still have a little money, and you can be tranquil, worthy Caballero; your recompense will be as if you had saved King Don Sancho, your august ancestor."[41] Bémolisant judged that romantic language was appropriate, and that one does not speak to a man of Navarre, however scant a hidalgo,

---

[41] Sancho I was king of Portugal from 1185 to 1212.

as one speaks to a Marseille street-porter or an Auvergnat water-carrier.

The old man allowed himself to be flattered and discussed the price of his small service. They soon fell into accord, however, and when the bargain was concluded the artist asked whether there was some shelter in which one might sleep—but the house only had that one room, and the travelers had no other recourse than to lie down in the darkest corner on the *esteras*—the coarse mats covering the bare ground.

They were beginning to get drowsy, in spite of the numerous insects that took their bodies for pasture, when the sound of a guitar that was being strummed caused the artist to open his eyes.

The spectacle was worth the trouble. Fuliginous and reeking lamps had been set on the ground which illuminated from below a tall young woman whose black hair was decked with a rose and twisted in a kiss-curl over her forehead. She adjusted her castanets and caused her satin corset to crack over her hip, as if to test the elasticity over her back.

Along the wall, men and women were ranged, cigarettes in their lips, while a flautist played a prelude of scales on a three-holed *chirola*, and another musician plucked the strings of his guitar.

Bémolisant raised his head. The mañola, hamstrings taut, launched into a *zoreico*, a primitive dance without attitudes, but rapid and brisk, to the accompanying rattle of the enraged castanets.

Ah, what rhythm!

For the moment, Bémolisant was all rhythm; he had learned rhythm on Spanish soil, where everything ends up in a bolero, and, willingly seizing a Basque drum or drawing *fin-de-siècle* chords from a guitar with the flight of his five thin fingers, he hammered out the victorious rhythm.

Under the oblique glimmer of the vacillating lamps, the great shadow of the dancer elongated, capricious and fantastic, over the poorly roughcast and blackened walls. Abandoning the old rhythms, she sometimes swayed on her hips, provoca-

299

tive and never weary, down to the ground, her throat extended for a kiss, the suddenly reared up as if to flee, with a laugh that displayed her white teeth, and exclamations that the musicians and the audience repeated.

The dances only ended with the exhaustion of the dancer and when the lamps went out for want of oil, but Bémolisant was already asleep again, snoring conscientiously, accompanying the last arpeggios of the guitar with a regular rhythmic purr.

He was sleeping profoundly when a vigorous hand came to shake him by the shoulder. It was necessary to get up and set forth on the march, silently, in the dark, along narrow paths on which the feet could hardly place themselves.

The smugglers took the lead, each one with a bale on his shoulder and a blunderbuss in his hand. The two Frenchmen brought up the rear, somewhat breathless and barely able to distinguish, under the tremulous light of the moon, the girl that the old smuggler had given them to serve as a guide, and who was marching in front of them with all the grace of her sixteen years, at a brisk pace, unhampered by her short skirt. Peppa turned round from time to time to check that they were following and to encourage them with a familiar appeal, and then she fell silent.

Dawn paled the high summits; the path plunged down into gorges. Undoubtedly they were on the French slopes, and it was a matter of keeping out of sight of the customs officers.

By virtue of what mischance did the band run into an ambush just as it emerged on to a small plateau on the saddle of a pass?

In the blink on an eye the alarm was given, but it was too late to change course; they were numerous, however, and the smugglers fell upon the enemy, daggers drawn, while two of them took cover behind a rock and leveled their blunderbusses.

Peppa, with a resolution that denoted a certain habitude to such adventures, had grabbed Bémolisant by the arm and dragged him into a clump of tall fir trees, while Pilesèche tried

300

to follow them, bumping into branches, his footing ill-assured on the slippers needles

The customs men were too buy fending off the Spaniards to pursue the fugitives, who hurried along, clinging on to rocks and branches.

The sound of gunshots gradually faded away in the distance, and they finally reached a muleteer's trail that led directly to the next village.

Peppa, anxious about the outcome of the battle in which her people were engaged, wanted to go back, and, after giving the Frenchmen her final instructions bade them adieu and wished them a successful end to their journey.

They were now in France, and in spite of their fatigue, hastening their pace, they resumed their route.

XIX. The End of an Auction

Elbows leaning on his work table and his head plunged into his open hands, Rosamour was trying to decipher a puzzle.

He had a photographic print in front of him in which all the letters were reproduced, one after another, without any apparent connection.

The letters, which stood out in white against the black background of the print, were, unfortunately, partly effaced, with lacunae where characters disappeared, scarcely leaving a nebulous trace, while the sponge that had passed over the inscription had striped it with broad milky streaks, endearing it illegible.

The photographic paper was curling at the edges, and in order to keep it flat, Rosamour has placed the paperweight he had picked up in Monsieur Grillard's laboratory, a nickel toad, on one edge, while a heavy ivory paper-knife maintained the opposite edge.

The agent concentrated all his attention on the characters, which, although belonging to a familiar alphabet, were nevertheless as many hieroglyphs.

By dint of patience, however, he had succeeded in transcribing the letters that seemed indubitable and replacing by
crosses those that were effaces, and had obtained the following inscription:

bfoomgtqklu++++esqnuo
+++agtb+++++ef++fy
esqnugnx++++et kgn+etc+
+gst+np+++pftofpcfyesk+
+++++ihoskenc++tec x+
++dbvetvaugn ugtjpsutu++
++++

His eyes fatigued by that difficult decipherment, and
without allowing himself to be put off by the numerous lacunae in his transcription, the agent set about considering the
physiognomy of that sequence of letters, while reflecting that
the invalid must not have searched very hard for his cryptographic system and must have used the simplest.

Following a familiar method, it was necessary to look to
see whether any group of letters was reproduced several times.
In fact, each of the ternaries *esq*, *qnu* and *yes* was reproduced
twice. After that, it was necessary to test whether the cryptogram might have been composed simply by means of a key of
three letters or numbers. Rosamour thus began to separate the
letters into groups of three, taking account as much as possible
of the effaced characters.

If his hypothesis was correct, each of those groups of
characters ought to correspond to the key—which is to say
that all the first letters of the various groups came from the
same alphabet; in the same way, all the second letters had
been formed by a second alphabet, and similarly for the third.

Having separated out the list of first letters he looked to
see which one was repeated most frequently; it was *e*. Now, in
French—as in the majority of European languages, in fact—it
is *e* that is most frequently repeated letter; it followed that the

first letters of the groups had not been subject to any alteration.

It was different for the other two series of letters; in the second, the f was most frequently repeated, and in the third it was *g*, which indicated that the *e* of the natural language was indicated in one case by *f* and in the other by *g*. Now, *e f* and *g* follow one another in the ordinary alphabet, so the key to the ternary might be 123, indicating that the second letter was displaced by one rank and the third by two.

Nothing was simpler. The clever fellow shrugged his shoulders before such ingenuity, and reproached himself for not having searched sooner for what the document might contain, which he swiftly transcribed as follows:

Bemoletpilt...eronto...meta... ee..evrnotev... esixm.. sa.. ess. mor... perienceveri...... heoriem... redu... datestamentetinstru......

Alas, alas! The puzzle was still as puzzling as it had been before the decipherment.

A few words were easy to recognize; firstly there was a question of *Bemol...* and *Pil...*; the word *mort*—death—was recognizable, and testament. *Experience*—experiment—was also definable, but what experiment? And did the letters *veri*, which followed it, mean that the experiment verified the *(t)heorie*: the theory?

"Good," said the agent. "Monsieur Grillard carried out an experiment that might lead to his death. He mentions his testament and his instructions. But all that doesn't say a great deal, and certainly isn't sufficiently explicit..."

After reflection and with a significant grimace, he added: "It doesn't explain anything at all. As many question marks as before! I really can't present myself armed with this incomplete and incoherent cryptogram."

Again he plunged his head into his hands, his eyes obstinately fixed on those shreds of phrases, whose image was dancing in his congested brain, his nerves taut to the point of exasperation, while his temples were throbbing.

The truncated words filed past before his eyes, and he completed them with the most bizarre assemblages. He read in them whatever he wished, instantly demolishing what he had painstakingly edified, without, alas, the help of logic. He adapted new syllables to them, trying the most unusual combinations, but it was all devoid of meaning, and his overheated imagination, drawing away from the immediate goal, went back to the beginning of the most mysterious and bizarre affair that he had ever encountered.

He saw himself before the magistrate again; he saw himself, presumptuous and sure of is method, the scientific method. "The fugitives," he had said, "I have at the end of a telegraphic wire...the key item of evidence, the cadaver—doubtless a cadaver—I shall envelop with my tightest deductions: it can't escape me..."

But the fugitives were at the bottom of the sea!

And the cadaver was still undiscoverable!

Finally, he saw himself in the home of the young widow, whose dolor had moved him from the start, and whose gentle face haunted him more than was reasonable now.

Abruptly his thought found a bifurcation there, and set off along the flowery paths of idyll. The career that he had embraced had brought him nothing but disappointments; lassitude took hold of him; he dreamed of a tranquil life in perfumed fields. A farm by the seaside, with a discreet and tender housewife, children playing barefoot in the grass...

His dream came back to the young woman whose sad eyes had troubled him so much. Was she not the good farmer's wife he needed?

And why not?

The satisfactions that the poor woman had found with her first husband would not leave her eternal regrets, and since Bémolisant was dead—oh, quite dead, since the sea does not yield its prey—it was quite permissible to dream of a new union in which they would both be perfectly happy...

Eyes half-closed, Rosamour let his domestic fantasy run down that slope, and smiled, as of the odorous breeze was already rustling the foliage in his orchard, in the midst of which the image of Hélène floated.

And it went on…and on…when his gaze, staring, encountered the piece of paper again—the infernal piece of paper that retained the indecipherable mystery.

Suddenly plunged back into reality, he felt a surge of irresistible anger rising within him. Oh, the idyll was a long way off. The professional gripped him again...

What! There was an obstacle that he could not overcome! A grain of sand, a mere nothing, was stopping him!

He stood up, furiously, pushing back his armchair, and started pacing pack and forth. The carpet stifled the noise of his footfalls, which hit the floor violently, but he talked aloud, hurling insults at people and things, insulting himself, showing his fist to the four walls…

It was, in brief, one of those sudden fits of anger that serve as a safety-valve for our irascible machine, and which rise, and rise, with an increasing din, until the final explosion...

It did not help him to decipher the cryptogram. But it relieved all his slowly-accumulated frustrations.

The objects that came to hand flew across the room, and, finally seizing the little nickel toad that was holding down the photographic print, he hurled it at the floor in its turn, violently...

But what the…?

It seemed that the impact had animated the metal!

The stunned toad hopped, awkwardly throwing itself between Rosamour's legs—who, opening his eyes wide, moved his feet out of the way to avoid the contact of the disgusting creature.

What a singular dream! Was he going mad?

And abruptly, he brought his heel down on the gray back of the toad, which he crushed with a curt sound. But immediately, recovering possession of himself, passing his hand over his forehead to drive away the last residues of anger, he leaned over his victim and examined it,

The animal had shiny metal scales on its back, and on the carpet lay a thin envelope of nickel. The paperweight had merely been an animal imprisoned within a frail pellicle of metal.

Suddenly, light dawned in his brain, illuminating an entire sheaf of facts incomprehensible until then. The statue! Why should the statue not also be the chrysalis of a living being?

Was not the experiment to which the cryptogram referred the metallization of a human being? And had not the two supposed criminals fled, frightened by the horrible operation in which they had doubtless collaborated?

But is not the most urgent thing to go and rid the man who was buried alive of the rigid envelope that enclosed his body? A cadaver, evidently…for a human being does not have the strength of resistance of a vulgar toad. The crucial piece of evidence is there; it will be revealed at the propitious moment, and will display the flair and science of the detective.

Damnation! The statue is about to be sold at auction, with the aid of a great reinforcement of advertising that does honor to the ingenuity of Jean Saure, the *fin-de-siècle* journalist. Imagine the face of the buyer!

And Rosamour arranges in his imagination an entire spectacular *coup de théâtre*, for the public exhibition, in the midst of which he will cry: "Stop! You're buying a statue and you're being given a man. A man can't be sold—there's an error in the merchandise! Rosamour is a great detective!"

Content with that discovery, the agent picket up his cane and his hat, and went out to go see Madame Bémolisant, whom it was necessary to tranquillize.

The young woman was accustomed to seeing in him an amiable savior, and had conceived a grateful sympathy for him. When he appeared, it was like a ray of sunshine that suddenly illuminated her sad interior. She often invited him to dinner; he was so cheerful, so full of delicate attentions for

Madame Legris, who was quite delighted by them, and even for the baby, which he dandled on his knees—with the consequence that he had gradually introduced himself into the life of the widow, and his presence was desired when it was anticipated.

That day, Hélène welcomed him with a smile, glad to see her friend at a moment when a certain discouragement had overtaken her. And he set about consoling her, talking to her about the future that would open the doors of a new life to her. He made discreet allusions to the dreams he had glimpsed of a communal existence.

Blushing, she closed his mouth with a word; but he told himself that she was gradually getting used to the idea, and, without insisting on his premature projects, he told her about his discovery.

"You see!" she exclaimed. "My husband couldn't be a murderer!"

"Eh? He's as good as, if he participated in the operation."

"He wouldn't only have been yielding to his uncle's demands."

"Does one obey a madman when he says: *kill me?*"

Hélène was about to reply, but, summoned by the doorbell, she ran to open the door of the apartment.

The door was scarcely ajar when two tall, thin bodies, clad in an incongruous fashion, slipped through the narrow gap, with a backward glance to make sure that they were not pursued.

The young woman had uttered an exclamation, and she stared at them, trembling, without daring to speak, nailed to the spot by stupor.

Those bizarre individuals with hirsute beards and dusty, stained garments, were Pilesèche and Bémolisant—or perhaps their ghosts—emerged from the waves that had engulfed them, suddenly surging forth to come and reproach her for her forgetfulness.

"It's me," said the artist. "It's really me. You thought you'd never see me again, didn't you? But anything can happen..."

The first shock having passed, she threw herself into his arms.

"Oh, Népomucène, what joy! What surprise! You...you, alive!"

The other kissed her, and let himself fall into a chair, exhausted. "Don't speak so loudly. What if someone were to hear?" And as he perceived Rosamour, who emerged from the next room and came forward, Bémolisant suddenly sat up straight, galvanized. "The police!" he cried, his voice whistling in distress.

And Rosamour, in his turn, furious at that untimely appearance, which wrecked all his plans, exclaimed: "You! What are you doing here? Why aren't you dead? Was it necessary to come back to dishonor your wife?"

Hélène looked at him, astonished and anxious. What? Hadn't he said just now that they weren't guilty?

"Not guilty!" replied the agent, with bitter scorn. "Not guilty of having lent their collaboration to a mortal experiment! Certainly, the law will want to arrest such accomplices! Tell the examining magistrate about scientific experiments! Come on—they have only to run away, and since no one is worrying about them any longer, since they're believed to be dead, they can live in some obscure corner where they'll be forgotten, these resuscitated dead men..."

But Pilesèche spoke in his turn. "What do you mean, collaborating in a mortal experiment? Monsieur Grillard left proof that we had nothing to do with it; before disappearing, he wrote a cryptographic declaration on the laboratory blackboard..."

"I know that," the agent interrupted, impatiently.

"Well, if you know that, you know the terms of the declaration?"

"Yes, certainly, but..."

"Me, I have the translation..." He took out his wallet.

Professional instinct gripped Rosamour again; his expression cleared; he was curious to know how Pilesèche had deciphered the inscription, and was already no longer thinking about the annoyance cause to him by the reappearance of the two phantoms.

"Come on, let's see," he said. "Aha! It's complete—no lacunae."

"I copied the inscription before passing the sponge over it."

Rosamour read: *Bémol et Pil trouveront cops métallisé. Enlèveront enveloppe six mois après. Si mort, experience vérifie pas théorie. Maître Durand a testament et instructions.* Which is to say: Bémol and Pil will find body metalized. Remove envelope after six months. If dead, experiment does not verify theory. Maître Durand has testament and instructions.

"Perfect," said the agent. "But who will persuade the examining magistrate that this isn't a document made up for the needs of the case?"

"You, Monsieur Rosamour," said Hélène, intervening very judiciously, "since you photographed the half-effaced inscription. It will be easy for you to clarify the matter. And you know, I no longer understand you; you've given me enough signs of devotion for me nor to doubt you any longer, and yet, since the arrival of these unfortunates, you haven't ceased to attack them. When they weren't here you wanted to search for them everywhere; they appear and it's almost with threats that you greet them. Come on, find our cordial sympathy again, and help us to get out of this cruel situation."

Rosamour was not a bad fellow, and was not a man who, for having seen the equilibrium of barely-sketched dream shattered, would abandon himself for long to an initial burst of spite. Thus, he immediately promised his most active collaboration, already sketching out a plan of campaign that would get him back into the Sûreté with the honors of war. Had he not untangled all the threads of the mysterious affair and put his hands on the actors in the drama, at the same time as the victim?

In truth, hazard had played a greater role in that than science.

Pilesèche wanted to go immediately and rid his former employer of his hermetic envelope. "He's alive," he never ceased repeating. "He's still alive, and we have to get him out as soon as possible."

Bémolisant could scarcely believe it, but he was shaken by the laboratory assistant's superb confidence. As for Rosamour, he was content to shrug his shoulders at the idea. Nevertheless, whatever condition the fellow was to be found in, it was time to hasten the solution.

Just then, Jean Saure arrived with news. The time was approaching when the statue would be put up for auction in the newspaper's dispatch room, which was already full of people—the All Paris of the premières. He had been astonished not to see his friend Rosamour arrive.

The latter brought him up to date with the situation and instructed him to run and inform the head of the Sûreté that, if he would care to be present at the sale on the stroke of three o'clock, he would take responsibility for showing him the so-called criminals for which Boissonnald had sought so ineffectively, and also the so-called victim.

In the meantime, the dispatch room presented the most animated appearance.

The statue had been placed well in view, on a pedestal covered in red velvet, in front of a small platform where the auctioneer as chatting with a few collectors while awaiting the time of the sale.

On chairs scattered throughout the room, ladies in beautiful dresses, lorgnettes raised, were chatting and laughing. There was an indescribable hubbub of pearly laughter, subtle compliments and society gossip, all overlapping.

The head of the Sûreté had not hesitated to accompany the journalist. On arrival at the threshold of the dispatch room, he found himself face to face with Rosamour, who said to him, smiling: "This is my revenge, Monsieur." At the same time, he stood aside to reveal two individuals dressed in costumes that were half-Spanish and half-naval—for they had not had time to change out of the borrowed clothes that had permitted them to make their journey. "These are the famous criminals that you believed to be dead. I have brought them to you as a gesture of good will; I'm handing them over to you."

The head of the Sûreté glanced behind him to make sure that he had two agents there ready to take possession of the two bandits. Rosamour noticed the movement.

"Oh," he said, "do me the favor of leaving them at liberty for the moment; I'll answer for them, and you'll doubtless be inviting them to return home tranquilly in a little while."

Accompanied by the magistrate they had all gone through the vestibule and through the door-curtain on hearing the voice of the auctioneer repeating bids and warming up the auction.

"Come on, Messieurs, this statue in a masterpiece by an artist now dead, who will make no more. We're at eighteen thousand francs; who'll make it nineteen…?"

"And now," said Rosamour, "would you like me to show you Monsieur Grillard? Come with me."

Two or three collectors had been disputing the statue, but the battle had slowed and the auctioneer, his hammer raised, was about to confirm the sale.

"No one else? At twenty thousand! That's all? Sold!"

At the same time, the hammer fell on the nickel breast, which rendered a dull sound, and, as if the impact, feeble though it was, had reawakened a dormant life in the statue, the metal began to quiver under increasing vibrations. The limbs stirred, as if to break their rigid articulations. The torso rose up in a supreme effort.

There was a confused rumor in the room. Everyone had risen to their feet, terrified by such a prodigy.

Suddenly, like a suit of armor opening and falling away, the pellicle of nickel cracked everywhere; a specter sat up, frightful to behold, the eyes bulging from their orbits, blackened skin appearing under the metallic scales, which fell away like dead skin from a leper.

He projected his arms forward, uttered a loud cry and fell back upon the red velvet.

This time, the man was really dead.

The ladies fled, screaming, jostling one another at the door in an indescribable tumult, while Pilesèche tried to fray a passage toward his former master. He was torn between the horror of the spectacle and scientific curiosity.

The experiment had succeeded!

Conclusion

The author could have closed this story with the last lines of the preceding chapter, for the abrupt discovery that put an end to the mystery of the nickel statue was the conclusion of the whole dramatic adventure, and the reader will easily divine that Rosamour had no difficult in exonerating the two unfortunates he had taken under his aegis from the suspicions that had so cruelly weighed upon them.

He handled things so skillfully, moreover, that his own role in the affair took on the most brilliant appearance. He was the one who had contrived everything and discovered everything; he was the authentic *deus ex machina*; the Sûreté had no more to do than make their apologies to him for having treated him so badly, and reintegrate him into the ranks, with a promotion.

Privately, Rosamour was perhaps less proud. He confessed that after having taken to much pride in his personal science, he had owed his eventual success to chance alone. A little modesty is never unbefitting; he promised himself that if future. He will undoubtedly have important cases to work on in future, for his has conquered the complete confidence of his superiors and the officers of the court, who no longer swear by anyone but him.

Bémolisant has renounced decadent sculpture and, for the love of rhythm that the Spaniards had awoken in him, he has returned to music. The heritage of Uncle Népomucène, in any case, permits him that new fantasy, and even Madame Legris, to whom that windfall has brought serenity, forgives his flights into blue skies inaccessible to vulgar souls.

As for Pilesèche, he is continuing his experiments in physiology and hypnotism; he has devoted a veritable cult to the venerable scientist who proved, by his autovivisection, that the occlusion of living beings of the primate class is as facile as realizing that of a mere toad.[42]

Nevertheless, if the author of this story dared to offer any advice to his readers, it would be to engage them not to try it at home.

---

[42] But was he reunited with poor Miss Adda, who probably received no apology from Rosamour for his stupidity in not realizing that she had, in fact, found the missing scientist for him? Surely we are entitled to be told, and perhaps entitled to take it for granted that she did, in fact, marry Pilesèche and live happily ever after.

Pierre de Nolhac: *The Night of Pius XII*
(1932)

On that hot dry Roman night, His Holiness Pius XII[43] woke up, as usual, in his study. The large windows overlooking the city allowed stifling air to enter. The old man felt fatigue arriving, and his eyelids became heavy with drowsiness...

It was almost midnight. The duty chamberlain came in and announced the news: Il Duce had just been assassinated.

The Pope closed his book, got up and, with his arms crossed over his white robe, seemed self-absorbed. The hero who was dead had had his moment in the history of the Church and merited a double prayer. Then the pontiff's eyes interrogated: When? How? By whom? But the tragic event remained devoid of detail; the telephone had only transmitted a few words, and the apparatus was no longer responding.

Pius XII gazed at the city. The Alban hills seemed to be suspended on the horizon. A slender ray of moonlight wandered over cupolas, leaving the quotidian illumination all of its brightness. A singular silence had, however, arrested the nocturnal rumor; the abandoned cafes and deserted streets were

---

[43] The Pius XII to which this story refers is not Eugenio Capelli, who became the Pius XII of our history when he was elected in 1939, the story having been published before that date; given that the reigning Pope at that time was Pius XI, who had assumed that title in 1922, however, that title would have seemed the logical one to attribute to a near-future Pope. It was also in 1922 Benito Mussolini became prime minister of Italy, although he did not become "Il Duce" until 1925.

divined in an instant, the last hastily-closed shutters covering the shop-windows.

Abruptly and simultaneously, the lights on the seven hills went out. The electric current had been cut off. The Pope thought about the terror that descended upon Rome on the day of Caesar's death.

Successive detonations broke the silence and, almost at the same time, three sheaves of flame sprang forth over the city. The nuclei of the fires were visible.

"That's the Ministry of the Interior, The Communication Centre, and the Palais de Venise, without a doubt," said the young priest.

Red reflections could, in fact, be seen on the marble of the monument to Victor Emanuel overlooking the Capitol.

Soon, the Quirinal was in flames. The Revolution was master in Rome.

A sound of footsteps and speech filled the antechamber. The Cardinal Secretary of State appeared with the governor of the Vatican City and a few prelates. At the same time, a bullet fired from Saint Peter's Square whistled through a window and was flattened out by the ceiling.

"That's a warning," said the governor. "The mob isn't far away."

A troop was coming through Borgo, singing long-forgotten songs, and groups carrying torches were seen forming in the square and invading the colonnades.

The cardinal spoke to Pius XII in a low voice, as if to vanquish a hesitation.

"Your Holiness's duty is not only to us," he said. "It's to the world that his life and the freedom of his speech belongs. The hour of sacrifice has come…everything is ready."

The Pope's gaze consulted the great crucifix on the wall.

"Let's go," he said.

The Holy Father, in a black cassock, had taken the head of the group. They went down the steps, traversed the Court of

St. Damasus and reached the bronze door via the marble staircase. The Swiss Guards who were barricading it turned toward him, and the young men's acclamation, requesting one last blessing, covered the threats from outside.

The door had just been shaken by a violent blow, which resounded for a long time in the galleries. Unhurriedly, the Pope went into St. Peter's by the interior passage, where all of the awakened Vatican joined him.

No noise any longer reached the immense nave, full of darkness, The lamps of the tomb of the Apostles were the sole points of light. Pius XII knelt down for a long time in the sacred place, and no one could tell what information he received from the pontiffs buried in the crypt, the long chain of martyrs and confessors of the faith of which he was the last link. The entire silent prayer of the centuries rose up around him, and from the sumptuous monuments of the basilica, at that decisive moment, the counsel of great humility seemed to emerge.

A few moments later, the inhabitants of the Vatican City gathered at the aviation post. The Pope announced that the pilot would return that same day. He embraced the cardinals, extended his hand over the tearful old servants, and then took the arm of the Cardinal Secretary of State. The two old men climbed into the cockpit together.

The engine roared, and the airplane rose into the sky of Rome, tracing its route among the stars.

It was four o'clock in the afternoon. In his beautiful study at the Hôtel de Ville, the Maire of Avignon sponged his brow, fatigued by having expedited, in such oppressive heat, so many current affairs that he would have preferred to allow to run on.

There were recently-emptied beer-bottles amid the files, and although he was in his shirt-sleeves in order to keep cool, the magistrate thought that a big city imposes heavy duties on its elected officials.

He was allowing himself to slide toward a reparative siesta when the usher knocked. Two priests with foreign accents were at the door and insisted on being seen. Even though he only belonged the most moderate Revolutionary Socialist Party in Avignon, the Maire was not "pro-priest," but he was courteous to foreigners. He shook his pipe, put his jacket on and offered seats to the two cassocks who came in.

One of the priests was short; he sat down without saying a word, with a singular majesty. The other, tall and vigorous beneath his white hair, spoke without embarrassment.

"Monsieur le Maire," he said, "His Holiness Pope Pius XII accepts your invitation. Circumstances have obliged him to quit Rome, and he accepts with gratitude the hospitality that you offer him in the Palais d'Avignon."

"What invitation, Monsieur l'Abbé?" said the Maire. "I don't understand the allusion."

The foreigner took an old newspaper clipping from a wallet and handed it to the Maire, who read aloud:

"*When the Holy Father wishes, when he has had enough of living in a land of dictatorship and tyranny, let him return for a sojourn in the Comtat; we take pleasure in offering him accommodation in the ancient papal palace. The reds here will rejoice in giving him a good welcome.*"

At the bottom of the article was his own signature.

"That's true," he said. "I'd forgotten that *galéjade*."[44]

"I don't understand that word," said the priest, "but I know that Provençals are men of their word and that they respect misfortune."

"Since that's the case," the Maire replied, "We'll honor our promise. I'll alert the curator of the Palais. He'll expect you in an hour, and will doubtless give satisfaction to the desire of Monsieur..."

He stood up, not knowing how to conclude the sentence, and bowed hesitantly to the man who had not spoken.

Having dismissed the strange visitors he telephoned the curator. "I'm sending you two lunatics, who don't seem ma-

---

[44] *Galéjade* is a Provençal dialect term referring to a kind of joke or tall story.

317

levolent. If you can't get rid of them, put them up in the Palais tonight."

When he went out into the courtyard, however, the latest edition of the Marseilles newspapers was being touted loudly. He found information in large print therein, which gave him pause for thought:

The telegraph from Turin, where the King of Italy is resident, announces that graved events must have occurred in Rome. Il Duce has been assassinated. Details are lacking. All telephonic and aerial communications with the capital are cut off.

"Damn!" said the Maire. "I've got a big affair on my hands."

Little attention was paid on the streets of Avignon to the two priests who asked a passer-by the way to the Archbishop-ric. No one knew what was said in the Monseigneur's drawing room during the hour they spent there, nor was their arrival at the Palais noticed, at the moment when the last visitors were leaving.

Dr. Colombe was not merely a scholarly historian of the monument confided to his care but also a moving spirit who was capable of dreaming. The newspapers had just opened up to him the dream that he had often formulated of receiving a Papal visit.

When the two priests introduced themselves to him, he had no difficulty recognizing them, and placed himself under the orders of the Sovereign Pontiff.

"We want," said the later, "before accepting the hospital-ity of Milord the Archbishop, to do honor the appeal that was once addressed to us in the name of the people of Avignon. We shall spend tonight, with your permission, under the roof of our venerated predecessors."

The curator unhooked his bundle of keys and conducted the Pope through the vast deserted rooms. On the way, he in-dicated the steps and passages that would take him, if he so wished to the Angel Tower, the library and the Chapel of St. John.

"I offer to Your Holiness," he said, finally, "the bedchamber of Clement VI and John XXII. It's the smallest of our rooms and the least comfortable. I'll have two camp beds set up for you here. The Holy Father will be perfectly tranquil, and no noise will hinder his sleep."

The visitors gazed with astonishment at the profane hunting scenes that covered the walls.

"These paintings are our most precious treasures," said the doctor. "They were the décor of private audiences. The memories with which this room is crowded render it particularly dear to us."

The Pope smiled and went to the window. The setting sun reddened the roofs that huddled beneath the high walls. A golden light covered Provence. Pius XII extended his arms as if to embrace the beautiful country and murmured: "The Vicar of Christ is at home everywhere that he finds his children. Nowhere is the Papacy in exile."

Avignon will never forget the weeks of that sojourn. The people, who are not astonished by anything, found it perfectly natural that the Pontiff had returned.

On the very first morning, at dawn, all the bells in the diocese sounded the great carillon, and the people on the other side of the Rhône wondered what unexpected festival was putting the land of the Mistral in a festive mood.

Then the series of pilgrimages to our Midi began. Whole parishes arrived from the mountains or the sea, in carts, in automobiles, and most often on foot in the white dust, led by exuberant priests who sowed enthusiasm along the roads. The Archbishopric was never empty of these rustic visitors, who brought ecstatic eyes, and medallions for blessing.

There was a rush from every region on the day when it became known that Pius XII would give the apostolic blessing from the height of the Rocher des Doms. The night before, fifty thousand people slept on the pavement under the stars.

Whoever did not see that fête has never seen anything. The hills, the squares and the windows were overflowing with people. The city was clad in yellow and white oriflammes from the stalls in the street to the summits of the towers.

During the ceremony, tambourines and tabors accompanied the canticles, and the Pope's ears heard more Provençal than Latin. Then, the white robes and the bishops descended into the streets again, swallowed up by a tumultuous and good humored crowd. The black, white and gray penitents rubbed shoulders with the municipal council without hostility. As it was not a procession but a cortege, the Maire was able to take part in it without violating his edicts. Delighted with his city's good luck, he flattered himself with the thought that he had brought it about.

In any case, there was more in Avignon than parties. Hearts became papal again, and the most miscreant, in order to make amends, whistled the familiar couplets of the old song of Clement V in the cafés. There was even talk of definitively fitting out the old palace and the millions to spend danced in the imagination of architects.

It was more serious, a few days later, when the French and foreign cardinals were seen arriving. When Poznan, Cologne and Westminster were present, Pius XII held a Consistory.

The affairs of the Church were in dire need of one. Those in Italy were hopeful; the provinces faithful to the House of Savoy had rid themselves of Soviet Republics; the army and militias were preparing to march on Rome; the great kingdom would not perish.

However, the return of the Pope to the Vatican seemed impossible. Destruction had completed the work of pillage. It was said that the Raphael frescos once spared by Charles V's knights had been lacerated. Even the Archives had been destroyed, burned or thrown into the Tiber. An entire history had disappeared with them and crumbled into the past.

The government in Paris was not unembarrassed. The Pope had thanked it without saying a word about his intentions. The religious effervescence of the Midi, which the prefects had declared "a straw fire," was beginning to cause anxiety. Would it influence the imminent elections? It was to be feared so. At least there was no danger of any interpellation in the Chambres; the habit had set in of only convening them rarely, which permitted government.

The Ministry sent the Republic's finest diplomat to Avignon. That was the President himself. A southerner, like so many others, an alert mind and a disabused freemason, he came to salute deferentially the man whom the press unanimously described as "the foremost moral authority in the world."

The archbishopric's visitor went to the prefecture, and the meeting lasted a long time. All that was learned was that the pontiff had received urgent invitations to go to America, where several states of the Union were offering installations worthy of the Church of Rome, Pius XII had refused the installations, but had agreed to cross the Ocean.

The Council of Ministers breathed out; the Republic was no longer in peril! And the only change that the President remarked on his return from the trip was that low masses were sometimes held on Sundays at the Madeleine.

On the day when the dreadnought that came to fetch him quit the coast of America, Pius XII crossed the Pont d'Avignon and traveled through the Languedoc. The parishes sounded the passage of the autos from one bell-tower to the next, and the Pope paused at the threshold of churches to bless the children. In the Montagne Noire, Catholics and Protestants lined both sides of the road, the former clutching rosaries and the later offering flowers.

At Toulouse, the pontifical high mass celebrated at Saint Sernin was quite an event. Pius XI wanted to make the pious visit to Lourdes that five Popes had desired for such a long time; around the miraculous grotto, a hundred thousand people proclaimed their fidelity to him. On both sides of the Pyrenees the Basque country testified its own with arches of foliage set up at the entrances to towns.

The Pope headed for Santiago de Compostela following the route of the Medieval pilgrims, still decorated with its chapels and calvaries. Entire provinces watched him pass by on their knees. He waited in the illustrious monastery, beside the relics of the apostle, for the promised vessel to anchor at Corunna.

On the staged decks of the iron ship, white-clad crews were on parade. To the accompaniment of cannon shots, cheers from the shore mingled with the solemn Anglo-Saxon hurrahs as the Star and Stripes carried the Church toward a new destiny...

At daybreak, when he was woken up by the bells of St. Peter's, His Holiness Pius XII asked for news from the Palais de Venise. Il Duce, in perfect health, had just mounted his horse for his daily excursion.

Pierre de Nolhac: *A Lovely Summer's Day*
(1932)

On coming out of the Academy, where our session was brief, I go over the Pont des Arts. The physician has recommended that I take a short walk every day. We have been working on the *Dictionnaire*; the letter A is going to take a long time, and my age leaves me little hope of reaching the letter B.

There is hardly anyone in Paris that August. There are four of us, with our director Pierre Benoît. He has grown old without losing his gaiety; it distracted us from care with public affairs, which are going badly. Although our colleague Herriot has been President of the Republic for some time, nothing has been settled. Strikes are multiplying in the vicinity of Paris; the Bourse is at a new low; I no longer have an automobile.[45] Although one is accustomed to such crises, the gravity of this one seems astonishing; even our old administration seems out of kilter. For two hours it has been impossible to obtain any telephonic communication from the Institut.

I watch the Seine flowing in that placid afternoon. A slight breeze is agitating the foliage on the quay. There is not a

---

[45] When this future-set story was written, the Radical Édouard Herriot (1872-1957) must have served at least one term as Prime Minister out of the three he served between 1924 and 1932, but he was never elected President of the Republic. The novelist Pierre Benoît (1888-1962) was elected to the Académie in 1931; Pierre de Nolhac (who had been elected in 1922), undoubtedly considered him to be a trifle downmarket, and the suggestion of his appointment to direct the committee updating the Académie's official dictionary of the French language is sarcastic.

cloud in the pure sky of our dear city. It really is a lovely summer's day.

At the exit from the bridge I find a surprising barrier of policemen. There are bare-headed individuals among them who appear to be assisting them in their service. I am asked for my papers. That is truly incredible. I stand on my dignity: "Member of the Acad…"

"Let the old man pass," says a voice. "He won't bother anyone."

I pass on, a trifle shocked. Monsieur Chiappe's agents used to be more polite.[46]

How restful it is in the courtyard of the Louvre, and what beautiful solitude! Two centuries of the noblest history of France are inscribed on these walls. One feels glad to belong to a nation that leaves such monuments to its glory. "At your own risk," said that imbecile of a Brigadier—as if there were any risk in taking a taxi to the Palais-Royal!

Anyway, there are no taxis in the square—no circulation at all. I notice that the Ministry of Finance is guarded by a troop similar to the one of the bridge.

I go to buy my *Débats* from the kiosk whose seller is familiar to me, but her display is empty and she is in the process of closing up.

"No papers today, my dear Monsieur."

The idea of going home on foot scarcely makes me. The Avenue Hoche is a long way off. I decide to take the Metro, but there too, no one is allowed in.

"But I can hear the trains moving," I say.

"That's not for you, it's for the service."

A singular service that obliges Parisians, in broad daylight, to walk for three kilometers. Doubtless I'll find vehicles

---

[46] The notoriously right-wing Jean Chiappe (1876-1940) was the head of the Sûreté during the 1920s and Prefect of Police during the early 1930s, until he was sacked in February 1934, occasioning a large demonstration of support that degenerated into a riot.

in the Rue Saint-Honoré, and I'll take advantage of it to go into my bookshop, which ought to have a small order waiting for me.

"Here's your book, Maître," says the clerk at Giraud-Badin, "You're just in time, we're about to close the shop, like all the neighbors. Anyway, we haven't sold a book for a week. It's not worth the trouble of staying in Paris—you'd be better off in the country."

The fellow puts up the shutters, and I perceive that, indeed, almost all the shop windows are already sealed off. There are very few people in the streets. It's a rare pleasure nowadays to be able to leaf through a book on the sidewalk. Mine is a delight. It's an incunabula for which I've been searching for a long time, the exceedingly rare edition of the letters of Aeneas Silvius, which must have been printed in Rome by Eucharius Silber in 1490 or thereabouts. It has no date on the colophon, but its beautiful characters justify the supposition.

Perhaps I encounter other barriers, but the only one that stops me seriously is in the Rue Royale. There is no means of getting through that one, and Aeneas Silvius and I are turned away rather harshly. What can I do? Fortunately, I perceive someone that I recognize in an animated and noisy group. It really is Octave, our electrician, who comes to my house to repair the wiring and the lights, and stays for a little chat. What is the worthy fellow doing here, bare-headed like the others? He seems to be giving orders.

I call out to him: "Octave! Monsieur Octave!"

He comes toward me, astonished and condescending. I ask him to get me out of difficulty.

"That's easy," he said. "I'm just about to carry out my inspection in your direction. We'll go together. You're in luck, for you'd never have got home on a day like today."

We cross the street and soon reach the Champs-Élysées.

"What the devil is all this?" I ask him. "What's happening in Paris? I no longer recognize it."

"Why," he says, laughing, "it's the Revolution. It's started, hasn't it? We've chosen a good time, and you have to admit that it's rather successful."

"We had no inkling of it at the Institut."

"You never have any inkling of anything at the Institut," Octave replied, indulgently. "Fortunately, the world doesn't need astronomers to turn."

All the openings to the sewers are guarded. At every post, Octave exchanges a few words, and while we go up the avenue he explains things to me.

"It's quite simple, you see. We have friends everywhere, the sewer workers foremost among them. A thirteen forty-five, our zero hour, as you say in your wars, all the electric cables were cut. The airwaves have been jammed. Paris is completely cut off. No orders are being transmitted except ours."

"What about the police?"

"The police! The majority are with us and the rest are directing traffic. That's their métier, isn't ii?"

"Oh!" I said, nonplussed. "It's you who are maintaining order?"

"And how! Look at our cyclists going by. Hey, Charlot, are you coming from the Prefecture? What did the Prefect say when he was banged up?"

The cyclist drew away triumphantly, a black flag on his handlebars.

Octave continued. "So, at thirteen fifty, our men were at all the strategic points. The Metro transported many of them, like good employees who seemed to be on their way to the office. At each Ministry, however, a *coup de théâtre*. From the manholes in the sidewalk, up the iron ladders, strong crews surge forth with sturdy cudgels. At the same time, our ushers close the doors. Not a single clerk can get in. Same thing for the banks. Everything is going well. Method, you see, method! Then again, the ministries were well hollowed-out!"

"Come on, Octave, at least respect the French language."

We go past the *Figaro*.

"F   the French language," says Octave, roundly. He points at the carefully-guarded building.

"Look, there's a barber who won't get in our way anymore. He's shaved for the last time this morning."

Higher up it's the old *Revue de Paris*. It was about to publish a major study of mine, "L'Humanisme éternel" on the fifteenth.

Workers appear at the windows of the offices, throwing proofs and manuscripts down in to the roadway. An editor comes out without a hat, his face bloodied.

"Literary quarrels," Octave explains. "The shop's been closed. Others will go the same way."

"Surely not the *Revue des Deux-Mondes*!" I protest. "It's an institution. No regime would dare to touch it!"

He seems amazed, looks at me for a moment, and bursts out laughing.

"You're magnificent, dear Maître. You still believe in your papers. They don't interest anyone any more. All that's worn out, obsolete, dead and gone. The cinema, with a nice, amusing daily rumor, will be sufficient for our comrades. And you'll see, you can write for us."

Alas, I think, what future is there for intelligence? What will become of "L'Humanisme éternel"? A double anxiety.

The man is following another train of thought, for he takes out his watch.

"Seventeen thirty! Your ministers will be peeved when they've been collected at the doors. Everyone's taking a stroll today—it's such lovely weather! A pity we haven't got our hands on your Foreign Affairs, whose banqueting in Switzerland or the Colonies, whose palavering in the colonies, nor all those who are taking the waters, at the seaside or at their lady friends' châteaux." He pointed at a carriage coming down the avenue. "But there's the general, picked up at the Porte de Saint-Cloud on his way back from Versailles. He won't be sleeping at the Invalides anymore."

"You can't have done that to Général Gouraud, I'm sure," I say, with an indignation that was beginning to grow. "He'd have shot you down first!"[47]

"We'll see about that! But you no longer have Gouraud or anyone else—nothing but the toads at the end of the bridge. And if there's only those birds to defend you..."

"I disregard those discourteous metaphors for the national representation. "There's also the army," I say. "Our barracks..."

"Let's talk about them. Naturally, the class is liberated. The fellows don't need to be told twice. Look, see how happy they are!"

At that moment, a cheerful troop of soldiers comes down the Champs-Élysées, arms linked, singing a hymn in which I don't recognize: the *Marseillaise*.

"But what have you done with the Élysée?"

"The President of your Republic? He's in Lyon, at the coronation of the rose-bushes. The comrades will furnish him with roses today, thorns and all."

"What! The provinces..."

"Of course! Marseilles, Nantes, Le Havre are all hotting up now. It might be a little harder there than here, where everything's going along peacefully."

"Peacefully!"

"Certainly. It was necessary to expedite a few agents who weren't very obliging at the bank when the Governor was taken down to the vaults. We'll have to hope that'll be all. We're not *muzjiks*. The people's revolution will have clean hands. It's not like yours, meaning no reproach."

"Mine?" I exclaim.

"That's right—the bourgeois one...89...93...the Rights of Man, the humbug. It's us who are claiming them, the Rights of Man..."

---

[47] Henri Gouraud (1867-1946) who had distinguished himself during the Great War, was the military governor of Paris from 1923 to 1937.

Octave is in full swing, he's opening his generous heart. Nevertheless, a little snigger causes me some anxiety.

"There's a few we'd like to stick up against the wall, though, like the others…your Blum, for example.[48] In the meantime, our delegate to Justice has just opened the prisons. It's not that we like murderers, if there are any in there, but it's necessary to make room, isn't it?"

We have reached the Arc de la Grande Armée.

I salute our past.

Where have the times gone when France shed her blood for the emancipation of peoples? What has become of that epic of liberty, served by arms, which Rude's sublime stone renders so present?[49] How far we have traveled since them, and how uncomprehending these people seem of our memories! What do I, an old liberal, have in common with the violent and determined man marching beside me?

Nevertheless, I ask him: "In sum, Octave, tell me where your revolution is heading? What are you going to do with Paris, and how will you hold on to it?"

"It's quite simple." *Determined* is definitely the right word. "What's demolished isn't rebuilt. You're asking me what our plans are? The factories are ours, virtually, as you say; how are you going to take them back? And you'll see that we're practical. Our locksmiths will get busy first thing in the morning. All the apartments whose shutters we see closed will be occupied by families from Saint-Ouen, Saint-Denis and

---

[48] Léon Blum (1872-1950) was a moderate left politician, who eventually served three terms as prime minister between 1936 and 1947, after the present story was written. Throughout the twenties and for much of the thirties he edited the Socialist newspaper *Le Populaire*.

[49] François Rude (1784-1855) sculpted the frieze and one of the most famous groups on the Arc de Triomphe, "Départ des volontaires de 1792," more commonly known as "La Marseillaise."

Pantin. There's no lack of tenants. As for those that are still inhabited, we'll share."

I make a fearful gesture.

"We don't want to be disagreeable to anyone," Octave adds. "In your place, for example, where there are so many bedrooms and drawing rooms full of books, I want you to have someone good. I'll send you my wife and kid. That way, you won't be inconvenienced."

I dare not testify my gratitude, having a horror of children who touch books and disturb papers. But Octave continues, benevolently: "You can also have my sister-in-law—only two small kids. "He adds, maliciously: "You're worried that she'll be in the way? She's not difficult. You'll be quite snug."

And as my savior leaves me in the hands of my tearful concierge, he adds, with one last smile: "You'll like my brother-in-law. He's one of you—a type-setter at *L'Humanité*. There's someone who'll appreciate your library!"[50]

---

[50] When the story was written, *L'Humanité* was still the daily newspaper of the French Communist Party.

Pierre de Nolhac: *Babel at Ferney*
(1932)

The League of Nations triumphed. Its work was applauded; peace reigned over the world, the terrible war threatened
for so long had been avoided. Nationalisms had calmed down;
raw materials were distributed as well as they could be; the
borders were almost fixed; budgets were almost equilibrated;
and the peoples, on the whole, were almost content.

For those fortunate results, believers thanked Providence;
skeptics attributed them to the force of circumstances, and the
League of Nations, attributed the honor, as is only just, to the
League of Nations.

There was one slight shadow over the scene of felicity: at
the moment when the 595th session opened, there was no significant question on the agenda. Success had exhausted them
all, and the functionaries, whose number had been vastly increased by all the work surrounding that powerful organization, were searching in vain for a pretext to increase their sala-
ries. The ingrate nations thought that they were paid well
enough by the shine of the services they had rendered to humanity.

The question of prestige was more serious, and the Supreme Council was preoccupied by it. What subject of discourse was going to animate the sessions in the Palais des Nations, before their audience of elite men and sparkling ladies?
How could it be demonstrated that speech was still necessary
as the ornamentation of truth? The older members had difficulty resigning themselves to not opening a great debate.

Remaining loquacious after having once been eloquent,
the venerable Permanent President continued to maintain the
moral authority of France in spite of the somnolence to which
his advanced age gave him the right. But that mind, fertile in

resources for so many years, admitted that the crisis was redoubtable.[51]

They turned to the International Committee on Intellectual Cooperation, which, as everyone knows, includes the most agile intelligences in the world, but even the ICIC recognized its impotence. It had given so much effort to the difficult coordinations that its glorious mill had never ceased to grind. It was presently occupied in unifying a system of punctuation in the various typographies of the world, but that affair of periods and commas, important as it was, could only impassion serious minds.

It was, however, from that direction that salvation came. The thirty-third sub-committee of the ICIC had just found a viable claim.

The Free State of Greenland was bemoaning the poverty of its artistic collections. Its newly-constructed museum, built at great expense of the rarest woods, only enclosed at present a few polar bear skins, admittedly magnificent. No esthetic information could be derived from such remains. Was it not just, however, that a young nation, avid for progress, should savor more elevated enjoyments? It appealed to the spirit of solidarity that now united human beings, and made energetic pleas for its fair share of common treasures.

How could such a moving request be refused? How could that cry for beauty uttered from beyond the sixty-fifth degree of north latitude go unanswered?

It was immediately evident that the greatest principles were involved. Several countries adhered without hesitation to a better division of the world's works of art. Iceland, Patagonia and the New Hebrides supported the Greenland claim. Official wireless messages criss-crossed the planet, and it was easy to anticipate that a majority of less favored nations would

---

[51] The Presidency of the Assembly of the League of Nations was rotated frequently, but the Secretary General served for longer periods; Eric Drummond, Earl of Perth held the position from 1920 to 1933.

rapidly constitute and aliment their plaints with numerous deliberations.

The report that was urgently demanded was a great success. In the midst of an attentive emotion, the delegate of independent Manchuria read a paper that he had had the delicacy of writing in Japanese in order that it might be better understood. It concluded firmly in favor of the request: "The League of Nations has brought about the equitable division of wheat, gold and radium; it remains for it to complete that of the wealth of art, which is no less indispensable to human life."

Elected with enthusiasm, imbued with the pure doctrine of the ICIC, the new Committee for the Wealth of Art promised the League of Nations a considerable plenary session.

Whence came the ingenious idea of basing the high commissioners charged with elaborating the plan for the great reform at Ferney?[52] Perhaps it was some erudite and rancorous memory who remembered having seen Voltaire ranged among the adversaries of the League of Nations His remark was, in fact, rather unfortunate: "I shall believe in perpetual peace on the day the hawks cease to eat pigeons."

The opportunity had arisen to inflict on the shade of the Seigneur de Ferney the spectacle of universal concord.

A simpler reason sufficed for the public. It seemed to everyone that it was necessary to isolate the deliberations from the various pressures of already-overexcited opinion. Nowhere was serenity better assured than in that old philosopher's her-

---

[52] The fortunes of the French commune of Fernex, in the Jura, close to the border with Switzerland, were dramatically changed when the great philosopher Voltaire decided to make his home there in 1759, purchased the estate and changed its name to Ferney because he thought too many places in the region had names ending in x. He built a château there, financed the building of a church (perhaps a trifle ironically), set up numerous cottage industries and effectively created a small town. He lived there until his death in 1778.

mitage, not far from Geneva, which remained a temple of human wisdom.

On that spring afternoon, reporters from all the world's newspapers, contained with great difficulty by the gendarmerie, were crowding the streets of the village, impatient to telephone, cable or send their sensational inexactitudes by wireless telegraph.

Inside the house, when the magnesium flashed, the photographic plates recorded a picturesque audience. Through the French Windows opening to the garden, the card-table was visible at which the great man had played whist with the whole of Europe. All around, on the Louis XV armchairs, the representatives of the powers displayed their coats. Secretaries and interpreters made a crown of smiles. Standing out in a graceful group against the pale background of the wood paneling, a dozen stenographers were touching up their lipstick. History would learn, by virtue of the indiscretion of the camera, that the envoy of the Chicago *Times*, hidden under a banquette, was taking clandestine notes.

Having tossed back his fine white hair, the Permanent President rose to his feet for the inaugural speech. "Messieurs," he said, "I declare the memorable meeting open." And the stenographers, pencils in hand, felt themselves swooning at the first chords of the melody

"Let me first thank you all for having chosen, for this historic discussion, a corner of French soil which will forever know the memory of a powerful philosopher. The democracy of my country has always honored the illustrious Voltaire as a precursor, for no one served the immortal principles of the Revolution better."

"What revolution is he talking about?" one delegate whispered in the ears of his neighbors, but none of them was able to reply.

Having evoked in emotional terms the Calas and Dreyfus affairs, the orator declared himself to be a partisan of the renationalized redivision of art, the privilege of which could not

334

be retained by nations that had no other entitlement than their antiquity.

"France, Messieurs, is determined to remain at the head of the irresistible movement that is drawing minds toward a better justice. A great producer of a sublime aliment, she is ready to be generous to the fraternal hands that are extended toward us. Messieurs, no one in this enclosure"—his gesture amplified the small philosophical drawing room—is in any doubt that it will aid the definitive solidification of the peace of peoples, for which you have worked untiringly..."

The unexpected adverb announced a cadence that the orator was not given the time to complete. He sat down in the midst of a noisy ovation, while, behind its wall, the press rejoiced in that good omen.

Less optimistic, the neighborhood sparrows, alarmed by the racket, prudently flew over the Swiss frontier.

The representative of the Iberian Federation, having risen to his feet, gave a magnificent assurance that the artistic treasures of his land, accumulated over centuries, would all be at the assembly's disposal.

Such a sumptuous gesture provoked a flood of generous declarations. Nations that possessed nothing but their good will were seen distributing it with lavish eloquence.

Such effusions testified once again to the native bounty of the human species. But, ignorance being the mother of ingratitude, no one thought about the posthumous revenge offered to Jean-Jacques[53] in the very house of the rival who had maltreated him so many times.

"We shall pass on to the drafting of the articles," pronounced the President—who, with that duty accomplished, closed his eyes and quietly absented himself.

Gazes were transferred to the Scandinavian spectacles of an eminent jurist, celebrated for the clarity of his style and his

---

[53] i.e., Rousseau.

fluent command of the Genevese idiom. His formula was ready.

"Article One. The esthetic contingent applied to the museums of each people is based on the numerical coefficient of its national agglomeration."

No one could have put it better. While the crowded translators multiplied misinterpretations in various languages, the customary epithets—charming, excellent, decisive—circulated around the armchairs.

One sole opposition as manifest: the Italian delegate, a young descendant of the Doges, declared the question untimely and badly posed—but that attitude, clearly Fascist, did not provoke any storm.

The Reich took responsibility for transporting the works of art; its technical power of organization was imposing, and it retained a team of disposable generals whose had been in charge of occupied regions during the Great War.

"What will your noble nation bring to the stock to be created for the common find?" asked one delegate.

Dr. Kirtius seemed surprised by that indiscreet question.

"The figure of the population of Germany," he said, "gives it the right to be among the receiving party, not the donating party. It awaits its share of the generosities of the League of Nations, and in any case, it is poorer than is believed; there are forgeries in the Museum of Berlin. Perhaps we would consent to a few exchanges."

"The golden tiara of Saitapharnes might be attributed to you," someone suggested.[54]

---

[54] The Louvre purchased a golden tiara that had allegedly belonged to the Scythian king Saitapharnes in 1896. Its authenticity was challenged by the German archaeologist Adolf Furtwängler, and the Louvre's attempts to defend its authenticity foundered when the Russian goldsmith who had made it demonstrated his claim by making an identical duplicate, and thus became famous.

As the doctor did not appear to grasp that compensation, someone told him that German hypercriticism had recently established the authenticity of the ancient sculpting of that marvel, in spite of the claims made by the impostor who said that he had forged it.

That petty argument changed the mood. Each of the nations interrogated thereafter made reservations in its own concern, and when Yugoslavia observed that Belgium held a prodigious amount of beautiful things unjustified by the number of its inhabitants, Baron Claës de Tirlemont took it very ill and said dryly that certain peoples born yesterday ought not to have a voice in the matter.

"There are thirty-five Rubens in the Brussels Museum," the Balkan insisted. "That's enough for the entire world!"

A few eyes gleamed with the covetousness that Bossuet called concupiscence. Figures and statistics flew through the air; precisions, albeit fictitious, were launched by connoisseurs.

"Thirty Memlings in Bruges! Forty Jordaens in Antwerp! Is such possessiveness tolerable in our modern societies?"

The worthy Baron exploded. Already apoplectic, he went crimson, and while people hastened to reach his cravat, he murmured: "The barbarians! The barbarians!"

He was carried away in the midst of the tumult. Holland, sensing too many Rembrandts on its conscience, slipped away through the back door, while the President, abruptly reawakened, was congratulated on the serenity of the debate.

Disdainful until then, Great Britain declared, on the contrary, declared that the discussion had become indecent, by virtue of the unjustified presence of petty nations. But Greece retorted bitterly that it was still waiting for the restitution of the Parthenon, which was still turning to dust under the skies of London.

Good conduct buckled. One aggressive voice threw out this menacing aphorism: "Peoples have the right to dispose of the superfluity of others."

"There will be war tomorrow!" yapped a prophet.

That was all too accurate. They separated in disorder. All hope of a plenary session was lost.

The bees in the garden remained mistresses of the manufacture of sweetness. In his gilded frame, Voltaire smiled without benevolence, and the consternated stenographers dared not read back their scandalous shorthand.

Pierre de Nolhac: *A Season in Auvergne*
(1932)

Royat, 21 July

This golf course in the mountains is a charming corner of Auvergne. You, my dear husband, who like that game, will be able to play more than one round when you come to look for your darling Claude at the end of the season. The course is superb and descends in a slope toward the valley of Royat, which is hidden from sight, but the view extends all the way to the plain of Limagne, unfurling to infinity. One can see a part of the town of Clermont, dominated by the two steeples of its cathedral, which project upwards on the horizon.

I can imagine you contemplating that peaceful scene, full of light, and see you bounding over the grass, club in hand, to the very place where I am writing. It is a very agreeable chalet, where I am sitting next to the excellent Brazilian family that you know, and who chaperone me at the palace.

I am surrounded by rather pleasant cocktails, which do not prevent me from drinking the delicious local milk. We shall go back down to lie in the sun by means of a beautiful winding path, which run through the fir-trees around an old extinct volcano named Gravenoire. Here and there, quarries open from which the somber stone known as pozzolan is obtained. The entire country in admirable in its coloration, which would tempt the most daring water colorists...

22 July

My cure has commenced. The carbonated baths are amusing; they project innumerable bubbles over our skin, which warm you up very quickly. My heartbeat will soon regularize, the doctor says. Even when cured, it will still beat more rapidly for you...

23 July

Your friends the Jacques Bardoux came to fetch me in the auto to take me for an excursion to the volcanic hills. We went through a valley streaming with springs to a vast plateau on which the entire row of extinct volcanoes is lined up. The Puy-de-Dôme looms over them all with its imposing mass. One makes the tour through the woods and rapidly becomes familiar with these singular mountains. Some are rounded, others flattened at the top—where, it appears, the extinct mouths of the monsters are—some covered with forests, the others bare and savage. The Auvergnats seem proud to point out to you, from that high Gallic summit, several lakes that are, it appears, ancient craters.

We took tea at Saint-Saturnin, where there is an old château, a Roman church and your friends' pretty house. They read me the verses of a local poet in which the fields of lava we traversed are described, disordered blocks of which were caught in the last eruption. The local name for it is *cheire*, which is the same word as *sciarra*, which designates the same thing in Sicily around Mount Etna.

I have copied the end of the poem for you:

The earth has reflowered on the savage slopes
Of mysterious mountains that were volcanoes,
But the Cheire, witness to the ancient days of the world,
Reveals the secrets that it seeks to hide:
The distant fire, the menacing, groaning wave.
It reminds our thoughts that the profound flame,
Is eating away eternally at its prison of rock.

You like poetry; those lines have enchanted me.

24 July

Another excursion: after the mountains, the plain. We have traversed the broad and lush Limagne, extended between two chains, in all directions, firstly to visit Thiers, its wooden houses, and its cutlers, and then to reach Vichy along the bank of a river with a pretty name, the Dore. The great Vichy is always noisy, elegant and agitated.

On the way back we saw the geyser that everyone talks about, which is truly something extraordinary. It sprang up suddenly the first time, but the peasants, fearing that their fields would be flooded, had almost blocked the orifice. A few days ago, the jet reappeared, and roses up more than a hundred meters. The water is as hot as that of the numerous mineral springs that are the fortune of the region. If you arrive soon enough you will undoubtedly see that astonishing spectacle, to which the crowds are flocking. I'm delighted to have been there.

While coming back toward Royat we admired the long chain of the volcanic hills standing out against the setting sun. The undulating line of craters seemed to be tormented by a magnificent eruption.

25 July

The waters of the Auvergne definitely have surprises in store.

I heard his morning, in confidence, from the good woman with the pink ribbons who dries me when I come out of the bath, that the wells have become so hot that they require cooling down. The mixture hasn't rendered the bath any less pleasant.

Your letters are a great joy to me. Do you have good tires with which to travel the roads of Poland? Clermont is the great manufactory of those necessary objects; entire districts are devoted to it there, but the black city retains its character of a Jansenist city, with its steep and narrow streets, its old lava houses, its sculpted blazons and its views of the mountain at every street corner. I shall be your guide when you come to meet me.

341

26 July

I must tell you about last night's event, in order that you won't be anxious if the newspapers bring you news of it.

At about three o'clock in the morning we had a slight earthquake. Woken up by the first tremor, I was thrown out of bed by the second. In an instant, the entire palace was out of bed, and pajamas were flying along the corridors. I went back to bed, very sagely in the dark, because the electricity, of course....

In the morning, we learned about the incidents. Our Brazilians had had a terrible fright. The system of bells is out of action, the glassware severely compromised, the conversations rather feverish, but your Claude is intact. Someone has gone to pillage the shops in Clermont in order to acquire candles, and our little tables are illuminated in a picturesque fashion at diner.

The establishment remained closed today.

27 July

I would be entirely content, for you know how curious I am, if I did not see so much fear around me. An unexpected spectacle has been promised to us, and we shall have good seats.

The mountain that I mentioned to you once, Gravenoire, is smoking like a chimney. The mouth, closed for centuries, is in the process of reopening. The plume of smoke was visible this morning, and some courageous people made the ascent. Courage is in a minority, however, and a number of precipitate departures were announced today. I've seen pyramids of exotic trunks. You will doubtless approve of my not taking part in that panic...

28 July

It really is an eruption! Muffled detonations announced it all through the nights, and I can assure you that no one got much sleep. This morning the mountain is entirely enveloped in smoke. Two large flows are emerging from it. One of them

342

is heading toward the village, the other taking aim at the hotels. The flow that is devouring my beautiful fir trees is descending with an impressive rhythm. If it doesn't slow down the lava will reach our drawing rooms within three days. It's said that the Puy de la Nugère, which overlooks Châtel-Guyon, is also on fire.

Everyone is leaving. The season is ruined. Brazil has bid me farewell, and the two Americans have followed. I've decided to go back to Paris and I'd go this evening if I weren't waiting impatiently for a letter from you. I shall go look for it at the post office tomorrow morning, and catch the twelve-fifty train from Clermont.

A bientôt. Come back soon.

In the newspapers of 29 July the following article appeared:

An unprecedented catastrophe has overwhelmed one of the most beautiful French provinces. The Limagne has disappeared!

The volcanic reawakening announced yesterday has provoked a cataclysm that is still unexplained. The great Auvergnat plain has sunk, and in a matter of minutes, the subterranean waters have covered it in its entirety.

Large towns—Clermont, Riom, Vichy—are under water, as are hundreds of small towns and villages. The number of victims is estimated at four hundred thousand. The eruption of the two mountains has abruptly ceased.

The airplanes that have flown over the hot sea have perceived, beneath the surface, the tragic map of that unfortunate region. The steeples and roof of Clermont cathedral form a strange islet therein. The chain of volcanic hills is reflected in hat immense lake. One can distinguish, on the railway lines, the trains seized in progress at exactly twelve fifty-five.

Pierre de Nolhac: *The Journal of Dr. J. H. Smithson*
of the University of Seattle (Wash.)
(1932)

Four days to see Europe is too few. To be sure, we go quickly; one can fly from Warsaw to Bucharest in an hour. This little country is monotonous, but, by searching hard, a cultivated American can find material for instruction here.

I should like to know the past of the nations that have formed these new United States; I would enjoy my voyage more—but humankind has such a long history that it cannot be embraced in its entirety. The rhythm of the world accelerates, and the last hundred years have accumulated more changes than the previous thousand.

The annals of our own States—of my own Idaho, for example—have been abundantly laden since our revolutions. In the twentieth century, America went to make war in Europe; they still remember that here. My great-grandfather, a singular man, took part in it when he was twenty, and my father still talked about that war. Today, it's no longer anything but a date to our schoolchildren.

Scarcely informed with regard to events that are much more relevant to us, how can we interest ourselves in the adventures of the rest of the world? Enormous extents of history have crumbled behind us; human memory no longer refers to them.

I can scarcely recognize in Europe the cradle of civilization that was described to us. Its soul has become foreign to us. We, who give the highest priority to ideal values and the disinterested curiosity of the mind, cannot understand that anyone can disdain, after once having known them, the treasures of art and thought. What a display there is here of industrial cities, what masses of perishable goods, what a brutal

344

search for pleasure! The eyes of the traveler are wounded everywhere.

I would not have prolonged my excursion if I had not perceived, here and there, a few traces of a curious past: a site escaped from the encumbrance of iron, an abandoned monument that amuses my archeological incompetence.

I am concluding my flights in Paris. Will I discover there, under its banal opulence, secret beauties speaking to me heart? I have already classified its most ancient edifices chronologically. The Panthéon and the Arc de Triomphe evidently date from Roman times. The temple of Montmartre is no less ancient, and I gaze with respect at the dome that the great Napoléon built to shelter his tomb.

An antiquated church like Notre-Dame attracts me by virtue of its religious mystery. But places of prayer are less frequented than our beautiful American cathedrals, so bright and vibrant, where the piety of our people is affirmed. On this continent of the East, it seems to be stifled beneath the materialistic indifference of the masses, too proud of technological progress to raise themselves to divine concerns.

How can a European of France support the fever of production and competition that leaves him no repose? We govern matter, as he does, but we do not submit our souls to it. Since the harsh economic crises that shook our ancient egotism, it seems that a little of the old America of Washington and Lincoln has reappeared. Our families have become patriarchal again. They are united and laborious. Nature surrounds them and enchants them. The benefits of the new world are employed in according us the leisure to live.

Let us glorify our great Universities of the Pacific, which complete the spiritualization of that great people! Heirs of Greco-Latin Humanism, the masters who transmit wisdom with knowledge form the complete human being. They furnish an ideal. Here, who reads poets? Beneath the sky that saw Homer and Keats born, no one reads them anymore. In our homeland, students and workers have them on their bookshelves. The verses that I compose are as popular throughout

Idaho as the songs of our musicians. What can become of a nation that replaces poetry with business, and no longer knows the price of anything that serves no purpose?

These enormous cities, which still call themselves capitals, have one common feature: it appears as soon as one flies over them. The center is restricted. Composed of narrow and stifling streets. As they draw away, the streets become wider, the green spaces multiply and the air there becomes respirable. Paris, today the greatest city, since its inhabitants approach fifteen millions, extends from the Oise to the Marne. Woods cover its hills; the one at Saint-Germain, on the Seine, is quite pretty. The traces of old roads guide the aerial traveler toward what is known as the South-Western Faubourg, where there are a few curiosities to visit.

One descends into a round space. In the center there is one of the statues of horsemen that are fairly frequent in Europe. It is said that this one represents our General Lafayette; I think that it is more likely to be the ancient king of the country who had the nearby château built. That building makes the depths of this faubourg very populous. Our American tourists have maintained the custom of coming to see it. Like them, I've visited two large halls, one of which, still decorated, resembles an old theater; they serve as schools of electricity. The middle of the château, which a warden opens for you, contains fairly small rooms with paintings whose significance escapes us today. They have, in any case, almost all deteriorated over time, and the part of the edifice that is no longer in use is threatened with ruin. Everyone detaches a piece of marble or bronze to take away, out of habit.

I was lingering over a few reflections on the fragility of the human glories of which traces remain here, and promising myself that I would study them one day in my books when a very old man with an affable manner came toward me. He was crossing the courtyard, keys in hand, and offered to let me into the garden. I still had an hour to spare before nightfall, and I accepted.

The deserted garden pleased me at first by virtue of its majesty. The further I advanced on the terrace, the more I divined that the disdained château must have been, in its time, something magnificent. The long façades presented a precise harmony; was that what the historians call "French taste"? I had never sensed so well that grandeur is not the same as enormity. The lines remained intact, even though the corroded stone was cruelly giving evidence of abandonment.

Why has that useless façade been maintained, since no one any longer comes to look at it? Two large ponds full of green-tinted water still reflected it confusedly, and I understood what nobility its image had had in the purity of those mirrors. Bronze figures, still lying on the disjointed edges, seemed to be to be more beautiful than any familiar to me.

One of them, a tall and slender woman playing with a child, stared at me strangely, as if to inspire a tender nostalgia in me. With one gaze, it has populated the entire garden.

I walked along the pathways, traces of which were barely conserved amid the long grass. Shots growing at random obstructed the way. A wilderness covered what had once been lawns. Staircases, fountains and colonnades were crumbling under the thickets, allowing the whole plan that had distributed them to be divined.

At every step, however, a mysterious statue appeared, which revealed under the moss the most perfect workmanship. More than one, fallen from its pedestal, was lying down, it limbs scattered. I dared not touch them; respect stopped me before those symbols.

Were they the divinities of old to which those woods were consecrated? Or allegorical effigies of forgotten heroes? Or merely simple ornaments imagined for a sumptuous dwelling? I inclined toward the first of those hypotheses—and as magic persists in the images of abolished gods, I hastened my footsteps under the branches, not daring to interrogate the enigma of the marbles further.

The great silence was only troubled by the leap of a squirrel or the passage of some unknown animal. The shadows thickened in the foliage, making the solitude more oppressive. I don't know how, lost in that labyrinth, I found myself back on the terrace, facing a perspective open to a distant horizon. A long canal was shining there in the light of the sun, which was about to disappear.

When I turned round I saw the fire of the sunset flamboyant in all the windows from one end of the château to the other: a fugitive apotheosis, which only lasted for an instant, but which will illuminate my memory forever.

I had visited the past; henceforth, that past lived within me. What it had allowed me to glimpse—those resuscitated gods, those uncertain shadows—would not abandon me again.

The old man who had introduced me signaled to me that he was about to leave. I asked him to tell me the name of the strange place. He looked at me, slightly surprised.

"It's Versailles, Monsieur."

SF & FANTASY

Adolphe Alhaiza. *Cybele*
Alphonse Allais. *The Adventures of Captain Cap*
Henri Allorge. *The Great Cataclysm*
Guy d'Armen. *Doc Ardan: The City of Gold and Lepers*
G.-J. Arnaud. *The Ice Company*
André Arnyvelde. *The Ark; The Mutilated Bacchus*
Charles Asselineau. *The Double Life*
Henri Austruy. *The Eupantophone; The Olotelepan; The Petitpaon Era*
Barillet-Lagargousse. *The Final War*
Cyprien Bérard. *The Vampire Lord Ruthwen*
S. Henry Berthoud. *Martyrs of Science*
Aloysius Bertrand. *Gaspard de la Nuit*
Richard Bessière. *The Gardens of the Apocalypse; The Masters of Silence*
Chevalier de Béthune. *The World of Mercury*
Albert Bleunard. *Ever Smaller*
Félix Bodin. *The Novel of the Future*
Louis Boussenard. *Monsieur Synthesis*
Alphonse Brown. *City of Glass; The Conquest of the Air*
Émile Calvet. *In a Thousand Years*
André Caroff. *The Terror of Madame Atomos; Miss Atomos; The Return of Madame Atomos; The Mistake of Madame Atomos; The Monsters of Madame Atomos; The Revenge of Madame Atomos; The Resurrection of Madame Atomos; The Mark of Madame Atomos; The Spheres of Madame Atomos; The Wrath of Madame Atomos* (w/M. & Sylvie Stéphan)
Félicien Champsaur. *Homo-Deus; The Human Arrow; Nora, The Ape-Woman; Ouha, King of the Apes; Pharaoh's Wife*
Didier de Chousy. *Ignis*
Jules Clarétie. *Obsession*
Michel Corday. *The Eternal Flame*
André Couvreur. *Caresco, Superman; The Exploits of Professor Tornada* (3 vols.); *The Necessary Evil*
Camille Debans. *The Misfortunes of John Bull*
Captain Danrit. *Undersea Odyssey*
C. I. Defontenay. *Star (Psi Cassiopeia)*
Charles Derennes. *The People of the Pole*

Georges Dodds (anthologist). *The Missing Link*
Charles Dodeman. *The Silent Bomb*
Harry Dickson. *The Heir of Dracula; Harry Dickson vs. The Spider*
Jules Dornay. *Lord Ruthven Begins*
Alfred Driou. *The Adventures of a Parisian Aeronaut*
Sâr Dubnotal *vs. Jack the Ripper; The Astral Trail*
Odette Dulac. *The War of the Sexes*
Alexandre Dumas. *The Return of Lord Ruthven*
Renée Dunan. *Baal; The Ultimate Pleasure*
J.-C. Dunyach. *The Night Orchid; The Thieves of Silence*
Henri Duvernois. *The Man Who Found Himself*
Achille Eyraud. *Voyage to Venus*
Henri Falk. *The Age of Lead*
Paul Féval. *Anne of the Isles; Knightshade; Revenants; Vampire City; The Vampire Countess; The Wandering Jew's Daughter*
Paul Féval, *fils. Felifax, the Tiger-Man*
Charles de Fieux. *Lamékis*
Fernand Fleuret. *Jim Click*
Louis Forest. *Someone is Stealing Children in Paris*
Arnould Galopin. *Doctor Omega; Doctor Omega and the Shadowmen* (anthology)
Judith Gautier. *Isoline and the Serpent-Flower*
H. Gayar. *The Marvelous Adventures of Serge Myrandhal on Mars*
G.L. Gick. *Harry Dickson and the Werewolf of Rutherford Grange*
Delphine de Girardin. *Balzac's Cane*
Léon Gozlan. *The Vampire of the Val-de-Grâce*
Jules Gros. *The Fossil Man*
Edmond Haraucourt. *Daah, the First Human; Illusions of Immortality*
Nathalie Henneberg. *The Green Gods*
Eugène Hennebert. *The Enchanted City*
Jules Hoche. *The Maker of Men and His Formula*
V. Hugo, P. Foucher & P. Meurice. *The Hunchback of Notre-Dame*
Romain d'Huissier. *Hexagon: Dark Matter*
Jules Janin. *The Magnetized Corpse*
Michel Jeury. *Chronolysis*
Gustave Kahn. *The Tale of Gold and Silence*
Gérard Klein. *The Mote in Time's Eye*
Fernand Kolney. *Love in 5000 Years*
Paul Lacroix. *Danse Macabre*
Louis-Guillaume de La Follie. *The Unpretentious Philosopher*

Jean de La Hire. *The Fiery Wheel; Enter the Nyctalope; The Nyctalope on Mars; The Nyctalope vs. Lucifer; The Nyctalope Steps In; Night of the Nyctalope; Return of the Nyctalope*
Etienne-Léon de Lamothe-Langon. *The Virgin Vampire*
André Laurie. *Spiridon*
Gabriel de Lautrec. *The Vengeance of the Oval Portrait*
Alain le Drimeur. *The Future City*
Georges Le Faure & Henri de Graffigny. *The Extraordinary Adventures of a Russian Scientist Across the Solar System* (2 vols.)
Gustave Le Rouge. *The Dominion of the World* (w/Gustave Guitton) (4 vols.); *The Mysterious Doctor Cornelius* (3 vols.); *The Vampires of Mars*
Jules Lermina. *The Battle of Strasbourg; Mysteryville; Panic in Paris; The Secret of Zippelius; To-Ho and the Gold Destroyers*
André Lichtenberger. *The Centaurs; The Children of the Crab*
Maurice Limat. *Mephista*
Listonai. *The Philosophical Voyager*
Jean-Marc & Randy Lofficier. *Edgar Allan Poe on Mars; The Katrina Protocol; Pacifica; Robonocchio; Return of the Nyctalope;* (anthologists) *Tales of the Shadowmen 1-12; The Vampire Almanac* (2 vols.)
Ch. Lomon & P.-B. Gheuzi. *The Last Days of Atlantis*
Xavier Mauméjean. *The League of Heroes*
Joseph Méry. *The Tower of Destiny*
Hippolyte Mettais. *Paris Before the Deluge; The Year 5865*
Louise Michel. *The Human Microbes; The New World*
Tony Moilin. *Paris in the Year 2000*
José Moselli. *Illa's End*
John-Antoine Nau. *Enemy Force*
Marie Nizet. *Captain Vampire*
Charles Nodier. *Trilby and The Crumb Fairy*
C. Nodier, A. Beraud & Toussaint-Merle. *Frankenstein*
Henri de Parville. *An Inhabitant of the Planet Mars*
Gaston de Pawlowski. *Journey to the Land of the 4th Dimension*
Georges Pellerin. *The World in 2000 Years*
Ernest Pérochon. *The Frenetic People*
Pierre Pelot. *The Child Who Walked on the Sky*
J. Polidori, C. Nodier, E. Scribe. *Lord Ruthven the Vampire*
P.-A. Ponson du Terrail. *The Immortal Woman; The Vampire and the Devil's Son*
Georges Price. *The Missing Men of the* Sirius

Edgar Quinet. *Ahasuerus; The Enchanter Merlin*

Henri de Régnier. *A Surfeit of Mirrors*

Maurice Renard. *The Blue Peril; Doctor Lerne; The Doctored Man; A Man Among the Microbes; The Master of Light*

Jean Richepin. *The Crazy Corner; The Wing*

Albert Robida. *The Adventures of Saturnin Farandoul; Chalet in the Sky; The Clock of the Centuries; The Electric Life; The Engineer Von Satanas*

J.-H. Rosny Aîné. *Helgvor of the Blue River; The Givreuse Enigma; The Mysterious Force; The Navigators of Space; Vamireh; The World of the Variants; The Young Vampire*

Marcel Rouff. *Journey to the Inverted World*

Marie-Anne de Roumier-Robert. *The Voyage of Lord Seaton to the Seven Planets*

Léonie Rouzade. *The World Turned Upside Down*

Han Ryner. *The Human Ant; The Superhumans*

Frank Schildiner. *The Quest of Frankenstein*

Pierre de Selenes: *An Unknown World*

Angelo de Sorr. *The Vampires of London*

Brian Stableford. *The Empire of the Necromancers (1. The Shadow of Frankenstein; 2. Frankenstein and the Vampire Countess; 3. Frankenstein in London); Eurydice's Lament; The New Faust at the Tragicomique; Sherlock Holmes and The Vampires of Eternity; The Stones of Camelot; The Wayward Muse.* (anthologist) *News from the Moon; The Germans on Venus; The Supreme Progress; The World Above the World; Nemoville; Investigations of the Future; The Conqueror of Death; The Revolt of the Machines; The Man With the Blue Face; The Aerial Valley; The New Moon*

Jacques Spitz. *The Eye of Purgatory*

Kurt Steiner. *Ortog*

Eugène Thébault. *Radio-Terror*

C.-F. Tiphaigne de La Roche. *Amilec*

Simon Tyssot de Patot. *The Strange Voyages of Jacques Massé and Pierre de Mésange*

Louis Ulbach. *Prince Bonifacio*

Théo Varlet. *The Castaways of Eros; The Golden Rock.; The Martian Epic* (w/Octave Joncquel); *Timeslip Troopers* (w/André Blandin); *The Xenobiotic Invasion*

Pierre Véron. *The Merchants of Health*

Paul Vibert. *The Mysterious Fluid*

Villiers de l'Isle-Adam. *The Scaffold; The Vampire Soul*

Gaston de Wailly. *The Murderer of the World*
Philippe Ward. *Artahe ; Manhattan Ghost* (w/Mickael Laguerre); *The Song of Montségur* (w/Sylvie Miller)

Victor Margueritte. *The Bacheloress; The Companion; The Couple*

MYSTERIES & THRILLERS

M. Allain & P. Souvestre. *The Daughter of Fantômas*
A. Anicet-Bourgeois & Lucien Dabril. *Rocambole*
A. Bernède. *Belphegor*; *Judex* (w/Louis Feuillade); *The Return of Judex* (w/Louis Feuillade); *The Shadow of Judex* (anthology)
A. Bisson & G. Livet. *Nick Carter vs. Fantômas*
V. Darlay & H. de Gorsse. *Arsène Lupin vs. Sherlock Holmes: The Stage Play*
Séamas Duffy. *Sherlock Holmes in Paris*
Paul Féval. *The Black Coats (The Parisian Jungle; Heart of Steel; The Sword-Swallower; 'Salem Street; The Invisible Weapon; The Companions of the Treasure; The Cadet Gang); Gentlemen of the Night; John Devil*
Émile Gaboriau. *Monsieur Lecoq*
Goron & Émile Gautier. *Spawn of the Penitentiary*
Paul d'Ivoi. *Around the World on Five Sous* (w/Henri Chabrillat)
Rick Lai. *Shadows of the Opera: Retribution in Blood; Sisters of the Shadows: The Curse of Cagliostro*
Steve Leadley. *Sherlock Holmes: The Circle of Blood*
Maurice Leblanc. *Arsène Lupin vs. Countess Cagliostro; Arsène Lupin vs. Sherlock Holmes (1. The Blonde Phantom; 2. The Hollow Needle); The Island of the Thirty Coffin; 813; The Many Faces of Arsène Lupin* (anthology)
Gaston Leroux. *Chéri-Bibi; The Phantom of the Opera; Rouletabille & the Mystery of the Yellow Room; Rouletabille at Krupp's*
Richard Marsh. *The Complete Adventures of Judith Lee*
William Patrick Maynard. *The Terror of Fu Manchu; The Destiny of Fu Manchu*
Frank J. Morlok. *Sherlock Holmes: The Grand Horizontals; Sherlock Holmes vs Jack the Ripper*
Jean Petithuguenin. *The Adventures of Ethel King*
Antonin Reschal. *The Adventures of Miss Boston*
P. de Wattyne & Y. Walter. *Sherlock Holmes vs. Fantômas*
David White. *Fantômas in America*

Pierre Yrondy. *The Adventures of Thérèse Arnaud*

SCREENPLAYS

Mike Baron. *The Iron Triangle*
Emma Bull & Will Shetterly. *Nightspeeder; War for the Oaks*
Gerry Conway & Roy Thomas. *Doc Dynamo*
Steve Englehart. *Majorca*
James Hudnall. *The Devastator*
Jean-Marc & Randy Lofficier. *Royal Flush*
J.-M. & R. Lofficier & Marc Agapit. *Despair*
J.-M. & R. Lofficier & Joël Houssin. *City*
Andrew Paquette. *Peripheral Vision*
Robert L. Robinson, Jr. *Judex*
R. Thomas, J. Hendler & L. Sprague de Camp. *Rivers of Time*

NON-FICTION

Stephen R. Bissette. *Blur 1-5. Green Mountain Cinema 1; Teen Angels*
Win Scott Eckert. *Crossovers* (2 vols.)
Randy Lofficier. *Over Here*
Jean-Marc & Randy Lofficier. *Shadowmen* (2 vols.)

ART BOOKS

Jean-Pierre Normand. *Science Fiction Illustrations*
Raven Okeefe. *Raven's L'il Critters; Rave's Faves*
Randy Lofficier & Raven Okeefe. *If Your Possum Go Daylight...*
Daniele Serra. *Illusions*